MAGGOTS

A binman's woeful tale

Frank Roberts

Bagwash Books

First published in Great Britain in 2008 by

Bagwash Books

Copyright 2007 Frank Roberts

ISBN 978-0-9558249-0-6

Printed and bound in Great Britain by
DPS Partnership Ltd
www.dpsltd.net

Front cover illustration by Sandra

Dedicated to my children, Lucy, Arthur and Edward

Chapter 1

The Huckett household was awake and preparing for a new day. The future was looking bright, the future was looking green, at least it was for Councillor Professor Cyril Huckett who was full of civic pride and a desire to build a community in which all could take part. This was the new motto of Cheatham Borough Council. Cyril, the soon to be appointed Lead Councillor for Waste was brimming over with excitement. There was just one more meeting to attend and his job was in the bag and there were such wonderful things he wanted to achieve.

Cyril sat and pondered some of the words he would be hearing about during the next four years. His political party had just been re-elected with a landslide majority and everyone was full of the joys of spring.

'Miranda, my love, have you ever considered how fascinating the English language is?' Cyril asked but before she had time to answer he went on, 'there are just so many double entendres, like for instance, the words, *refuse* and *litter*.' Miranda was not really listening; there was always so much to do each morning before one could get away to work. She allowed him to ramble on, pretending to be interested. 'Take *Refuse*, for example, my dear,' Cyril continued. Miranda was not at all keen to take refuse anywhere so early in the morning but there really was no way of stopping Cyril once in full flow, 'the dictionary says it means to withhold acceptance but it also describes items which are worthless. We know it better as, *waste*.' Miranda had an inkling where this was heading but after so many years another of Cyril's ramblings would not matter, she supposed. It was Cyril's new and all consuming passion and she would allow it to wash over her like before, 'yes, waste,' he was at it again, 'you see my ultimate aim is to have no waste in Cheatham. Zero waste! What do you think about that then Miranda?' Cyril purred.

Miranda stopped fluffing up the cushions and stared after Cyril. Had she misheard? Probably not, knowing Cyril as well as she did, she decided to humour him. He was bound to grow out of this crazy idea like all the others from way back when. It would just be a bee in his bonnet for a short time until something else grabbed his fancy.

'That's wonderful, Cyril, quite impossible but nevertheless a wonderful concept, my dear.' How Cyril hated his wife's grip on reality. Cyril carried on with his in depth thoughts on the English language.

'Well now, moving on, what about the word, *litter?*' Cyril was determined, Miranda thought, to slow her down. She could think of nothing worse than having to think about litter before breakfast. There was enough of it outside in the street without bringing it into her living room as well.

'Cyril, we all know what the word, litter, means. Please lets just leave it for now,' she pleaded.

'Miranda, it's of vital interest to me in my new role. I'm the Cheatham champion for litter. What I was trying to say was that litter can be misinterpreted. It can mean a group of young animals newly born, a kind of stretcher carried by men, an indoor toilet or it can be another name for refuse, known to you and me, as waste. Interesting isn't it?' Cyril was smiling.

Miranda was almost in tears at the thought of the next four or five years. Luckily, the need to research recycling and litter still further at the central library forced Cyril to forgo his quest for the etymological beginnings of litter words.

'Darling, where's my left shoe? Have you seen it? He asked like a small child.

'Your left shoe, Cyril, is next to the right one,' exclaimed an exasperated middle aged woman from the hallway of an elegant, if dilapidated five bedroomed detached house in the leafy haven of Pucks Knoll Close. Councillor Professor Huckett looked around him, his eyes eventually resting on a brown brogue sitting peacefully on his threadbare red carpet which had become just a memory of the deep crimson pile it had once been. Of course neither Cyril Huckett nor his wife would ever themselves have purchased a crimson red carpet with deep shag pile. It had been there when they moved in twenty eight years before and had been a lot thicker and softer then. Being Cyril Huckett, he insisted on wearing it out completely before they considered a replacement. Cyril applied the same environmentally friendly philosophy to all the house's furnishings. The house itself had been purchased with a decent and timely donation from Cyril's father and a substantial win on a horse at a point to point race meeting, the latter providing the deposit. The bet was the first and last time Mrs Huckett had been allowed to risk money on anything. The bulk of the house purchase money had come, it must be said from Mr Huckett senior who having achieved the exulted position of President of the Royal Society of Actuaries, had enjoyed a profitable career in the insurance profession until his unexpected death from scratching himself on his hybrid roses. He developed tetanus and died a death that even he could not have foreseen in his actuarial capacity. Luckily, prior to the accident, he had written his last will and testament, most of which had been in Cyril's favour.

Cyril, a pillar of English society and bearing a name of Anglo Saxon origin, was a councillor of five years standing. He was fifty eight years young and really looking forward to his second term in office. The Liberal Independent Party or LIPs as it was better known or even, The Liberal Independent and Environmentalists or LIEs as it was otherwise known by the opposition, had more than held power, it had secured a landslide at the last election improving on the previous landslide four years earlier. The poor Tories had been routed although they had managed to hold onto their true blue Member of Parliament. Cyril wanted waste at the top of the new LIP agenda. He was an environmentalist in both thought and deed and created no waste himself only opportunities for recycling. Recycled materials were indeed valuable materials from which even more valuable products could be made. Councillor Huckett's family produced only one half of a black sack of waste each six weeks. The rest of his Party were in awe of his miraculous achievement and of him being named the Environment Councillor of the Year for the second year in succession. On both occasions Cyril had taken the announcement of the award, which was made by the Mayor at full Council with the Press in attendance, with such humility, although on both occasions he just happened to have his meagre black sack of waste beneath his chair, which he instantly projected into the air and swung around like the proverbial cat for all to see and admire.

At the last full council meeting before the election, the Mayor had read out the accolade adding his own generous praise.

'This first class award could not have been given to a more *tip top*, environmentally caring person than my own honourable and learned friend of many years standing, Professor Cyril Huckett,' gushed Marcus Bullman,

Cheatham's first citizen. The Tory and Labour opposition had a job to stop themselves being violently sick over their microphones. Cyril, on the otherhand smiled broadly and reminded himself that he only ever played to win. You never get anything for coming second, he mused. The announcement of the Environment Councillor of The Year was followed by the usual congratulatory clapping and cheering by the party faithful. Many of these political crusaders were still relatively wet behind the ears in spite having served a term already. Unlike the Tories, they did not seem to understand the political etiquette of such occasions which was evidenced particularly by the way they dressed down rather than up, wearing corduroys, opened necked shirts and very casual jackets and that was just the ladies. It was also suggested that they not only lacked the wherewithal but the breeding too.

The recent election landslide had reduced the Tories to just a fragment of their former selves. From over forty councillors they had sunk to a mere five. The same had happened to the Labour Party who made up for their shortage in numbers by the sheer volume of silly questions they tabled and the routine heckling at Council committees and anywhere else that they thought political capital might be gained. Both the minority parties tended to push this accepted practice to the limit by inviting a few vociferous friends along to participate whenever the public were allowed entry. Whatever local Cheatham people felt about the opposition parties' politics, they could be sure that both would do their utmost to make public meetings as entertaining as possible. The problem with having won such an overwhelming majority was that the Liberal Independents no longer had anyone to fight. They could have whatever they wanted and in many ways this situation was leading instead to a little bit of competition between themselves. Sir David Hooper, the Council's Leader had his work cut out for him just trying to keep the peace between the rival factions. Nevertheless, they did all agree that they did a jolly good job for the London Borough of Cheatham and with this self inflicted pat on the back and the general agreement of all forty five LIP councillors, their first task was to pass a by-law paying themselves a salary. The Leader, naturally, being a full time member of the team and Council lynch pin, voted a barely adequate remuneration for himself of fifty thousand pounds a year, plus expenses, as would be considered right and proper.

Dr. Miranda Huckett at fifty five years of age had been Cyril's loyal wife for over thirty years but did not share his level of interest in civic affairs. Miranda had a proper job as a psychiatrist. The job itself was not all that exciting, in fact, it could be rather depressing. The highest number of suicides in the medical profession was amongst psychiatrists. She was also studying hypnotism and clinical psychology in order to have a little extra cash of her own. Private practice was big business and it would enable her to salt away some cash for those little things one finds one needs in retirement. It was so frustrating to live with a man who was so mean. As far as Cyril was concerned, Miranda was working on a new research project. It was better that way, she assured herself. She was also, it has to be said, absolutely delighted that Cyril had taken up politics with a vengeance upon semi-retirement. The very idea of Cyril being at home all day fully retired filled her with morbid dread. Being a psychiatrist she was well aware of the problems faced by wives when their restive husbands packed up work; half the money and twice the husband! If politics kept him busy and out from under her feet for the next few years, it could only be a good thing.

Councillor Huckett, having located his brown brogue shoe, set off for the first of the Party's post election soirees. The meeting was not due to start until the evening but being as keen as mustard, Cyril had lots of research to do for the new job, which he so hoped would soon be his and this warranted several hours in Cheatham's reference library. All members of the local Party would be at the evening meeting. It was the occasion when most of the Party's plans for the coming four years would be discussed and prioritised and Cyril knew full well that having been returned to power with an even bigger majority, some of those more difficult election manifesto issues would now be consigned to the back boiler. This was all to the good as Cyril had a master plan for waste and recycling which would need all the resources the Council could muster.

Councillor Professor Huckett, as he preferred to be known was an advocate of car sharing which would have been his chosen form of transport had he not arrived earlier in the day to use the library. He would not allow himself to own a car, being an environmentalist he could not be seen advocating a form of transport which relied upon the use of fossil fuels. Rather, he preferred to arrange for Jim Bowen, another councillor with whom he shared the responsibility for the Stonebridge Ward, to pick him up in his new racing green VW Polo whenever appropriate. This was good, because it showed that the councillors were in favour of sharing car rides and reducing pollution particularly with the current debate on how to be carbon neutral and reduce Climate Change.

Dr. Miranda Huckett did own a car. She drove one of those sweet old Jaguar 204 saloons in signal red with matching red leather seats, which the devil himself could not persuade her to give up. Built in 1967, it was over thirty years old and therefore qualified for an exemption from car tax. The road tax exemption and the chance to save money pleased her husband no end and being an ex public school boy this particular model fitted the educated class that he liked to think that he belonged to. Keeping an old car, in spite of the thick black smoke that poured out from the exhaust pipe whenever it moved, helped him appear conscientious about making things last as long as possible rather than readily adding to the waste mountain. He was always banging on to his colleagues about repairing rather than replacing with new. In spite of his altruistic outpourings, it rankled with Miranda that his tight-fisted nature meant he rarely agreed to pay for her long lasting car to be serviced even though he enjoyed its facilities almost as much as she did.

The Cheatham LIP councillors arrived for their first Group Meeting of the new administration. The floppy jumpers had infiltrated the ranks to some degree but most did at least wear socks and the men had shaved making themselves look respectable. Our own Councillor Huckett wore a pair of much lived in light brown corduroy trousers. They used to be dark brown but had been through the wash so many times over the years that they had definitely faded. A cowboy brown check shirt and a green rope stitch jumper completed the ensemble. The sandals of his youth had been replaced by the brogues, good stout shoes that lasted forever and were also serviceable for working in the garden. The lady LIP councillors were just about presentable in their charity shop outfits. They were not exactly this season's haute couture but some of the ladies to their credit sported the merest hint of makeup, although one of the LIP babes had managed to smear it on her teeth which showed beautifully when she smiled. Sadly, just like the LIP men, the ladies lacked style and presence. The Party women then, were just that little bit less drab than their counterparts in the local Labour Party and certainly less glamorous than their political colleagues in the Tories.

The Party meeting was a full house and there was a definite air of excitement. The noise from chatter and the clink of glasses was deafening as Cyril got himself a drink and surveyed the crowd. The Mayor, Marcus Bullman OBE, a retired sales executive for a diary manufacturer was sixty-eight and another environmentalist and was standing just in front of Cyril chatting to a new council member. He had been awarded an OBE for his services to local government or as staff in the Chief Executive's department called it, *for other buggers' efforts*. Marcus, everyone agreed was a very nice man, full of basic family values and prepared mostly to go with the flow. It would have been impossible to predict at this time that after a few months of plain sailing his mayoral year would take a turn for the worse. Tussles and revelations would allow his closest friends to see a totally different side to him. Marcus was a civic junkie and as Mayor, liked to make an entrance. So when his mace bearer, the long suffering Mrs Carter who had seen many a Mayor come and go, suggested that he might need a gimmick if he wanted to be remembered in the annals of Cheatham's history, he thought long and hard about how he would achieve this.

Mrs Carter recalled that during one Tory mayoral year the Mayor had ridden his horse into the shopping centre fully attired in his civic regalia looking every inch a Lord Mayor such as the likes of Dick Whittington. More recently the LIP had appointed a female to the mayoral office who often turned up at engagements wearing her nurse's uniform to show that mayors' were just ordinary people having to earn a daily crust like other council tax payers. This sentiment was decidedly lost on Cheatham's residents. They did not understand the LIP philosophy for wanting to be, *ordinary*. The majority believed that the Mayor was as close as they would ever come to meeting royalty and were quite plainly disappointed when the presidential styled Bentley had been sold off in favour of a leased family saloon car albeit highly polished and having a place for the Cheatham crest and flag. Marcus deliberated for several days, finally deciding that he would ride his way into the Cheatham hall of fame, on a bike. This mode of transport would show his commitment to conserving the environment and make a splash around town at the same time.

The Mayor's decision was, with hindsight, one that in later years would cause hearty laughter in the town's drinking houses. Riding a Council bike certainly turned out to be a good way of getting into the Cheatham council archives. As his 'reign' continued, His Honour the Mayor was often seen arriving at mayoral engagements on a bicycle complete with crash helmet and a high visibility belt tied around his waist. He was unperturbed about arriving at official engagements in a sweat, even on hot summer days when he spent many hours opening fetes and carnivals dripping with perspiration and smelling slightly off. The Mayoress, luckily for her, declined to tag along on her own bike on the basis that she was in frightful demand at the Cheatham Citizens Advice Bureau where she worked as a solicitor. Two smelly officials would have been simply too much for most welcoming crowds. The Mayoress, Virginia Bullman was tall and slender and in her youth could have been a supermodel of the ilk of Elle Macpherson but instead she had chosen a legal career where her litigation skills made her exceptionally useful. The Bullmans' had three sons, who had all attended private schools, married well and sown their seeds for a decent Britain. A fourth son had kind of dropped out of polite society and for a while had worked as one of Cheatham's refuse collectors managing to get the sack for theft and unruly behaviour which included being lippy to the supervisors. The matter was quietly swept under the carpet to avoid the Press getting hold of it for which Marcus was eternally grateful. If the incident had been more widely reported, he would not have been made Mayor of Cheatham, he felt sure. He owed a favour to the Waste Management Section and they knew it.

The LIP of Cheatham were obviously green which one would expect to have seen feature strongly in their manifesto. Environmental Sustainability was an area that other parties had not thought to go into until the LIP arrived with their landslide election results. Tory and Labour councils throughout the length and breadth of Britain worried about more pressing problems such as housing, the elderly and health care. The Environment was the new kid on the block and if the real truth be known, the LIP still being relatively new to government, did not fully understand the workings of Social Services and Education, although to be fair, there was the odd councillor who on occasion had a stab at it. Cyril Huckett agreed wholeheartedly with the green priorities of the LIP manifesto and was the brainchild behind the developing Waste and Recycling Policy. He had no intention of allowing the LIP to pay lip service to his all embracing plans. It was, Cyril believed, his plans for a waste recycling revolution that had hurled the Party back into power with such a large majority and knowing this he fully intended dotting all the i's and crossing all the t's along the way.

Cyril often reminded himself and others that he was a professor of palaeoecology, the study of fossil ecology. He was semi-retired, granted, but the academic life was a training of the mind for life. As well as his own London University department, he was also a guest lecturer at the local Cheatham College of Further Education at which he gave short *snap shot* talks on how to grow runner beans the size of marrows and valuable gardening advice on how to make local residents as self sufficient as himself. All very community spirited since he was not interested in money, he told himself. He could get by without the little extras. His wife, however, no longer thought that way. She was gearing up for a retirement in comfort, with or without Cyril. Although, it must be said that on occasions, she still thought he had a certain rugged, handsome look about him with his long, fly away white hair. If one added a white moustache he would have resembled Albert Einstein she believed but without the stunning intellect, she conceded. When he was younger, he looked a little like a Michael Heseltine with his golden locks in what was known as his mace throwing era, she often wistfully reminded herself.

The Mayor, Marcus Bullman was wily with a greying beard and crooked discoloured teeth. He had an unfortunate leery smile that didn't exactly say, *trust me, I'm a councillor*. In spite of his looks, the local electorate had voted for him yet again. Marcus had an eye for the ladies. In particular he had a penchant for Cheatham's Chief Executive whom he usually found some pressing need to speak to on a daily basis. In his eyes, the Chief Executive, Maisie Atichitawomba could do no wrong. The very thought of her sent him into raptures. She was divorced, black and incredibly fat all of which he liked very much and she was not at all bothered about smelly cyclists. She also liked a good time. Alas, as the first citizen of Cheatham, Marcus had standards to maintain and naturally the Chief Executive, as the first officer of the Council had her own reputation to uphold, although she also believed that where there's a will there's a way. Maisie was uncompromising in her insistence that the councillors would behave and obey the councillors' code of conduct. She was, however, prepared to make an exception for Marcus, whom she knew marvelled at her fat bosom in which he regularly dreamt of cradling his head especially after a heavy day of civic duties.

In Maisie's experience, most mayors' asked for things which were so much more difficult to provide and usually meant asking the Finance Committee for more money, like an increase in the mayoress' clothing allowance. This was not the way of Marcus Bullman. All Marcus wanted was a romantic tryst or put more simply, her body. Maisie tended to be rather hands on and ahead of the game. She had noticed his admiring looks, his flirty gazes and drooling and given it some serious thought. OK, he was older, not exactly a Mel Gibson but she could do worse. He would, she felt sure prove ready and willing and at their ages, *beggars can't be choosers*. A mayoral year only lasted twelve months and then there would be another mayor coming along, a bit like buses really, she smiled; easy come, easy go. Do as I say rather than do as I do, was her new motto. As a lawyer in a previous life if anyone could get herself out of a legal scrap in a divorce case, it was her own good self. As Chief Executive, her main task was to make sure all departments ran smoothly with the officers left alone to run the Council. It was not uncommon to overhear a bamboozled councillor asking the simple question, *who runs this damn Council, us or the staff?* The staff knew unquestionably that left to their own devices, the councillors would have the town in ruins within weeks. It's not to say that the councillors' hearts were not in the right places; it's just that although the lights were usually on, there was often nobody at home!

The Council's Leader, the distinguished Sir David Hooper had the misfortune to be nicknamed *Pooper Scooper Hooper* because of a serious interest in dog shit. The Council's super dog shit shovelling machine, which went by the name of Fido was Sir David's pride and joy and being an upstanding and admiral public servant and having a penchant for this particular subject he took up residents' complaints with gusto. Sir David knew that dogs' mess won or lost votes and that in every satisfaction survey concern about dogs' shit came out on top. With the need to set and maintain standards of cleanliness he set tonnage targets for recovered dogs' doings and was therefore distraught when Fido hit a tree and was damaged beyond repair. Sir David's other desire was a determination to make sure that his political administration operated without scandal. He worked fervently to keep fellow councillors under his thumb and prided himself on being a naval man, running the Council as a 'tight ship', everything Ship Shape and Bristol Fashion. Sadly, the extent of Sir David's naval experience had been the Sea Cadets as a teenager and his modas operandi was a rowing boat around the Isle of Wight during his summer holidays.

Cyril's post election Group Meeting was held at the Todgers Bar at the local golf club and began with informal chit chat and several glasses of champagne to celebrate victory. The elected members had seated themselves around the walls facing the bar where Sir David stood ready to start the meeting proper. He took a swig of Dutch courage and brought the meeting to order.

'Ladies and gentlemen, we're here tonight to consider our individual talents.' The Leader was middle aged with a florid complexion, moustache, goatee, on the stout side and height challenged at just five feet four inches tall. He was developing a beer gut from all the propping up of bars on Council business and seldom showed signs of being interested in anything energetic apart from the removal of dog dirt. He trusted no one, having read several books on boardroom power struggles and back stabbing sagas. Of one thing he was sure, he intended to stay at the helm of his ship come what may. Sir David continued with his rallying address.

'On Monday, I will be meeting the Chief Executive,' at the mention of Maisie's name, The Mayor came over all funny and let out a sigh. The Mayoress, who was there to show solidarity and to enjoy some of the splendid champagne they always served on such occasions, nudged him believing her husband was already showing the first signs of boredom. Sir David continued. 'We must not be too shy to volunteer for unfamiliar departments. We must place ourselves where our talents will be used to the best advantage,' Sir David encouraged. The Mayor was convinced that the Chief Executive's Department was where he could certainly put his talents to good use. He was quite sure that he would rise to any challenge that the voluptuous Maisie Atichitawomba could throw at him. She was going to make his mayoral year one of his best yet and he had to acknowledge that dwelling on her soft, rounded form was at that very moment causing consternation in his charity shop trousers.

An eccentric, retired lady head teacher with a voice suggesting she took no prisoners stood up and addressed the Chair. Councillor Edith Dickopf was born of German parents and now lived with her ailing father. He was in his eighties with more than a touch of senile dementia. Councillor Dickopf had done the decent thing and given up her top job at just forty five years of age to take care of her dear old dad. The extra time on her hands provided the perfect reason for her to enter the world of politics as a local councillor. Councillor Dickopf took the stage.

'Leader, with respect, I think we should just remind ourselves of our manifesto before we go any further. We need to maximise our time by putting members in the most appropriate positions which may not necessarily be where they would like to be most of all. I would like to interpret our victory as an analogy to the well known Pareto Principal. This is where the workers, that's us in the model, must produce results for their employees, in our case the local electorate. We have a contract with the public to deliver our manifesto but results, as is conventional in principal-agent theory, depend not only on the effort that the worker exerts, but also on a random component, being the economic environment, the weather or whatever.' There was a thud as Major Councillor Prentice-Peabody, an ex-Tory, slipped off his chair and onto the floor waking from his slumbers in shock. Councillor Prentice-Peabody at seventy four had crossed the proverbial political floor. He had felt that residents in his ward were becoming just a bit too sympathetic with the LIP and decided just in the nick of time to jump ship. He changed his political alleviation and was swept back into power whereas his fellow Tory ward councillors who regarded Prentice-Peabody as a traitor, were not. Prentice-Peabody's mishap provided only a short respite for the assembled LIP from the Dickopf lecture.

The glazed faces of those present suggested nobody in the room had the slightest interest in the ramblings of Pareto or Councillor Dickopf. Life was far too short and there was still some alcohol left to drink. Unfortunately, they all knew Edith to be forthright, stubborn and inclined to go on a bit and if truth be told, no one was brave enough to stop her. She dug her heels in and rattled on undeterred.

'A teacher's performance is measured by his pupils' exam results but his pupil's innate ability is a random variable,' Edith paused for breath before going on, 'the point that I'm trying to make is that we're all in this together. We need the support of our residents even though they are variable and we must in turn support them by delivering our manifesto principals as soon as possible.' Councillor Hooper was gasping for a drink and had reversed his carcass to the bar for a swig of something whilst Edith continued with her thought provoking tirade. Politely, the Leader thanked her for her comments and made a secret pact to avoid sitting on any committee that she was on in the future. Little cliques were forming to try to understand what the hell Edith had been going on about. The Leader restored order and there followed some discussion on the various committees that were up for grabs. The main committees were the Strategy Committee, where councillors agreed to future policies; the Performance Committee where policies previously agreed by the Strategy Committee were measured and achievements noted or corrective action sanctioned and lastly but not least, the Scrutiny Committee, where they studied the plans for any proposed new service to make sure that they were watertight.

There were many other committees and working parties to appoint; all rather boring but necessary. There was the Cemeteries Board, the four Area Committees where local planning applications for the usual two storey house extensions were rubber stamped; the school governing bodies and various working parties that met ad hoc. One such was the focus group aimed at, *helping older people live longer.* The Leader was losing his concentration having had a few glasses of bubbly and having left his spectacles in his office.

'And finally, we need a volunteer for the, *'Increasing the number of lone parents from disadvantaged areas'* working party,' Sir David Hooper stopped as he became aware of complete silence, which gradually gave way to titters. The Mayor's concentration was drifting. He rather agreed with the Leader and liked the novel idea of increasing the number of lone parents. His imagination ran riot as he thought of one rather large lady in particular whom he dreamed of experimenting on. Sir David, realising at once that he had misread, began again, 'sorry about that, too many glasses of the fizzy stuff no doubt,' he excused himself, 'I should have said, 'Increasing the number of lone parents from disadvantaged areas and people with disabilities *into work,*' he corrected as a sigh of relief swept across the room.

By the time the meeting finished Cyril had managed to get himself the plum job he had coveted and was officially appointed the Lead Councillor for Waste. He would be able to change the borough and make inroads on the world. Cheatham would shortly become the most talked about borough in London if not the whole of the UK for its recycling programme. The LIP would be seen as a party with truly green credentials. He telephoned Miranda from the Todgers Bar to let her know the good news.

'That's wonderful, dear. Would you like me to get you any books from the library about waste when I'm next there?' Miranda humoured him, pleased that she could be sure Cyril would be fully occupied for sometime to come. It would leave her to concentrate on the things that were really important like her own life. Miranda was very strong willed when it came to her own professional interests and could be just as stubborn about that as her husband was about his sustainability issues.

Cyril's co-ward councillor, Councillor Bowen had been awarded Libraries as his special responsibility and took great joy in announcing his early thoughts to his colleagues.

'I want to see the local gypsies looked after and I want the mobile library to visit at least three times a week so those poor, deprived children have the chance to read books like other more fortunate kids in our borough. And that's not all. I want the gypsies to have an internet service so that they can surf the web like everyone else,' Councillor Huckett stopped Bowen in his tracks.

'Jim, I think that we must refer to them as *travellers* now even though many don't travel at all, worst luck! Political correctness, you know.' Cyril took another sip of his drink and as he did so the ex-headteacher Dickopf chipped in offering her own impassioned thoughts on the subject.

'Do you think that the public will wear free internet services for *the travellers*? I mean, many of our Council Tax paying families aren't connected to the internet. Do you think it would be fair?'

'Fair! What's fair to do with it? It's about creating opportunities,' Councillor Bowen said feeling angered at such mutinous comments by a political colleague. As an ex-computer person who had been eased out of his job when his company had downsized, he felt he was the expert here. To his credit he had given over much of his new found spare time to helping young people or young men to be more precise, become computer literate. Those listening to Jim were stunned by his outburst.

Councillor Jim Bowen was thirty years old, slim built with ginger hair and a slight hook to his nose that made him look a bit like a Roman. The libraries appointment, would his close friends thought, help restore his self esteem. It had not helped that he had married at twenty five only to discover a latent tendency for men rather than the fairer sex. The marriage had lasted less than a year when he walked out to set up home with Damien, a librarian with Cheatham's neighbouring council, the London Borough of Padwick. The Council was an institution which took its equal opportunities policy seriously and Jim's gayness had not counted against him when he had put himself forward for selection as a candidate. Cyril, on the otherhand did not really approve of homosexuality. Being a horticulturist it was anathema to his belief and expertise on cross pollination and the ability to reproduce. However, for the good of the Party and since he did not have any choice in the matter he had accepted the inevitable with good grace.

The LIP were still mulling over Jim's idea to parachute the travellers into the modern world when Edith Dickopf spoke for the majority.

'It won't look good in the local paper will it?' Edith could not help herself, she just had to have her say, 'I mean you can just see the headline, *Council chucks fifty thousand pounds at travellers for computers*. It will cause a riot. We might as well go and cut our wrists now, Jim, because if we've a spare fifty thousand pounds lying around I think the electorate would much rather we spent it on Social Services. A favourite for me would be to support the carers of elderly parents.' This was a subject Edith Dickopf knew lots about. At this juncture Major Prentice-Peabody tuned in to the discussion. Still feeling sleepy, he considered as best he could in his inebriated state, the possibility of being an aged parent himself. He lived in his daughter's granny flat. Could she claim for him he wondered? Don't ask, don't get! He would speak to the Executive Head of Social Services in the morning.

Councillor Huckett, knowing something about the nation's growing waste problem had recently had the travellers drawn to his attention on another matter. He'd seen the dreadful mountains of waste they had left behind on Cheatham's biggest housing estate, The Beverly. Being, as he believed the more mature and experienced councillor out of the two of them, he adopted a fatherly attitude to the young Bowen in order to make him see reason.

'Easy Tiger! Residents are already forking out over one hundred thousand pounds each year to clear up after the travellers as they move around the borough,' Cyril advised, 'the local people are already unhappy about them and only last week we evicted some from Britannia Way. The pile of rubbish and smelly disease ridden defecations left behind by just four families is going to cost the Council a bomb,' Cyril expressed his view with relish. Edith wrinkled her face in horror at the thought of piles of steaming faeces whilst Councillor Bowen was becoming hot under the collar at seeing his brilliant new idea flushed down the pan before he had had any chance of putting fat on the bones. He rallied to his own defence.

'Well that's why we need more educational services for them, besides, *Live and Let Live,* that's what my old grandmother used to say,' Councillor Bowen was indignant.

Cyril and Councillor Bowen thought the debate was over but Edith Dickopf had other ideas and wanted to add another pennyworth.

'I thought the gypsies,' she shook her head, 'I'm so sorry, *travellers,* were in any case rather richer than most of us because, correct me if I'm wrong, but they never pay any taxes to government or council? I once had a couple of children in my school that came from a local gypsy caravan site in Hounslow. They had a home computer before anyone else and they came to school in a rather nice Mercedes motor car as I recall.' Dickopf, both defiant and smug at being able to quote a real life experience finished off by going for Bowen's jugular, 'yes, and it was whilst those children were at the school that some of our expensive micro chip thingys went missing. The police found some fingerprints which they said belonged to someone called Delaney? They never caught anyone red handed and interestingly, the break-ins stopped about the same time that the travellers moved on,' Edith announced triumphantly.

Jim Bowen was growing rather fed up with what he saw as extremely irksome criticism of his revolutionary plans. He felt quite sure that his idea would make Cheatham great. It would be a first and he would get his name in the educational press and perhaps great honours would follow. Several councillors in the room were secretly thinking about their own egotistical aims with regard to their privileged positions as council members. Cyril was one such councillor and he was quite sure he would leave his mark on waste and his name in the history books before this administration came to an end.

Chapter 2

Early in June on Friday the 13th, a date usually associated with disasters, the Council's waste managers and supervisors met their new Lead Councillor for Waste. Cyril was as keen as mustard to start discussions on the future of waste management in Cheatham. Around the table with Cyril were John Dingle, The Executive Head of Waste Management and the two service managers for Refuse Collection and Street Cleansing who were respectively, Reggie Turner and Gary Newton, and Recycling Officer, Adrian Moses-Pomfrey. Three senior supervisors had also been given a three lined whip to attend and these were Micky Brown for Waste, Gary Green for Street Cleansing and last and certainly least, Micky 'Slump' Smith, Toilets and Pest Control. Slump was in an 'acting up' position. The previous occupant of the post had recently left for a better job with neighbouring council, Padwick. Cyril had stopped any permanent reappointment until he had had time to consider any necessary re-structuring that might benefit his long term plans for his new responsibilities. Other reluctant invitees to this ominous get-together were a selection of lowly supervisors. Gary Biddles, Larry Wright and Mick, the Ice Man Davies, his nickname evolving from his main duty of arranging the collection of old fridges and freezers recently reclassified as hazardous waste because of something called CFCs. Mick Davies knew little about CFCs but his new exulted position made him a prime mover within the Council.

Professor Huckett listened attentively as John Dingle went round the table and introduced his staff one by one. Cyril was quite confused by the time Dingle had finished. He thought they all looked somewhat scruffy and wondered fleetingly whether paying the staff a bit more might attract a better calibre of officer? Another look round the table at the careworn, unshaven supervisors who looked as though they could give as good as they got in any pub brawl, decided him on quickly moving the meeting forward. Dwelling on staffing issues at this stage would not be a good idea and a strike during his first few weeks in the job would sully his reputation for sure. Cyril put his thoughts on staff intellect to one side for the moment and having introduced himself began revealing his recycling goals and service aspirations for the coming year.

'It seems to me we need a strategy,' Cyril announced, 'we need to have a plan of how we're going to get to eighty five percent recycling within the next twelve months.' The faces around the table, with the exception of Cyril's became pale and mouths were hanging open. What was all this about eighty five percent recycling?

'With respect, Councillor,' a perplexed Executive Head of Waste Management interjected, if rather weakly, 'we've never, as far as I am aware, adopted a target of eighty five percent recycling. We can't even meet ten percent at the moment,' he said driving the point home. He removed his spectacles, small round frames that made him look a little like Rudyard Kipling. He gave them a cursory clean with a real white cotton handkerchief with the name, John, neatly embroidered in royal blue in one corner and then carefully returned them to the bridge of his nose whilst he awaited a response from Cyril.

The quiet interlude seemed to last for ages. Embarrassed waste supervisors shuffled in their seats and fumbled with their pens, their mobile phones or took gulps of water from the tumblers in front of them. A phone sprung into life with the sound of the Eurythmics pop group hit, *Here comes the rain,* in retrospect an appropriate choice of music. Cyril made a plea for everyone to switch off their phones or at least switch them to vibration mode. Micky Brown, Senior Supervisor for Waste, motioned for everyone to do as Cyril had asked and then broke the ice by cracking a joke.

'...that way if yer phone rings, you get a little bit of enjoyment and no one else gets annoyed.' There were a few chuckles although Cyril's expression remained impassive and Micky sensed he had said quite enough from the look on the councillor's face. He turned to Reggie, 'doesn't that man have a sense of humour?' He whispered. The rest of the team were quietly wondering the same thing and dreading the months ahead.

There was a general feeling of, *here we go again* and what did these councillors think they were doing? They knew absolutely nothing about running a service; just think they can waltz in and take over. Dingle just wanted a quiet life and all this fighting talk about an eighty five percent recycling rate was frightening the shit out of him and he felt threatened. He tried telling Cyril some simple home truths.

'Councillor, if I might just take a few minutes to explain our current situation?' An almost apologetic Dingle began, 'when Compulsory Competitive Tendering arrived, the in-house service team was awarded the contract. We've worked consistently hard to maintain services with sparse resources and we were glad to keep the contract in-house but to do so meant cutting corners and well, to be frank, we haven't the crews or the vehicles to offer any increase in services,' a despairing Dingle saw the blank look on Cyril's face.

'CCT! What the devil has that to do with now? We all know about CCT. It went out of the window when Best Value walked in through the door,' Cyril had read all the Best Value performance and monitoring papers he could lay his hands on and considered himself an expert not to be trifled with. 'We must think ahead now to the future, be progressive, forward thinkers and all that. I want Cheatham to be first, right at the top of the recycling league tables. Do we all understand this?' The team were stunned into another silence and all fiddling with paper clips and mobile phones ceased. Cyril felt unrest bristling in the room and decided some sort of conciliatory measures were necessary. 'Young man,' he called, addressing the Ice Man, 'please, do pour us all some coffee,' pointing towards the vacuum flasks sitting on a trolley at the other end of the room.

The coffee pouring break allowed a suitable lapse of time for ruffled feathers to become settled again and Cyril then set about addressing this heathen bunch that had the audacity to call themselves a Waste Management Team.

'Look,' Cyril began, 'I have read up quite comprehensively on the new Best Value Review requirement and it seems to me it's all about these ruddy little things called, Performance Indicators. We all have to show that we're trying our level best to meet them. Of course, if we show that we can exceed them the government will give us an easier ride when it comes to allocating money to us council wide,' he stopped momentarily thinking that they probably didn't have a clue what he was on about. He would have to molly coddle them and explain it in simple terms. 'It's called the Standard Spending Assessment, that's the grant they give councils at the beginning of each financial year, although, I do believe they've just changed it to FSA or Formula Spending Assessment but you don't need to worry about that,' he told them. Cyril wisely decided not to cloud the issue by bringing in complicated explanations about formulas and how richer boroughs should compensate poorer ones, 'you see all councils get a third of their money from the council tax and the other two thirds from the government in grants and business rates.' He stopped abruptly, deciding that all this was not only irrelevant to the matter in hand but most probably boring the pants off them. He changed tack, 'of course the bad news is, if we don't meet the Performance Indicators, we could be given a nasty little tag that says we're one of the under performing councils, a bit like Padwick and the problems they had with their Education Department and we all know what happened there, don't we?' Everyone sat still. Most could not think for the life of them what had happened in Padwick and did not care, the exceptions being Dingle and of course the only college educated person in the room, Adrian Moses-Pomfrey.

The mention of Padwick as a failing council did indeed fill Dingle with horror, sending shivers coursing down his spine. He could not comprehend an independent body marching in on government instructions to take over his patch at a time when he had rather high hopes of getting his early retirement package through. Adrian, on the other hand was more positive. He did not believe that he would be around long enough for any government body to come in and tarnish his good name. His career progression was already planned out and he would be looking for promotion elsewhere within two years. Cyril noted that the assembled throng were still attentive and thought his cunning ploy to frighten the buggers into thinking big had worked relatively well.

Their throats now lubricated with coffee and caffeine, they were agog, sitting up and looking reasonably attentive at Cyril and awaiting his next revolutionary idea. The new Lead Councillor launched into his revolutionary concepts for recycling but it was not long before the motley crew around him were feeling weary again and showing sure signs of battle fatigue. Micky Brown sat quietly pondering Cyril's ramblings finally deciding that he had sat there for long enough. Believing that in the face of adversity it was probably better to be positive, he spoke up.
   'Councillor, if I might make so bold, what sort of things do you want us to do to increase recycling? We're all for recycling, me and the boys, just tell us what you want. Providing you've got some money to back up your ideas we'll do what we can. I'll tell you now though, unless the men get some decent vehicles and more pay they won't be doing nuffink extra,' Micky's gruff and assertive manner had been formulated by over thirty years of continuous and heavy smoking. He reinforced his words by tapping his cigarette lighter on the wholesome oak table in what was a tastefully furnished Civic Offices meeting room, taking care not to knock over his corporate green Beryl Ware cup of coffee.

Cyril was about to speak but was prevented from getting a word in by Reggie Turner, Refuse Manager who spoke in support of Micky Brown.
   'Micky's absolutely right, Councillor Huckett. The men have been doing overtime for months to help out and they're sick of it. We're having a terrible time getting the work in some days. Over the past five weeks we've been to hell and back trying to complete all the rounds. This has been mostly down to driver shortages. We book replacement drivers from the agencies but they don't turn up. Why? Because we simply don't pay them enough! HGV drivers can get good regular and highly paid work anywhere else but from this council,' Reggie paused, he could see several heads around the table nodding in agreement, 'having a constant stream of agency drivers causes us other

headaches too,' he barracked, 'we get so much damage to the vehicles. Charlie Pratt in the Transport Workshop charges it up to Waste Management's budget as what he calls *abusive damage*. That means, Councillor, we can't claim it off the insurance. It costs us a small fortune every year,' Reggie lamented, having started life as a dustman and progressing through the ranks to reach the dizzy heights of manager, he knew mostly what he was talking about. He claimed with some kind of pride that his family were originally pikies, a fact that was confirmed by his swarthy and hirsute appearance. His grandfather had wanted better for his family and put himself on the local council's housing list and the rest is history as Reg would often say as he thought about his cosy three bedroomed semi-detached house in a tree lined road in Padwick.

The meeting continued and trainee supervisor, Gary Biddles shifted uncomfortably in his seat. Biddles was what one might call, a penny short of a pound but he had reached his exalted position because his dad had worked on the council, man and boy as a road digger when councils still had such departments. Biddle's crew cut hair revealed beads of sweat trickling down his face. This was because as usual, he was still wearing his council issue winter anorak. Some people believed that it might be glued to his back since you never saw Biddles without it. The summer heat was getting the better of him in this airless meeting room. He was an *outside* sort of person and could not for the life of him imagine why he had been summoned to this high powered meeting at the civic nerve centre and in the presence of an elected member. Cyril was actually thinking more or less along the same lines about Gary as he watched him fidget.

'Would, Gary is it?' Cyril knew it could only be Gary, Larry or Mick.

'Biddles, Councillor. That's Gary Biddles, Sir,' Reggie confirmed.

'Would Mr Biddles like to take his coat off? You may find it a little cooler,' Cyril suggested thinking he would get more satisfaction out of talking to a brick wall. Gary Biddles, not one to make a scene complied with Cyril's wishes and removed his coat revealing several tatoos of a macabre and sinister nature the most benign of which read, *I love Carol*, enclosed in a big blue heart and a curious sort of multi pointed star on the third finger of his right hand. Cyril was rooted to his seat. He felt that as Lead Councillor for Waste he had his work cut out for him and so must this woman, Carol?

Cyril decided to persevere and try once more to get through to these numbskulls.

'When I say we need a strategy, it's not as vague as it sounds. I do have some ideas, if perhaps radical ones that I would like to share with you. You might also like to know that I recently went on what they call a Project Management course. Great stuff this Project Management. You see it's all about understanding the nature of a project, building a kind of road map so you know what to do, when. There are also wonderful little management tools called, Critical Path, Gantt and PERT charts,' Cyril was allowing himself to be carried away on a wave of enthusiasm for his new found knowledge. John Dingle heard the word, pert and looked up. There was only one *pert* he had heard of before and that was how Mrs Dingle's breasts had been when they had first married. Casting Mrs Dingle's breasts to the back of his mind, he commented on Cyril's pie in the sky ideas.

'Councillor, all this planning sounds rather risky. Shouldn't we wait a bit until we know how the Strategy Committee feel about sweeping away the refuse service as everyone has come to know it, in favour of one which is brand new and totally untested?' He watched Cyril Huckett's face closely.

'You're quite right, John. A journey towards an eighty-five percent recycling rate is guaranteed to be full of unknowns but as I see it, without risk. Obviously, in due course, we'll need to run proposals through the Strategy Committee but not until we've investigated fully the costs and feasibility of any plans. This will, I'm afraid make extensive work for you, Adrian and quite a few of you here and the work will need to be done swiftly, twenty four-seven as they say in the States, eh Adrian?' Cyril said this with such verve and in the best American accent he could muster. 'I aim to increase our current recycling rate of eight percent, sevenfold in the next six months. You will all be pleased to hear that I do have a longer term plan to get us to eighty five percent in the next twelve months or so. We must all be prepared to put our shoulders to the wheel, pull out all the stops and I don't want any cock-ups along the way. You can tell the men they can forget about strike action whilst they're about it.' A masterful Cyril warned.

Micky 'Slump' Smith, Acting Toilets and Pest Control was nodding off to sleep. He had been on lates the night before and had started at 6am that morning. Following a nudge from Cleansing Manager, Gary Newton he was jolted into a state of semi-awakeness and with toilets constantly on his brain started shouting gibberish....

'What stop-cocks. Strike! Are we on strike?' Slump looked around the table bewildered and Cyril was filled with despair. Gary Newton intervened to give some meaning to his colleague's outburst.

'Slump,' Gary could see that Cyril's mind was working overtime trying to work out who or what the devil was *Slump,* 'err, sorry Councillor, I mean, my colleague here, Micky Smith has a point. How do we ensure that the whole workforce doesn't take strike action? They're at breaking point already. Is there anymore money available to keep them sweet? The Unions are not as militant as some of our inner London friends but they're being pushed to the edge. We must do something to placate them or face the music,' Gary Newton explained. Cyril did not want complications. He had a few ideas which he intended to bandy around for effect. Money was dirty lucre which he had no intention of discussing at this point in any detail and certainly not with a room full of morons like this lot. What's more, he most certainly was not going to be stymied by a few lack lustre senior council officers or even worse, those from *below stairs* like supervisors, drivers and those only interested in task and finish. He wanted staff with verve and enthusiasm.

Cyril had a moral duty to the people he had been elected to serve. There was a little thought at the back of his mind about a possible New Year's Honour, which he would be truly overjoyed to collect should one ever be bestowed upon him. With regard to his new merry band of men he considered the best option was to humour them. It would not hurt to give them some small ray of hope to cling on to, he thought.

'I'll mention extra resources to the Head of Finance and the Leader on Saturday morning. We're all attending a community conference to discuss policy matters,' Cyril was anxious to get to the real meat of the meeting. He wanted no Luddites on his new team rather only progressive thinkers, which was beginning to look an extremely unlikely possibility. Cyril decided it was now time to dive into the deep end knowing full well that once he had revealed his hand completely the next few months would be quite an uphill struggle.

'I've been throwing a few ideas around and this is what I think we might take a closer look at,' Cyril held his pencil in his right hand and sort of twirled it around as he spoke, 'please don't think these ideas are in any particular order of importance. I think that we'll have to adopt several ideas. We are unlikely to reach such an ambitious eighty five percent recycling rate with just one new radical service.' Cyril was leading up to his *raison d'être*, his *piece de resistance*, or the icing on the Liberal Independent's cherry cake. All eyes and ears were focussed on him as he unfolded his grand plan. He stood up to look more authoritative and in his mind he could hear Churchill's thundering voice going on about, *fighting them on the beaches*....I suppose I'm a bit like the venerable war leader, leading Cheatham's Waste Management Section into battle against waste, he thought to himself.

Cyril relished his new position and took a deep breath before starting his spiel.

'First I want us to undertake what they call a SWOT analysis. What we do is list all our ideas and misgivings under the headings, Strengths, Weaknesses, Opportunities and Threats. We'll do that next time when you've had time to think about it. Whatever we decide, I want Adrian to arrange for all the boy scouts and girl guides to help us by door stepping, that's spreading the word about recycling... we'll pay them well to knock on every door in the borough and tell residents they will recycle or face heavy fines,' Cyril sniggered; this idea was an absolute corker. Adrian Moses-Pomfrey regarded the Lead Councillor with a worried frown.

'Councillor, how can we fine residents for not recycling when we've no idea whether they're recycling or not? The only way they can recycle at the moment is by taking their paper and glass to the few recycling centres that we have,' Adrian explained.

'I'm coming to that, Adrian,' Cyril glared momentarily at the Recycling Officer. Anyone who opposed him immediately became the enemy. He took a deep breath and gave Adrian a very sickly smile. He had noticed that Adrian appeared to be a very smart member of the team, in the fashion sense that is. Today he was wearing a sage green blazer which Cyril thought appropriate to his environmental role. He had also been advised by Mr Dingle that Adrian had a degree and was not only an Associate Member of the Chartered Institution of Wastes Management but was well on his way to becoming a member of some new environmental assessment body. Cyril felt that he must be the only educated person in the whole of the Waste Management Section. He might have to nurture this boy to his way of thinking. It was always a good idea to take someone who wanted to get on in the world under your wing. Worked for both parties, he believed.

Cyril swallowed his pride and congratulated his Recycling Officer for being on the ball.

'Good work, Adrian. I knew I couldn't catch you out!' Cyril humoured. 'Whatever we decide to do we will of course need to enhance our network of bring sites,' Cyril emphasised the word *bring*. Dingle noticed the complete look of utter incomprehension on the supervisors' faces.

'Councillor Huckett is referring to our District Recycling Centres. In the trade they're known as *bring sites*, because people *bring* paper and glass to them!' Dingle smiled condescendingly at his team and then at Cyril and then cast his eyes down on his notepad feeling resigned to ask for early retirement as soon as he thought it might be accepted. This was inspite of the fact that deep down inside he heard a little voice saying, *you're not a real man unless you work until you're sixty five.* However, another voice, which was growing ever louder as the days grew longer said, *I've only got four thousand three hundred and eighty days left before I reach my three score years and ten and drop off the end of this world.* The latter always got the better of him.

Cyril, still standing, went on with his illuminating lecture on the future of recycling in Cheatham.

'We'll introduce a garden waste collection service throughout the year and a kerbside service for everything that residents can possibly recycle. This might mean two, three or even four bins per household, who knows? We'll do whatever is necessary and we'll go the extra mile as they say on the Government's Beacon Scheme. We'll put Cheatham on the recycling map if it's the last thing we do,' Cyril said taking another good look at his new team and shuddering inwardly. They could easily be the death of him, he thought unkindly. Reggie looked worried too as he could see nothing but gloom and doom ahead.

'Councillor, excuse me, I think I'm probably being a bit dense today. I seem to have missed something,' Cyril looked at Reggie and was prepared to take Reggie's word as regards his level of intelligence, 'how will we introduce these services when we haven't got enough trucks to run the current services? I think we've come back to the old chestnuts again, vehicles and staffing levels. We'll need more of both. There's simply no way of getting around it,' Reggie was dying for a fag.

'Yes, yes; I know we need to address the problem of vehicles and I do have a cunning plan up my sleeve. The government wants local councils to move to greener fleet transport and I thought that we might get hold of some of that European dosh that's splashing about for just this type of project. I've already taken the liberty of asking the Transport Manager to arrange a meeting with one of those European grant advisors and if we play our cards right, before you know it, we'll have a fleet of vehicles running on natural gas and all paid for by those bureaucrats in Brussels!' Cyril gave himself the proverbial pat on the back for coming up with his so called, *cunning plan.* The others were decidedly reticent on the subject.

Mick, the Ice Man Davies was not normally known for his shy approach to life and his quiet contemplation of Cyril's cunning plan came to an abrupt end when he was overcome by an irresistible urge to point out one of the basic requirements for using gas fuelled vehicles.

'Sir, won't we need to get gas from somewhere if we have gas vehicles?' If he was anything he was blunt was Mick Davies. Cyril reflected for a second or two and whilst he did so, Gary Biddles seized the opportunity to give the meeting the benefit of his own learned thoughts on the subject.

'I fink that's what me mum says is putting the cart before the 'orse, or in this case the refuse freighter before the gas filling station!' Biddles' face beamed. With the exception of John Dingle and Cyril, they all laughed. Even Adrian allowed his lips to pucker ever so slightly. Cyril was beaten and he knew it. On this occasion he would have to acknowledge defeat.

'Young man, you are absolutely correct,' Cyril answered, hiding his contempt for this silly oaf, who besides not knowing the rudiments of good manners had no idea how to make himself presentable in certain respectable company. Cyril was remembering the dirty council issue jacket that had been stuck fast to Biddle's back at the start of the meeting and believed the man to be a complete anorak! This last thought made Cyril smirk which was short lived since everyone was watching him and waiting for his answer. 'I haven't fully investigated the fuelling aspects yet but I will ask Charlie Pratt to fix up a meeting with the Gas Board ASAP,' Cyril gritted his teeth in defiance. He found the need to rely on these plonkers a bit daunting and sensed that he was not in for an easy ride. What he must get across to them was that his word was law. Either they learn to do it my way or it's the highway for each and every one of them! He told himself. He would find some loophole in the Council's Employment Law!

Adrian, being the nearest to a professional waste expert that Cheatham had, asked Cyril to elaborate on some of his ideas.

'Councillor, how do you see us picking up the kerbside recyclables, boxes or bags?'

'Neither! I want to use wheeled bins; small wheeled bins and I want to collect the non-recyclable waste just once a month but the recyclable materials, every two weeks,' Cyril was playing to the audience and you could have heard a pin drop, 'of course, we'll have to get the Council to agree to a capital grant to purchase the wheeled bins. Reginald, I want you to make some enquiries on the prices for one hundred thousand small bins. We mustn't let them have bins which are so obviously the right size for their families because basically, we can't trust them. We want wheeled bins which are just a little bit bigger than a normal dustbin. Working together with the girl guides, boy scouts or whoever's interested in earning a few bob, we'll soon have the buggers recycling as much as possible,' Cyril looked around his new friends for approval.

Blank looks stared back at Cyril although there was one half-hearted smile from Mr Dingle, who thought it wise if he wanted to stay in his job until the next election.

'Councillor, I'm concerned about your rush towards an eighty five percent recycling rate. Getting the basic infrastructure in place usually takes a bit of time and as I understand it, no major project and this one would indeed be a project of enormous proportions, has ever been installed on time, within budget and with the same staff that were there at the beginning. I think that we should bear these things in mind when we are racing ahead on such an ambitious recycling programme. Twelve months to do it all in is no time at all. It bothers me just a tad that some of us could get our fingers burnt, Dingle said. He was already feeling a tightness in his chest and just prayed that when Armageddon came his own fingers would not be anywhere near the fire.

'I hear what you're saying, Mr Dinghy, ehm, John,' Cyril said getting the name wrong and not bothering to comment further. Dingle however had not finished with Cyril yet.

'Councillor, perhaps at least it would be wise to consider collecting the non recyclable waste a little more frequently than once a month? Residents are used to having a regular service and I'm thinking in particular of problems we might get in the hot summer months,' Dingle suggested as an enormous sigh of relief escaped from everyone in the room except the new Lead Councillor for Waste.

Cyril suddenly felt queasy. The thought that they might be reproaching him or worse, making fun of him was sick-making in the extreme. He reminded himself that he was the Lead Councillor for Waste, for goodness sake; nevertheless, sensing the mood he decided it might be best to concede just a little ground.

'I suppose you might be right. Let's make the collections of general waste fortnightly. How's that sound?' What the hell, Cyril thought privately, he could always reverse it at a later date. Dingle still had more to say. Being a diplomat and used to compiling letters to residents which never quite answered the question, he decided to enlarge on his own views.

'Councillor, might I suggest that we don't use the 'F' word. Instead of referring to fortnightly collections, the term, *alternate weekly* might be preferential? That way we can sell the idea to residents as still being a frequent and regular service. They'll still get a collection each week, just not for general waste. What do you think?' He felt decidedly nervous about the revolutionary changes Cyril was proposing.

'Jolly good, Mr Dinghy, John, I like it,' Cyril said. Dingle smiled graciously wondering if Cyril would ever get his name right.

As the meeting came to an end, Cyril gave out a number of tasks that required research before the next meeting, a week hence. He thanked all for their kind attention and support and closed the meeting at 1.30pm. There was a rush for the door as the team made a dash for the car park and a fag. Cyril looked around and admired the room. He knew he would not have liked the makeshift, cramped depot office that the supervisors were forced to work out of at 6am each morning. What with its faded carpet that was in worse condition than the one he had in his own home and which was covered with ground in cigarette ash and any other muck that was walked in on the boots of the supervisors, it could only be described as a tip. Neither the carpet nor the office saw a vacuum cleaner for months at a time, the cleaner having been one of the first casualties of the last round of budget cuts. Cyril watched the team leave and his thoughts on his new colleagues were not what you might call, magnanimous.

'What a mediocre lot they are,' he muttered quietly as they left, 'still, I suppose every pyramid has to have a base!'

A bemused and hungry Waste Management Team made their weary way to the exit and lit up their fags in an effort to suck in enough nicotine to get them through the rest of the day. Once their addictions had been satisfied they shared themselves around the available cars to return to the depot to see the last of the crews clocking off for the day. Micky Brown took Slump, Reggie, Larry and Mick Davies, whilst Gary Newton took Gary Green and Gary Biddles. Before setting off Micky looked squarely at those in the back and warned them not to fiddle with his handles or anything else in his prized MK 3 Cortina otherwise *he'd kill 'em*. It seemed to do the trick. They kept their hands to themselves. The chatter at first was of the next day's friendly football match until Larry made a request to drive back via Wales Road and Powys Court.

'Why do we need to make a detour to Wales Road?' Slump demanded. His main job was looking after the public toilets and right at this moment he was desperate for one himself.

'They've got some problems with their bulk bins,' Larry said winking furiously, knocking the side of his nose with a well placed finger.

'Oh, come on Lal, tell us what's going on,' Reggie urged.

'Well, a little bird told me that Lolita Baby Doll Reynolds has a luxury flat there,' Larry explained excitedly.

'You're joking? Not the Lolita Baby Doll Reynolds?' Reggie shrieked although in reality he didn't have a clue who Lolita was. Larry revealed all.

'For those less well informed like my friend, Reg here, Lolita is a lady with rather large mammaries who has appeared in the adult recreational press in some interesting positions, in the raw usually. Anyway, the caretaker at Powys Court has a maggot infestation which I think needs Slump's attention immediately,' Larry was again knocking the side of his nose. The others thought it best to humour him and allowed the request to proceed. Gary Newton heard about the proposed detour via his radio but went straight back to the depot with the other two Garys moaning in his ear about wasted opportunities.

At Powys Court half of the Waste Management Team poured out of Micky Brown's car. Onlookers would have believed the caretaker's request had been answered in what could only be described as overkill. Slump ran over to a hedge to relieve himself whilst the others opened up the binstore and took a look inside. The bulk bin had indeed missed a collection and probably a few more too. There was a trail of maggots coming from the bin and a very sickening stink. Reggie used his mobile phone to summon a bulk bin freighter and within minutes they were there, upending the bin and solving the problem in one fell swoop but not before a couple of rats had been spotted at the back of the binstore. Ignoring the rats, the supervisors and the bulk bin crew had another ciggy and chatted about the footy until interrupted by impatient honking coming from behind the freighter. The normal raucous response from the team was evident immediately and the driver of the freighter let out an *F* word which did not refer to the dreaded fortnightly collection which Cyril and John Dingle had discussed earlier. A rather over cooked tanned woman of about twenty five years of age with long golden tresses straight out of a bottle and huge breasts straight out of a cosmetic surgeon's clinic sat at the steering wheel of an up market sports car.

'Oy get that thing out of me way,' the wench shouted. This was Lolita. All eyes were on her bulging breasts which seemed to be impersonating large water melons and contained with great difficulty within her low fronted pink T-shirt.

Micky Brown was the first to regain his grip on reality and taking the cigarette out of his mouth, motioned the freighter driver to move the truck to one side so that Lolita could drive into her parking space. Larry was almost coming in his pants whilst Slump, who seemed to have a touch of the runs, had almost done the same. Lolita was only interested in men if they were paying to look and these freaks most definitely were not. Stepping out of her car with few concerns about her modesty she allowed the boys to see more of her thighs than a proper lady might have wished. She locked the car and swung the strap of her leopard print bag over her shoulder as she walked with difficulty in six inch red plastic stilettos towards the apartment's entrance. One of the rats ran headlong towards Lolita, who screamed and ran backwards into Larry's arms. He held her tight, enjoying the soft warm feel of her hard up against him.

'It's OK love, we're dealing with it,' Reggie shouted. Lolita's breasts were shaking all of their own accord due mostly to their silicone implants and were still the focus of attention for the men standing on the forecourt. Reggie grabbed a boomerang, which for some unknown reason was lying in the cab and chucked it at the rat hitting it on the head, knocking it out in one go. The driver's mate picked the rat up by the tail, threw it into the hopper and pressed the button to start the ram. Lolita was grateful and after extracting herself from Larry's grasp offered the boys half-priced tickets for her Soho strip show.

Lolita was all they could talk about for the remainder of the trip back to the depot.

'I bet she turns a few heads when she goes out shopping,' Mick Davies said.

'Turns my stomach more like,' Reggie responded, being the older hen pecked married man in denial, 'that was one ugly lady and I don't go much on her personality neither,' he added.

'Who cares about her personality? It's her Bristol Cities we're all interested in. Weapons of Mass Destruction if ever I saw any,' Larry drooled.

'Yeah, well dictators everywhere had better watch out, that's all I can say,' Reg added.

'You miserable old sod, Reg,' Larry shouted.

To add to the day's excitement on the final lap to the depot, Micky's phone started to ring. He answered it using the arms free paraphernalia that Reggie had insisted all the supervisors use to avoid getting points on their licences. He heard a familiar voice at the other end.

'Hello boss! Look in yer mirror,' the voice demanded. Micky did as he was asked. Coming up close behind his car was a refuse freighter, fleet number HR6 and the smiling faces of one of Micky's crews waving like loonies at the occupants of the MK 3 Cortina. By the time they returned to the depot they all felt that life had some redeeming features. Micky Brown carefully filed away their half price group voucher for tickets to Lolita's seedy strip club and as he caught site of Gary Newton leaving the office, he called to him.

'Oy, Gar, I need a quote from you,' Micky shouted but before he could finish his sentence, Gary had flung his arm up into the air and started reciting.

'To be or not to be... that is the question...'

'I don't mean that kind of a quote you idiot. I want a price for clearing up a fly tip in Needham High Street,' Micky called back laughing. It was too late. It would have to wait until tomorrow as Gary was already inside his car in his own private world.

Chapter 3

One evening Cyril sat at his dining room table opening his post including his invitation to attend the Mayor's Parlour for an important event. He read the gold embossed card out to Miranda.

The Worshipful, the Mayor of the London Borough of Cheatham requests the pleasure of the company of Councillor Professor Cyril Huckett and Dr. Mrs Miranda Huckett on Tuesday 17 June at a reception to mark the launch of the Council's new Environmental Statement.

The environmental enthusiasts in the local LIP had been working on their new environmental policies for some time and were looking forward to publishing them. The Statement would give the Party carte blanche reasons to push through their priorities over the next four years. Party members had, of course, consulted with residents on the proposed new policies and somewhere in the bowels of the Council's Policy and Research Unit there was a man with a database proving that at least one hundred residents had been asked pertinent questions such as, *do you want a nicer, cleaner, greener place to live?* Naturally, there was always a positive reply which only served to inspire Cheatham's councillors even more.

Miranda was only half listening to Cyril as he proudly read out their invitation. She had been catching up with some reading of her own, a steamy novel about a couple engaging in wife swapping sessions, which she believed was her professional duty to read. It would, she felt, assist her in understanding the sexual frustrations of her patients. Repetitive and compulsive sex was a major specialism of hers and a condition that she was seeing much more of. Not that her patients were actually enjoying the fruits of this complaint in her consulting room but rather laying themselves bare in the professional sense. The administration of alcohol was probably frowned upon by other medics but this method of getting her clients to unwind was Miranda's own and it was her own little bit of risk taking in the NHS world of bureaucracy. It certainly did wonders for her because at the end of the day following all those accounts of sex in wardrobes, sex in lifts and in fact sex anywhere at all she felt that she had actually had sex herself.

Miranda's novel stirred something deep down inside her that Cyril hadn't stirred for years but grudgingly she looked up from her book and tried to look interested in Cyril's invitation.

'So what's the Environmental Statement all about then, dear?' Miranda realised she had a duty to Cyril too.

'This and that you know. Anything really that makes the environment in which we live better,' Cyril said, feeling that he was keeping his wife from something far more interesting. Miranda, not wanting to be quite so transparent, shut her book.

'No Cyril, I don't know,' Miranda said looking quizzical.

'Sustainability, my dear, that's what it's all about. We want to improve local sustainability by, for example, increasing the amount of insulation residents have in their lofts and persuading them to adopt new whole life attitudes to the way they do things, like recycling more, buying products with less packaging and re-using things like yoghurt pots,' Cyril enthused.

Miranda was horrified. Cyril did not allow her to buy yoghurt because the Council could not recycle the pots and the thought of all those poor little plastic pots ending up in landfill sites was too much to tolerate. Having none of his own, however, had never stopped Cyril from obtaining yoghurt pots from other sources. He collected them up from his neighbours, thus preventing them from being wasted and then put them to good use in his greenhouse germinating his seedlings in them. The greenhouse was full of yoghurt pots, the shed was full of yoghurt pots and all around the perimeter of the detached house was an army of little pots and tubs, not just ex-yoghurt but margarine, ice-cream and anything else that may have started off as a plastic food container. Miranda hated them and the abhorrent thought that Cyril might suddenly feel that he must practice what he preached, even more intently than he did now, filled her dread.

Getting back to the subject of the invitation, Cyril reminded Miranda that she was expected to accompany him to the event.

'What about the 17June then, my sweet? Will you come? I need to reply,' Cyril asked. How Miranda hated it when he turned on the charm. It was so uncharacteristic.

'No dear, sorry pet. That's my volunteer counselling night at the Royal,' she explained.

Cyril was baffled. This volunteer counselling was obviously something else that Miranda had forgotten to tell him about. Miranda offered her services twice a week as a volunteer counsellor for hospital staff at the Cheatham Royal Infirmary. This charity work of Miranda's was to help hospital staff coping with depression largely because they were not having enough sex due to their long and tiresome hours.

The Environmental Statement launch event arrived and Chief Executive, Maisie Atichitwomba who had an office just across the corridor from the Mayor's, slipped across to see Marcus in his regalia, a penguin styled jacket, hat, cloak and interestingly tight breeches knotted at the knees. The mace bearer was just pinning the chain of office around the Mayor's neck when Maisie dismissed the elderly woman with a wave of her right hand.

'I'll finish that, Mrs Carter. You just slip away home and have an early night,' she suggested. Mrs Carter did not need telling twice. After driving her little red Nissan Micra all around town in an effort to keep up with the bicycling Mayor, she was what is commonly referred to as, all shagged out. Maisie, on the other hand was feeling randy. Her voluptuous figure was always so warm and soft and gave off a gentle perfume that reminded the Mayor of his cruise to the Caribbean Islands the previous winter. Maisie's choice of costume for the evening's celebrations was a magnificent multi-coloured Nigerian frock complete with turban in greens, oranges and yellows which caused Marcus' heart to flutter.

The Chief Executive positioned Marcus' tie and allowed her hands to slide beneath his cloak where she gave his ceremonial jacket a little tug.

'There. Can't have you looking like you're pregnant underneath your cloak can we?' She teased. Marcus bit his tongue at this remark. He allowed himself to be drawn ever closer to this warm, friendly, black mother of two. Maisie had never actually been to the Caribbean. She had been born in Britain forty eight years before around the time of Jamaica's independence. In fact the Jamaican independence had been partly responsible for her being born at all. Her late father had been so worried that once independent the likes of him would not be able to be British anymore that he jumped ship in Liverpool and set up home in South London. He met a nice girl from British Guyana and after enjoying local celebrations to mark Jamaica's new independent status went home drunk and enjoyed the fruits of this other British colony. Maisie was the little sapling they produced.

Marcus could feel Maisie's chubby hands through his ceremonial breeches, which made him feel quite light headed and he wanted the moment to last for ever. The light headedness was coupled with a frothy leak down below in his mayoral breeches and he prayed his cloak would hide any damp patches. Maisie was just removing her hands from beneath the Mayor's cloak when Councillor Edith Dickopf, the first of the invited guests to arrive, swept in.
  'Hello Marcus,' Edith said, her face beaming, 'tonight we're putting the Council on the environmental map. It will be a mammoth task but we know we can do it,' Edith always was so enthusiastic Marcus thought wishing she had not mentioned the word, mammoth with Maisie hovering in the background. In his reoccurring nightly dream he always found his hands trapped in Maisie's plentiful bosom and any words referring to gigantism reminded him of this. 'Where's the Press? I thought I saw a photographer as I came out of the lift,' Edith asked feeling that the Party must make the most of any publicity they could get hold of. She marched off to find him. Photographers! Marcus hoped not. He had had his eyes shut when Maisie had been fiddling beneath his cloak. What would the locals make of a picture of himself and the Chief Executive, up close and personal and him in his funny clothes?

At the appointed time the invited guests gathered to hear the Mayor speak. Glasses of wine in one hand and nibbles in the other they waited eagerly to be told about the bright new future Cheatham faced with the new administration which was now in a stronger position than ever before.
  'This new Environmental Statement will cover every aspect of life in the borough. We will adopt a Green Travel Plan which will make our roads safer and reduce the number of people killed each year,' the Mayor spoke enthusiastically as supportive clapping from the Party faithful could be heard in the background. 'We will provide services that will encourage residents to live greener lifestyles. There will be a lot more household recycling, environmentally friendly weed killers and organic composting of kitchen waste,' and so it went on. Twenty minutes later, the Mayor was coming to a climax in more ways than one as he watched Maisie mouthing the word, *sex*. What she was actually trying to tell him was that he had forgotten to tell everyone about the revolutionary idea that was Statement Number Six. After concentrating hard he understood. 'Ah yes, and last but not least I want to say a few words about Statement Six, working with the local Travelling Community. We are about social inclusion and with this in mind we will be offering the local traveller population free internet access and mobile library facilities.' The Mayor's speech was greeted with more enthusiastic applause by Party stalwarts.

The Council's Leader, the normally morose Councillor Sir David Hooper spoke next. He had cheered himself up for the big occasion by wearing a beige jumper with a racy stripe down one side.
  'Ladies and gentlemen, it is never any good saying we'll do all these wonderful things if we don't have the support of our residents,' he began, this

time keeping his eyes glued to the piece of paper in front of him, 'we'll do our best to encourage residents to support our new green agenda and in return we will make Cheatham a better place to live.' A newspaper reporter from the Cheatham Echo on his first important job took this opportunity to quiz the Councillor.

'Can I ask you, Sir David, how you will make the borough's roads safer?' The cub reporter asked.

'We want to get people out of their cars. What we plan to do is make it more difficult for them to drive round the borough. Lots more speed bumps and hidden cameras, higher parking charges and many areas where we'll no longer allow parking of any kind,' Sir David said realising too late that the canny reporter would not miss an opportunity to report every word.

Sir David thought on his feet and came back with a softener to butter up the reporter.

'We are, naturally, only responding to residents comments. Whenever we survey them they tell us the two things that really annoy them are traffic and dog fouling. I would like to point out that the Council will be practising what it preaches. Staff will have their car allowances cut back and they will be encouraged to use environmentally friendly means of travel such as public transport whenever practicable,' he told them proudly not hearing the low hum of discontent arising from the contingent of senior staff at the back of the hall. John Dingle had become white with silent rage and turning to a sixty something Head of Meals on Wheels, whispered in her ear.

'Just let him try and touch my car allowance,' he threatened.

'You're quite right, John. They won't get me on any bike either!' The surly Social Services matron returned.

The Mayor had announced that Councillor Dickopf would be chairing a special working party to look at improving the overall cost-effectiveness of the Council's environmental wish list and the public would be advised as the programme progressed. Cyril made a mental note to meet with Edith as soon as possible to sound out some of his ideas for putting Cheatham at the top of the recycling tree. He needed friends where the money was. In the meantime the evening was still young and there was still time to pose for a few Press photos with the Leader, the Mayor and with Councillor Tom Merryweather who had responsibility for the getting the public to Take Part and Take Pride. Later still Cyril chatted to the Head of Parks, Melvin Cherry on the use of pesticides, a topic that as a horticulturalist he had firm beliefs on. Melvin had seen enough slugs and snails to last him a lifetime and he had no patience with Cyril's ideology that the little beggars should be allowed to live freely. Once Cyril was in full flow there was not much chance of getting him to put a plug in it. As a university professor and a lecturer in botanical sciences, even in semi-retirement the old adage once an academic, always an academic rang true.

Marcus was circulating and just as he joined Cyril and Melvin Cherry the conversation had turned to pollination.

'Did you know that fruits can be dry or juicy?' Cyril asked an unwilling Mr Cherry.

'Yes,' a dour Head of Parks admitted, hoping that that would be the end of it but Cyril continued.

'Dry fruits are soft and juicy at first but they dry out as they ripen,' Cyril said, raising his voice as the effects of the wine filtered through his arterial system to his brain. Marcus' attention was pricked. He thought Cyril's description of dry fruits rather fitted his wife, Virginia. She had been a stunner in her youth but he saw her now as a dried up pod that had popped open allowing all of her seeds to shrivel. 'Incidentally,' Cyril kept up the momentum, 'did you know that flowers which are pollinated by birds are nearly always red?' Cyril took Cherry's nod as approval and glancing intently at Marcus began to talk about the problems of cross-pollination, or rather what happen when the wrong pollen is trapped by an inappropriate plant from another species. 'Of course the seed usually dies although there are some interesting varieties such as the Deadnettle. Their flowers have nectar right at the bottom of the petals and only bees of the right sort with very long tongues can reach it. Nature usually has a way for making sure only flowers of a particular species get together and reproduce,' Cyril bored. Cherry made his excuses and went off to get another glass of wine. Marcus, on the other hand was convinced that Cyril had rumbled him and his affections for Maisie. He was pissed and rounded on Cyril.

'I don't want her to have my babies, you bloody fool. I just want to sample her nectar,' Marcus roared. Cyril was taken aback. The Mayor, he knew, was never one to hold his liquor.

Chapter 4

Early mornings at the depot were frantic and the morning after the Environmental Statement's launch was no different. All those actually arriving at the depot at 6am could put their hands on their hearts and say they knew nothing about the Environmental Statement nor wanted to. They had more important issues to deal with. It was pouring with rain for a start and three vital vehicles had starting problems and they were five drivers down. Micky Brown and Gary Green were on duty. The allocation office was a dingy kind of place but a little better in the summertime when it was at least light at 6am. It also had very little space for all the supervisors to sit comfortably in together. There was only one computer and that crashed most days because the wiring kept getting eaten by rats or squirrels. Temperature control was non-existent and as a result it was freezing in winter and boiling in summer. At this time in the morning the supervisors usually stood inside the office whilst the crews awaited their orders outside, next to a large sliding window. To the right of the window was a scrawled notice which read, *I can only please one person each day. Today is not your day. Tomorrow is not looking good either.* A plastic roof covered the assembly area so the crews stayed dry but in winter they always complained about Brass Monkey Syndrome as the wind rushed through.

At this time in the morning there might be up to sixty men waiting outside at any one time for their orders. Apart from the chatter of the supervisors from inside the office, the only other noise was the groan of the fax machine as urgent jobs from all around the borough came rushing in. The radios were silent at this ungodly hour but within a short time the criss-cross of messages sent through radio control at the Civic Offices would add considerably to the background noise and the officers' stress levels.

'Good Morning Transport,' an unshaven Micky Brown telephoned the workshop where the fitters had also started at 6am. He could hear Elvis singing Jailhouse Rock in the background, 'Christ Almighty, Workshops!' Micky shrieked, reaching up and giving an almighty shove to a stuffed toy gibbon hanging from the ceiling on a piece of grubby string, 'it's a bit early in the day for such excessive music. Turn it down now will yer. I can't 'ear meself speak,' he moaned, brushing a hand over his coarse whiskers and dodging the gibbon as it swung back again. Attached to the gibbon was a laminated note which read, is it Friday yet? Mick noticed this for the first time in ages and grinned, if only!

Ever since the in-house Direct Service Organisation had won the contract there had been trouble making ends meet. In order to compete with external contractors such as the big boys in the industry, costs and corners had been cut with no investment in manpower or vehicles. The crews had been delighted to keep their Council jobs because they knew full well that private business paid a lot less. Their colleagues in neighbouring boroughs were always out on strike, it was an easier decision for them to make because they were less well looked after in the first place and therefore had less to lose.

'I hope you've got a lot of lead in your pencil and a very long piece of paper,' Micky tormented Terry Deadman, the senior fitter, 'W67 Dennis Eagle, bin lift has no power; W82 Jack Allen, ram not packing; C13, Unlucky for some! Gully sucker not sucking. We're already behind with the trade waste collections from yesterday so Terry, as soon as you can with W67. I've got

Gary Green here who wants a word with yer,' Micky said handing the phone to Gary.

'Tel, I need the gully sucker back ASAP because I've got that new Councillor Bowen on my back. Some old bag in 'is road has made a formal complaint about her bloody drains being blocked. I'd really appreciate it mate as I've got to meet with Bowen after the football and I don't want 'im to have a go at me again,' Gary explained.

'We'll do our best but we're short staffed just like you are. One of my blokes has had to take the hired glass recycling vehicle back for a service and Charlie's away in Epsom on a Health and Safety course,' Terry sounded desperate and it was only 6.15am.

During the CCT era the Transport Workshop had been deemed *de minimus* and was saved from going out to tender but now the new Best Value regime brought all the worries back again as they had to constantly review how well they compared with other workshops and with no extra money the staff felt jaded.

'Come off it, Tel, I know Chas has gone to see the gee gees at Epsom. You can't pull the wool over our eyes. If I'd have known, I'd 'ave got 'im to put a bet on for me,' Mick teased. The Charlie referred to was Charlie Pratt, the Transport Manager. Terry was not laughing.

'Well I suppose we'd better get cracking; put W67 in bay two and the gully in bay five,' Terry sounded resigned to another day like the one before.

Time was pressing and Micky went outside to the Must Work Ltd. employment agency representative to see who they had brought along today.

'Right, I'll have you, you, you and you,' Micky pointed to four burly blokes. Holidays and sickness were endemic in the summer months and most of the agency workers turning up each morning were found work. The chosen four were to be refuse loaders picking up black sacks and throwing them in the back of the freighters. There were around two thousand households on each round so they needed to be fit.

'Alison, did you get me any HGV drivers?' Micky bellowed across the yard as the agency's rep walked towards the coffee machine positioned near the Transport Workshop.

'Mick, have I ever let you down?' She shouted back, cigarette in hand and coffee in the other.

'Yeah, every bloody day. When are you gonna get me some decent drivers? That one you gave me last week...' Micky was not given the opportunity to finish.

'Yes, alright Mick. I've had enough of you reminding me about Fred Haines. Sorry about him but he came to us with good references,' Alison defended, arriving back at the allocation office window.

Alison was not a bit concerned by Micky's gruff manner; she was used to it. Micky, she knew, liked to make his point.

'Listen to me, my darling,' Mick said, 'when I say I need drivers, I mean proper qualified drivers. Larry Wright interviewed four of your recommended so called drivers last week and two of 'em didn't even have driving licences. I have it on very good authority that one of 'em didn't 'ave a licence because he'd failed the bloody theory. You lot had better pull yer socks up or else we're parting company,' Mick admonished, 'and another thing, when we want loaders, we want good strong men. Eighty percent of that bunch you sent us for temporary six month contracts were bleeding bank managers with lily white hands.

'I'm sorry Micky. That's all I can say. We'll try to do better and by the way, FU,' Alison said taking a drag on her fag.

'Fuck you? What kind of talk is that from a lady?' Micky yelled.

'What the 'ell are you talking about, Mick? I said FU, Flies Undone, mate,' Alison smiled pointing at Micky's crotch.

Gary Green handed out the work folders and radios.

'Gar, it's your turn to check their kit,' Micky called. Each morning a supervisor checked the agency blokes to make sure they had been kitted out with steel capped boots and protective trousers, gloves and reflective vests. Gary Green went outside and taking a puff on his fag inspected the troops, recording their names and any pieces of kit they were missing. The Council would charge the agency later for any items that the Council had to give them. This morning the agency had provided just two drivers and Mick, who was losing confidence with Must Work Ltd., checked their driving licences himself. Gary allocated the daily intake to appropriate crews and found just one sad would-be loader left in the yard wondering if he had a job for the day.

'I can use you, mate,' Gary said, 'you'll have to litter pick though, d'yer mind that?' On receiving a positive response Gary went to get a litter picker.

At 7.30am the supervisors on the later shift arrived.

'What time do you bloody well call this?' Micky Brown grunted as Gary Biddles and the Ice Man approached the office; Biddles was smiling broadly with his security entry pass at the ready. The Ice Man had to rely on Biddles at this point because he was busy rearranging his crotch having suffered a call of nature as he entered the yard. 'Anyways, now you're 'ere make the blinking tea,' Micky called out to Biddles.

Everyone knew Micky's bark was worse than his bite. He was actually a caring family man and had moved heaven and earth to be at the hospital when each of his grandchildren had been born. He even took the older children on holiday with him to give his daughter a break.

'What was all that about a Fred Haines? Gary Green asked.

'Oh, you weren't 'ere was you? Last week Alison brought this guy along, said he'd worked for Medidrug, the drugstore chain and was used to doing long runs up and down the country with articulated lorries and tankers. Within one hour he'd demolished a house wall and taken a chunk out of the weighbridge at the tip. Insurance are dealing with it. No wonder our premium goes up every bloody year,' Micky moaned, staring into his mug, which was now full of very weak tea.

'Did you put any sugar in this?' Mick shouted at Biddles.

''Ow many do you take for God's sake? I put three in,' Biddles may have been just a youngster in Micky Brown's books but he could give as good as he got.

'This is awful muck,' Micky moaned, 'my Susan brought some of those sachets of cappuccino the other day, bloody good an all. I'll bring some in tomorrow. I don't want your brew anymore. It's like drinking dishwater,' Mick said screwing up his face at Biddles.

'It's hot and wet and that's all I care about,' Biddles replied.

The chat returned to their favourite subject, the football.

'What time we meeting in the park today?' Ice Man asked.

'3.30pm. As soon as the last crews are in. Slump will cover for any delayed crew and get the missed bins crew out on the late run,' Micky Brown was rubbing his hands with glee, 'we're gonna thrash 'em today,' he insisted, showing one of his wicked smiles.

'Is Gadget playing? Ice Man enquired. They all laughed.

'Yeah he's playing. Do you know last week he scored in the opposition's goal. Someone set up a *We Hate Gadget Club* and Gadget put up his hand to join. That guy is simply unbelievable,' Mick said stubbing out his cigarette, his fifth that morning. All the supervisors left the office except Micky, having a few last minute things to do. He bellowed at Mick Davies.

'Ice Man, don't you forget you need to be here at 12.30pm to see the crews in. Slump will be here in time for you to leave for the footy,' Micky's voice boomed in the direction of the hired Luton taillift van that the Ice Man used for collecting the fridges.

'You can count on me, Mick!' The Ice Man returned as his van door slammed shut.

Just as Mick was packing away the endless paperwork associated with a large workforce, a call came in over the radio.

'Mick, I collected the gully guzzler from Transport at 11am this morning and it's sucking all right but I can't get it to go in a straight line,' a worried driver reported; Mick sighed heavily.

'Jesus Christ, Sam. Don't drive it. Park it up and wait until I get Transport out to you; OK, mate?' Reluctantly Sam said he would wait knowing it could be several hours before a fitter arrived. Meanwhile Micky got on the blower to Terry Deadman and read the riot act about sending out vehicles that were not fit for purpose. Terry got the message and Micky was finally free to go and do the things that senior refuse supervisors do before preparing mentally for the footy.

The football went well, that is for Parks. The five-a-side friendly was still that even though Parks thrashed Waste Management within one inch of their lives. The Crooked Billet, just across from the football pitch was the venue for an after match beer and sandwich. Reggie had joined the team as a supporter and watched them from the side, shouting advice when he thought they warranted it.

'We could make this match a bigger event; invite the wives and have a drink afterwards one Saturday?' Reggie was seriously contemplating making it a formal social event which was quite unusual for him because he always had a good excuse for missing the Christmas party and any other such event where loud music and jocularity were involved.

'No Reg,' Micky Brown defended their friendly games, 'thanks for the thought but we just like to let off steam a bit. We don't want to make it formal. It all gets too stressful,' Micky explained looking at the others for support.

'Mick's right, Reg. It's nice of you to think about us but we'd rather just leave it as a friendly,' Larry reinforced Mick's sentiments.

Reggie was still not satisfied. Human Resources had had consultants in and all managers had been tasked to put together a buddy programme, where staff get to know each other better and feel loved by their co-workers.

'Has anyone got any other ideas for a social event then? What about a quiz evening or rounders perhaps?' Reginald Turner was about the same age as Micky Brown, fifty something. He smoked heavily like most of the supervisors and croaked liked them too. Reggie had long greasy hair streaked with grey that was usually tied back in a pony tail. He resembled a market trader more than a council manager which probably helped the workforce identify with him.

The only reason that Reggie was a manager, Micky reckoned, was because he always managed to say precisely the right thing at the right time. To add insult to injury, his words of wisdom were usually those he had heard someone else utter; no original thoughts of his own, Micky often teased him about it to his face.

'What's all this crap about wanting to organise social events then, Reg? You hate social events,' Micky insisted, taking another drag on his ciggy.

'It's all about workforce wellbeing, Mick,' Reggie explained, 'I'm supposed to do something to raise morale. It's one of my appraisal objectives set by Dingle last week. I'm supposed to appraise you lot now, bloody nonsense, it is really. This Council wouldn't know what morale was if it bit it on the bloody arse,' Reggie sounded defeatist although the Ice Man had just thought of a cracking idea to build morale.

'Lolita, Baby Doll Reynolds is what we should do,' the Ice Man exclaimed.

'Yeah right, we'd all like to do her,' a woeful Larry Wright lamented.

' No you pillock, Lar, I mean lets take those half price tickets and go and see Lolita at that place in the West End,' the Ice Man said watching the smiles spread across the faces seated round the pub table. Micky was volunteered to make enquires about available Lolita dates. The outing was to be offered to all depot staff but without their partners, a good boys night out.

Gary Green was roused by his mobile phone. It was Councillor Jim Bowen.

'Sorry chaps, I need to go. I've been asked to show Councillor Bowen round the new mobile library vehicle. Libraries are closed today so there aren't any library staff to do the honours. Bowen's off on a fact finding tour of American libraries tomorrow and wants to have a peep before he goes. See you tomorrow folks,' he said, dashing off to get his van.

Gary Green drove into the depot at breakneck speed. On arrival he parked and rushed over to the neatly dressed Councillor standing relaxed and smiling by the allocation office and showing no sign of being irritated at having had to wait around for twenty minutes. This, Gary soon realised was due to the fact that the Councillor had been thrilled to meet the late crew, a mixed bunch returning to the yard at the end of the missed bins collection. In particular, he had been bowled over by their driver, Richard Holmes. Late twenties and built like an Adonis with blonde hair and a healthy tan, his oiled and rippling muscles proclaimed him as someone to die for if you were that way inclined. By the time Councillor Bowen had arrived and asked him where he could find Gary Green, Richard had changed out of his protective clothing and put on his civvies, which were rather tight around the nether regions and produced a rather pronounced bulge at his groin.

Richard claimed to be bisexual and there seemed to be a mutual attraction growing between himself and the councillor. He asked sheepishly if he might have a look inside the mobile library, sort of tag along and since Gary did not want an argument in front of a councillor, he agreed. He was only there himself because he had drawn the short straw and unluckily signed for the vehicle when it had first arrived.

'Councillor, I think you'll find the issue and discharge system interesting. It's computerised and very hi-tech. The vehicle will have internet access, or so

I am told,' Gary was no computer expert but he could use a PC for rudimentary things like letters and could even make up a basic table.

'Yes, I particularly wanted internet access as I'm very keen that the travellers' at the Lemon Grove camp site have free access,' he explained. Gary made no comment.

The councillor admired the internal decoration of the mobile library and was especially taken by a neat vending machine cleverly wedged into a recess.

'Excellent,' he said pointing at the machine, 'people in areas that are more than three miles from a library building will be able to choose their books over a cup of coffee. I have a great feeling about this library. It'll be a real community asset and provide a chance for neighbours to meet and have a chat,' the councillor enthused.

'I didn't think the mobile stopped long enough for that?' Gary remarked having spent years driving around the borough, making mental notes.

'Well then, we'll just have to change the schedule so that it does!' Councillor Bowen said assertively, eyeing the HGV driver lurking in the shadows of the oversized books.

Richard Holmes was mutually attracted to this fresh blood on the Council wearing the quaint tweed jacket topped with radiant ginger hair cut in the shape of a college boy number five. Gary, feeling uneasy about all the suggestive glances bouncing around him decided it was time to exit.

'Councillor, is there anything else you'd like to see tonight? It's just that my wife has a yoga class tonight and I'm babysitting…'

'I just want to have a quick look at the book stock,' the Councillor replied, 'but I'm sure Richard here could lock up, that's if you wouldn't mind Richard?' This was an offer not to be refused and he nodded eagerly. 'Right you are then, Gary, off you go. We'll manage on our own,' Jim Bowen said keeping an eye trained on the muscular body in the tight trousers. Gary smelled a rat but just wanted to get home and retain his harmonious household.

'Rich, put the keys through Workshop's letterbox. There's a tag on the bunch so they'll know what they are in the morning,' Gary said leaving the library vehicle, 'have a good trip, Councillor,' Gary called, waving as he walked down the yard to his van.

The councillor and Richard chatted happily in the silent yard for some time until Richard courageously asked if his new friend fancied a drink at the Raindrop, a pub just down the road.

'That's a gay pub. I go there sometimes with my friend,' suggested an excited Councillor Bowen.

'I drink there all the time,' Richard said moving closer to Jim, 'I'm surprised I haven't seen you there, Councillor?' Richard seductively rubbed his hand along Jim's
tweed sleeve, pouting slightly, 'nice material. I must get one,' he said sarcastically. Richard prided himself on being a trendy dresser and homely tweed was not really his scene. Was it the older, father figure look he was drawn to? Jim Bowen was enjoying being touched by this beautiful young macho thing with pulsating muscles and when lust finally got the better of the pair they left together in the Councillor's VW Polo, leaving Richard's battered old Ford Fiesta in the yard. They drove to Richard's flat above the local Tandoori restaurant, counting themselves as new best friends. The next

morning Gary Green was on the early shift and noticed Richard's car was still parked up the yard.

'Have a good night's sleep, Rich? Gary greeted him as he arrived for his shift. Richard kept his head down so that his blonde hair was nearly all you could see of him. 'That Councillor Bowen's a nice bloke, eh Rich?' Larry called out having been briefed by Gary on the previous evening's body language. Later, over a cup of coffee, they got stuck in.

'That Councillor Bowen's definitely got the hots for our Rich and Rich likes him too, I could tell. You should've seen the admiring looks they were giving each other. I'm not bothered but Charlie Pratt told me this morning that Bowen is supposed to be living with some chap who works for Padwick Borough Council,' Gary said, taking another drag on his fag.

'They tend to move around from one to another at the drop of a hat. What's that word, prom something?' Gary Biddles asked.

'Promiscuous, is the word you're searching for,' Micky said coming to Biddle's rescue.

'Yeah, that's it. My mum says it's why they 'ave so many of those sexually transmitted diseases,' Biddles enlightened them. GB was bordering on the edge of being a bit simple and at thirty still lived with his mum, Carol, the namesake of the tattoo Cyril had admired at the team meeting.

'Your mum says a lot of things, Biddles, mind you, she's usually right!' Micky Brown cackled. The merriment did not last long. Cyril's name was prominent on a piece if paper in front of him, which quickly led to a change in his countenance. 'Now what are we going to do with these silly buggers who think we're going to get everyone recycling eighty five percent in one bleeding year?' Micky said, looking like he had a headache coming on.

'That Huckett is a silly sod if you ask me,' chipped in Gary Newton, Street Cleaning's manager, 'the times have definitely changed. It wasn't that long ago that we were here to make sure that the electorate did what we told them to do and the elected councillors didn't interfere. Now all they want to do is take over,' Gary spoke from the heart and for them all. Another day of gloom and doom beckoned.

Chapter 5

Cheatham's Chief Finance Officer was a woman at least that was the rumour circulating the Council's corridors. Miss Irene Bendover was tall and gangly with mousy brown hair and a demeanour that said she could drink you under the table any night, which was confirmed by the bags beneath her eyes. Her name, I. Bendover conjured up an amusing spectacle and she was the butt of so many jokes providing endless mirth amongst her staff. To say that Irene was careful with money was an understatement. The departmental directors found her a difficult character to deal with as she could turn quite nasty indeed, most felt that Miss Bendover was the Council's very own *axis of evil*.

Cyril was attending the Saturday Community Conference that he had referred to at his last team meeting and was joined by the event's Chair, Councillor Tom Merryweather, the Lead Councillor for community things. The day was pitched at showing community groups how they could become trailblazers and environmental champions leading Cheatham to greatness and encouraging everyone to do their bit. Merryweather got the ball rolling with a stirring opening.

'Local Agenda 21 is about taking forward the recommendations of the Earth Summit agreed in Rio over a decade ago. It's about appreciating the issues raised at Kyoto and the Johannesburg World Summit on Sustainable Development. Environmental problems affect us all and particularly the poorer family. Friends of the Earth have found that poorer families are more likely to live closer to polluting factories than richer families. By working together we can make sure that we don't have any polluting factories in Cheatham,' he explained.

Needham's Public Hall fell silent. The community spirited volunteers assembled were greatly affected by the Councillor's words. Cyril, however, could not at first understand the relevance of Merryweather's remarks since the borough did not have any polluting factories and few poor families. Although, on second thoughts, a population worried about the local environment was more likely to recycle more stuff.

'LA 21 gives us, the major stakeholders the power to change things; to carry the flag and show others the error of their ways. The ultimate aim of this conference is to get local people like us to sign on the dotted line and assist the Council with its Sustainability Action Plan. There will be no financial reward but the moral satisfaction will be endless as you will be doing so much to safeguard the future of your children and even reduce the effects of climate change,' Councillor Merryweather encouraged.

Merryweather's discourse paved the way for Sir David Hooper to address the crowd and offer his own six penny worth.

'I want to talk to you about trees. I plan to plant an urban forest in Cheatham because trees attract wildlife, clean the air and reduce the risk of flooding to some of our low lying areas where the River Pad runs into Padwick. To do this I need lots of Tree Wardens to plant, water and keep an eye on them,' Sir David spent ten minutes talking about trees gradually bringing the subject round to Cyril's pet topic, 'and not a million miles from trees, is recycling. Seventeen trees are needed to make a tonne of paper and we don't want to keep cutting the things down,' Cyril made a note of this interesting fact ready to impress the Waste Management Team. Sir David, having come to the end of his address, extended an arm to Cyril. 'My councillor, Cyril Huckett is working tirelessly to revolutionise our waste services and increase our recycling rate to eighty five percent in just one year!' Cheers arose from the audience, 'yes, I know it does sound like a tall order but Cyril has impressive plans and he has my blessing to put Cheatham on the recycling map. I need, however, to count on you all to support him in achieving the Council's manifesto on Waste and Recycling.'

Cyril rounded on Miss Bendover and Sir David Hooper during the conference coffee break.

'David, Irene, I need your advice. I had a meeting last week with the Waste Management Team about improving the recycling services but they're not keen to listen to me because they're under staffed and have horrendous problems with unreliable vehicles. This could put me in a spot of bother and I was wondering if there was any chance of a sub for Dingle's crews and a little bit extra for Charles Pratt in Transport who is in desperate need of a couple of additional fitters?' Cyril delivered his request with gravitas but Irene looked, as usual unmoved. Her appearance gave the impression that she had been pulled through a hedge backwards; her makeup was askew and staggering momentarily she gave Cyril one of her, *where did you creep out of my funny little friend,* stares. Her cup rattled noisily on its saucer as Cyril's request gave her the shivers.

'How much of a sub, as you call it, were you thinking of Councillor?' Irene's eyes were glued to Cyril's face whilst Sir David stood quietly drinking his coffee ignoring the contretemps going on around him.

'I'm afraid I can't say at the moment but I do want to make some drastic changes. I want to avoid industrial action that might arise on the pretext that my service changes will give them more work. The Union is pretty quick to tell them to down tools,' Cyril could see from the look on Irene's tired features that she was not sympathetic, 'our refuse vehicles are passed their sell by date and spend more time in the workshop than on the road,' Cyril continued, hoping to convince her.

Irene was irritated by these so called untrained professionals who just kept spending her money.

'Councillor, I am feeling your pain!' she said banging her chest with her hand. Cyril was unconvinced by this emotional outburst. 'I understand that a new refuse collection vehicle can cost upwards of one hundred thousand pounds,' Irene Bendover said glumly. Cyril felt a sudden need to lower his sights to accommodate this fiendish woman.

'Good second hand RCVs can be obtained at auction for about two thirds of the new price, even half the price and I suppose two reconditioned vehicles might do the trick for the moment,' he added hastily.

'So, the worse case scenario is you need an immediate one hundred thousand pounds. Would you like me to write you out a cheque?' Irene asked sarcastically. Cyril regarded her facial expression closely. She seemed to be getting ruddier, which was probably due to too much hot coffee, he concluded. Irene's offer of money dumbfounded him; was she really going to write him out a cheque then and there? It was then that she went for Cyril's proverbials.

'Money doesn't grow on trees, Councillor, even environmentally friendly ones like those The Leader was just talking about. I need a formal proposal from you and only then will I consider whether the money will be forthcoming. Anything you get in addition to your budget you will pay for next year!' Irene took a deep breath and smiled wickedly back at the sad, quaking apology for a man in her midst.

Cyril felt sure he had caught a glimpse of two bloodstained fangs in the mouth of *she who must be obeyed*. He looked again but they were gone and whilst he still had her attention, he racked his brains to remember exactly what else the Waste Management Team had told him they must have.

'We need a couple of loaders and at least five new HGV drivers to reduce our dependency on agency staff as well as the freighters we were just discussing,' Cyril rattled.

'Councillor Huckett, please send me a report detailing exactly what it is you want and I will consider our options,' Irene Bendover never bent over backwards to help her colleagues. She boasted truly executive accommodation mainly because she could squeeze money from somewhere else to pay for it. It was a strange thing but Irene's section never went over budget. Most believed it was because she knew the precise details of everyone else's budget and in particular who was likely to be underspent and therefore in a position to arrange virements according to her whims.

As Irene stepped away to get a refill, Sir David gave Cyril hope.

'Tough cookie that one but don't you worry, Cyril. I'll have a word with her in due course. Just let me know if you don't get any joy. We certainly can't have our fledgling manifesto floundering,' Sir David supported. Overhearing some of the conversation Irene returned and towering over Sir David, delivered her missive.

'Leader, I will take this opportunity to remind you that according to Section 114 of the Local Government Finance Act 1988, a Council Member must have regard to any relevant advice provided to him by an Authority's Chief Finance Officer acting in pursuance of her duties under section 5(2) of the Local Government and Housing Act 1989. I will of course be pleased to give you my advice at any time,' Irene said with a wry smile on her face as she flounced off to join one of the conference's break-out groups.

The Leader was annoyed at being talked to in this manner in front of Cyril. He made a mental note to search out suitable jobs that might attract Ms Bendover to pastures new. He was already drafting the most impeccable reference in his head and muttering obscenities under his breath he took his leave of Cyril and went to another of the workshops. On Monday morning Sir David spoke to his secretary, Pamela Peters.

'What was the name of that head hunting company that advertises in the Municipal Yearbook? I mean the one that's always looking for chief officer material and I think I remember the Greater London Authority was recruiting finance people just recently too. Check the GLA's website would you, Mrs P and let me know what you find,' Sir David said already feeling better. He would show that cocky Miss Bendover what he was made of.

Chapter 6

They say a week in politics is a long time but for Cheatham's Waste Management Team it could be an eternity. Stressed out from fighting fire with fire every day they filed into the Civic Offices exactly a week from their last meeting for another scintillating discussion on how to improve recycling. Cyril was late. His wife had taken the car and there was no way she was leaving work in order to run him to his 10am meeting. It had to be the bus and the bus was late. During his absence, the team drank coffee and chatted idly until Slump dipped into his pocket and brought out a crinkled sheet of paper.

'Mick, look at this picture and if you laugh it's because you're an evil bastard!' Slump said. They all crowded round as he revealed the photo of an elderly lady on a mobility scooter lying on her side in a ditch surrounded by workmen. The picture was funny and Mick could not help but allow his lips to pucker; the rest were in stitches too. 'You're all evil bastards!' Slump shouted

'Only because we don't know the lady in the picture. If it was my own mother I wouldn't laugh because I would be emotionally involved,' Mick explained.

John Dingle pretended not to hear the crude conversations going on around him and kept his head down trying to read through the minutes of the last meeting. Reg was making some kind of list that had not gone unnoticed by his team.

'What you up to Reg?' Micky asked loudly, 'you're lovely Juney making you get the shopping now as well as doing the dusting?' Micky laughed, 'get it? Reggie's a dustman or was until he became a high and mighty manager,' Mick crowed.

'Actually Mick, I'm baking a cake tonight. A Victoria jam and cream sponge; it's my speciality.' Reggie was making a list of the ingredients he needed to buy at the Co-op on his way home.

'Well, I've 'eard everyfink now,' Mick said surprised, 'why ain't you ever told us you made cakes before? You could have made us all cakes instead of those awful bloody things Gary Biddles brings in from his mum.' Micky knew how to wind Biddles up and Biddles was rising to the bait until Gary Green put an arm around his shoulders to placate him. Adrian Moses-Pomfrey bounced a knowing glance across the table at John Dingle. They were both taking in this picture of domestic bliss in the Turner household.

The incongruous image of a rotund, greasy haired Reggie plastered with flour and wearing a cotton apron rested uneasily in their minds.

'Well, come on then, Reg. How do yer make a sponge cake, pal?' Mick was not going to let this one go.

'This is serious business, Mick. It's therapeutic, helps to calm me after a day in the chicken shed.' The chicken shed was Reggie's way of describing the frantic way they worked and the awful conditions they had to do it in. With his voice croaky from his last ciggy, Reg began to explain his method for baking sponges.

'I take the butter, real butter mind, not margarine and blend in the caster sugar until it makes a fine paste. I then whisk in the eggs and the flour, sieved of course and...'

'Stop right there, mate,' Slump shouted. Reggie found it difficult to ignore Slump's interruption as his eyes were drawn to the words emblazoned across his T-shirt, *treat me like the slut I am.* He noted that the Acting Manager for Toilets was not in Council uniform. 'I always sieve the flour in a bit at a time with the eggs; stops it all curdling,' Slump added his culinary advice whilst turning an imaginary wooden spoon.

'Slump's right. It can curdle very easily. My mum always makes sure her pans are well greased before stuffing the mixture in,' Biddles said having watched his mother lovingly bake cakes on many an occasion.

Councillor Huckett had arrived in the middle of the cake baking discussion. He poured himself a coffee and joined them at the table. He listened attentively and could not believe his ears; he was working with a bunch of pansies, all of them. No one would ever catch Cyril making cakes. Women bake cakes. He coughed to let them know he was present.

'OK chaps, I'm so glad you could all make it,' he said, which begged the question of whether they had had any choice in the matter. 'Adrian, let's start with you and your research. What have you got for me? Delay is the enemy of progress,' Cyril chuckled, 'that's one of my own sayings. Rather good, I think,' he insisted. There was no sign that the assembled throng appreciated Cyril's way with words.

Adrian cleared his throat and began outlining some of the recycling schemes being implemented by other councils.

'Boxes are very popular. Residents put out papers, glass, plastic bottles and cans which are collected weekly or fortnightly and separated at the kerbside into a specially built vehicle or taken back to what is called a MRF, a Materials Recycling Facility or put simply a sorting facility. The good thing is that the collectors only take the items that are on the list. Anything that's not wanted and can't be marketed is left behind. Several councils using boxes have found their satisfaction rates soar,' Adrian enthused.

'How big are these boxes and will they get us to eighty five percent recycling?' Cyril asked.

'Usually they're about fifty litres. This means they're small enough to carry out to the kerbside and store indoors but reasonably large enough for a substantial amount of the household weekly waste,' Adrian was efficient in his research and Cyril was convinced that the graduate background was an asset but he was not all that pleased with Adrian's research outcomes.

'I want more recycling than *a substantial amount'*. We must maximise collections and find a way of doing so cheaply. We can't afford a weekly collection of both waste and recyclables,' Cyril said thinking about his wheelie bin idea again. Dingle could see the way things were going and thinking in terms of pleasing Cyril and his own request for early retirement he put across another possibility for Cyril to consider.

'Councillor, if we were to develop your interesting wheelie bin idea we might be able to economise by using just one set of vehicles. We would need to increase our fleet because emptying wheelie bins takes longer but we could use the waste vehicles one week and the same freighters the following week to pick up the recycling bins,' Dingle had been busy. He had his eyes on an upgrade before collecting his pension, 'we would also need to recruit more staff,' the Executive Head of Waste Management added. Mick Brown leaned towards Reggie and whispering, *arse licker*.

Reggie added grist to the mill reminding Cyril of his previous plea for more resources.

'Sorry to bring this up again Councillor, but you said you would find out if we could get any extra money for staff and vehicles? We're running around like blue arse flies, pardon my French,' Reg explained. The supervisors did look tired and Micky Brown was leaning his head against his hands.

'Well, as a matter of fact I did speak to the Chief Finance Officer, Irene Bendover,' Cyril began. A chuckle arose from Gary Biddles and was quickly snuffed out by a look from Councillor Huckett. 'She is quite prepared to consider any emergency funding we might require. What I need is a breakdown of the costs and the cheaper we can make it the better most probably. There is always the chance that we'll be made to go out to tender of course,' Councillor Huckett explained deciding not to share with them his venomous exchange with the Finance Department's witch.

The supervisors were not hugely in favour of too much change and worried about being pushed into purchasing equipment that they were not used to. Reggie Turner had an idea. John Dingle sat on the edge of his seat. He had a funny feeling Reggie was about to make a fool of himself.

'Having to tender won't matter. What we do is make the specification so tight that only a particular company can apply. Say for example we wanted to buy trade bins, since we like Appleby's bins we specify bins with Swedish handles. We say we want a particular capacity because we know that only Appleby makes that size. Get it? There's only one company that fits the bill and that's Appleby!' Reggie banged the table with his lighter, 'we get the supplier we want and the Council can say that it has adhered to the European procurement process,' Reg was pleased with himself but Dingle was not. He did not want councillors knowing that this was how they did things. Councillor Huckett, however, thought this was a very useful piece of knowledge for the future.

'Adrian, what materials do you think we should collect?' Cyril asked. He had a few ideas of his own but he understood the merit of letting others think that their opinion was important.

Adrian looked through his file and as usual he was ahead of the game having burnt the midnight oil.

'Well, Councillor, I would say newspapers and magazines for sure. In a borough like Cheatham where literacy standards are high, residents tend to buy a lot of newspapers. I would estimate that it must be in the region of thirty three percent of our waste; plastic bottle recycling is becoming a must too. I'm always getting requests from residents to collect plastics. Glass is a good one; it's heavy and could help our recycling rate enormously. Aluminium and steel cans are easy to collect...' Adrian was just getting into full flow but was interrupted by Cyril.

'Good work, young man,' Cyril thanked Adrian for his enthusiastic approach, 'I agree that paper is vital but I want all paper not just newspapers and magazines. Look at finding a suitable merchant for the cardboard and junk mail too. I want all those annoying leaflets that come tumbling through our letterboxes salvaged,' Cyril was on a roll now, 'I must say, I really would like to tackle plastics. I'd like to include margarine tubs, yoghurt pots and meat trays as well as the bottles. I don't care about the markets, if residents want them recycled then so do I,' Cyril was feeling triumphant.

Following a coffee and fag break, Dingle drew their attention to another challenge.

'I wonder if I might ask how you intend to sort all these materials? The markets are very specific and they only want clean materials. They won't tolerate contamination in the loads,' Dingle had a sneaky suspicion that the councillor had overlooked this major point and thought he might have managed to put a spoke in his wheels. Never let it be said that Cyril Huckett was not a reasonable man; he welcomed Dingle's question with open arms.

'Mr Dingle has raised an important issue here. Its real 'touching the void' stuff and Adrian, I bow to your professional knowledge on this matter. How do you think we should deal with such a mix of materials?' The team were still working out what 'touching the void' was all about.

'Well yes, Councillor, there are a number of these American inventions that I mentioned earlier known as Materials Recycling Facilities or MRFs. They use a series of conveyors and separating devices and literally sort the materials into whatever you want to sell on the recycling markets. I do believe that a flexible sorting plant that will allow us to add new materials when the time is right will stand us in good stead if there are sudden dips in market prices; recycling is known to have one of the most volatile markets for materials.' Adrian said in his most erudite manner. Cyril was agog; this boy was really something.

Adrian realised when he was on a winning streak and pressed on with his show of knowledge.

'I believe it is sometimes necessary to sort things by hand. Plastic bottles for instance, particularly if the facility is for a smallish borough like our own. The very large cities in the States and UK cities like our own Greenhill Gardenville have thousands of tonnes coming through each year so for them it's worthwhile investing in expensive automatic equipment, like lasers,' Adrian said noting that Cyril was bursting to come in here.

'What! Greenhill Gardenville already has one of these things, these sorting plants?' Cyril blurted. He was extremely annoyed to hear that he had been pipped at the winning post by new town upstarts, 'and what does one of these MRF things cost then and how did Greenhill flipping Gardenville get one before us?' Cyril looked as though he should have taken a pill to reduce his blood pressure and prevent him blowing a gasket.

Fortunately for Cyril, Adrian had the answer to his question. There no stopping this lad, Cyril was impressed.

'European money was how they did it; about eight million pounds of it. The European Union made a grant to get Britain off the bottom of the recycling ladder but it didn't work as it seems we're still there! We've a nasty reputation for being the *dirty man of Europe,* apparently,' Adrian said, frowning at the thought that Britain, the winner of two world wars and defender of so many nations could ever be called *the dirty man of anywhere,* 'Greenhill Gardenville, being a new town with no recycling whatsoever, was chosen as a good place to start. A completely new waste and recycling service was introduced in one go. Residents were so used to being surrounded by newness that they took to it like ducks to water. My own feelings are that we don't need anything as grand as the Greenhill state of the art plant. A scaled down version with lower costs would be adequate for Cheatham,' Adrian advised. Cyril's view of Adrian took a turn for the worse at this point. They were not singing from the same hymn sheet after all. Perhaps Adrian was too circumspect; probably something to do with his age.

'I want one of these MRF thingys and I want the best available. I want the most up to date machinery and I don't care how small Cheatham is, I want automatic sorting, lights, buzzers, bells, computerised monitoring, you name it, we're going to have it here in Cheatham. We're not going to be beaten by the likes of Greenhill Gardenville. Do you hear me everyone?' Cyril Huckett was at his most authoritative.

Dingle listened to Cyril's wish list with dread. His cheeks drained of colour as he tried to think how they might fund such a project with the government about to announce drastic cuts to Cheatham's Standard Spending Assessment.

'Councillor, to have one of these sorting factories we've got to be looking at an investment of around one and a half million pounds and that's if we already own the land on which we build the plant in the first place. If we don't, then I'm afraid the sky's the limit. We will need at least two to three million pounds of capital funds. In addition, we don't yet know exactly how much we'll need to implement a quad wheeled bin scheme, buy the bins, vehicles, extra staff and so on,' Dingle was feeling weary and made a suggestion that was greeted positively by all, 'Cyril, can I suggest that we break now and put together a few feasibility plans before meeting again this time next week? John Dingle only had a couple more years to go to retirement so he did not want ill thought out plans marring his remaining working life. His plan was still to get a few more points up the salary scale before putting in his request for early retirement. To do this he was quite prepared to introduce elephant recycling if this would get him an acceptable retirement package.

Before Dingle had finished speaking the team were on their feet; they all needed a fag. Cyril needed to present his outline plans to the Strategy Committee very soon and he must do this before presenting the Scrutiny Committee with his final costed plan. The Best Value Unit would also need to be involved at some stage and then there was the public to be consulted too. Cyril heaved a sigh as he contemplated the battles ahead and was secretly pleased to have a breathing space. He agreed to Dingle's suggestion to meet in a week's time and made his way upstairs to the LIP Group Room to seek a meeting with Councillor Dickopf. He needed to discuss cost-effectiveness with Edith as soon as possible and get her on his side before he tackled the Strategy and Scrutiny Committees. In his briefcase he just happened to have three bottles of his own home-made organic rhubarb wine which was over ten percent proof. Cyril used his entry card to gain access to the LIP Members' Only office.

Friday afternoons were usually quiet in the Members' Room and this Friday was no different. Edith was sitting at a desk drafting her paper on the Cost Effectiveness of the Social and Moral Affairs Committee or SMAC for short. This committee was supposed to be delivering a new Code of Conduct for Councillors and was charged with any number of other spurious jobs. The new code was aimed at putting an end to the increasing number of council catastrophes.

'Hello Edith,' Cyril announced his arrival. Edith was fully engrossed in reading the PC screen in front of her but on hearing Cyril's voice she stopped and looked up smiling.

'Oh Cyril, how are you? I didn't expect to see you here today,' her inflection made her sound just a little coquettish.

'I was here for a meeting with John Dingle and his team and I saw you come in a little while ago through the meeting room window. I wondered, Edith, if we might have a chat?' Edith Dickopf pushed her keyboard away and swung her chair round to face Cyril.

'How can I help you?' She cooed.

Edith was a little in awe of this member of academia. Having been in education herself she had a high regard for those who were part of the higher education system and university lecturers were at the top of her imaginary ladder.

'Edith, I want to make a difference here in Cheatham. Recycling and waste reduction are part of me. I think, eat and sleep waste minimisation. It's an integral part of my every day life,' Cyril laid himself bare in the poetic sense. Edith was nodding in agreement whilst fluttering her eye lashes and maintaining a sweet angelic smile that caught Cyril's attention. 'I really want to provide a service here in my own backyard that will help others like me feel they are doing their bit for the environment,' he spoke softly to her.

'Yes, yes, Cyril, I quite understand those sentiments but how can I help you?' Edith was listening intently. Cyril opened a reused plastic carrier bag and pulled out a bottle of his rhubarb wine and Edith went to find a couple of plastic cups.

Cyril told Edith of his plan for multi-materials collections and sorting facilities and the need for at least three million pounds of capital investment to say nothing of the increased revenue spend to sustain the current service. They emptied the first bottle.

'I say, Cyril, this wine of yours is jolly good. I feel quite light headed,' Edith admitted. Cyril was feeling quite jovial himself and opened a second bottle. They went on chatting and drinking.

'You see, Edith, in your capacity as Chair of the Cost-Effecti-vshness Committee,' Cyril had difficulty with his pronunciation, 'I know you can help me. You're friends with the Chairs of both the Sh-rategy and S-h-crutiny Committees and I just wondered if you might put a good word in for me?' Cyril needed to say no more. Edith was nodding her head in a very positive manner and Cyril, in his dazed state thought it might spin off in any direction.

'I do think you're wonderful, Cyril,' Edith said, acting just like a star-struck teenager and none too steady on her feet either, 'I think I'd better get myself home,' she said, dazed. Edith staggered towards her jacket hanging on a peg by the door, 'do you know Cedric, no its Cyril isn't it. Oops! Sorry. Now where was I? Ah yes, I was telling you, I read an interesting fact today. Did you know that according to Pareto, eighty percent of council spending is from only twenty percent of its cost centres?' Edith slurred and burped.

Cyril was getting bored with this fellow, Pareto. Edith was always throwing his words of wisdom into council discussions; it was as though she was married to the bloke. They walked with difficulty to the lifts and together they travelled down to what they thought was the ground floor. In their drunken state they had managed to bypass the ground floor and instead found themselves in the Civic Offices basement which was a mass of heating and air conditioning pipes and stacked with old desks and furniture no longer wanted by their previous owners. Stacked up against the walls were loads of cardboard boxes full of old computers waiting to be recycled. Without thinking much about what they were doing they stepped out of the lift and walked along the basement corridor still discussing Cyril's waste management revolution as best they could in their sloshed state. Their voices reverberated off the pipes and concrete floor and the strange resonance made Edith look up.

'We're in the basement, Cyril. It's quite scary down here isn't it,' she whispered. The next minute she was on the floor having slipped on some invisible banana skin.

Cyril put his arms around Edith and tried to pull her up off the floor and as he did so she threw her arms around his neck and kissed him passionately bringing him down on top of her. She would not let him go and soon enough he stopped resisting and gave in. Edith went further; without any warning, she pulled up her navy blue polka dotted pleated skirt and holding her breath, moved Cyril's hands to her thighs. Cyril was intoxicated in more ways than one feeling suspenders, lace stocking tops and frilly thong knickers. He could not see them but in his mind's eye they were crimson, a colour he thought matched this minx's personality. Was this really Edith Dickopf? She was indeed all woman. Cyril had never experienced this sort of tantalising behaviour for nigh on thirty years. He gripped Edith's flesh to be sure and he was indeed touching parts of Edith that no other councillor had ever touched before. Time seemed to stand still as the wine and the overwhelming passion welling up inside him took over and wedging her between cardboard boxes he became one with the Chair of the Cost Effectiveness Committee and knew instinctively that he was not her first.

Cyril sat momentarily on one of the boxes and held his head not believing what had just occurred. Edith beamed satisfaction from ear to ear revealing her slightly bucked teeth. She smoothed out her skirt, pulling her suspender belt back into place making it more comfortable to walk. She recovered her handbag from the concrete floor and finding her mirror and comb, she attempted to unruffle her mousy, chin length hair. Cyril adjusted his own clothing and once they were both decent, he ushered her along the corridor. As they approached the stairwell his eyes homed in on a metal object with a lens high up on the wall. Momentarily his brain did not register the piece of equipment and then suddenly he realised he was looking at a camera. He shuddered and was rendered speechless but for Edith's benefit he pointed to the offending object.

At the top of the stairs Edith found the ability to speak.
'Cyril, I think I'll just pop back to the Members' Room for my paperwork; I'll finish my report at home. Thank you for asking me to help you with the waste minimisation plans. Of course, I will do everything in my power to assist; just come and see me when you're ready,' Edith regarded the floor as she was too embarrassed to look Cyril in the eye. Cyril took the bus home during which he had time to reflect on the outcome of his recent amorous activities. You really could never tell with women. A picture of Miranda formed in his mind and he wondered just how stable his marriage might turn out to be if those cameras had been switched on.

Meanwhile, upstairs in the Chief Executive's office, Councillor Bullman had been enjoying a frothy cup of coffee with Maisie Atichitawomba. They were discussing the day's events and Marcus watched mesmerised as Maisie's breasts rose and fell with each breath that she took. Her low cut, tight fitting black frock, hem just above the knees was more like a sixties cocktail dress. Maisie's plentiful hips pushed the material to its extremes. Her large size however, did not concern Marcus in the least; he found her soft deep fleshy love handles rather comforting. He tried to get Maisie's flesh out of his mind.
'I opened the new swimming pool today and I believe it will be an asset to the borough. It's very welcoming; bright colours, modern changing rooms and so on and I understand from speaking to some of the children this afternoon that the water is nice and warm too. Pools thesedays are nothing like the dark, dank, freezing penny baths that I learnt to swim in,' Marcus was reminiscing for Maisie's benefit since she had not been around in the early fifties, 'I think with facilities like the Fishtails Leisure Centre, we might have

the makings of a few Olympic 2012 champions,' he said, trying to keep his randy feelings hidden.

Mrs Carter, the Mayor's mace bearer had also attended the gala and had seen it through different eyes, grumbling to Maisie about the immoral society we seemed to be developing.

'I don't know what the world's coming to. Those girls from that six form college have no idea of decency. Even if they were swimming in races there are costumes and costumes. It's the parents who are to blame if you ask me. When they all come home pregnant, they'll be sorry,' Mrs Carter prophesied. Remembering Mrs Carter's words, Maisie teased the Mayor.

'Marcus, would any of those prospective Olympic champions be breast stroke champions?' She asked. Marcus looked confused, 'oh, come on Marcus, I'm sure you enjoyed watching those nubile sixteen year olds in their skimpy, high leg, low fronted costumes?' Maisie suggested. Marcus smiled weakly thinking that it was the more mature woman he was interested in, not spotty teenagers.

Maisie decided it was time to take the plunge, metaphorically speaking and leaned over, placing her hand on Marcus' knee, she gave it a squeeze.

'Marcus, don't be shy with me. I'm going to get your innermost secrets out of you before the end of this mayoral year,' she coaxed.

'Oh, I do hope so, Maisie my dear. I would certainly like you to get something out of me,' he replied quietly as Maisie got up to answer the telephone.

'What sort of a security breach are we talking about?' Maisie asked, 'what dvd? I think you'd better come up to my office straight away and explain what the Dickens you're talking about,' she ordered, 'I'm sorry Marcus but I think we're about to have our tête-à-tête interrupted. Stay though, we can find out what this is all about together,' she said.

The uniformed security officer had been busy on the telephone throughout most of Cyril and Edith's hot and steamy rumble but had just caught the end of it on the security cameras as Cyril popped his cork. Being new in the post he could not put names to all the regular faces he saw coming through the Civic Offices so fortunately he had no idea as to the identity of the passionate couple he found himself snooping on. In actual fact, the camera was not positioned in the right place to give a close up of the couple's faces although someone who knew them well would have recognised them.

Maisie took the DVD and popped it into her player. The three of them, Maisie, Marcus and the security officer watched together. The middle aged couple came into camera at the point where Cyril was trying to drag Edith off the ground following her slip. It looked on camera as though he was dragging her to the cardboard boxes to have his wicked way with her. It was only when Maisie watched the piece of film again that she saw more clearly that it was Edith kissing Cyril and making the initial advances, which were definitely of a sexual nature. The security officer was intrigued to know why she was so interested in the finer detail of the activity but luckily declined to ask.

'Do you have any idea who the couple are?' Maisie asked casually, hoping the answer was going to be to her liking.

'None whatsoever;' the security officer answered shaking his head, 'but I could show it to Mike, my line manager. He's been here for yonks and if they're regulars here he will know them for sure.' Maisie jumped in to stop any further investigation into the matter.

'No, don't bother just now. They're probably just some wacky couple who've had too much to drink in the Civic Social Club. I knew this would happen if we opened it up to the public,' Maisie said.

Marcus had recognised Cyril's old corduroy trousers somewhere between his hips and knees. His flyaway hair was another give away. Edith Dickopf in her suspenders and lacy underwear had been more difficult. The words, brazen hussy ran through the Mayor's mind and brought a saucy smile to his face.

'I'll hang on to the disc as you probably have a second copy?' Maisie asked, fishing.

'No Mam. This is the only copy,' the security officer said making his way to the door apologising that since he was the only one on duty he needed to get back to the security desk straightaway.

The coast clear, Maisie turned to Marcus for advice.

'Marcus, what are we going to do? This is a disciplinary offence; no indeed, it's worse than that, it's an immediate suspension. How could they be so stupid? The morons!' Maisie bellowed.

'They're not staff and before you say anything, yes, I know there is a similar procedure for erring councillors but they haven't harmed anyone else except possibly themselves and the good thing is only you and I know their identities.'

Marcus took the disc and wiped it clean preventing nasty embarrassing moments later on.

'But Marcus,' Maisie was still feeling agitated, 'Edith is supposed to be looking into the value of SMAC for heavens sake,' she reminded.

'Let's be thankful then that Edith's committee is SMAC and not SWALC, Sealed with a Loving Kiss,' Marcus mocked thinking it was time he had a bit of the action. Before too long, Marcus was getting stuck in with some juicy slobbering along Maisie's neckline going down as far as he could before being hindered by her dress. Maisie, too, was starting to relax and enjoy.

'I suppose if we've cleaned the dvd at least I won't have to make an embarrassing written allegation to the Standards Board for England or an even more embarrassing statement to the local press about the reasons for the sudden withdrawal of two councillors. Silly me! I really shouldn't be using that word, *withdrawal* should I?' They fell about laughing.

Cyril and Edith both received telephone calls summoning them immediately to the Chief Executive's office for a friendly chat. They decided independently to use the East Entrance thus avoiding the Security Desk. They were seen at different times and although Maisie had made the calls, it was decided that Marcus would deal with Cyril and Maisie would speak to Edith. Both interviews were kept short and sweet and went straight to the point, which was that they must not get caught a second time.

Back at the yard, Friday's workload was also drawing to a close and had for once been less eventful than Cyril's. On Fridays, the crews finished a little bit earlier than the rest of the week and most had checked in by 2pm. For the supervisors it was time for a cuppa before heading home for the weekend.

'You'll never guess what Gary Green told me earlier? He only had a complaint from some woman at Rosemary House about Estate Cleaning Team B,' Larry said as he grabbed the attentions of his colleagues assembled in the allocation office. Micky Brown, Gary Biddles, the Ice Man and Bobby Dalton, an HGV driver on the commercial waste who doubled up as the union shop steward waited with baited breath for Larry to go on, 'apparently, this woman came out of her flat to find one of our cleaners urinating in a bucket. She's made a complaint about that but says he was exposing himself as well and if that's not enough, she's also accused him of being the owner of a two foot turd she found in the hallway,' Larry revealed.

'Well of course he was exposing himself. If he needed a pee he couldn't avoid it,' Bobby said. knowing what it was like to work outside and need a loo.

'She should think herself lucky he wasn't peeing on the floor or in her doorway,' the Ice Man added.

The supervisors had gone back to discussing the state of the universe and finishing their tea when a telephone call interrupted their Friday afternoon mirth.

'Hello, Battersea Dogs Home. How can I help?' Biddles asked trying to be clever. The resident at the other end was not amused and neither was Micky.

'Oy Biddles, do as I say and not as I do, yer silly pup,' he yelled. Biddles owned up.

'Madam, I'm sorry about that. You have come through to Waste Management. How can I be of assistance?' The lady had a penetrating voice and the others could hear her clearly without having to ask Gary to repeat the conversation.

'I put my bin out and you missed me again. This is the third time I've had to report it. Why can't you get it right? I pay my Council Tax...,' the message was given over in the usual irate and aggressive style that the team had grown extremely fond of.

'Tell the lady she's been lost in the system. It never fails to wind them up!' Bobby suggested and then, 'no, on second thoughts don't do that you'll get a bollocking. Tell her you'll deal with it personally, she'll love it!' He chuckled.

Biddles looked to Mick for a definitive way to proceed. He wasn't disappointed.

'We've got a crew doing missed bins in the morning. Put it on their list to do,' Mick ordered, smiling, 'I know I'm not perfect but I'm bloody close,' he joked leaving his mug on the draining board and picking up the local newspaper.

'See this picture of Adrian Moses-Pumphrey or Pomfrey or whatever 'is bleeding name is?' Mick Davies asked, 'he's in 'ere opening a new recycling centre at the Cracknell Superstore, you know the new one on the bypass? That'll upset old Huckett as he's rather partial to a bit of publicity that one is. Mark my words, there'll be tears before bedtime when he sees he wasn't invited to have his own face in the newspaper,' even the Ice Man had noted Councillor Huckett's hell bent drive for boosting his own already inflated ego and on this occasion their Recycling Officer had eclipsed him; recycling was going to be bad news for some. Agreeing with Mick's sentiments they made their way home, Mick dusting the bonnet of his MK3 Cortina adoringly with his sleeve before jumping into the driver's seat.

On the Saturday morning of Cyril's fateful basement rendezvous week, the Huckett's had breakfast together. It was just tea, wholemeal toast and marmalade as was usual and a chance to catch up and chat about the whereabouts and doings of their children. They were never able to discuss, *Question Time* or the latest documentary on Jack the Ripper because they didn't own a television set. It was part of Cyril's own brand of snobbery and in keeping with the illusion that very clever people in the academic world simply did not require stimulation from one. Television was for common people who turned into couch potatoes as a result of endless viewing. Academics like the Hucketts' passed their time reading good quality newspapers and learned journals.

'Cyril, have you seen this picture in the local paper?' Miranda asked. Cyril was suddenly convulsed and struck by a form of paralysis. His cup was suspended in mid-air and he was unable to put his arm into reverse and return his cup to its saucer. He was sweating like a pig and his thoughts were propelled instantly back to the events of yesterday and the Civic Offices basement. It just could not be possible, could it? It happened less than twenty four hours ago. Even the local paper was unable to work that fast?

The strained look on Cyril's face told Miranda that he hadn't seen the picture.

'Oh really, Cyril, I know it's unthinkable that there should be a feature on recycling and you're not the star of the show but do you have to look as if you've been seriously wounded? I really think you must make that appointment with the optician. You must have spent a good hour first thing this morning scrutinising every sentence so how on earth you missed this photo I do not know,' Miranda sighed. She could not understand how Cyril got through the day let alone managed as a councillor. He took the paper from her and there in front of his eyes was a photograph of Adrian Moses-Pomfrey with the store manager about to cut a green ribbon and officially open a new car park recycling centre. Thank God for Adrian Moses-Pomfrey, thought Cyril. He would strangle Edith the next time he was alone with her except that he never intended to be alone with her again.

Chapter 7

Following Cyril's escapade in the Civic Offices basement he considered it might be better to lie low for a few days. A year would have been preferable but he did have Council business to attend to and a reputation to rebuild as Maisie and the Mayor would see it. A meeting was timetabled with the Leader, Sir David Hooper and other lead councillors and he felt he should force himself to resurface for that.

'Good to see you're alright, Cyril. I understand from Pamela that she's had difficulty contacting you this week,' the Leader said but noting Cyril's indifferent facial expression and after what seemed like an eternity, the Leader started the meeting.

'I just wanted to have a catch up session with you all just to see how we're all getting along with our strategic plans. I had rather hoped that Edith would be here,' he said, clinging to the hope that someone might offer an explanation for her absence but with several executive officers shrugging their shoulders, he realised his hope was in vain. Cyril was praying hard that she would not turn up late. 'Edith will be playing a crucial role in deciding on the cost-effectiveness of your little projects. She is, as you all know, working very closely with the Best Value Unit. Yes, I know Best Value isn't just about the most cost effective or cheapest contract anymore but about all round good value as encompassed in the four C's – Challenge, Compare, Compete and for the life of me, I can't think what the fourth beggar is. Anyone remember?' The Leader paused for a suitable length of time but no one appeared to have the fourth C on the tip of their tongues so he continued. 'We'll go around the table and perhaps you can each give a résumé of where you are. Jim, perhaps you could start by telling us something about your recent trip to the States?'

A fresh faced Jim Bowen, Lead Councillor for Libraries cleared his throat and sat upright in readiness to speak.

'Thank you, Leader. I must begin by stating that the trip was not a jolly,' smiles, winks and murmurings around the table could be summed up as, *pull the other one, its got bells on,* 'it was a whistle stop tour of some of the main libraries in Washington and New York State, which included small town libraries. I found good book stocks, lots of parking, which I suppose you would expect in the States,' he knew they would not like the sound of 'lots' of car parking with their manifesto to reduce car usage in the borough and he proceeded with less gusto, choosing his words very carefully, 'I am of course aware that we want to get residents out of their cars and onto public transport and indeed that the LIP manifesto clearly states a desire to reduce the need for large car parks and five car families. USA mobile libraries are really something, enormous stocks of CDs and so on. One even had two foldaway beds so that the driver and librarian could keep their mileage down by not returning to base each evening,' knowing smiles flashed across the table.

'That wouldn't be much good to us, would it?' Tom Merryweather piped up, 'Cheatham only covers twelve square miles,' he said, laughing heartily.

Towards the end of his report, Jim mentioned that he had come across a place that had offered residents a kerbside collection for their recyclables but they had turned it down.

'They preferred instead to take their waste to a depot known colloquially as 'the dump', because apparently they saw the weekly trip as a chance to get to know their neighbours and have a chat. An enterprising entrepreneur had even set up a coffee stall making it quite a community hub. I was wondering if it might catch on here in Cheatham? It could save the Council a bob or two,' he suggested. The Leader liked what he heard. Residents taking ownership of their waste and delivering it to a central location would indeed save tonnes of council money.

'How about it, Cyril? Do you think it would work here and could we pick up brownie points for Community Development?' Sir David asked. Cyril struggled for an answer wanting to put his large hands around the Leader's neck and squeeze hard feeling that his plans were under threat.

'Well, as a matter of fact, Leader, I've undertaken some research myself,' Cyril managed to think up an alternative idea, 'coincidentally one of the British paper mills has spent a fortune on a survey of recycling habits,' by chance Cyril had skimmed through one of Adrian's reports, 'apparently people recycle more if it's collected from their doorstep, just like the general rubbish.'

'It does seem sensible,' Councillor Merryweather supported Cyril, 'I wouldn't load my car up and drive miles with a load of rubbish in the back. Empty cat food cans are frightfully smelly and I should know, because my wife has seven of the feline monsters,' he explained with feeling.

Sir David did not like cats or dogs in any shape or form but he noted that Tom Merryweather always got an acceptable majority which was probably down to his wife's popularity with Cheatham's cat lovers.

'Talking about smelly cat food cans has reminded me of something else that's been bothering me of late,' the Leader began, 'the Dogs (Fouling of Land) Act or whatever it's called,' Cyril sat up thinking that this question was directed at him but the Leader turned instead to Councillor Jack Goodenough, the councillor in charge of Environmental Health, 'Jack, what are we doing about this? Are we going to start fining owners on the spot if dogs are caught defecating on the pavement? There are lots of votes in dog shit especially from the mothers of young children and we should always remember that,' Sir David told them.

Some say LIP won the last election on its dogs' mess manifesto. There had been some silly comments about the phraseology used like, *pulling out all the stops; tabling a motion* and so on in relation to dog poo and Councillor Goodenough did his best to put a cohesive reply to the Leader.

'David, it's not as easy as it seems. In order to fine a dog owner for falling foul of the law you have to see the four legged blighters do the business and this doesn't happen very often. Dog owners can smell a council officer a mile off and they run like the clappers. In addition, if a resident sees a dog do it, they have to follow them home and report the dog's address to the Police and be prepared to stand witness in court. This doesn't go down too well in the good neighbour stakes,' Jack said pouring himself a glass of water. All this talk about dogs' mess had made him rather dry.

The Leader admired a photograph of Fido, the Council's poo scooping machine used to shovel up dogs' doings. It showed the honourable Sir David against the scenic backdrop of Cheatham High Street adorned with a crash helmet and sat astride Fido. There was also a vacuum cleaner attachment to the back, which was used to suck up the unmentionables.

'I want some action on this Act,' Sir David said sharply, 'I want dogs kept out of most parks and large signs put up clearly stating this,' the Leader ordered.

'I don't think dogs can read can they,' Cyril whispered in Councillor Merryweather's ear.

'No, but knowing David he'll have the signs written in doggy language, woof, woof, ruff, bark.' Goodenough muttered. Sir David was still going strong.

'I want headlines in the local papers about this Act and I want some poor sod made a scapegoat and fined out of all proportion sending a message to all bloody dog owners. I also want to be part of any targeted publicity. Buy another five Fidos and get dogs mess on the front pages as soon as possible,' the Leader said finishing his lecture and asking Cyril to outline his waste minimisation plans.

The next day Cyril decided to drop in at the depot. Councillor Bowen had an appointment with the Transport Manager to discuss maintenance charges for the mobile library fleet enabling Cyril to cadge a lift. This meeting was carefully planned to coincide with the time the crews arrived back from their rounds. Bowen parked his VW Polo in a prominent place hoping that a certain sexy person with rippling muscles would spot it. Parting company with his fellow ward councillor, Cyril made his way to the allocation office. Micky Brown and Reggie were there and somewhat taken aback by the Councillor's unannounced arrival. The door was being wedged open by a fire extinguisher so Cyril was able to stroll in taking them all by surprise.

'This is a pleasure, Councillor,' Reggie said finding his voice, 'what can we do for you?' He croaked.

'I've got some ideas Reginald, which I rather wanted to share with you and Mr Dingle. I suppose he's at Civic is he?' Cyril was never sure where his staff were garrisoned.

'He certainly is,' Reggie answered gleefully.

'Yep, that's how we like it to be,' piped up Micky, coughing.

'I suppose Adrian's not here either?' Cyril looked at the weathered, coarse and harassed faces of his Waste Management staff and knew he had chosen a bad day. Still, he was there now and intended to make the best of it, 'is there somewhere comfortable we can sit and chat?' Cyril asked, looking around at the rinky-dink furnishings and knowing he was going to be disappointed.

A mangled settee and a couple of uninvitingly grubby chairs salvaged from the tip were all that was on offer. Cyril decided that the settee would have to do.

'I've been thinking that perhaps we should visit a few councils and waste companies and get some ideas. I was wondering about a trip up north to Crappendale City Council? They recently started something called a treble wheeled bin scheme and I believe it's working rather well. The last I read in the Municipal Times was that they'd hit a forty five percent recycling rate from day one. Eighty five percent is what I'm after and these commercial bodes could tell us how to do it,' Cyril said, rather hoping they might offer him a coffee. They didn't.

'Sounds like a good idea Councillor but we can't all go because someone has to mind the shop,' Reggie said, being practical. Cyril looked strangely baffled as he had not reckoned on conscientiousness being a depot commodity.

'I need you to come, Reginald, together with Adrian and Mr Dingle and you might want to bring one of your drivers to see what he makes of any new schemes we see. The crews are at the rock face and I'm sure they'll have some important comments to make,' Cyril said knowingly.

Gary Newton breezed into the office wearing a smart suit which made him look decidedly swanky and enabled the ensuing silence to be broken.

'Oy oy, why my son are you dressed up like a tart then, Gar?' Micky asked in the only way that Micky Brown would ask.

'Leave him alone, Mick,' Reg requested, 'Gar's had an interview today, aint yer mate?' Reggie explained.

'Yes, that's right. I went for that job over at Padwick, Contract Manager for Street Cleansing. Not much different to what I'm doing here actually but more pay and less work,' Gary shot a glance at the councillor. Cyril shut his eyes momentarily and prayed quietly that they would not all be spurred on to apply for job re-evaluations and end up costing the Council more money at this important juncture in his tenure. Mick, as always managed to have the last word.

'Gary, what's wrong with it 'ere mate? You can't deny the insults are quite good in Cheatham,' he glanced across at Cyril who was pretending not to have heard a word and who then steered the conversation back to his anticipated fact finding tour.

'Good, that's settled then,' Cyril concluded, 'I'll ask Adrian to make the arrangements ASAP. Now I wonder how long Jim Bowen's going to be,' Cyril said as he looked out into the yard.

Micky Brown did eventually make Cyril a mug of tea which he drank whilst listening to the banter across the counter as the men returned from their day's work. Micky called Kelly Dinhern, the depot's clerical support, in from the Transport Office to help with the crews wanting to clock off.

'Hi Yer baby,' yelled a loader who would have easily passed for a skeleton, he was so thin and scrawny, 'I'm not sure if I'm gonna be in tomorrow love, as my wife's 'aving stomach pains. I just hope she 'aint pregnant again. If she is I'm leaving home,' the skinny bloke stated defiantly as he handed in his completed worksheet, folder and freighter keys.

'Wayne, if she's pregnant I think you might have had something to do with it, don't you?' Kelly replied in her squeaky voice, wagging a finger at Wayne as he stared glumly back at her.

'Yeah I suppose so,' Wayne agreed, 'although it could have been the milkman,' he added looking dead pan.

Conscious of the fact that Councillor Huckett was still there waiting for his friend, Micky busied himself with correspondence.

'Councillor Huckett, you'll like this. It's a letter of praise, although it's a bit difficult to understand exactly what the old gent is going on about. We have to be masters of telepathy down 'ere, Councillor you know. This old gent is ninety seven years old and he says, a big thank you to Cheatham Council for collecting his old cooker last week,' Micky looked up to see Cyril's face beaming, 'but then the letter goes on and I quote...my toilet is broken so where do I stand?' Micky looked mystified.

'As far away as possible or else he'll have very wet feet!' Joked Reg, 'working here is just like playing a game of Cluedo,' he added.

'Yeah, Reg and you'd make a good Mrs Scarlet,' Micky bantered.

'I think that one is definitely for Housing,' Micky said placing it in an internal circulation envelope and dropping it in his Out Tray.

If Cyril thought the day could not get any worse, he was wrong. One of the sweepers arrived at the office window minus his contract uniform.

'Hi Mick, alright if I have a quick practice before I go home?' He asked. Micky tossed a look in Cyril's direction and thought for a second.

'I can't see why not, mate. Give Councillor Huckett a treat,' he said smiling. Cyril thought he was more likely to give him an irritating rash if anything at all. The young sweeper ran off to a cupboard in the entrance hall and reappeared carrying a diggeridoo.

'Love a duck,' Cyril was uncharacteristically heard to exclaim. The sweeper leaned against an oil drum in the yard and started blowing down a large hollowed out wooden tree which made some very deep throbbing sounds, not unlike, Cyril thought, the calls of the bittern which he had often heard in his youth booming on field trips to Norfolk.

Cyril listened to the sweeper's music for fifteen minutes although it seemed like a lot longer. Looking at his watch, he decided that he had been serenaded enough and stopped the sweeper playing in mid flow to speak to Micky.

'Ehm, Micky, I heard the other day about a council in the West Country that's introducing a special song for its workers. How do you think a special song for the refuse crews would go down? Do you think it would help morale and build a feeling of belonging amongst them?' Cyril asked. Micky did not need time to think. The sheer horror of Cyril's suggestion showed immediately on his face. He was not going to be turned into a namby pamby for anyone's sense of belonging.

'Councillor, d'yer mean like those Americans do; hands on breast and thanks be to God for Cheatham, that kind of thing?' Micky could not quite believe the stupidity of this man standing before him. Did he really think that refuse crews, known the world over for their indifference to society's rules and regulations, applauded for their superb knowledge of parts of the English language that others have only heard rumours of and noted for their outstanding musical abilities especially after a night in the Eagle pub, would be the slightest bit interested in singing a mediocre corporate song before starting work at the ungodly hour of 6am on cold, frosty mornings? The idea beggared belief. For sometime he was lost for words and eventually decided to treat the suggestion with the disdain it deserved. 'You're funny Councillor, very funny,' he laughed, pointing at Cyril, 'you'll go down well 'ere if you come up with jokes like that one,' Micky laughed. Cyril got the message and with his pride wounded, he wandered out to Jim Bowen's car.

As Cyril left the office, Micky's attention was diverted to a radio call.

'Mick, is Gary Green there? Only you're not going to believe this, mate. That job at the Dover Road Recreation Ground, you'll never guess what it was?' Before Mick had a chance to answer, the driver of Mobile Street Cleaning Team Three was back on the radio, 'it was only a bloody giraffe. No kidding Micky, a giraffe! It was a deceased baby giraffe, I'll give you that, but even so, it was enormous. We couldn't get it in the transit, Mick,' the hysterical driver reported.

'Have you got it inside the van now, Trev?' Micky asked confused and wondering why he was asking. They had to be pulling his leg as there were no zoos round Cheatham that a giraffe could have escaped from. If they were pulling the giraffe's leg, he thought, it would have been a very long leg at that!

'Yeah thanks, Micky. We've managed after a fashion to get the poor animal in the van. It doesn't look too dignified though. Heaven knows where it came from,' Trevor said.

'Gary's not here at the minute, Trev. I'll call him up and get him over to you,' Micky offered.

'Thanks again, Mick. We'll wait for instructions. I supposed we'll have to take it to the clinical incinerator in Padwick will we, Micky?'

'Yeah, I think so Trev, unless Cyril Huckett has heard of a way of recycling dead giraffes or maybe wants to compost it in 'is back garden,' Mick said looking at Cyril who was still standing in the yard.

'What Micky? I didn't catch what yer said,' Trevor asked.

'No matter Trev, I was being facetious,' Micky laughed.

'What's facetious, Mick?' Trevor asked. Micky shook his head.

'Never mind Trev, I'll see you when you get back. Over and out,' Micky called, closing the call down.

Since Jim Bowen's car was unlocked, Cyril decided to take advantage and sit inside and wait for him there. The radio worked without the need for the ignition key so he took the liberty to tune in to Classic FM. He drifted off in contemplative mood to the rhythm of Beethoven's Pastoral Symphony quite forgetting that he was sitting in the middle of the depot's car park. A dark shadow loomed over the near side passenger window which was followed by a rap tap on the glass, causing Cyril to snap out of his trance. He turned his head towards the window to see a young man with dyed blonde hair looking back at him. Still stunned, he wound down the window and waited for the young man to speak.

'Hi, I thought this was Jim Bowen's car,' the masculine blonde bombshell said, flashing his muscles and wearing designer sunglasses, 'in fact from behind I thought you were Jim Bowen.' The young man was smiling broadly and Cyril detected just a hint of campness in his tone.

'No, I, ehm Yes, I mean this is Jim Bowen's car. I'm waiting for him. He's with Charlie Pratt, the Transport Manager. He'll be along very soon if you need to speak to him,' Cyril, still startled, managed to reply.

'No worries. Just tell him that Richard Holmes was asking after him. Tell him to give me a call, OK? Thanks mate,' he said, pursing his lips and mouthing a kiss at Cyril before leaving.

Cyril nodded as the cocky young man walked nonchalantly away, throwing his contract uniform jacket with the Cheatham council logo of a dove, a wolf's head and a crab over his shoulder. Cyril thought for a few seconds about this impromptu meeting realising that Richard was one of Councillor Jim's little secrets, an illicit liaison since he already had a partner, Damien, living with him. It suddenly dawned on him that perhaps Richard had found Cyril attractive too.

'Well I don't know what the world is coming to; first Edith and then some gay guy! My life used to be so boring and predictable,' Cyril whispered. Slowly a titter started which soon gave way to a howl as he contemplated more fully the occurrences of the past few days. Jim arrived to find Cyril clutching his sides in some discomfort from all the laughter. 'Your lover boy came by to see you; he said for you to give him a call. I must say he's rather a dish!' Cyril winked at Jim, 'I almost fancied him myself. Mind you,' Cyril teased, 'I think he liked the look of me too.' Cyril was still laughing as Jim, mystified by Cyril's reaction to Richard slid into the driver's seat and drove out through the gates, the tears still coursing down Cyril's cheeks.

Adrian, duly informed of Cyril's wish to make a fact finding tour, set about making arrangements. Bill Sterling, the Council's Best Value Co-ordinator explained that there would be a handful of councillors joining the expedition.

Tom Merryweather wanted to look at the sustainability factor; Edith Dickopf was cajoled by Irene Bendover into going, because the shelling out of money would be inevitable in any future recycling plans. The Cheatham Queen of the Dark Arts wanted the councillor responsible for cost effectiveness right in there from the beginning as no way was Ms Bendover for the high jump at some later date because of ill thought out plans. Being comparatively young for a Chief of Finance she intended on having a long career. No financial blunders would occur during her watch. Sir David Hooper was set on going on the trip as a finger in every pie was his way and Jim Bowen had decided to tag along to check out Crappendale City Council's library services although more probably because the provocative Richard Holmes, exemplary HGV driver extraordinaire had volunteered to drive the minibus. There were two other members invited on the trip chosen primarily for their availability rather than their knowledge of recycling. These were Major Prentice-Peabody, the ex-Tory and now member of the LIP and Alfie Leadbetter, a Labour councillor. The LIP worked hard at showing a united and transparent front, hence the desire for cross party involvement. The Mayor had put his name down believing that the Chief Executive might be accompanying the party but when he realised this was not the case he quickly backtracked. Maisie was having her bunions treated on those days and would not be going anywhere for a while.

Cyril was sent the list of attendees and shivered when he saw Edith's name at the top. He had done his utmost to stay away from her; he could not deny that he had enjoyed their dalliance in the Civic Offices' basement but he must now consider his marital position and ignore any romantic feelings he might have for Edith. As he thought about his earlier actions a song from his university drinking days surfaced and he found himself humming the tune to *dirty Gerty from number thirty;* what a siren that woman had turned out to be; just thinking about her seemed to be releasing pent up pressure from inside.

John Dingle was unnerved not knowing precisely what the councillors were up to before he had worked out what they needed to be up to. He met with Adrian and Reggie to find out how the plans for the trip were progressing.

'Adrian, how did they find out about Crappendale City Council's new service?' John was peering over his glasses at Adrian.

'I have no idea, Mr Dingle. I didn't even know about the scheme myself,' an exasperated Recycling Officer replied. Reggie sat there quietly wishing most definitely that they had not found out about Crappendale because now he would have to ask his Juney for permission to sleep away from the marital bed for a night. June had a nasty suspicious mind and coupled with a growing interest in kinky sex, it was putting a strain on their marriage. Reggie could not find enough excuses to fend off his wife's constant carnal desires. Her new interest scared the living daylights out of him. Some of the magazines she was buying could make a man go blind.

The Executive Head of Waste usually liked to be one step ahead but with Cyril in cohorts with Adrian who was racing away with things, he was feeling a sense of failure.

'Where else does the party want to go?' Dingle asked. Adrian pulled out some papers from a very smart leather wallet.

'Besides Crappendale, they say they would like to visit a go-ahead commercial company moving from merely waste disposal to a greater emphasis on recycling and recovery. I thought Aurelia Waste Handling Ltd. would be a good one to visit. Aurelia is on our way back south and it has its own landfill sites and interesting waste reduction plans or so I've heard. They've also had a lot of professional press coverage recently regarding their plans for something called, *In Vessel Composting* and a ring of sorting plants around London. They're importing a lot of their ideas and equipment from Europe and America,' Adrian said, reinforcing his confidence in industry. John Dingle looked on it as the innocence of youth.

John Dingle had to admit that Adrian had used his initiative in recognising that cramming in too much at once would mean more time away from home and an excessive bill for bed and breakfast paid for by the local tax payer. He also had to concede that allowing Adrian to lead on this project had saved him having to do it all himself. Adrian had even badgered Charlie Pratt for a corporate bus at a very cheap rate saving them a considerable sum on the transport costs. Dingle could not help but remind himself how selfless this young professional was turning out to be even offering to drive the bus himself if Richard could not be released from his usual job on the trade bins.

Dingle, Adrian and Reggie were sat around Reggie's computer to check out the Aurelia Waste Handling Ltd. website as Adrian wanted to demonstrate the company's professionalism.

'You'll love it, Mr Dingle. It's one of those all singing and all dancing sites, lots of moving pictures. Little trucks drive across the screen and tip their waste in a big hole on the other side,' Adrian described the website excitedly. John tried to seem interested but computers were a headache and skating the internet or was it surfing, was quite beyond him. He was one of those *older* managers, constantly humiliated by having to ask the youngsters on the team how the new technology worked. It was much the same for Reggie too.

'Good God, Reggie,' Adrian shrieked, 'what have you been up to?'

'What's up?' A startled Reg turned from chatting with John to see what was causing his colleague to kick up such a rumpus. Both Dingle and Reg stared at the computer screen bewildered as a stream of pornographic pictures flowed across it. There were breasts of all shapes and sizes, the prevailing size being thirty eight GG, and they were all in full colour. Reggie was in a state of shock as he fought to disassociate himself from the graphic images in front of him.

'This is nothing to do with me. I ain't taking the blame for this. I've been set up,' Reggie said, his croaky voice faltering. He was very glad that June was not there. She would never have believed his innocence and worse still, she would have wanted to make notes for use later on!

'I'm calling out IT,' Reggie shouted, making sure his eyes did not rest on the sexy participants in the pictures. Adrian and John had difficulty tearing their eyes away and continued to watch the blatant, sexually charged scenes flash passed.

Kelly was sorting out timesheets for the Wages Section and on hearing Reggie blaspheme came over to see what all the fuss was about. Adrian, the knight in shining armour, sprung into action and gallantly tried to protect her honour by raising his hand in a halt gesture.

'Kelly, please don't come over here. It's not nice. In fact it's very offensive!' Adrian was apologetic for the behaviour of his colleague's computer but Kelly came over anyway, believing that she was a woman of the world and that there could not possibly be any pictures that would offend in the slightest.

Standing about two metres away from the screen she burst into uncontrollable laughter.

'Is that it?' She asked, still laughing. No one answered and she returned to her desk still chortling.

The IT Officer came as soon as he received Reggie's telephone call and checked Reggie's PC. He wanted to know who had access to passwords, the dates when Reggie had been away on holiday and so many other things. Adrian explained exactly what he had been doing when the pictures began cascading across the screen.

'and then they were coming through so fast I just couldn't 'x' them out quick enough,' Adrian explained. Reggie was concerned that at no time did the IT Officer confirm that Reggie had not put all this stuff into his machine himself. John Dingle with an amused expression on his face was glued to the screen. Reggie looked on in disbelief; here was a respectable local government officer completely mesmerised by saucy pictures.

'If he keeps turning his head around that fast, he'll get whiplash,' Reggie whispered to the IT Officer in despair.

'I believe images of this type which cascade like this are referred to as, *angels*,' the IT officer sounded knowledgeable which was not surprising since he was supposed to be a computer guru, Dingle thought, 'Reggie, I'm taking the innards of your PC away. They'll be locked up for tonight and the incident will be investigated fully in the morning. I'm a bit worried that someone may get wind of being discovered and try to erase the evidence,' he explained, looking directly at Reggie.

'This must surely have been someone clever who knows their way around computers, which lets me out because I can just about get my head around Word for Windows,' Reggie said, trying hard to exclude himself. The IT officer had an answer for him.

'Not clever enough, I'm afraid. If he was clever, he would've known that every time someone accesses a website through the Council's server, he leaves a trail of historic information behind him,' the IT Officer beamed back with a sarcastic grin on his face.

John Dingle was fascinated. If only he had known that all this entertainment was just the push of a few buttons away.

'How would one get to know how to find these website addresses?' He asked. The IT Officer, Reggie and Adrian just stared at him in utter disbelief.

'It's a sackable offence you know,' the IT Officer rounded on poor Mr Dingle as he removed the offending piece of machinery and left the office taking the product of twenty first century communications with him. Reggie, completely gutted by the perceived suggestion that he might be responsible, wandered downstairs to the allocation office to see if he could be of use there. Dingle took the opportunity to have a quiet word with Adrian.

'Who'd you think would have done such a thing?' He asked.

'Strange, isn't it? I can only say that if I hadn't asked to use Reggie's PC, we would still be unaware of what was on his computer!' No more was said until the IT expert returned the next day.

Dingle, Adrian and Reggie reconvened the next morning with Bill Sterling, the Best Value Coordinator who told them how well the arrangements were dove tailing together.

'Thanks for sending me that list of Crappendale hotels. I've booked a four star hotel conveniently near to the Crappendale City Council's offices. The one you originally circled, Adrian, didn't have a swimming pool with gym and Jacuzzi and one of the party told me he must have these and a double room overlooking the town square otherwise he wouldn't be going,' Bill explained.

'Who was that?' An outraged Adrian asked. He had always thought that the LIP were dedicated to the cause and worried less about the finer things in life.

'Jim Bowen,' Bill replied with a large sigh, 'I'm afraid those American hotels he stayed in on his recent trip to the States have spoilt him. He did say, to his credit, that he would be prepared to share with the minibus driver, Richard, so I suppose we shouldn't be too hard on him. He'll be saving the Council a bit of money by doing that,' the unassuming Best Value Co-ordinator remarked. Adrian sighed as he was reminded that there did seem to be rather a lot of wanton sexual appetites on display in the circles that he frequented of late. Was all local government like this? Industry would be far less complicated, he was sure. In six months time he would start making overtures to some of the big guns and at the same time start buying the National Waste News, the weekly jobs paper.

Later that day the IT Officer came with the Head of IT to speak to Reggie and John Dingle. Adrian was not invited since it really was no business of his.

'Well, what have you found out?' John asked. He believed Reggie was innocent, of course he did, but someone had been abusing the Council's property.

'It seems the stuff was downloaded via a computer address in Education. Does anyone outside Waste Management know your password Reg?'

'No, absolutely not, there isn't any reason for anyone to know it,' Reggie said conveniently forgetting his wife, June, who worked part time for Education.

'We've asked the Schools' Admin Manager to make some enquiries and we should know by the end of the morning. We'll keep you informed,' the Head of IT said.

The vital parts of Reggie's computer were returned forthwith and at midday the unpalatable news was delivered that June was the culprit and had been suspended immediately. Reg went home to face his sexy blonde babe in whose mouth butter had never melted. Now he found her for once in her life completely subdued. June was left in no doubt about the depth of Reggie's anger and filled with remorse she cried relentlessly. Reggie could never stomach a women crying and to be honest had never witnessed this one crying before. He took her in his arms and being June, she took advantage by pulling him upstairs to the bedroom. This sultry housewife and part time Education Department clerical officer dragged Reggie onto the bed and demonstrated some of the new, exciting and extremely intimate movements she had learnt on the internet. Reggie was left not knowing whether to laugh or cry.

The Council was swift to act and Marcus Bullman received notification of June's misdemeanour within a couple of days. Besides being the Mayor he was also the Chair of The Moral Behaviour of Councillors and Staff Disciplinary Sub-Committee, an off shoot of The Social and Moral Affairs Committee which was usually more famous for its evening buffets than for its guidance on acceptable ways to behave. It was this Sub-Committee which was charged with hearing the case of June Turner v The Council. The Sub-

Committee's findings would have a bearing on the disciplinary action meted out to Mrs Turner. The hearing did not take long since June spared Reggie any further embarrassment by pleading guilty to abusing council equipment and the flagrant misuse of work time and to causing pictures of a sordid and explicit sexual nature to be placed in the public domain. Pictures from the internet websites that June had downloaded were shown to the Sub-Committee members who in spite of being good actors could not prevent their sheer delight showing through at having something as stimulating as pornographic images of consenting adults to examine.

The Sub-Committee adjourned sentencing until the end of the week and June, supported by her devoted and now extremely well satisfied husband, left the building. They both kept their heads bowed low in a display of penitence. Bobby Dalton, trades union steward followed on closely behind. The very next day Marcus received a private visit from the union representative who wanted to clarify a few minor points about the proceedings before sentencing. This done, Bobby stopped to chat.

'I was talking to some of the men at the depot recently. Yeah, seems they get some really thick people turning up for jobs. Not only thick, very often they're just bone idle or even worse, just plain dishonest,' Bobby said. Marcus was shaking his head not being quite sure where this conversation was going. He pretended to be sympathetic.

'Really,' Marcus uttered in a disinterested way.

'Yeah, apparently they had some councillor's son down there a few months ago. He didn't stay long though. They had to sack 'im because he was pinching the equipment and flogging it at some boot sale or so they tell me. You'd think councillors' sons would know how to behave, wouldn't you?' Bobby commented. 'Those supervisors are a good lot though. They could 'ave gone straight to the local rag or much worse, the fuzz. They still could if they were just a little bit revengeful. The local papers would have gone to town on it, don't you think Mr Mayor?'

'Certainly would. We don't want any scandal now do we?' Marcus felt a large frog in his throat.

'Well, thanks for clearing up those points on the Staff Behaviour Code for me. I'm not so hot on the legal aspects of some of these council rulings. I'm better at understanding 'uman nature meself,' Bobby Dalton explained lighting up a small cigar as they reached the entrance. He shook the Mayor's hand and left with a distinct smirk on his face.

Marcus was in a bit of a stew. Revelations about his errant son would not do his political career any good at all. He made a beeline for Maisie's flat where she sat him down and brewed him a refreshing cup of Earl Grey tea and massaged his shoulders until he was feeling calmer. Always one step ahead she gave everyone the impression that she had read the book and seen the video, the latter of course, Marcus certainly knew to be true. Wow! And how! She was certainly a girl who liked her films alright. Marcus chuckled to himself as she went to get him a hot towel to absorb the excess massage oil from his shoulders.

Armed with the ex-lawyer's advice, Marcus suggested the Sub-Committee be lenient since it was a first offence and limit the punishment to a written warning. They were surprised at Marcus since he was usually all for the squeaky clean image that the LIP constantly tried to project. They were, however, quite happy to yield to the Mayor's wishes. Personnel were directed to write a letter to Mrs Turner that same day with copies naturally to her line managers and to John Dingle. Sadly, it is not easy to keep secrets in a council depot. With girls like Kelly in the office, Reg would have to expect the worse. Kelly could talk for England if necessary and still not get jaw ache. It was an art.

Reggie, naturally, did not say a word to his colleagues but he knew that it was only a matter of time before the leg pulling would start. Being the brow beaten husband was bad enough without everyone thinking his Juney was a nymphomaniac as well. He would never live that down. The supervisors were the first to rib him on the titillating affair.

'We're all a bit surprised about you Reg. They say you 'ave to watch the quiet ones, don't they?' Slump teased.

'Yeah, why didn't you tell us you knew how to find the dirty stuff on the internet, Reg? We'd 'ave bought you a pint in exchange for the info,' Mick Davies was just leaving the office with his fridge collection sheets but felt he must have a dig. It was just too good an opportunity to miss.

'Reg, I 'ear those pictures you pulled off the internet were more fruity than one of your cakes, mate,' Micky Brown was facing the other way with his back to Reggie and laughing quietly. Reg prayed it would all pass quickly. Mick offered an olive branch.

'Reg, I'm meeting Round Five at Rosie's Café for some breakfast if you wanna join us?' He called as he left the office with a clip board and a first aid box for the crew.

'Thanks Mick, but I'd better get on with this bleeding wheeled bin pricing work for Huckett. Have a bacon sarny for me whilst you're there will yer, mate!' Reggie called back.

Chapter 8

The Crappendale City tour date dawned. Richard, the blonde bombshell but careful driver had spent the night with his young councillor lover, Jim Bowen. Damien, the latter's more usual partner was away visiting his mother and what the eye didn't see, the heart didn't grieve over, he cogitated as he dropped Richie off at the depot to collect the Crappendale bound bus. The workshop was so snowed under with repairs to refuse freighters that it had been impossible to find the time to repair the Council's twelve seater minibus. A few eyebrows were raised as Richie climbed out of the councillor's car at the depot so early in the morning and a few more for different reasons when he eventually arrived at the Civic Offices driving what looked like a day ambulance complete with wheelchair secured at the back.

The Best Value Co-ordinator, Bill Sterling, a young man of a similar age to Adrian, late twenties but with a more weedy appearance was to assist councillors in the evaluation of the different services they were due to see. Bill slipped easily into the role of organiser-in-charge ticking off the names of councillors and officers as they boarded the bus. Maisie, hobbling in some discomfort with her bunion problem made her way to the front steps assisted by Marcus to wish them all bon voyage. They stood unknowingly at first midst the pile of cigarette ends that Reggie, in his anxious state had created, blissfully unaware that he had been standing beneath a warning sign about new fixed penalty fines for cigarette litter.

The group's first destination was expected to be the Crappendale City Council's Civic Offices and the mainly motorway journey was expected to take around four hours. Cyril sat at the front and put his rucksack on the seat beside him so preventing Edith from sitting next to him. There was plenty of room in the bus for each delegate to have a pair of seats to themselves so nobody thought anything of Cyril's insistence at hogging two seats. There was some discussion enroute about waste processes until Major Prentice-Peabody changed the subject asking Cyril which chemical worked best to rid the garden of bindweed.

'The best way is to pull it up by hand,' Cyril advised, wearing his academic hat. The Major at seventy four looked disappointed with Cyril's answer.

'Not for me,' the Major muttered under cover of the noisy engine. Cyril continued.

'It isn't a good idea to use chemicals but if you must, try using one of the glyphosate group. I suggested these to the Street Cleaning Team and I must say they're using them quite successfully,' Cyril said realising that this fact had not been publicised, a serious slip up to his mind. He would contact the Press Office about getting a press release and a photograph of himself into the local papers as soon as they returned from their trip.

Bill Sterling had been listening to Cyril's advice with interest. A recent council survey of residents undertaken by Papillon Opinion Polls on council services had clearly indicated that there was a distinct drop in weed removal satisfaction levels. The opinion poll survey had included questions like, how satisfied are you with the Street Scene? The answers thrown up were a cause for grave concern. Respondents had indicated that over eighty percent of those surveyed were unhappy about the forest of weeds lapping their properties during the summer months. In fact it had been so bad that one resident had made a comment about being able to shake hands with the weeds in his road!

'Councillor, how does the glyphosate substance work?' Bill Sterling asked.

'It just kills the top of the plant. Doesn't feed into the root or the soil and so therefore doesn't do any environmental damage at all,' Cyril said knowingly. John Dingle listened with interest to the weeding conversation for the simple reason that Best Value Co-ordinators seldom take an interest in topics such as weed killing without reason. Usually these reasons culminate in councillors placing the blame for service failures round the neck of a council officer, such as himself.

Bill Sterling was an expert himself in the area of resident satisfaction levels and was chomping at the bit to reveal Cheatham's latest poll results.

'Councillor Huckett, the results of our as yet unpublished household survey show that we're just not dealing with the weed problem well enough for residents' liking. This glyphosate stuff, it's just not good enough,' he suggested. Cyril looked mortified but Bill was not finished yet. He still had some salt to rub into Cyril's wound. 'I'm told the roots survive and as soon as they think the weeding staff have gone away, they pop up again.' Bill was revelling in Cyril's discomfort whereas the Major, who had started the conversation in the first place had nodded off.

John Dingle felt the need to wade into the weeding discussion.

'May I make a suggestion, Councillor and Bill? I'm just about to re-organise some parts of the Street Cleaning Service so there's more team working,' John used the 'T' word. All councillors loved to hear the team word used in any combination, team player, team building and so on. It did the trick, Dingle was on to a winner. 'I would like to propose that we look at a return to using the good old fashion garden hoe,' Dingle suggested, 'I think we'll be able to manage with the new working arrangement that I'm planning,' he sounded confident and looked directly at Cyril, 'it's a tried and tested way of doing things and Cyril, if you wouldn't mind, I'd rather like to put out a piece about how you've re-introduced it as a means of reducing the Council's use of harmful chemicals and preserving the local environment. Adrian will sort it out as soon as we return. Won't you Adrian?' Dingle asked rhetorically. Adrian nodded. Cyril was grateful to John who he knew understood councillors' needs to receive local acclaim for purely egotistical reasons. One hundred Brownie points to me, I think, Dingle considered.

"Fucking Ada, what a bunch of wankers,' Labour Councillor Alfie muttered under his breath, 'if it's not broke, don't fix it is my motto. Glyphosate, my fanny. Stick to manual labour and keep the working man in a job is my philosophy,' he concluded in his own quaint way.

'A new technical term from Alfie, everyone,' Cyril replied, dissipating the sudden strained atmosphere.

Many comfort breaks later primarily for the benefit of the coffin dodging Major Prentice-Peabody who along with a kind of narcolepsy also suffered a bladder problem, the party arrived at the Sunrise Hotel in the middle of Crappendale Town Centre. Relief swept across their faces as soon as the engine was switched off. Battered, bruised and shaken by the unsophisticated ride in the Social Services day ambulance they stumbled out of the vehicle and into the hotel foyer. Bill took charge ensuring that everyone was checked in, knew their room numbers and what the dinner arrangements were.

Cyril had successfully ignored Edith so far and was feeling quietly pleased with himself. The wily spinster, however, was feeling lucky. She was in room 288 which was right next door to Cyril, in 290. Feeling drained after the journey Cyril showered, flipped through that evening's menu and then flaked out on his emperor sized bed until nearer dinner time. At 7.15 pm, the doors to rooms 288 and 290 opened simultaneously and quite by accident Cyril found himself alone in the corridor with Edith. A sudden flush of heat usually kept for menopausal women struck him as he tried in vain to engage her in polite conversation.

'Good evening, Edith. I wonder what's on the dinner menu tonight?' Cyril could not have picked a duller subject for conversation as Edith for one thing was certainly not thinking about food.

'Cyril, we've adjoining doors between our rooms,' she exclaimed, 'I expect the two rooms double up as a family suite during school holidays but could be cosy at other times,' she said reaching out and squeezing his hand. Cyril sharply withdrew it wondering if this woman had any scruples at all. Remembering the last time they had been in a lift together Cyril could not help noticing that Edith was using the wall lined mirrors to steal glances at his private parts. Strangely this had the effect of awakening within him a great sense of yearning for something other than duck encroute with fresh garden peas.

Reggie found himself billeted with John and Adrian, which was not anyone's idea of fun but it was a large room with three single beds and ensuite facilities. He had telephoned June on arrival and given her his room number so she could keep tabs on him. Reg knew exactly where he stood. Throughout dinner he clock-watched hoping he would be allowed to get through his meal before having to report back by mobile phone. After dinner he had the hotel room to himself as Adrian was keen to discuss the merits of nappy recycling with Bill Sterling. Relaxing in a bedroom armchair he flicked through the TV channels finding one that was particularly risqué called, 'Intimate Techniques'. Two could play at June's game, he decided.

John Dingle excused himself after dinner from any polite chit chat for a stroll though the town. The sly old fox wanted to do some window shopping research into Crappendale's street walkers. It was just a morbid curiosity of his, no more. Adrian meanwhile, having tired of discussing nappies made use of the hotel sauna and then repaired to the hotel's library to quietly read his notes for the next day's visits. He had thought for a few brief minutes of undertaking this task in his room but with of his line manager watching porn he decided against it. Around midnight, the Leader found Dingle in the foyer and joined him for another wander outside, this time around the City's main square. The Leader's mission was to see how well Crappendale managed to keep its main thoroughfare clear of dogs' muck. He had a few questions he was saving up on the topic for the City's Cleansing Director.

Cyril, in spite of trying to fend off Edith's advances eventually found himself giving in to her invitation to join her for a night cap in the bar. All those around him had witnessed the damsel's request and not wanting to be deemed caddish he felt he could not refuse. He ordered a gin and tonic for her or *mother's ruin*, thought Cyril sarcastically. They settled in leather club armchairs at the far end of the room. Councillor Prentice-Peabody was already asleep in another armchair and Leadbetter was looking around for someone with whom he could pick a fight.

'Who is looking after your father whilst you're away?' Cyril asked Edith, trying to make polite conversation.

'Respite care, Cyril,' she answered loudly, 'the Council takes him into Imperial House every third weekend and for several other occasional breaks throughout the year. It's a Godsend. It allows me some "me" time,' she said touching his thigh, 'and actually Cyril, I was wondering if you would like to come round and see my tomatoes? I know you're keen on organic vegetables and I've a few other soft fruits worth seeing too although some of them have suffered recently from a penetration of fungus,' she said winking at Cyril. 'Dad will be away again next week, Wednesday to Saturday. Perhaps you'd like to pop round and pick up one of my peaches? I can also offer you several bunches of fat juicy grapes for your wine making. Are you tempted Cyril?' Edith asked using her most alluring tones. The drink was clearly going to her head.

'Infestation, Edith. Your fruits are suffering from an infestation not a penetration, my dear!' Cyril corrected her. Merryweather and Sir David were seated at the bar and noticed Edith's hands all over Cyril's leg. Cyril noted their concerned looks and on seeing the clock was approaching midnight took leave to visit the gents. On his return he stopped by his colleagues and suggested that Edith was completely ratted and he would do the decent thing and get her back to her room.

Edith was wide awake by the time the pair arrived outside Room 288 but being a complete hussy she pretended to need Cyril's assistance to negotiate the key in her lock. Once inside she stumbled across to the bed and stood there as in a stupor, clinging onto the bedspread until she had managed to steady herself. Cyril planted her handbag on the dressing table and busied himself drawing the curtains, turning on the light, in fact anything to put off the evil moment when he might have to help her into bed. Whilst his back was turned Edith stripped off her frilly white blouse and black pleated skirt, another from her dated wardrobe revealing along with the bulges of middle age another set of sexy lingerie in blood red.

Cyril turned and walking over to the bed and faced with a sea of crimson, visibly shook, unsure whether he should stay or go. All these thoughts were academic because in a thrice she had pulled him out of his procrastination and down on top of her. Later, devoid of energy for further engagement they laid on the bed chatting like two young love birds. Edith's eyes glazed over and she prattled away as one does in the aftermath of successful coupling.

'Cyril, do you think that youngsters believe that people of our age are incapable of doing it anymore? What do you think they'd say if they could have seen us tonight?' Edith giggled.

'Bloody lucky,' he replied simply. The conversation ebbed to be replaced by a deep and comforting slumber.

The ebullient Bill Sterling was in the hotel lobby at 9.30 am sharp. He ushered his party out of the breakfast room and rounding up the odd stray still reading the newspaper, he positioned them for the off. The Cheatham party walked across the square to the Crappendale City Council offices, a tourist site in themselves being all glass, brass and sparkly in the sunlight. The visitors, feeling like out of town cousins looked up and admired the swanky building and wondered how they might also wangle having a new civic office complex built to such remarkably high environmental standards. The moment passed as they were beckoned inside by Crappendale's Director of

Cleansing, Jake Samson who outlined the Council's treble wheeled bin service to them. The Cheatham party heard how Crappendale collected general waste every week in a dark cherry red coloured bin whilst garden and food waste were collected fortnightly in a strawberry red bin. Newspapers were also collected fortnightly in an attractive salmon pink bin. The residents were apparently beside themselves with happiness at having a service that had trebled the City's recycling rate overnight and on collection days painted the town red in a literal sense.

The natives seemed friendly enough and the Cheatham party soon felt that they were amongst chums and relaxed. The Leader started the ball rolling with a pertinent question.

'Jake, do the residents ever put the wrong waste in the recycling bins?' Jake looked surprised at being asked this and Sir David suddenly felt daft asking it, 'silly question, I can tell. Probably not a major concern here,' Sir David said smiling at Jake. Jake returned the smile and Cyril, who was already convinced that a variation on this theme would work back home moved the conversation on to other practicalities such as markets. Edith wanted value for money information especially as she would have to report to Irene on her return. With this in mind, she hogged the Director of Cleansing for a considerable time, grilling him on the minutiae of the financial operation. The icing on the day's cake was being taken to see Crappendale's bins being collected.

'Waste of time, if you ask me,' Leadbetter and Prentice-Peabody mumbled in unison, believing that if you have been lucky enough within your lifetime to have witnessed one bin being emptied you will undoubtedly have seen enough. Not so for the rest of the party and particularly Sir David, who, striding along the quiet tree lined cul de sac known as Acacia Avenue was like a kid with a new toy, lifting the lids of each and every bin he came to and noting an abundance of cornflake boxes, tabloid newspapers, baked bean cans and so on. He also made a mental note of several items he had spotted that Crappendale didn't have on their wanted list which surprised him following his earlier conversation.

'Jake,' Sir David called out holding what resembled a yogurt pot up in the air, 'can this be recycled?' Sir David liked yoghurt and found it rather annoying that he was unable to recycle them at home. Cyril pricked his ears up too. Miranda would be so happy with him if he could give her this one good bit of news. Recycling yoghurt pots meant less clutter at home and that at least would be greeted with joy by his long suffering wife. Jake Samson contemplated the yoghurt pot issue.

'Yes, Sir David, they can be recycled although generally across the UK there are no facilities for them. However, Crappendale has taken this problem seriously and I think I can say that we're light years ahead of any other local authority in the country. We've invested in a project that will revolutionise the polystyrene and polypropylene markets. It's still top secret, I might add, so I must ask you and your party to keep mum about it until we launch it in the Recycling Press. Today Crappendale, tomorrow the world!' He enthused, swinging his arms around to indicate the wide ranging effect that Crappendale's technological breakthrough would have. 'Pete Digby, our more than competent Recycling Officer will fill you in with the details. Pete please, over to you,' Jake said putting poor old Pete under the spotlight.

Pete was often ribbed by his colleagues as the plastic bottle man because the shortened form of his name, Pete, was similar to a well known abbreviation for polyethylene tetrachloride more usually known as fizzy drinks bottles or PETe. Pete felt secretly honoured to be asked to elucidate on their wonderful forward thinking project and he made a little celebratory bow before beginning. Smiling broadly he proceeded to baffle the Cheatham guests with science.

'As Mr Samson said it's a top secret research project. We've joined up with a partner from a local plastic company who has put much of the money up front to pay for the project. It's a local company called *Plastipot* which usually makes yoghurt pots. The company has a legal obligation to recycle yoghurt pots because they come within the Packaging Regulations as containers,' Pete spied Prentice-Peabody covering his mouth as he yawned for a third time. The Cheatham delegation frowned at the Major's discourteous behaviour. Pete continued, 'the project is a beauty and is not far off from being launched. It's Crappendale coup de grace!'

Jake was pleased to have his Recycling Officer there to explain the technical details because he, for the life of him, knew absolutely nothing about plastics reprocessing and long may it continue. Pete got stuck into the PR exercise.

'We have designers working very closely with our engineers to make a strong material that can be moulded out of used yoghurt pots and margarine tubs into imitation full sized trees for the Street Scene. They won't need pruning, there are no dropped leaves in the autumn and no one gets asthma from the blossom,' Pete enthused, 'the only problem we have is that there's just one colour at the moment and that's brown,' he lamented.

'But what's wrong with brown? Trees are brown,' the Leader remarked.

'Yes Sir David, but we currently have to make the leaves brown too so unfortunately it looks like autumn all year,' Pete explained. The Leader was soon asking a second question.

'Do you think plastic trees will deter dogs from peeing up them?' The Leader asked, gleefully.

'Thinking about your favourite subject again, David?' Councillor Leadbetter quipped.

The Crappendale contingent made up of Recycling Officer, two city councillors, the Director of Cleansing and the roundsmen emptying the bins watched Alfie Leadbetter picking his nose. It was not a pretty sight and they began to wonder what sort of a hole their visitors had crawled out of. Time was moving on and Jake had high hopes that his visitors would shortly be doing the same.

'Sir David, Crappendale is embarking on cutting edge technology here. We're about to make scientific history. Our plastic tree invention will create vast markets for recyclable materials and help the cause of all local authority recycling departments. We're prepared to stick our necks out and be counted. Our trees will be like the five hundred year old oak tree that King Charles the Second hid in. It will be both reliable and long lasting and could save councils a fortune!' Jake Samson emphasised the last sentence. Alfie had had enough of this silly conversation.

'What the bloody hell are we talking about here? You can't be serious. Making trees out of plastic yoghurt pots! Bollocks! I must be 'earing things. What council in its right mind makes trees out of bloody plastic pots for God's sake! I've heard every ruddy thing under the sun now. Where will you put these bloody things?' Councillor Leadbetter was a plain speaker, 'if you're short of an idea, I think I can help you out there,' he insisted.

'Oh, please, Councillor Leadbetter, don't hold back on our account; say what you really think,' the Leader said sarcastically, ignoring the dumbfounded expressions on the faces of their new friends.

Cyril suggested quietly to Alfie that he apologise to their hosts and Jake overhearing, intervened to save the day.

'Please, no need to do any such thing,' he implored, 'we really do intend to use them to replace street trees and eventually we're hoping to make them in many different mock species and plant them wherever real trees would normally have been planted. We also aim to let residents choose exactly what type of tree they have in their roads,' Jake finished. John Dingle, who was being his usual charming, tactful and patient self was standing beside Alfie.

'Perhaps Councillor Leadbetter, we should see the plastic trees as an extension to the already popular artificial plastic flower market. Thesedays they're quite exquisite. I remember in the sixties my mother received the free gift of a very simple red plastic tulip with her box of washing powder and it stayed on show in our home for years after,' John reminisced, even humming the tune for the washing powder commercial.

Alfie was rapidly losing his rag and distanced himself from Dingle the sentimental old fool that he now took him to be. He moved forward to hear the continuing discussion going on between Cyril and Crappendale's Director of Cleansing.

'You did say that the trees will only be available in brown?' Cyril was being pulled between his ideals as a botanist and his desires as an environmentalist and recycling champion.

'Yes I did but of course we're still running trials at the moment,' Jake replied, 'our blueprint tree, in the Council's nursery is an ornamental cherry and our scientists are confident that they'll shortly make a breakthrough with regard to attaching pink blossom, which will of course be made from even more yoghurt pots. Our design team is quite sure that in due course they'll be able to reproduce a plastic lime tree without all that annoying sticky stuff they spit out, usually all over residents' cars. Crappendale City will be launching its plastic street tree in a few months time and I will make sure that you receive an invite,' Jake added.

Pete Digby offered some technical data on the plastic trees in his own excitable manner.

'Each tree uses two million plastic pots and costs zilch compared to proper trees which need careful planting, watering and pruning. This end use for plastic pots and tubs will put a stop to any future potential yoghurt pot mountain,' he was so keen that the Cheatham delegation could not fail to be impressed. The Leader made a few enthusiastic notes of his own.

'I like your idea, Jake,' he said turning to the director, 'I wonder if you've given any thought to producing plastic dogs out of yoghurt pots? A plastic dog would always be there, never get muddy or bark and be cheap to feed. In my book anything is better than the flesh and bone ones that shit all over Cheatham. Just think of it, a world without any canine mess to clear up and no germs left on the pavement either,' the Leader explained. A silent pause ensured. Dingle could see something of interest here for himself. His satisfaction ratings for Street Cleaning and dog waste removal would shoot through the roof of the local government opinion poll league tables and his early retirement pension would most definitely be in the bank. He placed the Crappendale director's business card in his wallet.

Flushed with a liquid lunch the Cheatham group took their leave and in an uncharacteristically merry mood began singing a medley of *the sun has got his hat on* followed by *there's a hole in my bucket, dear Edith* and interspersed with cap naps and a final rendition of *black bird singing in the dead of night*, made their way south again. Their next visit was to Aurelia Waste Handling Ltd. which was on the outskirts of North West London. Aurelia had built up its business by working on the principle that *where there's muck, there's brass,* realising at the right time that the money of the future was in recycling. The government had spotted Aurelia's potential and snapped up its offer to research various new technologies on behalf of the Department of Waste, Wind and Water or DWWW as it was better known. By late afternoon the now sober Cheatham delegation was signing in at Aurelia's main reception and being shown into the company's Education Suite where tea and biscuits awaited them.

Jim had managed to avoid the Crappendale wheelie bin visit by arranging a tour of the City's libraries instead but he was now stuck with nowhere else to go. He could either stay in the day ambulance and read his newspaper or join the visit to Aurelia. He decided to do the latter and invited Richard to come in with him for refreshments. The two of them wandered round the Education Room looking at the photographic exhibition of the various projects undertaken by Aurelia for the DWWW. As a mark of respect for the company and the serious nature of the trip, Richard's rippling muscles were covered demurely by a long sleeved shirt. He gave Jim the occasional knowing smile as they traversed the room daintily drinking from their cups like ladies at a Conservative Association coffee morning. A sudden gasp emitted by Richard made everyone look over. His eyes had alighted on the unfortunate picture of a fluffy rabbit looking rather floppy.

'I had a rabbit like that one once called Cuddles. I came home from school one day to find my dad had cooked it,' Richard revealed. No one said anything. You could have heard a pin drop until Alfie piped up, breaking the silence.

'The mistake you made son was giving it a name!' Alfie croaked. The situation was eased by
Aurelia's Education Officer, Judy Craig who came into the room at that moment.

'Ah good, I see you've found our black museum,' Judy said, looking rather prim and proper in a navy two piece suit, 'that poor unfortunate animal was found in a household dustbin we were sorting through. We were analysing waste for another council,' she explained, 'it's surprising what some people throw out isn't it?' She said eyeing Richard with suspicion as Jim tried to put a comforting arm around his friend.

'What happened to this poor creature?' Edith asked.

'It was crushed in a freighter,' Judy explained.

Judy rabbitted on about the usual housekeeping arrangements whilst Alfie engaged the Major, sitting next to him, in conversation at the back of the room.

'I used to work in the building trade you know,' Alfie began, 'that's an industry that's actually been recycling for years and years. But you know why they did it don't you?' Alfie was holding the Major's attention, which was usually difficult, 'they did it because they made money out of selling salvaged wood, fireplaces and bricks,' Alfie explained.

'You're right there,' the Major said, suddenly aroused. Alfie had obviously struck a chord because Prentice-Peabody suddenly seemed to have some life in him. 'I owned a building firm until I retired. We used to clean buildings, like the stone work on big office blocks. We use to use sand for shot blasting until it was banned because of the dust. Then we used copper slag. Nothing stays the same,' the Major recalled wistfully. 'Now I believe they use some recycled glass stuff. I suppose it must be better for the environment,' the Major nodded.

'Copper slag eh!' Alfie said rubbing his chin and staring at Jim's Bowen's ginger hair as he sat in the front row still trying to console his sensitive lover.

Judy gave an introduction to the beginnings of the Aurelia Waste Handling Company.

'Aurelia is a family based company, one of the few that are left. Most of the others have been gobbled up by the big boys in recent years,' she explained. Jim was impressed because he would have liked the opportunity to meet some of these big boys. Judy continued, 'the company was started by Antoine Aurelia, a Frenchman who came to Britain in the thirties and cleared houses with his horse and cart. His wife used to help. They could always be seen trotting through the town with their cart loaded up with all kinds of rubbish. On they'd go to the local tip and back again for more and remember the tips in those days were nothing like the civil engineered sites we know today. They were muddy and when I say muddy, I mean muddy,' Judy spoke with feeling, she was a star performer. Edith was starting to feel irritated and wished she would just get on with it. 'Today the company is fortunate to work under the direction of Antoine's son, Augustus,' Judy said with a discernible twinkle in her eye at the mention of Augustus' name.

At length Judy got to the real business of the day, explaining how important it would be in the future to get to grips with recycling and in particular biodegradable waste. Cyril was interested in this because he had an intense dislike of people who put this stuff in the dustbin when they could have composted it in their back gardens. In fact, more to the point he could not understand why anyone should have food waste in the first place. *Waste not; want not,* his mother always taught him. Hot roast on Sundays, cold on Mondays. There was always someone in Africa going hungry, lectured the old Mrs Huckett. Cyril always kept a beady eye on Miranda but convenience food and over-indulgence were just not in the Huckett vocabulary. Lovely word, *over-indulgence,* Cyril thought and Edith had given it an entirely new meaning. Strewth. No need to take out gym membership whilst Edith was around! He gladly admitted to himself.

Judy continued to overwhelm them with her knowledge.

'Biodegradable waste is now the subject of a European Directive. We must reduce what we send to landfill by at least twenty five percent in the next three years. We can do this by composting at a central site or getting people to compost at home,' she explained. Sir David was deliberating on whether she might be thinking of a career move in the direction of local government and more specifically, Cheatham Borough Council. He may just mention that he would like to have her details before they leave. He stroked his goatee beard and wondered if perhaps she liked yoghurt too?

'You mentioned composting,' Alfie Leadbetter began, 'did you compost the rabbit?' Alfie was laughing but he was the only one. Richard grimaced. Judy, treating Alfie's question with the disdain it deserved, ignored it.

'Did you know that Londoners consume almost three times their fair share of the Earth's resources? If everybody lived the life of an average Londoner we would need at least another three Earths.' Aurelia's Education Officer paused for a second whilst she drew herself up to her full five feet two inches and in doing so pushed out her chest putting a strain on the already tight red, striped blouse nestling below her smart corporate navy jacket. 'Councillor Leadbetter, you are obviously interested in the processing of biodegradable waste so you might be interested to know that each Londoner ate their way through seven hundred kilograms of food last year and over eighty percent of this was from outside the UK. Another interesting fact is that every Londoner produces over half a tonne of household rubbish each year. It's up to councils like Cheatham to become leading lights and carry the baton for new technologies,' she concluded. Sir David and Cyril both liked this analogy and nodded enthusiastically.

Judy invited questions and Cyril dived in first.
'What services can Aurelia offer local authorities such as Cheatham?' He asked boldly.
'Aurelia has developed a fully enclosed windrow composting plant with heat extraction by very clever technological means. You can deliver your garden waste to us or we can collect it from you,' a broad smile swept across Judy's face, 'and we're very cheap, or rather, very good value for money, I should say,' she said, 'and we'll even let you buy back the soil conditioner that we make from your garden waste. The public love to buy it. It'll be a great awareness raising gimmick,' she suggested, 'and even more exciting, we'll shortly be able to take your residual waste and send it through our experimental Trashnox Optics Separation System,' she revealed, enticingly.

Judy switched on her computer to illustrate Aurelia's carefully planned new technologies programme and projected a short film of moving conveyors and machines that munched and crunched onto the white wall in front of the Cheatham delegation. At the end of each conveyor was a pile of glass fragments, plastic bits, sheets of paper and many others materials awaiting despatch to manufacturers. Judy's voice provided commentary for the film.
'This is the secret project that we've been working on for the DWWW. We take mixed recyclables and separate them out into glass, paper, plastics, metals and wood. We even have plans for dealing with nappy waste if it's brought in to us separately. Yes, that's right, even little baby's poos which of course get diverted to the composting plant whilst the plastic bits of the nappy are recycled,' she excitedly related. The Leader admired the way she said the word, *poos* in public. Some people would have difficulty with that, he thought. The dog poo problem also needed a public airing and the more people talked about it in the cold light of day the better. It was a philosophy he had been nurturing for some time.

'Are the materials easily sold? What I mean is do they meet the manufacturers' specifications?' Adrian ventured to ask. Good old Adrian, thought Dingle, he is the only one as usual, to ask the pertinent question. Judy was hesitant.
'Well yes and no. We haven't managed to sell everything we've produced so far but I'm sure we will in due course. We've sold the glass though,' Judy just hoped that they wouldn't pry any further.
'Where did you say you sold the glass?' Cyril asked.

'I didn't, but since you ask, we've sold, ehm, given it actually, to Italy for their vineyards. I believe they're very pleased to have it,' she said glancing at her watch. It must surely be time for them to leave now, she hoped. Prentice-Peabody nudged Alfie.

'Vineyards! I bet the bloody ground sparkles in the moonlight alright. What do yer think, Alfie eh?' The Major laughed under his breath, 'bloody grapes will grow in anything. Hardly a quality product, I'd say, what?' Heads turn towards the Major and he shut up. The ensuring silence signalled the end of the visit and time for the group to make their way in an orderly fashion back to their bus. Bill Sterling feeling highly embarrassed following the rude behaviour of some of his party was left to thank Judy and Aurelia for their hospitality.

On the bus ride around the M25 Councillor Merryweather, who had been intrigued by the technological possibilities for waste but nevertheless had reservations about allowing it to take over from public participation spoke out.

'I can't see how the public would be involved in taking responsibility for their waste with Aurelia's ideas. If all they need to do is put their rubbish out in a sack or bin as they do now, where's the good environmental practice and attitude change in that? The whole point about Local Agenda Twenty One is that local people learn how to be responsible and believe wholeheartedly that every little helps. All Aurelia is doing is making it easy for them to go on being as pig headed about the environment as they always have been. The *chuck it away society* will not change if we don't make them actually take part,' he rambled.

Tom Merryweather wanted to go further than just have Cheatham's residents take part. He wanted any initiative imposed by the Council to be implemented and operated by local people which he believed to be the true meaning of local democracy. He had plans for a Standing Community Conference where the local people get to make the big decisions and *Sir* Tom Merryweather sounded rather fun. It was just a passing thought, you understand. Cyril could see that Councillor Merryweather's ideals might well detract from his own popularity and status in the wider waste management world and he would need to make sure that Merryweather was restrained and kept from being quite so vociferous. He would have to handle the situation with kid gloves as it did not do to fall out with colleagues.

Edith, Prentice-Peabody and Alfie Leadbetter had an alternative view on how responsible residents should behave. Prentice-Peabody spoke on behalf of them all.

'I'm in favour of any system which doesn't require me to give it much thought. A system that even the village idiot can understand is the one which will get my vote. Afterall, there's no point in using new technologies if you don't make them work for you,' Peabody explained. Edith smiled in agreement with the Major and Alfie nodded his own approval, the latter being too fagged to wade into any more arguments. Cyril and Tom decided that they had no intention of asking the Major for his opinion so his views were academic. On arrival back at the Civic Offices they agreed to hold a debriefing session as soon as possible to appraise the various options available. Edith would then need to consider carefully the cost effectiveness of their chosen scheme.

Whilst the information seeking party were away Marcus and Maisie were busy creating a bit of a stir themselves. Maisie had watched the party depart for Crappendale and had then checked in at the hospital for the minor operation to have her bunions sliced or chopped off or whatever it is they do to bunions to get rid of the infernal pain. Maisie Atichitawomba was a large lady and her size made her bunions even more of a problem. The pain some days was excruciating. Marcus had a little bit of a sadistic nature and there were times when he quite enjoyed seeing the object of his affections wince. On such occasions he would prankishly pinch her love handles hard causing her to flinch and sending her rolls of blubber shivering down her body. Mrs Carter watched these shenanigans on a daily basis and her own interpretation of this show of affection was that they were just a pair of silly twerps. At such times she diplomatically remembered the mace needed polishing or the tyres on the mayoral bicycle needed pumping. Marcus, as luck would have it, was visiting Maisie's hospital at 2.30pm that same afternoon. The NHS Trust which administered Cheatham's Royal Infirmary had invited him to open a newly refurbished geriatric ward named after his good self.

Marcus had started to enjoy the brand new mayoral Bentley foisted on him by his wife in her role as mayoress. Virginia had simply refused to undertake any more civic duties unless she was allowed to do so in style. He had to admit there was a certain something that the Bentley added to each occasion and especially today as it glided onto the hospital forecourt to be greeted by a bevy of nurses in smart uniforms. The hospital administrator welcomed him and introduced him to Sister Brenda who was in charge of the new ward. Normally Virginia would have accompanied him on such occasions but due to a prior engagement she was unable to do so. How lucky was that? Marcus asked himself as he toured the new ward and admired the therapy garden with its raised beds for the longer term patient to plant bulbs in. He chatted uneasily with a few patients feeling distracted by the fact that he would rather be elsewhere in the hospital. Eventually he found the courage to ask Mrs Carter to find out where the minor operations ward was situated. Mrs Carter was no fool and knew precisely what he was up to. She took Sister Brenda aside and in order to avoid any embarrassment suggested that Marcus had a relative on the ward that he wished to make a speedy and very private visit to.

The Mayor carried out his official duty drawing back a curtain in the foyer to reveal a brass plaque.
'I am very honoured to be invited to open the Marcus Bullman Ward and indeed to have a ward named after me at all...' Marcus said all the usual things about the good work that the hospital did and how he was looking forward to hearing wonderful things about the new ward in the future. Someone at the back motioned that refreshments were ready and that was the signal for Marcus to wind up his speech. As he moved away, he glanced back at the plaque, The Marcus Bullman Geriatric Suite, he read. If he was honest, he did not like the sound of that at all. The ward sister suggested everyone adjourn to the Nurses' Room for refreshments. This gave Marcus the chance he had been waiting for and he slipped away for ten minutes of nooky.

Marcus found Maisie in a private room relaxing with her feet protected by a metal cage listening to the soulful voice of her favourite crooner, Barry White. Her dreamy mood was interrupted as Marcus' familiar face appeared around the door. To say she was surprised would be an understatement but her surprise was intensified still further when she found herself gazing at his crotch.

'Marcus what are you doing here and what's that bulge in your pocket, or are you just pleased to see me?' She chuckled.

'Hello my petal. I've brought you something special to make your stay more enjoyable,' he said mischievously pushing his hand into his trouser pocket and pulling out the biggest flesh coloured dildo Maisie had ever seen. She burst into her deep throaty laughter and looked beyond Marcus to see if the coast was clear. The bedclothes did the rumba as Marcus engaged the dildo. The fireworks only ceased when he accidentally nudged Maisie's de-bunioned left foot causing her to yelp so loud that they must have heard it upstairs in obstetrics. They listened but no one came running and once the pain had subsided they continued in fits of giggles. Time was of the essence and soon Marcus was making himself tidy. His now one abiding thought was to get back to the Nurses' Room at top speed for a cup of tea and a fairy cake.

It was just as Marcus was kissing Maisie goodbye when the door to her private room opened. A nurse approached with a fresh jug of water. Marcus dropped the dildo, still glistening from recent use and watched as it rolled around on the floor. Good naturedly, the nurse picked up the roly poly object and realising at once what it was, dropped it and went into a state of apoplexy, fleeing the room shrieking at the top of her voice.

'Oh Lord!' Marcus exclaimed. Maisie did not look all that pleased with the turn of events herself. Still wearing his chain of office he picked up the artificial penis with the battery inside still vibrating and shoved it at Maisie who hastily hid it beneath the bedclothes. The Mayor then hurried away for his tea, speeding down the corridor at an undignified rate of knots using one hand to hold his mayoral chain firmly down against his chest to stop it hitting him in the face. Maisie hastily wrapped the appendage in a scarf and said a prayer thanking God she was due to go home in the morning.

The following week a nurse called Sadie sat in the waiting room of the nurses' psychiatric counselling room. She wanted to speak to a professional about her anxieties.

'I'm not sure if I can cope anymore. I've never thought of myself as a prude but I suppose I must be. After seeing what I saw I no longer know what normal behaviour is,' Sadie chided herself.

'Well my dear,' the kind middle-aged lady began, 'tell me in your own time, what do you mean exactly by, *after seeing what you saw*?' The doctor encouraged. The nurse looked uncertain and so the doctor did her best to reassure her. 'My dear, anything you say within these four walls is confidential.' Sadie hesitated for a few seconds before finding the dutch courage to go on.

'I went into room twenty three, that's one of the private rooms on the first floor and there was this mayor in there with a black lady and they'd been at it! I know because I saw it rolling on the floor as I walked into the room. They were as flabbergasted as I was. I know this because they were quite flushed and the bedclothes were all over the place,' Sadie was looking pretty flushed herself and losing her calm. 'What should I do? Should I write to the papers or just say nothing?' The psychiatrist had seen cases like this before. It was such a shame to see the stress that these poor creatures were under. Put simply they were just run into the ground with the pressures of work overload. The NHS should be ashamed of itself. Miranda put on a tape of relaxing rain forest music and invited Sadie to allow any nasty thoughts to pour out of her mind into the ether.

'What do you mean by, a mare. Was there a horse in the room or did you see a black lady riding a horse?' The psychiatrist was beginning to think that this little nurse needed rather more specialist help than she could give her in just one short clinical session.

'What horse? I'm talking about *the Mayor*, the one that's always pictured in the papers,' recounted a now visibly distraught Sadie. 'I'm telling you he was in room twenty three with a black lady who was lying in the bed and they'd been doing things with an artificial flesh coloured penis,' the young nurse, near collapse blurted out. Dr. Miranda Huckett sat back in her chair and tried to visualise the spectacle. The image of a large flesh coloured dildo kept filling her head and blocking her from saying anything constructive for quite some time. Her brain was in a spin. There was only one Mayor of Cheatham and there was indeed only one black lady at the Council's helm. Cyril had muttered once or twice about how well the Mayor and Mrs Atichitawomba seemed to be getting along. Maisie must be the black lady that Sadie had referred to. The reality gradually dawned on Miranda as she pictured this first citizen of Cheatham engaged in what she would term inappropriate public activities. She, too, like little Nurse Sadie, felt in a quandary.

Miranda procrastinated, probably for the first time in her professional life. What would her husband Cyril say to this? He would be shocked. The Council's reputation would suffer for sure and perhaps Cyril's credibility too. As a doctor she was subject to the confidentiality clause and could not repeat Sadie's accusation. In the meantime, Nurse Sadie was sitting in front of her expecting an answer and sobbing into Miranda's box of man sized paper hankies.

'You know, Sadie, sometimes it's better to be kind to ourselves and try very hard to forget something nasty that we think we've seen. Sometimes we haven't seen at all what we thought we'd seen. Sometimes the brain gets confused. I would like you to come back at four thirty this afternoon when your shift finishes and we'll try out a little bit of alternative therapy. Would you like that?' Miranda was smiling sweetly as analysts do when they are trying to gain their clients trust or extract money, although the latter was naturally not the case here. She must try and eradicate this girl's wretched experience from her memory and thus any danger to the Party, for Cyril's sake if nothing more.

Miranda's altruistic nature and basic bluntness was getting the better of her. She had been thinking that Nurse Sadie was a touch on the chubby side, too many chips and burgers no doubt. Having just studied the relationship between diet and mental ill health, Miranda thought she would put her other theory into practice.

'I'm recommending that you look at your diet, Sadie. Studies have found that young people like yourself can very easily be deficient in thiamine and see things that are not really there, get confused and anxious, a bit like you are now.' Miranda would have made a good salesperson not unlike the Mayor successfully selling his diaries in his hey day. She went on, 'now my dear, I want you to see the dietician although I would recommend that you immediately start eating more eggs, grains and cereals and I don't think you should mention the exact reason for your coming to see me. It'll be our little secret, OK?' Miranda smiled sweetly remembering the Council's potentially precarious position if Sadie's explosive revelations were to get out into the public domain. Putting an arm around Sadie's shoulders, Miranda escorted the nurse to the door, 'come back and see me at four thirty pm and remember to stay focused on your work,' Miranda called as Sadie made her way snuffling down the corridor. *Staying focussed on her work* was actually what had caused the trouble in the first place, Miranda thought to herself.

Chapter 9

Back at the depot the natives were getting restless. The trip to see Lolita was approaching and the air was alive with excitement.

'Cut that out, Brewer,' Micky Brown shouted at the radio microphone, 'it's a disciplinary offence to hog the airwaves, you know that. I've told you enough times before; now get off,' Micky stood no nonsense.

'Brewer's been a right pain for the past couple of days, Mick. He keeps singing on the radio. It's so difficult for the other crews to speak to me when he's having a go. It's been like Radio Brewer!' Kelly started checking through some of the paper work.

'Yeah, I know gel. Brewer's just a bloody nuisance. If we weren't so short of drivers I'd find some way of giving him the push,' Micky agreed, making his way over to the window to deal with returning crews.

Gary Green arrived and started sifting through the In Tray.

'We've got a memo here from John Dingle. The Strategy Committee has given the OK for us to pick up incontinence pads with the general rubbish instead of paying for a clinical waste collection; it's too expensive, apparently,' Gary said reading the memo. Micky stared back at Gary for several seconds before replying.

'What is it about me? Do I have a notice on my forehead that says, *Give me more to do, I haven't got enough?*' Micky sighed and wrinkled his brow as Gary started to laugh at his colleague's depression. Mick picked up another piece of paper lying on the counter. 'I've got another note here about WEEE collections,' Micky said emphasising the word WEEE and then laughing in a croaky voice that easily equalled Reggie's, 'it says the UK has to meet a minimum collection target of four kilos per person,' he read, not realising that he was being overheard. A driver standing at the window felt he must contribute to the debate.

'What's this? We ain't collecting piss now are we?' Littleton, the grubby driver shrieked, 'my Aunt Fanny, what will they think of next? That Councillor Huckett chap's the type that would eat his own scabs rather than allow them to go to waste!' Littleton said sniggering.

'I've told you before Littleton, get lost!' Micky shouted, 'don't eavesdrop, OK? Watch my lips; this is nothing to do with you!' Micky was finding it hard to keep a straight face. 'We're not talking about wee, you stupid prick-head. WEEE stands for Waste Electrical and Electronic Equipment. Everyone knows that, dimwit,' Micky said, pointing towards the gate hoping that Littleton would get the message and go home.

Gary and Micky watched as Littleton finally left the yard and then returned their thoughts to the beckoning night of adult pleasures.

'How many 'ave we got going to Soho on Friday night?' Gary asked unaware of more flapping ears elsewhere in the office. Kelly looked up from her paperwork afraid that she might have missed something, which nudged Micky to react swiftly to throw her off the scent.

'You mean Dougy's stag night in that new Hidlebury pub?' Micky said, winking at Gary. 'Fifteen at the last count, I think, Gazza, me old matey,' Micky said, nonchalantly.

'Is Reg coming?' Gary asked knowing the answer before Micky had a chance to reply.

'Whatta yer think? That Juney of his wouldn't let him out of her sight. How he managed to go on that trip to Crappendale without her blowing a gasket beats me,' Mickey sighed. His own wife was so much more reasonable he thought.

'It's probably just as well as we all know Reg is such a miserable sod at the best of times,' Gary replied.

Friday night arrived and fifteen blokes all shaved, showered and splattered with *Man of the Night* cologne turned up at the depot to board a community bus. Gary Newton was driving and the man making up the party numbers was the union steward, Bobby Dalton. As they left the yard, there were cries of, *where's that Dougy?* Over the general din came the reply, *Dougy who?* Raucous laughter followed since they had all tanked up before arriving at the depot and this transcended the Rolling Stones' number, *Can't Get No Satisfaction,* which was playing at that moment on the in-bus radio. The night was balmy as were most of those travelling on the bus. As soon as they arrived at the Pink Mojo Club the beer was flowing. It was not cheap but then this was supposed to be a good night out with the boys. The Club lighting was discreet and the younger men in the Cheatham party were making friends with a few unattached ladies who had been brave enough to enter such a den of iniquity so full of horny men. Larry Wright had decided to throw caution to the wind. At thirty something he had a partner of twelve years standing and three children but with his quaffed black hair held down with lashings of gel resembling a Teddy boy, it didn't take him long to find a partner to dance with.

Larry Wright's dance partner was called Samantha and if you looked closely you might be forgiven for thinking she was only about fifteen. Larry applied logic, accepting that since it was an over twenty one's night there was absolutely no way she could be under the age of consent. Samantha had waist length blonde hair and felt absolutely gorgeous to Larry's sweaty wandering hands. He could feel her bra through her tight red top and a beautiful bum beneath her equally tight sequinned jeans. Unable to resist her he was soon kissing her and looking for somewhere far more private to retire to. The music continued for another half hour, as did Larry Wright and nubile Samantha.

The warm up comedian came up on stage and told a few blue jokes and was followed by a few run of the mill strippers. The boys from the dust began to get impatient; these mediocre strippers were not what they had come to see.

'LOLITA, LOLITA, LOLITA...,' they called in chorus as the alcohol took hold.

'Let's see yer tits honey,' Brian Brewer shouted hoarsely, a bottle of beer in his hand.

'Come on, COME ON, Come on, COME ON,' Gary Biddles chanted as though he was at some premier football club. Just for a change he was not wearing his anorak; instead he had put his tattoos on display. A new tattoo had appeared on his left arm which read, *I love Lolita* and these words were written on a three inch tattoo of a penis. Biddle's mum Carol was unaware of this additional artwork and he knew there would be hell to pay when she did.

Finally, Lolita appeared and the club was filled with frenzied shouting and whistling. Lolita's act was announced by the master of ceremonies but the clubbers saw her attributes come around the corner before they saw the rest her. The men thought her act was definitely more sophisticated than any other so far and were deliriously focussed on her person as she moved seductively to the music, dressed as a mermaid. Her costume did not remain in one piece for long as she stylishly cast off the fishy tail and several of the silvery blue scales. One by one the scales came off revealing a pretty brassiere which hardly contained her large breasts. A white rabbit fur piece hid her nether region, which was also peeled away in due course. Lolita's polished act included giving the honour of removing the rabbit fur to one poor sod sat at the front with his tongue hanging out. The room went suddenly silent as a minute silver G-string was revealed. Several signs around the room saying, Do Not Touch were ignored. Lolita was used to the feelings her act aroused and her lithe body slunk away just out of reach each time one of them made a grab at her. Gary Green was invited up on stage to unhook her sequin encrusted bra allowing the free fall of her massive bosoms.

'They're the biggest boobs I've ever seen in my whole life,' a rather drunk Slump Smith remarked, 'they must weigh half a tonne each at least,' he said running his hands over imaginary breasts on his own chest.

'Ditto,' the Ice Man whimpered, definitely not feeling as cool as ice at that moment.

'I wish she'd talk dirty to me,' Biddles said ruefully.

'You listen to your mum,' a fatherly Micky Brown advised. He seemed to be the only one who had managed to keep control of himself. He had rather fancied the stripper before Lolita, a Miss Sofia, a Turk from Istanbul but thoughts were private so no one would ever know.

Gary Newton was feeling tired. He was only on the lemonade and absolutely sober being tea total, which was probably why the men had petitioned him to be their driver. He looked at his watch and signalled to the others that perhaps it was time to leave.

'Yeah, alright Gary, I'm coming,' Micky called, 'Biddles will round 'em up. Go on Biddles, get on with it,' and then turning back to Gary, 'sorry you didn't get that job at Padwick, Gar. It was a bit of a while ago now I suppose but I just want to say, Gar, that I appreciate your being my friend and colleague,' Micky slurred, 'and in any case Gar, I think you'd agree that the Cheatham job's OK; it's the work that gets you down!' Gary knew for certain that it was time to head back.

Lolita had made a real fuss over her dustmen; sitting on their laps and making them feel like they were the most important men in the club, she had made them feel like kings. The dishevelled Cheatham party slouched their way back to the bus and Gary was forced to listen to a mixture of snoring, giggling, singing and chatter all along the route home.

'I think the union should inform management that we want social well-being, morale boosting trips to see Lolita every six months. It would be like a council treat for a great bunch of workers. What d'yer say Bobby boy or should that be booby boy?' Someone was heard to shout. Laughter filled the bus as Bobby tried on a pair of enormous false plastic knockers purchased at a club kiosk. Gary Biddles was sick as they stopped to drop someone off.

'Sod it!' Micky swore and turning to the only other person on the bus who was completely sober, their driver, 'Gary, get the duty mobile cleansing unit out to give this bus a bloody good clean before we hand it back on Monday, mate,' he ordered. The smell was making the rest of them want to puke too.

'Right, will do, Mick,' Gary Newton replied, driving on to the next home on the list. Gary Biddles had stopped throwing up and was sitting silently with an old piece of towelling over his mouth, an old rag that had been left on the bus for wiping the windows, hoping he could make it home without divulging more of his stomach contents.

The usual Monday blues were ominously absent. Micky Brown was singing, which was always a good sign especially at 6.30am in the morning. Sickness was slightly down for the first time in weeks and less than ten people were needed from Must Work Ltd. Alison was there to offer her help.

'What's 'appened to Eddy Baker? I had a job for 'im today?' Micky asked Alison.

'His wife rang the agency and left a message to say he'd had a bottle in his face on Saturday night. Don't know when we'll see him again to be honest. It sounded like he's got quite a few stitches,' Alison explained through the office window whilst smoking her cigarette outside in the yard. Gary Biddles had just arrived wearing his council issue anorak even though the temperatures were expected to soar to twenty six centigrade at midday. Before he could get himself inside the office, Micky had spotted him.

'Gordon Bennett, Biddles! Why the fucking 'ell are you wearing that coat? Excuse the technical term, Alison my love,' Micky exclaimed, sweeping his eyes up to the ceiling in disbelief.

'The weatherman on the telly last night suggested we might be in for a summer storm and I'm like the boy scouts, Mick, I like to be prepared,' Gary explained, smiling broadly. After acknowledging Alison, he swiped his card to gain entry to the building and joined Micky inside.

'How are yer feeling, Micky?' Biddles asked, winking furiously and swinging his hips in a suggestive manner.

'I'm fine, son. What about yerself? Sick as a dog you were on Saturday night. I hope your mum didn't give you a hard time,' Micky chuckled as he checked the radio sets sitting in their charging holsters. Alison was listening intrigued by the turn of the conversation.

'What 'ave you cheeky lot been up to, then?' She asked suspiciously. Biddles, who was brimming over with excitement allowed his enthusiasm for their night on the tiles to gush out.

'Only went to see Lolita, Baby Doll Reynolds at the Pink Mojo Club didn't we, Micky?' Gary was pretending to be holding two large melons. Alison got the picture.

'That Lolita is a sex pot. I'd like to show her a few ways of doing things,' Gary insisted boldly.

'Get out of it, son, you're far too young!' Micky countered.

Slump arrived at this point and was bursting to chip in.

'I'm a sex addict, me. Sexual practices, there is nothing I don't know about,' Slump boasted. He was breadth challenged or put another way, fat, hence the nickname, *Slump*.

'Next you'll be saying that practise makes perfect,' Micky Brown laughed, 'oh, and by the way Slump, when you call in on your radio, you sound as though you've got your head stuck down one of your toilets. When you've got a minute get that radio technician back pronto to look at this blinking radio control box. It cost a flipping fortune and it's never sodding worked properly,' Micky grumbled. Kelly arrived at 8am.

'Right Babe, take over here for me whilst I catch up with all this bloody paperwork. We've got seven blokes off apparently with sunstroke from the weekend, if you can believe that?' Mick said sarcastically. He looked out into the yard. Alison was still there greeting her agency staff one by one as they arrived. 'Alison! Bring the rest of your men over, lovey,' Micky yelled through the window. Most had already gone out but Mick found that he still needed a few bodies to get up to full strength. Alison brought her bunch of workers over for inspection whilst Kelly meanwhile, settled herself into the radio hot seat. Slump left the office saying he'd be back with a surprise!

'Hi everyone!' Kelly announced her presence to the crews on open channel, 'I'm here for the next half hour if you need me,' she said sounding rather like a mother hen.

'I need yer, darling. Get yer knickers off, I'll be there in a jiffy, sweetheart,' came the gruff order from one crew member over the airwaves. Micky recognised the voice as belonging to Littleton. He swung round, taking the microphone from Kelly.

'If I have to tell you again, Littleton, it'll be curtains for you, matey, comprehendy?' Micky was cross and rough diamond he might be but he liked the ladies to be treated right.

'Thanks Mick,' Kelly said getting back to the radio.

'That's alright Kel. I'm not doing it for you, love. I'm doing it because I can't stand that bastard Littleton,' the Senior Supervisor growled, 'anyway, be careful if you go outside today Kel. We're expecting a summer thunder storm.'

'Rain, Mick? I wasn't born yesterday you know. I do know about rain,' a confused Kelly answered.

'OK, my little flower. It's just, well, you know what happens when flowers get drenched in the rain don't you?' Mick teased. Kelly smiled broadly at Micky's compliment.

'Oh, Mick, you lovely man. You've made me come over all funny. That was a really lovely thing to say,' she squeaked. Micky smiled contentedly. It didn't cost the earth to say something nice once in a while, he believed.

Later that morning the radio traffic was still heavy.

'Twenty three can you hear me? Come in twenty three,' Mick called.

'Twenty three here, Mick. What can we do yer for?' A representative from Crew 23 answered.

'What did you find at Tomb Lane, anything?' Mick had asked a mobile team to go and investigate following a call from a resident reporting an obstruction in the road.

'It's a bloody fly tip Mick, about eight yards of it. We're getting on top of it slowly,' the mobile team reassured. Micky listened as his eyes suddenly caught sight of a shiny yellow thing coming towards him from across the yard. It was Slump, his belly overhanging his trousers because his shirt was too short to cover his girth. This was quite normal but now it was partially covered by a bright yellow kipper tie and high visibility reflective vest.

'Blimey, what on earth has Slump put on? He wasn't wearing that at 7am this morning,' Mick exclaimed to Biddles and Gary Newton who were in the office with him, 'I hope you've got yer sunglasses with yer today Biddles,' Mick quipped. Gary glanced out through the window and smiled as he watched Slump waddle over.

'I think I'll go and make the tea,' Biddles suggested and then added, 'Mick, the crew did say that they were getting on top of it, didn't they?' He said laughing childishly as he thrust his hips in a bonking like movement.

'Biddles! Do you have to put a sexual connotation on everything that happens?' An exasperated Mick asked, raising his voice at the depot idiot who treated Mick's remark like water off a duck's back and got on with making the tea.

'Good on yer Biddles! Make mine two sugars will yer,' Slump shouted as he entered the office. 'Well what do yer think?' Slump paraded his new tie so that everyone could get a good butchers at it. It was ghastly but he liked it. The bright yellow background was complemented by three green slimy monsters from another galaxy gliding up from the bottom. Slump was a good lad, Mick thought, but a rice pudding had more fashion sense. At this point Reggie arrived carrying a tin containing a dozen iced sponge cakes, which he had made with his own hands for their morning coffee breaks. He put the tin down on the bench in front of the window.

'Good morning everybody,' he called cheerily adding, 'Mick, I think we need a serious chat,' motioning in the direction of Kelly's empty seat.

'Kel's just gone upstairs, Reg, to make some toast. She won't be long, mucker,' Mick explained, taking a quick look at page three in the newspaper that was lying around on the bench, on account of his needing to keep abreast of things.

'Get Kelly to cover for another hour,' Reggie suggested, looking concerned.

'You obviously want something off your chest in a hurry, Reg,' Micky said, his choice of words influenced by the voluptuous model staring up at him from the daily rag. Reggie was silent.

'KELLY, come on down 'ere love, you're needed,' Micky shouted up the stairs. He rejoined Reggie and as he did so heard the pitiful strains of one of his driver's on the radio.

'Houston, are you there Houston? Come in Houston,' the driver called. Mick rolled his eyes and on hearing Kelly's feet on the stairs, locked the window shut to prevent thieving Toms with wandering fingers reaching in and stealing the spare radios, their iced dainties or whatever else they could get hold of from outside. Kelly dealt with 'Houston' as Micky and Reg went upstairs.

'What's up, Reg? Juney find out about some woman you took a fancy to in Crappendale?' Mick sometimes forgot his scruples.

'Get off it. Chance would have been a fine thing,' Reggie sighed.

Mick and Reggie were interrupted by a piercing scream and their door being flung open. Kelly came running in, flushed and outraged.

'That bastard just pinched my bottom,' she blurted. Mick was speechless. Kelly usually gave as good as she got.

'Who, my darling, has pinched your divine little bottom?' Mick asked sweetly. Kelly was not to be placated.

'Biddles, that great stupid lout, that's who. I want to report him, make an official complaint. Harassment or something they call it.' Kelly had recently read the Council's dictum on the definition of sexual harassment and this normally calm young woman who considered herself a woman of the world had changed her tune dramatically. Micky understood her anger at having her shapely rump end pinched but was at a loss to know how to deal with it. He made her a cup of coffee in the only clean mug he could find whilst he thought about it.

Gary Newton had arrived in the middle of the commotion and found himself left to operate the radio in Kelly's absence, Slump having left swiftly with Biddles.

'Biddles is a silly fool. He doesn't mean any harm, Kel. Let me get 'im and make 'im apologise?' Mick suggested. Kelly would not be consoled and eventually Mick left her to find Reg, who could not stand tears and had taken the opportunity to wander outside, take a call on his mobile and have a smoke until the fuss had died down.

Kelly was adamant that she wanted to lodge a complaint against her assailant and raise the baton for women everywhere. Reluctantly Mick was forced to contact Personnel who decided that the only course of action was to make a full report on the incident and suspend the simpleton Biddles on full pay with immediate effect.

'This is so unfair,' Micky said to Reggie, 'Kelly's probably suffering from women's monthly troubles, PMT or something. She'll feel differently in the morning. That poor bugger Biddles didn't mean to offend,' Mick was upset about just how seriously the incident was being taken.

'It shouldn't take long to clear up, Mick. I'll get Kelly to write out her complaint and we'll whip it over to Personnel and get Gary back as soon as possible,' Reggie was also surprised at how harshly Gary had been dealt with and felt so relieved that his Juney had got off so lightly.

'Personnel, Personnel, bloody Anti-personnel if you ask me,' Micky cursed.

With the bottom pinching incident out of the way for the minute, Reggie, Micky and now Gary Newton, sat down to talk.

'Following our visits last week to Crappendale and Aurelia, Huckett and Dingle were talking on the way home of introducing wheeled bins, which I know we already knew he was considering,' Reggie began, 'the fortnightly rubbish collection is still firmly fixed in his mind. Crappendale City Council has convinced him that it's the way to go. Trouble is he thinks we can collect a lot more than we originally talked about. Now he wants wood, furniture, rubble and engine oil all collected on separate collections and oh yes, he wants to enter into a partnership with Crappendale to recycle yoghurt pots to make them into plastic trees!' Some sort of dropped jaw syndrome seemed to grip Reg's colleagues. 'OK, OK, I know it sounds daft but they've told Pooper Scooper Hooper and Huckett et al that they've got some research project going. Mad as hatters, the lot of them are if you ask me. Alfie Leadbetter thought so anyway,' Reggie said, tormenting himself by playing with an unlit cigarette held between his fingers in the full knowledge that he was not allowed to light up on council premises.

Mick being the optimist consoled them with a prediction.

'He'll most probably have changed his mind by next week, Reg. I wouldn't lose any sleep over it,' Micky said.

'Mick's right, Reg. If they want all these new services they'll just 'ave to give us the men and the vehicles. To be honest, the street cleaning guys would love to have wheeled bins. We'd get a lot less mess to clear up after those foxes and cats have been at the black sacks,' Gary Newton was only speaking common sense and Reggie knew it. Having been in the trade for a few years he knew the pitfalls of introducing new and untried schemes.

'Yeah but we all know what usually happens is they give us extra work and expect us to manage without any extra funding. In fact it's worse than that, they somehow find a reason for not recruiting to vacant posts for months and then say, *well you managed for all this time without, we'll just cut the post altogether*,' Reggie had been there many times before and the others had too.

As if Reggie's revelation wasn't enough he went on to tell them the really bad news.

'In addition, Hooper, the stupid sod, is keen for Huckett to look into used nappy recycling. *Used nappies*. Can you believe that? Apparently if you weigh the nappies from one baby over a two year period it would be equivalent to the weight of a small car,' Reggie had at least learned one interesting fact on the trip, his colleagues pondered.

'Looks like Littleton was right after all. The Council will soon be collecting piss,' Micky remembered.

'Oh, I forgot to ask, Mick, how did the Lolita night go?' Reg inquired.

'Great, but you'd probably better ask Gary Biddles because he obviously thinks that he's still there,' Micky said sorrowfully. They all had appointments elsewhere in the borough and walked downstairs and out to their vans still discussing the Biddles v Kelly saga unable to comes to terms with the speed at which Biddles had fallen foul of the Council's rules. Before unlocking his van Micky turned and shouted back towards the allocation office.

'Kelly, love, get the Ice Man on the blower and remind 'im to buy those bloody lottery tickets this week,' he insisted.

'OK, Mick,' the blonde dolly bird replied and then, 'Micky, here catch,' she shouted, throwing Micky his yellow vest which was compulsory uniform when out on duty.

Chapter 10

Sir David arranged a debriefing session as promised with Cyril, Tom and Edith following the Crappendale trip to discuss Cheatham's future environmental direction. Irene was also invited to comment on the financial aspects of the Members' wish list. Cyril wanted maximum recycling; raising the game for all London boroughs by introducing several ideas they had seen at first hand on the grand tour. Councillor Tom Merryweather wanted similar results but with the maximum use of community groups and public involvement. Irene Bendover wanted maximum everything but with minimum of spend.

Tom Merryweather explained the importance of involving residents. He wanted everyone to be able to take part, take pride and high participation rates because this would be good for his Community Action Reports. Edith wanted the best for her beloved LIP, her beloved Professor Cyril and at a cost she thought Cheatham could afford. Cyril was first to put his suggestion forward.

'I've spent the past few nights lying awake trying to think things through, haven't had a wink of sleep,' Cyril said rubbing his eyes. Edith smiled to herself thinking that perhaps he should have popped round to her place. She knew a few night games they could have played which usually induced sleep. They do say a problem shared is a problem halved, she thought. In any case she was more than willing to chew on Cyril's problem, literally speaking of course, although Cyril's problem, she had to admit was of gigantic proportions. A smile had crept across her face and realising others were wondering what on earth was so funny she changed her expression, sat bolt upright and began to write some notes.

Cyril's plan was now for each house to have four bins.

'I have a quote from our Waste Management Team for the purchase of four wheeled bins per household and another for the purchase of the specialist vehicles we'll need for the collections. I'd like to see us introduce an alternate weekly frequency for non-recyclable rubbish,' Cyril carefully avoided the dreaded 'F' word even when speaking to the converted as it always seemed to send shivers down spines. He still thought longingly about his original wish to have the general rubbish collected monthly but in order to avoid hostilities breaking out he was careful not to mention it. 'The recycling collections will be leading edge stuff for paper, cardboard, plastics, cans, glass and textiles. We'll have another set of vehicles for building materials, scrap metal and wood and another for garden waste and finally, one for furniture, engine oil and anything else. I think, for the latter, a flatbed lorry with a taillift would be best in order to stop the furniture getting damaged by the rams in the RCV's,' Cyril explained as Edith sighed inwardly. If only Cyril would refrain from using that word, *ram*. How masterful he sounded, she thought. Irene, however, was still contemplating the Councillor's reference to *leading edge* collections.

'Councillor, do you really mean, *leading edge*? Are we sure that your plans are error proof? I wonder if it wouldn't be better to describe your plans as *bleeding edge*?' Irene could be sarcastic without even trying. Cyril decided not to grace Irene's question with a verbal reply at this stage.

Cyril continued completely unaware of the stirring in Edith's loins.

'The flatbeds will also be useful to my colleague, Jim Bowen. Jim is planning to work with Social Services to provide the Lemon Grove travellers site with a supply of good serviceable clothing along with internet access. On days when the flatbeds are not collecting recyclable materials, they can visit Lemon Grove and distribute second hand clothing,' Cyril suggested, which surprised Edith who thought she had made her views on travellers quite clear at their earlier Party meetings.

'Cyril, are you sure Jim still wants to do that?' Edith asked indignantly and watched as Cyril just shrugged his shoulders and nodded in the affirmative. Edith felt disappointed and lost interest in the meeting as Cyril prattled on about the Landfill Directive and how they must now reduce the amount of biodegradable waste that they send to landfill. Failure to meet their targets would result in the Council being fined obscene amounts of money.

Tom Merryweather had read the Mayor's Waste Strategy and clearly remembered that it encouraged community spirit. Residents should not only be encouraged to take part but to be part of the decision making process too. He thought he might take it one step further and get the residents to make the collections as well. Unemployment figures were low in Cheatham but it could be wiped out altogether.

'We should petition the DWWW to allow Cheatham to trial a work programme for the unemployed. If the unemployed don't co-operate, we'll get their benefits withdrawn. I would like to set up a limited company for the unemployed and the trouble makers in Cheatham. This would be a recycling company which would go into every street in the borough and collect the paper and glass and anything else we want collected,' Tom thought his idea was a cracker, 'we'll kill two birds with one stone and just think of the money we'll save! We wouldn't need to employ all those loaders you were talking about, Cyril, and think about the clout for Cheatham's Community Strategy,' Cllr Merryweather was ecstatic. 'Just think about it Cyril, we could have ex-managing directors working side by side with offenders doing Community Service. The whole community pulling together just like the old Dunkerque spirit,' he explained. The Chief Finance Officer started to take an interest. Her concentration had started to wander but any talk about saving money focussed her.

'Councillors,' Irene began, taking a fresh interest in the current topic of conversation, 'I wonder if you've ever thought about charging residents to have their waste picked up? I understand the Treasury is looking for a willing council prepared to take a risk and have a stab at it. There are all sorts of benefits we could get for being guinea pigs,' Irene said, positively glowing with the prospect of getting more money into her coffers. Sir David was also eagerly rubbing his hands together, the idea appealed to him too. It certainly warranted more research.

'It's true, we don't have any elections coming along and we've a thumping great majority; what do you think of that idea, Cyril, Tom, Edith?' Sir David asked enthusiastically.

'I think we really need to think this one through carefully,' Edith said, being the practical one, 'we may end up with more litter on our streets or residents dumping outside their neighbours' houses to avoid paying for extra waste. If I'm honest, I don't like this idea at all,' Edith sounded extremely sensible proving to Cyril that not all sex kittens are empty headed.

Cyril knew he would need bucket loads of dosh from somewhere to pay for his grandiose scheme. He reassured Irene, whom he knew lived outside the borough and who would not therefore be required to pay extra for her own waste, that he would consider her suggestion carefully. Irene agreed to get the full facts from the DWWW and to register a potential interest in officially considering such a system. It was obvious to her that she would need to burn the midnight oil on this research so stocking up on the gin and tonics and finding some way of conveniently setting said alcohol off against a suitable cost centre would require a bit of creative accounting.

Cyril called another meeting of his Waste Strategy Team, as he had come to regard it because the name, Waste Management Team, he felt was already sounding old hat. He set out his ideas for Cheatham's future recycling services and looking around the table realised that the guy with the anorak was missing. He hadn't exactly made much of an impact on the recycling debate in any case and therefore would not be missed.

'Adrian, I would rather like you to compile a report for the Performance Committee next Thursday night. Include your costings based on Reggie's prices for the wheeled bins and Charlie Pratt's estimate for new vehicles,' Cyril said turning to look at Reggie and Mick. 'I've good news for you all and especially for Reginald and Micky. Miss Bendover has agreed to put up ninety thousand pounds for two secondhand refuse freighters. Charlie will buy them at auction asap.'

'Thank you very much indeed, Councillor,' Reggie said trying to sound pleased.

'Yeah, thanks a lot, Councillor. Charlie had better make sure they've got bin lifting gear on the back otherwise they'll be no earthly good to us especially if we're going down the wheeled bin route,' Micky Brown replied caustically. Cyril glumly scribbled a note on his pad of recycled paper.

Not to be deterred by a load of cocky dustmen Cyril decided to let them have the full benefit of the comparative research he had carried out on our European cousins.

'I think I should tell you I've heard about a German vehicle that lifts five bins every four seconds and can do an incredible four hundred and fifty bins every hour. There is a substantial cost involved but then you will need fewer crews,' Cyril said, noticing incredulous looks on his Strategy Team's faces.

'But, Councillor,' John Dingle sounded apologetic, 'we will of course need to pass all these ideas of yours through the Union. The workforce need to be consulted before we ask them to take on new working practices, afterall they are only human. The Union will make the decision on whether the workforce can comfortably deal with four hundred and fifty bins an hour,' John sensed the imminent danger of a mass walk out. 'The Ice Man worked closely with the Union and no doubt much of their meeting would be leaked. Micky Brown was choking on his water. He had enough trouble getting them to do two hundred and fifty black sacks an hour.

'They'll ave to grow bloody wings,' Micky muttered under his breath to Reg.

'Councillor, what size bin were you thinking of having as the standard size and in what circumstances will we allow households to have a bigger bin?' Adrian asked. 'It's a well known fact that residents will fill whatever size of bin you give them. Padwick Borough Council is really kicking itself for giving everyone a refuse bin big enough for a family of ten,' Adrian elaborated.

'Good point, Adrian,' Cyril said, considering this new dilemma, 'I think we'll give them each a bin that's only just big enough to take one black sack of waste. They will, after all said and done, have a recycling bin for papers, plastics and so on, the latter being the most voluminous items in the domestic dustbins,' Cyril said, unable to resist adding some of his newly gained knowledge. 'I've read several reports on the contents of the average household dustbin and they all seem to agree that around eighty four percent is packaging. Food waste can be composted at home and before any of you say I'm wrong, let me just tell you that I have also read about a wonderful machine that residents can have on their balcony or in their garden that uses bugs to break down cooked food and spit it out as a compost,' Cyril explained. 'My door step recycling scheme will also enable bricks, rubble, wood and batteries to be recycled too, so I don't see any problems with reaching an eighty five percent recycling rate, do you?' Cyril asked glibly. No one spoke but this was due mostly to the fact that their concentration had wandered about ten minutes before Cyril had started pontificating.

Micky Brown, unlike his workmates was paying attention and had an important question to put to Cyril.

'What about side waste such as black sacks put out next to the wheelies?'

'My good man,' Cyril could be annoyingly patronising at times, 'absolutely not! We'll leave them all behind,' he insisted, 'we simply can't have the residents getting away with extra waste, now can we?' Cyril smiled condescendingly. He thought this would please the crews who would be slowed down just emptying the wheelies and having to return them to each house. Larry Wright, being a deep thinker had a spoke to throw into Cyril's wheel.

'But what if Joe Bloggs has a party or decides to clear out his garage? Everyone does that from time to time, Councillor,' Larry said. Cyril felt that some of his new team were just not taking his strategy seriously.

'Gary,' Cyril said, pausing. He had spouted the wrong name, which was made known to him by subtle shuffling around the table, 'Larry,' he began again having latched onto the right name this time, 'party or not, we must stand firm. Residents can always take it to the Brookfields Lane Civic Amenity Site,' Cyril reminded, 'or should I say, Reuse and Recycling Centre nowadays?' Cyril looked at their blank expressions, 'I saw it somewhere; I rather like it and I think we should re-label Brookfields. Perhaps I can give that little job to you Adrian?' Cyril asked.

'Brookfields is bloody miles from anywhere,' the Ice Man whispered in Micky's ear.

'Would you like to share your thoughts with us?' Cyril asked a rather surprised Ice Man.

'I was just saying that we offer a very good service at Brookfields, Councillor Huckett,' the Ice Man answered nervously.

Micky Brown's mind was working overtime and he had thought of yet another slippery slope that might cause Huckett to end up arse over heels.

'Councillor, can I ask you about all the elderly people we have? At the moment there are well over five thousand on the *dead and dying* list. Wheeled bins will make life more difficult for a lot more. The d&d list could swell to ten thousand or more. There's no doubt about it, they'll slow everything down and mean we'll need more in the way of vehicles and crews,' Micky stated, pragmatic as usual. He knew how keen the Council was to help the aged. The local newspapers had reported that the Mayor, Marcus Bullman OBE, had adopted the *Help the Aged Stay Put At Home* charity for his fund raising events throughout his official year.

'Take no prisoners,' Cyril ignored the sentiments that might be attached to any such politically correct considerations to do with those less able than himself, 'of course, I'll admit that there will be a few exceptions to some rules but we route out the genuine ones; do you hear me?' Cyril barked.

Cyril noticed for the first time during the meeting a predominance of green shirts in several different shades covering the chests of his Waste Strategy Team. He liked it very much. A complete accident he was sure but he would speak to John Dingle later on the subject of uniforms for the officers too. The idea of officers wearing something similar to the colours used for the crews' protective clothing really appealed. Cyril returned to the question of the *dead & dying* list, he still had more to say on the matter.

'Make them see a doctor and get it in triplicate. Send someone to knock them all up and check whether they can or can't push their bins to the edge of their properties. Do whatever is necessary to kid them into giving themselves away. This is war on waste,' Cyril said, thumping his hand on the table, 'we can't afford malingerers.' John and the others were mortified at Cyril's phraseology, *knock them up?* What sort of educated person used that kind of language? They were not sure whether to laugh or cry.

The Waste Strategy Team sat in silence for what seemed an eternity. John knew he had to do something to ease the tension. Cyril's fighting talk could cost lives or at the very least a drop in staff morale to say nothing about the state of the elderly who could peg out trying to get their rubbish collected.

'Cyril, Marcus Bullman has pledged that this council will do all that it can to make life easier for the infirm and elderly. Might I suggest that when we release details of the new service we make a song and dance about the fact that the elderly and disabled will be *encouraged* to come forward and ask to have their bins walked to their front gates by the crews? This way you're bound to grow support rather than alienate a large section of the population,' John explained, sitting back and watching a smile form on the corners of Cyril's mouth. As visions of rickety old residents, thumping the depot gates with their sticks receded, the depot staff relaxed into their chairs.

'Sir, I don't mean to be difficult,' Slump began, 'but what about people like me who live in flats? Will we have the quadruplet wheeled bins because I see lots of problems if that's the case.

'I beg to differ young man,' Cyril answered stoically, 'but we'll research it if it'll make you feel better,' he said turning to the Recycling Officer. 'Adrian, organise a survey of all private blocks of flats in the borough. Where we can put them on the wheelies easily, we'll do it. We'll see how it works,' and then he added, 'you know, I've just thought of a jolly good idea. If wheelies are not practical we'll give them clear sacks so we can see what they're up to! We'll be able to see what class of wine they drink too. Those young stock market types are as drunk as lords most nights from what I've heard.' Cyril was laughing like a drain at his own joke whilst everyone else remained silent. Gary Newton brought Cyril to heel with another serious question.

'Councillor, I've been talking to Councillor Goodenough and it seems that incontinence pads and stoma bags have been declassified as clinical waste. The Performance Committee has agreed that it will be alright to put them in with the ordinary rubbish. If we allow this, a lot of people will need larger bins. Will these residents be a special case?'

'Gary,' Cyril got the name right only because Gary was the only one wearing his council name badge, 'I don't see why we need make any exceptions to this rule; suck it and see is my motto,' the team contemplated the thought of a *suck it and see* policy with regard to stoma bags.

At just before midday, Reggie, Larry, Gary, Gary, Micky, Micky and Mick left the company of the pompous Cyril Huckett and the obsequious John Dingle and bundled into Reggie's Volkswagen, Sharon.

'Oy Reg, you wouldn't get me driving a car with a gel's name!' The Ice Man quipped.

'Yeah, yeah, just get in will yer? I've got work to do,' Reggie shouted, starting the engine and checking that all the doors were shut. He noticed that one of the dashboard lights was on indicating a door ajar but before he could admonish them, Slump, who was suffering from hunger pains, called out an instruction.

'Stop at Wing Wong Willie's on the way back; I wanna get some chiss and fips for me dinna,' he shouted desperately. He was more at home with cleaning his toilets or catching rats than wheelie bins and composters.

'Shut that door properly and we might get there today,' Reg bellowed. The team arrived back at the yard clutching paper packets of chips, some with fish and some with meat pies. The car stank. Reggie wound down the electric windows.

'I don't know what June'll say when she gets a whiff of this car,' he worried. Gary Green was just getting out of the car.

'She'll say, what a wonderful perfume Reg, quite seductive, take me now,' Gary was winking as the rest turned their heads to glance back at Reg lighting his cigarette and staring grumpily after Gary.

On arrival at the depot they found the airwaves alive with radio communications. Bobby Dalton had been taken off his usual driving duties to cover whilst the supervisors met with Cyril at the Civic Offices and he was only just coping.

'Where's Kelly,' Micky asked, 'she was supposed to be 'ere with you,' he added.

'Don't know Mick. She was 'ere until about half and hour ago. I think she might 'ave gone to lunch.' Bobby was on the phone, on the radio and in between times trying to look at work sheets to see what and where the crews were supposed to be. Everyone was talking at once.

'Women! They are never where they should be,' Micky sighed, lighting up a ciggy.

'Micky, you're not supposed to...' Slump wasn't allowed to finish.

'Yeah, I bloody know, I'm not supposed to smoke in a council building anymore. Fucking 'ell what next,' and with that Micky went out into the yard leaving the others to relieve Bobby.

The radio was bubbling away with drivers making contact with the Cheatham nerve centre. Gary Green told everyone to stop prattling on for a minute and just listen.

'Tony, you're number one; Brewer, you're number two and Fisher, you're number three. When I say go, speak - number one, go..,' he ordered. Slump could not stop himself laughing whilst trying to deal with a resident on the telephone. Slump's enquirer was a fretful cat owner who wanted to know whether a stripped ginger moggy with an Asian look about it had been picked up.

'We picked up a ginger tom-cat in Rollo Street last Tuesday, madam,' Slump told the tearful lady as he flicked through the Dead Cats Book and found the entry. The distraught ex-cat owner wept.

'Thank you, young man. Where do I go to collect my cat's body?' Slump was stumped for a second.

'I'm afraid that won't be possible, madam,' Slump returned without much of a hint of compassion, 'the cleansing crew threw it in the back of the lorry. I expect you were hoping to bury it in your back garden were you?' Slump had never cared much for felines; nasty killers in his book, always catching baby birds.

Slump's explanation of events led to a good show of histrionics from the now ex-cat owner.

'Young man, my cat was not just an ordinary moggy,' the distraught caller finally managed, 'it was a wild animal, just three steps away from a tiger. That cat cost me three and a half thousand pounds and I want to collect some insurance money. I demand the Council write me a letter confirming that my cat is dead,' she barked. Slump was shocked.

'Madam, we can't be sure that it was your cat. The member of staff who picked it off the road is adamant that it had no special markings and there was no collar with an address. We believe it was just a straight forward ginger cat,' Slump explained, managing to get rid of the caller who had relapsed into another fit of crying.

'You're an idiot, Slump,' Micky chided, 'how many times have I told you, we never tell them the truth. Next you'll be telling 'em that Ginger was chucked on the dump and rolled flat by a ten tonne landfill tractor! Just say the cat has already been sent away for a dignified cremation. Never, never, let it be known that it was slung in the back of the lorry and landfilled! If you must, say it was, humanely disposed of. We'll get a complaint now,' Micky grumbled, feeling that he had not benefited at all from the fag he'd just smoked.

'Mick, how many ways are there to skin a cat?' Slump wondered dreamily. Micky was dumbfounded.

'I don't know and I don't bloody care!' Mick answered.

The Performance Committee met to consider several new initiatives one of them being the consideration of Cyril's recycling plans. The Committee was made up of councillors who included the Mayor and Edith Dickopf. It was advised by several chief officers and the Chief Finance Officer, Irene Bendover was a regular attendee. She looked her usual tired and drained self; sunken eyes circled by black and red blotches and as usual her hair had not seen a brush for at least twenty four hours. From across the table, Cyril detected a whiff of something on her breath that was most definitely a lot stronger than the water in her glass. Irene smiled sinisterly, unnerving him.

Cyril outlined his alternate weekly collection plan and his aim to provide each home in Cheatham with four wheeled bins. The Committee sat and listened attentively. Edith smiled serenely at Cyril from across the table.

'We'll need two hundred thousand wheeled bins; fifty thousand each for rubbish, dry recyclables, garden waste, wood, builders rubble and metal waste,' Cyril explained confidently, 'I think too, we should buy the best available in the way of vehicles. I've heard about a wonderful new model just coming off the production line at the Grossman Works in Hamburg. The new design is known in Europe as the *Rote Vogel* and runs on natural compressed gas. Our Transport Manager has already held a meeting with the Gas Board and I understand that they are very keen to invest in Cheatham. They're ready to install a fast fill station provided we make a commitment to put at least seventy five percent of our fleet onto gas within the next five years.' Cyril could see his fellow councillors were impressed and so they should be because his plan was going to make Cheatham great.

Cyril could see that Irene was straining to ask a question.

'Councillor, I'm sorry to bang on all the time about cost,' she fibbed, 'but what's the difference between using ordinary old freighters and these new fangled things you refer to?' Irene asked looking decidedly more inebriated than earlier.

'Irene, my dear,' Irene's heckles were already standing on end; she was no one's 'dear', 'it's not about money alone. The very principles of Best Value teach us that. All of us in this room want to do our bit for Climate Change and to do this we must consider the very best that technology can offer us. The Council is a major purchaser and must set an example to others,' Cyril felt his sustainability stand had triumphed over cost effectiveness at last but Irene's piercing stare unnerved him. He reached for his glass of water. It was tasteless and he felt he could do with some of the stuff that this bendy woman must be on right now.

Irene was not finished with Cyril yet.

'I would really like to know how much these new Grossman red thingy vehicles will cost?' Irene had cracked harder nuts than Cyril Huckett before now.

'Irene, I really don't think this is the time or place for an argument but if this information will assist you in getting a good night's sleep they cost around two hundred thousand pounds each but we'll only need five of them, possibly six at the most,' Cyril revealed. There was a gasp from the Bendover corner as she did the arithmetic.

'We need nearly one and a half million pounds for vehicles if you consider all the little extra costs that come with such things and we will need another two and a half million for bins. That's four million pounds at the very least not taking into account the extra staff and actually putting out the bins and all the literature explaining how the new service will work.' The stare was back, focussed steadfastly on Cyril who made up his mind that the time was ripe to drop the next clangor; in for a penny, in for a pound!

'Ah, Miss Bendover, I should add that we'll need somewhere to sort the materials too,' he said brazenly. Irene's expression best resembled simmering hatred..

Councillor Goodenough, as Chair of the meeting decided it was time to break the circle of spite between the Chief Officer and the Lead Councillor for Waste. He asked Cyril to explain what he meant by somewhere *to sort*.

'We'll need to have a special set of conveyors, trommels and shakers to loosen the materials in order to separate them prior to despatch to reprocessors. There are several different polymers used for plastic bottles, you know?' Cyril was blinding them with science and it seemed to be working and more importantly it momentarily stopped Miss Bendover from continuing her interrogation of Cyril's expected financial outlay. Irene, however, was like a dog with a bone and on her insistence they soon returned to the subject of costs. Cyril was on the crest of a local authority recycling breakthrough, which should he believed be a raison d'etre and so was at a complete lost to understand the workings of this woman's mind.

'Please do tell us how much, Councillor?' Irene nagged him. Cyril cleared his throat; this bloody witch needed putting down.

'I believe one can have a simple materials sorting facility for about a million pounds,' Cyril offered this servant of the Council. Anyone would think she owned the place, he thought privately.

Cyril boiled within knowing that he might have to justify himself yet again to this Council upstart; he was earning a living before she was born!

'But we're not talking about a simple materials thingy are we, Councillor?' Irene was tenacious if she was anything.

'You're quite right, Irene, to have the very best that money can buy...' Cyril began. Irene was thinking that he wanted the very best that *her* money could buy, 'we'll need to invest a good two million pounds but let me remind everyone that with this total investment of six million pounds, Cheatham will race to the top of the recycling league tables not to mention the honours that the government will bestow upon us. We'll get one of those special Beacon Status awards for being innovative and Irene, if I might make so bold, we'll probably get extra cash from the Treasury too,' Cyril concluded, hoping his last remark might satisfy her for a while at least.

An elderly lady from the Education Group, Councillor Mrs Pedder, with grey hair plaited and coiled around her temples had been listening carefully to Cyril's plans. His heavy spending would mean just one thing, less money for Education.

'Councillor Huckett, can we assume that if your schemes go ahead and we approve the spending of up to six million pounds of tax payers hard earned cash that there will be some sort of Education Centre, somewhere that we can take school children to do a bit of soul searching and understand exactly what recycling does for the environment? It is after all part of the national curriculum,' Mrs Pedder pointed out. She would have liked six million pounds to spend on her own department but if she could use some other fund to enhance her own facilities, so be it.

The fresh faced Jim Bowen was sitting next to Mrs Pedder and added his own thoughts.

'Yes Cyril, I think I know what Councillor Pedder is getting at as I have similar sympathies,' Mrs Pedder was quite sure that someone of Jim's sexual orientation could not in the least sympathise with her, 'if we could have an Interpretation Centre with computers showing exactly what was happening in the sorting plant without the children actually having to go there and get covered in dust, it would be an educational breakthrough as well as a recycling first. We could have little mock up machines that they could play with such as scaled down baling presses and ...' Councillor Bowen was interrupted by yet another councillor, the Chair of the Performance Committee, Jack Goodenough.

'I think I know what Jim means. A series of hands on experiments like they have at the Science Museum...' Goodenough went on for some time with his all illuminating description of what he had seen on his last visit to the museum with his grandsons. This was followed by a general discussion on exactly what a Waste Education Centre might contain and where it should be and even whether or not it should have yellow and green carpet to match the LIP colours. With all of these extra and naturally more urgent considerations to consider, the debate was prolonged by another thirty minutes.

The main reason for holding the meeting in the first place had been the revolutionary change in the way that rubbish would be collected and that now seemed to have been consigned to the back boiler. Cyril sat back exhausted, suffering from extreme disbelief. He allowed the debate or rather the free for all presently going on around him, to wash over him and shook his head unable to believe that they were actually more interested in the provision of toys and gadgets than whether they should spend six million pounds on the nuts and bolts of the project. At an opportune moment he managed to intervene and attempted to wind up the discussion by getting the Chair's attention and pointing to his wristwatch. Councillor Pedder had the last say.

'Oh yes, Chair. I've just had another super idea. Why don't we provide every child with one of those miniature desk top wheelie bins that manufacturers give away free at trade fairs? You know the ones that people stand on their desks and use as caddies for their pens and pencils? Kids love that sort of thing,' she enthused.

The discussion now back on course, Cyril ran with his ideas once again.

'You see, Councillors, we have the chance now to be revolutionary, *to think outside the box*, to be proactive for a change and we must take the bull by the horns before it's too late,' Cyril explained. The Mayor, who had arrived late, had sat quietly until now.

'May I ask about the proposed collection frequency? Marcus asked. 'I understand from what you've said that residents will only get their rubbish collected every fortnight. Is this so Councillor Huckett?' The Mayor twiddled his bow tie. He was not a regular member of the Performance Committee but as Mayor he had an honorary seat on all committees and in the event of indecision had the casting vote. Tonight Marcus had a personal interest in the waste issue and had felt it his duty to attend.

'Mr Mayor, there will be a collection every week; it's just that each week we'll be collecting different materials,' Cyril was still ignoring the F word which had been John's super idea to bamboozle his audience. The Press were scribbling away which unnerved Cyril somewhat.

'Don't you think that rubbish collected every other week will be a health hazard?' Marcus asked directly. Cyril was bamboozled now.

Cyril needed help and looked over at John Dingle who was at the meeting primarily to advise the Lead Member for Waste should a difficult situation arise such as now. Luckily, Dingle was frantically scribbling away too and shortly handed Cyril a scrap of paper.

'Mr Mayor, I plan to provide a free home composter to every house with a garden and to make seasonal collections of kitchen and garden waste during the hot summer months. This means that residents will have no need to have food waste rotting in their brown rubbish bins during the hottest months of the year. I've also asked my Waste Strategy Team to liaise with their colleagues in the Environmental Health Department to establish what health risks, if any, are associated with this type of collection,' Cyril explained.

'I would like it put on record that I, for one, have grave concerns about the health and safety of your proposed scheme, Councillor Huckett,' the Mayor kept it formal for the sake of the minutes, 'I don't think that two weekly collections of waste are acceptable,' the Mayor declared.

'Well, Mr Mayor, if I might just say that it was a great pity that you were unable to accompany us on our recent visit to Crappendale City because there we were able to see a similar scheme at first hand. It worked perfectly well without any health risks at all. But, Mr Mayor, I understand your concerns and I will personally make sure that we investigate them fully,' Cyril could see the OBE with his name on it floating away.

Thankfully for Cyril most of his political colleagues had been swayed by his promise to look very carefully at the environmental impacts of his recycling bonanza. Cyril's ideas would get Cheatham and the LIP mentioned in government despatches and for this reason alone they were considered to be worth taking a serious look at. Edith had listened attentively to the debate and felt some sympathy with Marcus' view but this femme fatale had her lusty sights focussed on Cyril, realising at the same time that she would have to convince Irene further down the line; a necessary evil she concluded as she glanced at the Chief Finance Officer, shaking her head and looking ready to cut her wrists at Cyril's proposed spending spree. A happy bunny, she was not, knowing that now she was being asked to find another twenty five thousand pounds for interactive web designers and fancy things for kids to play with at some idealistic Waste and Recycling Education Centre. It was such a pity, she thought, that the little bastards would not be allowed to play with real balers. A smile crept across her face as she considered the added bonus for the borough. Losing a few kids each year would keep the per capita spend on Education down. Her depression grew deeper when she remembered that she also had to finance things that looked like bloody daleks and were called home composters. Where were these costed? There was certainly no mention of them in the pre-agenda report submitted by Cyril for councillors to read before the meeting.

Jack Goodenough, being an affable sort of chap saw both sides of the argument and usually found a way of consoling the warring fractions by some sort of compromise. He tried to be helpful but on this occasion managed to throw another fly into the ointment, the emphasis being on the fly in this whole debacle as history would prove.

'What about consultation, Cyril,' and then looking directly at John Dingle he added, 'consultation, John?' John Dingle was surprised to hear his name spouted in the same breath as Cyril's, because officers were persona non grata at committee meetings, only allowed to speak when spoken to. They were like actors' understudies, waiting in the wings ready to make their grand entrance at an appropriate time, which was usually when lead councillors had dug themselves into a very deep hole and needed a lifeline thrown to them.

Edith was deep in thought trying to decide how she would vote, being totally split between supporting Cyril and Irene. She picked up on the suggestion of consultation and supported Jack by pushing Cyril for an answer.

'That's a good question. What about consultation, Cyril?' She demanded, 'we're expected to consult with our public aren't we? I think, Cyril, we should ask them whether they want your new scheme. That'll tell us whether we're truly in tune with our residents,' Edith suggested.

'Possibly,' Cyril agreed, 'I'll consider everything in good time,' he said without emotion. Meanwhile Jack, misinterpreting the Mayor's expression as one of utter dismay for what he had heard so far, asked for his views on the survey suggestion.

'Marcus would a survey help you to come to terms with Cyril's quadruplet Wheeled Bin Scheme?' He asked, waiting patiently for a reply. The Mayor by now had other weighty matters on his mind. Daydreaming about his next rendezvous with Maisie was clouding his concentration. 'Er, yes, of course, that would be perfect,' Marcus said his attention span at an end.

Dingle whispered an idea in Cyril's ear which Cyril then repeated out loud for the benefit of the meeting.

'Chair, I'd like to suggest we run a trial scheme to say, oh I don't know, lets say five thousand households and then survey those residents after three months. The sample households will have tried using the changed collection frequency and from them we should get a truer picture of how people really feel about it,' Cyril said holding his breath until everyone began nodding in favour of his idea.

'That's splendid, Cyril. Residents in some areas have been crying out for wheeled bins to stop the foxes getting at the old chicken carcasses in their black sacks.' Goodenough was looking for a way to stop the continuous stream of complaints about foxes and their annoying habit of leaving their calling card on residents' lawns. Cyril's own neighbour was one of them. His environmentally sound wild patch at the back of his garden housed five foxes at the last count or so his neighbour complained. She regularly rang Pest Control and always named Cyril as the culprit saying he would be the cause of an outbreak of legionnaire's disease or something equally as obnoxious spreading around Cheatham wholesale. Slump had taken several abusive calls from the neighbour about vermin setting up home in Cyril's garden and he was wondering how he might broach the subject with the Lead Councillor for Waste at their next so called, Waste Strategy Team meeting.

The Performance Committee meeting finished with a vote unanimously in favour of a wheeled bin trial. It was then left for Edith and Irene to put together a report making recommendations for the funding including the extensive borrowing of capital monies to the Strategy Committee, which was due to meet in a few days time. The meeting closed in time for all to retreat to the Council's Social Club, colloquially known as The Black Hole of Calcutta because of its dim lighting which was said by some to be a measure used by Irene to keep the Civic Offices' costs down to a minimum. Tom Merryweather also claimed the credit for the Social Club's energy saving measures, which he said reduced carbon dioxide emissions and therein assisted the government in its carbon reduction targets.

The following morning Cyril received a memo from Edith suggesting that in spite of the favourable outcome for a trial run, having now considered fully the financial implications there was no way she could endorse his recycling plans without substantial cuts to some of his other service areas. Cyril was counting on Edith's support as the wily old dog knew that if he had her backing he was more than likely to convince Irene Bendover to his way of thinking, probably unwillingly but likely. There was only one thing to do and that was to get Edith on the telephone immediately and discuss any of the more difficult areas of his plans. Be friendly but not overtly so, he decided.

'Edith, my dear, how are you this morning?' Cyril felt a fool asking her this when he had seen her just the evening before.

'I'm fine Cyril. I suppose you read my memo this morning?' Edith understood Cyril's motives entirely. It came with years of practice, trying to establish exactly what her pupils were guilty of without them having to say it out loud. Mind reading had become Edith's speciality.

'Ah, well yes my dear; I thought we might talk about your concerns, try and work out an acceptable way of introducing some of my ideas? Have coffee with me at Richelieu's in the High Street at 11am?'

'I've got a better idea. Dad's out this morning at the Granfers Club. Come round and I can show you the fruits of my loin, poetically speaking of course, in my conservatory.' Edith was giggling. Cyril was speechless.

'Well I'm not so sure I should, Edith.' Cyril said nervously. He was supposed to be on a mission to secure funding for his new scheme not after a bit of slap and tickle. Edith made up his mind for him.

'Come if you want your damn silly schemes or forget about them altogether,' the ex-headmistress retorted sharply. Blackmail is what this resembled to Cyril but then sometimes one has to do what one has to do, for Queen and country and all that. He took several deep breaths to help himself remain calm and collected.

Edith yanked Cyril into her lounge and before he had time to say, good morning, she was leading him into the conservatory losing no time at all in giving him a guided tour of her crops. She held out one of her cucumbers, still attached to its stem.

'What do you think about the size of this brute then, Cyril?' She asked, running her hand seductively up and down the length of the slender, shiny cue, squeezing it here and there, 'we could have some fun with this, ay? Who said size doesn't count?' She laughed. The real Edith was so unlike the image that she projected in public. Cyril had not come to discuss her cucumbers but realised that he was quite at her mercy. If the truth were known he really was amazed at the size of her large fleshy fruits. Nervously, his eyes were darting this way and that, trying to find something a bit less shaped like a sexual appendage on which to rest them. He admired her geraniums and tomatoes and shuddered at her little collection of meat eating Sundews and Venus Flytraps thinking there but for the grace of God go I!

It was a warm day and the windows were steaming up from the transpiring plants. Cyril undid the top buttons of his check shirt and pushed his fingers through his hair to revive himself a little. He turned to see Edith stripping off her caftan. Her perfume, Lilly of The Valley, a scent which betrayed her age, reminded Cyril of a fragrant garden and was pure heaven to his nostrils. This scarlet woman approached him and totally uninhibited, ran her hands over his body. Her tantalising touch, as she ran her hands between his legs was fatal. Cyril was delirious. They were soon lost in each other and Cyril, who was still thinking *outside the box*, was quickly brushing away the soil particles that littered the potting table and purposely, like a man possessed lifting Edith up onto it. They made love ravenously and not without a lot of sighing and grunting. The windows were streaming as water ran in rivulets down the panes creating clear spots where it was just possible to look in from outside and see the glorious ferns and little rosebuds which made up Edith's tropical paradise.

As fate would have it, Gary Biddles at this very hour was nearby earning a bit of extra cash by moonlighting. The disciplinary affair was still to be resolved and in the meantime he was still suspended on full pay. His mum Carol was furious with him and to prevent him hanging around the house all day and getting under her feet found him another part time job. This mum in a million also knew a man who needed someone to help him with lucrative house clearances and the odd bit of gardening work. Gary proffered his services as a labourer for cash in hand, no questions asked.

It was Friday and Gary's foray into manual work consisted of light gardening. He was told to go round to an old dear on the outskirts of Cheatham and cut her grass. It was a standing arrangement every Friday fortnight. The old lady was hard of hearing and did not hear his knock so using his initiative he went straight to the shed and found the petrol mower. Off he went up and down the garden following a sheet of instructions which reminded him to take great care trimming around the old lady's two old apples trees. A blackbird frightened out of the hedge by the noise flew up in front of him and looking up he noticed the big glass conservatory next door. Peering over the hedge it looked rather exotic as bits of palm tree trying to escape through the glass roof and the steamy interior came into view. He walked along the hedge until he came to a gap which was just big enough to squeeze his stout body through and stealthily he crept up to the steamy windows and strained his eyes to see through the condensing mist.

Gary had always fancied a conservatory full of tropical plants for his mum but his thoughts were interrupted by something pink moving rhythmically inside. He concentrated and it became clear to him that there was also something grey moving on top of the pink. The rivulets of water running down the glass caused a temporary clearing and he realised that his eyes were witnessing a naughty escapade. Mesmerised by the scene he froze with his nose stuck up against the window pane. After a couple of minutes he felt something hard inside his anorak pocket. It was the Waste Management digital camera which he had been using just prior to his sudden suspension. He seized the moment and placing the camera hard up against the window, took several shots of the harmonised bodies working within.

The rapid movements and accompanying shrieks of joy halted suddenly as camera flashes bounced back off the glass. The grey person straightened up and picking up a small towel lying on the bench behind him used it to cover his modesty. The pink person jumped down from the table and reached for her caftan, holding it close until a convenient time came when she could pop it over her head. Gary took one more photograph and stuffed the camera back inside his pocket hearing Edith emit an agonising scream as he did so. She dived beneath the potting table, where Cyril, still in shock had also hidden himself away. Cyril had spotted the anorak and a mental anguish overtook him as he remembered Waste Strategy Team. Clasping his head in his hands he cowered with Edith for several minutes until at last they thought the danger had passed.

For Cyril, this incident was the last straw. First it was the Civic security cameras and now that oaf with a camera. God, he was so unlucky! Gary Biddles was similarly unnerved at what he had witnessed and feeling confused he returned to the old lady's garden and his unfinished mowing. His concentration had gone and the lawn was anything but prettily cut. The old lady came outside to pay him but had to content herself with watching the silly bit of a boy running off down the road.

Chapter 11

By midday on Monday the allocation office was buzzing. Mickey was pulling out his hair with several breakdowns to deal with. Gary Newton was taking a telephone call from Gazza O'Neill, one of the so called, Rapid Response drivers.

'Gazza, what's up now? Where's the f------ radio I gave you this morning? I went to a lot of trouble to find you a replacement for the one you bloody lost yesterday,' Gary swore, which was quite out of character.

'I know, I'm sorry guv but I've had to use a call box because the bastard thing's been stolen,' Gazza apologised.

'Christ Almighty, Gazza, where the hell did you leave it?' Gary was short of decent radios and managers had been told to cut back to essential spending only. A set of radios would mean finding another thousand quid or more.

'It was in me lorry, guv and that's been stolen as well,' Gazza said relating his sorry tale and rendering Gary speechless. The cleansing crews were not noted for their academic prowess but this took the biscuit.

'Yeah, I'm sorry guv, I left it outside the Magistrate's Court while I went for a pee. It was gone when I got back,' Gazza explained without too many signs of remorse. Gary had to sit down. How many times had he drummed into his crews the need to lock up their vehicles whenever they had to leave them? He picked up the phone and rang the Council's Insurance Section, yet again.

Just as Gazza was sorted out, Gadget, one of the blokes on Weeding Team 'A' walked up to the office carrying a hoe. He was followed by three others singing, *I ho, I ho, it's off to work we go...* It was comical, as only street cleaners can be but Gary Newton was not amused.

'Now what?' Gary was just about to drink a soothing cup of camomile tea. Weeding Team 'A' did a little dance with their hoes and then Gadget presented Gary with a broken stick, which he thrust through the allocation window.

'Boss, these are no good. We've already gone through ten this week and there are only four of us. Can you get us some decent hoes, mate? The hardware shop down the road stocks better hoes than these,' Gadget explained emphasising the "h" sound on the word "hoes", 'the ones Gary Green gets from Stores are just no bleeding good at all,' he wailed pathetically for effect and was supported at this point by a general hum of approval from the rest of his team. Gary extended an arm out through the window.

'Giss 'em here,' he ordered, thinking the day could only get better, 'get another set from Stores for now and piss off back to work, you bloody morons,' Gary grimaced but was smiling inside and they knew it, 'I'll get you some stronger models tomorrow,' he condescended. Happy with their accomplishment, Weeding Team 'A' wended their way towards the Stores, a large shed at the bottom of the yard, still doing their little dance and singing at the tops of their voices.

Once the problems of the day had been sorted, Mickey Brown sat down with Gary Newton, Reggie, Adrian and John Dingle to discuss the Council's future recycling services. Dingle filled them in on the latest developments.

'Strategy Committee has agreed in principle to Cyril's plans. From what I gather, Edith Dickopf was a bit of a spanner in the works, wanted guarantees that proper performance indicators will be in place so that cost effectiveness can be measured. I believe Cyril had to go some way to appease her. How he did it no one knows but last night she couldn't have been more supportive, just like putty in his hands,' John said, looking relieved that at last they knew the direction of travel, as they say in the industry.

John Dingle's next bit if news was something else they had all been expecting.
"We've been told to implement a trial of the Quadruplet Wheeled Bin Scheme to about five thousand households as soon as possible. So, Adrian, I would like you to order twenty thousand bins from Plastibin Ltd., that's five thousand in each of the colours. If only life could be that simple, Micky Brown was thinking.
'Colours?' Micky asked.
'Yes, that's our next decision, I suppose,' John agreed.
'Grey for rubbish and I suggest green for dry recyclables,' Adrian called. No one disagreed with this.
'What about the third and fourth bins?' John remembered.
'Brown like earth which is what the garden waste becomes,' Micky offered.
'What about a nice yellow for the wood and other stuff?' Gary Newton suggested.
'You don't suppose Councillor Huckett will want to choose the colours himself do you?' Adrian asked.
'Yeah, Adrian's right, Mr Dingle. We'd better ask his lordship first. He won't like it if we let him think we've minds of our own,' Reggie said, searching his pockets frantically. He was itching for a ciggy.
'Where shall we put these blinking bins, then?' Micky asked indifferently.
'Ah yes. I think we're expected to find three suitable areas that roughly match the political interests in Cheatham. So I would say a bit of the Tory East, two thousand in the LIP heartland and the remainder in the bosom of Labour's stronghold, all the houses around the fringe of the Beverly Estate, which as we know isn't very large but big enough to provide us with most of our headaches,' John said contemplating the difficulties that would inevitably lie ahead.

Introducing Cyril's new service to the Labour stronghold was not going to be easy because the households there had not yet grasped the very basics of rubbish collection. Many residents still had trouble just remembering which day of the week to put their rubbish out to say nothing about making sure it was all contained within black sacks without gaping holes in the sides.
'I think Reg, Micky and Adrian had better work on defining the trial areas,' Dingle decided sounding doleful, 'Gary, I wonder if you could provide a couple of people to survey the areas? Walk the roads, count the households and check for stairs, access to back gardens etc. We mustn't forget that some households have nowhere to keep four wheeled bins. I will expect your people, Gary, to be on hand to advise residents during the trial and to monitor how it's working,' Dingle insisted. Public service still meant just that to this old fashioned public servant. He remembered the days when workers use to doff their caps and tug on their forelocks respectfully at their elders and betters and indeed the customer was always right.

Larry Wright and Gazza O'Neill, the latter being driver without a lorry, were volunteered to undertake the survey work. Mr Dingle was already anticipating the grilling he would get when the Scrutiny Committee met to consider the long term life of the scheme. His next job would be to get Cyril to elucidate on the preferred colours of the required wheelie bins. Micky Brown was also feeling irritated.

'I really don't like the sound of four wheelie bins per house. God knows what roads are going to look like on rubbish days, flipping ugly, I can tell yer,' he grumbled. The team meeting over, they all went downstairs and Micky made a beeline for his beloved Cortina MK3, which was sitting peacefully in the depot car park. The sight of this object of his affections brought a happy smile to his face and went someway to relieving the trepidation he felt about the future.

Larry and Gazza started walking the streets on behalf of the Refuse Section. The Council's Leader, Sir David, who liked very much to have his finger on the pulse, telephoned Dingle with regard to the type of literature the Council should distribute to residents on the new trial service.

'We need a really well laid out leaflet informing residents about the service and why we're doing it,' he explained to a weary Executive Head of Waste who could not help think he was being taught how to suck eggs, 'I've spoken to the Head of Communications and he suggests we form a working party to decide exactly how we tackle this urgent problem. I don't want any cock ups like the time your team sent out that notice saying, *the Council's Leader is personally interested in receiving any problems you might have with the disposal of dog dirt*. My front door,' he hesitated, 'I couldn't open it for two days because of the stacks of dog shit on my doorstep. The stench is still there,' he said with feeling.

'I am mindful of that occasion, Sir David,' Dingle admitted, faintly remembering the incident and keeping an eye firmly on his pension for which reason alone he was not keen to go there again, 'I think a working party is a very good idea. I'll speak to Communications and see if we can get something arranged in the next few days.

The Head of Communications was new. He was still at the stage of making himself known to all. He was not as tall as his predecessor and not nearly so outspoken, more a *company* man saying what was expected of him at all times. The previous post holder, Tim Baldwin whose job title as Press Officer had been subtlety different had been guilty of the most awful faux pas. One day when Sir David had been in another part of the office hidden behind a line of filing cabinets, the brazen Tim had made some reference to the Leader as, *Roly Poly Hooper* being that he did have a substantial roll of fat around his middle. Sir David had stood up at that point and made his presence known to the rest of the office and it was shortly after this event that the Press Office was restructured and the new post of Head of Communications established. Poor Tim, not surprisingly did not meet the selection criteria for shortlisting and not wishing to take a post on a lower grade gracefully accepted redundancy. They say that revenge is sweet and Tim left telling himself that Sir David may have won the battle but he was yet to win the war; he intended to live on and fight another day.

The Leader's new working party on how to best cascade information to residents on the new waste and recycling services met within a couple of days. Sir David met with Cyril, Dingle, Bill Sterling, Russell Webster, the new the Head of Communications and Maisie Atichitawomba. Maisie's presence served two purposes. She was head of the Council's staff and secondly, she could advise personally on the ethnicity value of any documentation thus compiled. Maisie chaired the meeting while Sir David's secretary, Pamela Peters took notes.

The Chief Executive got down to business in her usual brisk fashion.

'John, please tell us what you think are the most important issues to tell residents,' she prompted. John considered his reply carefully

'I would suggest that we set out clearly what they may and may not put into each of the bins. The public do get rather confused you know. I remember the Crappendale Director saying that although they'd told their residents they only wanted plastic bottles they still had people asking if plastic meat trays could go in the bin. It's very difficult not to be rude sometimes and say, well madam, is a plastic meat tray a bottle? One knows instinctively that it isn't, but it's....' Dingle was just getting into gear when Sir David interrupted his flow.

'Yes, yes, John, we haven't got all day. Lets get on with it. I want the literature to say why we're changing over to a four wheeled bin scheme. Cyril, can you draft something for me to look at by tomorrow midday? You know the sort of thing, landfill space running out, toxic juices getting into the water supplies; those sort of scary facts,' he suggested.

'David, I think you mean, leachate rather than toxic juices,' Cyril advised.

'Yes, yes, whatever,' the Leader snapped, 'and what are those bloody gases that are making our ozone layer disappear?'

'Methane is the word you're looking for,' Cyril answered feeling rather annoyed with the way his colleague seemed to be running away with things, Cyril's things in particular. He felt his toes were distinctly being trodden on.

The Leader, if he had noticed Cyril's dejected look was completely unfazed by it and moved on. He was reading a report which he was holding out in front of him having left his reading glasses at home, something that was becoming a habit.

'Oh, yes, this is a good one. I want it said that Europe is responsible for making us get up to speed on our recycling rates. Mention a few relevant European Directives and don't forget to add a bit about The Mayor of London's Waste Strategy and of course the government's revised Waste Strategy. We want all the credit and none of the blame for forking out, what is it, six million quid on waste minimisation measures? If you have too, frighten the buggers into taking our side and supporting our policies,' Sir David said eagerly.

Russell was unimpressed. Whilst he recognised that loyalty to his new employer was sacrosanct that did not include telling lies or putting the fear of God into residents. He had always prided himself on his fair reporting.

'Sir, may I just say that I don't think it is ever a good move to frighten the public. Putting *something of the night* into the way a council information leaflet reads is totally wrong in my view. You may turn the public completely against you. I think we should invite the local Press in for a cup of tea and a chat. It will give us the opportunity to explain the environmental credentials behind our wheeled bin scheme. It's best to get the Press on our side from the start in my experience. They'll want to take pictures and we can get Councillor Huckett to pose with some of his bins the week before the leaflets are delivered. Residents will be delighted to have been chosen. They'll feel privileged and I do believe that you'll get their support far more easily than sending them leaflets which frighten the life out of them,' the Head of Communications talked sense and Maisie supported him.

'Russell's right. I'll invite the Press along on Friday provided we can get a set of bins by then. What do you think, John? Will this be possible?' Maisie asked. Dingle nodded making a note on his pad as he did so. Maisie continued, 'I think we should go for a leaflet in four colours. That way we can illustrate each of the bins in all of the colours. What do you think, Cyril, David? In any case what colours have we gone for? Anyone know?'

Maisie glanced around the table. There were looks of consternation as they all put their thinking caps on.

'It's brown for general rubbish, black for garden waste, grey for dry recyclables and purple for wood and the rest,' Cyril bounced back leaving Sir David looking perturbed. The latter began to shake his head and corrected Cyril.

'No, that wasn't it at all. It was black for general waste, grey for garden waste, green for dry recyclables and a rather nice beige as I recall for the builders stuff,' the Leader said. He was unsure about the last one, might have been yellowish. Now it was the turn of Bill Sterling.

'Sorry to interrupt but I remember something about a red bin, I'm sure of it, for the general rubbish?'

'There certainly was never a red bin,' Sir David rebuked, 'we would never choose a socialist colour such as that.'

Pamela Peters sitting quietly at the end of the table trying to take notes was getting frustrated with the lack of clarity on what colours the bins had been ordered in and was about to lead a full scale one person revolt by throwing down her pencil when John raised his hand to stop the hearsay and put everyone in the picture.

'I think you'll find gentlemen, that in a set of minutes somewhere we agreed on the following: grey for the general waste, that is non-recyclable waste; green for the dry recyclable materials, brown for the garden waste and black for the wood, metal, builder's waste and that sort of thing,' Dingle desperately hoped that they would not change their minds at such a late stage. Just an hour before the meeting he had signed the order for twenty thousand wheeled bins, five thousand in each of the colours with a description of the waste for which they were meant etched on the front of each bin. Maisie was laughing her deep volcanic roar just like an imminent eruption from Mount Etna. Sir David asked her to share the joke with them.

'I was just thinking about that advert on the television some years ago. It was Maureen Lipman, advertising British Telecom, I think. She was buying a dress and the shop had it in all the colours and all the sizes...,' the faces around the table looked blankly back at her and she shut up and moved on to the next item on the agenda.

The Round Table Press Meeting was arranged for the end of the week as Maisie requested. The three local newspapers sent representatives to find out what it was the Council thought was so urgent that it needed to rush them to the Civic Offices on a Friday for God's sake! Divulging secret plans before they were either leaked by opposition members or officially announced at the time-tabled council meetings was not the LIP's usual manner of working. Russell Webster, the Council's mouthpiece, ushered them into a meeting room where a plate of biscuits and copious tea and coffee was laid out in waiting at the centre of an otherwise bare table.

'Good afternoon to you all,' Sir David barked, 'I'm so pleased you could come along. We want to let you know about a very big, some might say, revolutionary change that we want to make to the way we collect the rubbish. You may be aware that the European Union and indeed our own government are putting forward statutory recycling targets and there are lots of other laws coming into effect that relate to biodegradable, electrical and hazardous waste and so on. All these new laws mean that Cheatham must make drastic changes if it is to meet the targets and avoid being penalised by hefty fines,' Sir David explained, dearly hoping they would include this little remark in their next editions. How many times had he taken idiotic calls from unreasonable irate residents, upset about some trifle and the first thing they'd say to him was, 'I pay my council tax, so I have my rights,' or failing this they would quote the old chestnut, 'I pay your wages...', which in truth of course they now did since Cheatham's councillors all received a tidy sum of several thousand pounds each for expenses.

The Leader went on just for good effect, really rubbing in the legislative problems that Cheatham would soon be facing. In fact, he was prepared to throw anything into the ring to obfuscate the true problem and clear Cheatham councillors from being blamed for the higher taxes that residents would certainly have to pay in the end. Naturally, he left out the bit about the Cheatham councillors' ultimate aim of bathing in the sparking blue waters of success and glory for spearheading recycling. He also decided not to draw too much attention to the LIP goal of meeting both their own and the government's exacting targets ahead of time and being proclaimed not only the best in London at embracing new technologies but possibly the best in the whole of the United Kingdom.

It was apparent at times that Sir David was not an expert on waste management or human nature for that matter as he waffled on about waste minimisation.
    'It's not just all about recycling, indeed no. It's about educating the public to minimise their waste before they get to the point of making rubbish in the first place. It's called waste avoidance,' Cyril winced visibly as the Leader continued, 'buying multi-packs may be cheaper but they create more waste. They are also responsible for increasing our waste tonnages and filling up our landfill sites. If residents bought larger sizes overall we would have less packaging to dispose of.' Cyril was trying hard to keep an expressionless face but he knew exactly where Sir David was going next. They had had this discussion only a few evenings before over a pint in the Civic Offices Social Club. The Leader continued, 'Cheatham's residents must take responsibility for the global environmental problem and think less about themselves and how much they'll save on a so called, bogof or *buy one, get one free* or a pack of four tins of baked beans when they only need one tin,' Sir David finished speaking, expecting applause. There was none.

The Press had already made up their minds about the Leader; he was loony, absolutely off his rocker and no doubt about it. The Leader however was unconcerned about this prospect. All publicity is good publicity, keeps your name at the forefront of society he liked to believe and since secretly he was, like several of his colleagues, counting on the New Year's honours list for what would be in his case an additional honour, it could only be good for him. The honours nominee was never disclosed to the public. He knew this from his previous experience of getting his knighthood. This time round he would put a word in the direction of the local LIP Chair who just happened to be his sister. He also just happened to know that on the previous occasion his brother-in-law who had been Chair of the local Police Advisory Board at the time had written a very persuasive letter to the Queen's representative proclaiming Sir David's good works for the borough. This was just after Sir David had lent him some money for his new two bed extension to his country cottage. It was quite coincidental and there was nothing at all improper in it at all.

The Press posse had listened attentively to Sir David Hooper's introduction, sipping their cups of tea and making a few shorthand notes. Sir David now asked John Dingle to put some flesh on the bones of the proposed new scheme.

'The average dustbin contains around thirty percent paper, thirty percent food and garden waste, ten percent cans and plastic bottles and around four percent rag. There's another ten percent in glass bottles and jars,' Dingle announced. It never hurt to show you knew what you were talking about and he knew the Press just loved to have a few figures to work into their copy, 'we believe that we can reach our ambitious recycling rate by capturing most of this using separate wheeled bins. In Cheatham the paper content of our bins is probably higher at maybe thirty three percent, so you can see that these figures do vary from council to council. There are other materials such as wood and little bits of rubble and metal that we all throw out from time to time and we hope to capture these materials as well. With these extras we expect to meet in excess of the eighty five percent recycling rate that we've set ourselves.' There was a low gasp from around the room as the untidy group of journalists took in the enormity of the task ahead.

John felt pleased at the obvious impact his speech was having on the Press and continued even more enthusiastically.

'At the same time we'll be saving residents the job of carting it all the way to the civic amenity site,' he took a deep breath before getting to the scheme's nitty gritty. The reporters were still dumbstruck, 'basically, we'll be giving every house in Cheatham four small wheeled bins and if they'd like one, a composter for their garden waste. The bins will be colour coded and labelled as a memory aid, a grey bin for rubbish that we can't recycle *yet,*' he emphasised the word, yet; 'we'll be using a green bin for paper, card, cans, plastic bottles, glass and reusable clothing; brown for garden and kitchen waste and finally black for wood and metals, etcetera. The bins will be collected...,' before John could finish, Sir David stood up and left the room begging to be forgiven because he had a more pressing problem to deal with elsewhere. John had a sneaky feeling he knew why the Leader was leaving and it had nothing to do with other pressing problems. Rather more, it had all to do with fortnightly collections and difficult questions that would inevitably arise from the Press contingent. He rolled his eyes whilst all others in the room watched the figure of Sir David exit. Cyril, too, looked nervous but preoccupied himself with checking to see if his nails needed a manicure.

Following Pooper Scooper's hurried departure, Dingle surveyed the pack of dogs sitting at his feet and considered that they did look kind of aggressive. However, he reasoned, the show must go on and he checked his notes and continued.

'The rubbish collections will alternate with the dry recyclables and garden waste. This means rubbish one week and dry recyclables and garden waste the following week. The black bin for metals and wood will be collected once a month. We're researching the idea of having our very own sorting plant built or if that's not feasible to enter into a contract with a commercial operator. Other research we have been doing has centred on using biological bugs to eat the waste up,' Dingle explained, aware of disbelieving smiles on the faces of the hungry mob before him. 'It's a new technology,' he justified, 'the very latest technology will be needed to separate, sort or just break our waste down.' John wound up the presentation with a few slides of piles of waste which were always good for effect. He prayed silently that he had impressed them enough to make them forget the controversial bit about the *fortnightly* rubbish collections.

A pretty antipodean reporter flicked back her blonde hair and asked the first question.

'Don't you think it'll be a health hazard collecting waste once a fortnight? Aren't there laws against that sort of thing?' She asked in her innocent childlike way. Cyril winced for a second time that afternoon; he knew what was coming and shot a glance at Dingle as much as to say, *you answer it*.

'The EPA, ehm, the Environmental Protection Act, 1990,' John proceeded to explain, 'says that we can give residents a container and ask them to separate their waste according to how we wish to collect it. We are quite within our rights to do this,' he explained hoping the worst was over.

'Mr Dingle, you haven't answered my question, I don't think so anyway. What I asked was whether it's a health hazard?' Such a charming accent for such an annoying Sheila, thought Cyril.

'Well, no. It's not a health hazard. We've taken advice from our Environmental Health Department and our officers are quite happy with our proposed arrangements,' John retorted, 'we will of course monitor it in the hot summer months and we can always increase collections during those more difficult times if necessary,' he did not actually believe this because extra resources were never available but he did his best to reassure these journalistic bandits.

'Aren't flies and maggots going to be a problem?' The feisty blonde asked.

'Madam, we get residents ringing us to say they've got maggots even now when they're still on a weekly black sack collection. It's all about how you wrap your waste. If residents do this then there is very little chance of them getting maggots. In any case our experts in the field tell us that the gestation of a fly is longer than the fortnight between collections so it won't be a problem,' Dingle relaxed feeling a sense of relief that he might have won that round. The blonde was nodding, making notes and seemed happy with John's reply. Dingle took a chocolate bourbon biscuit and hoped he would have time to eat it.

Cyril liked to know who the enemy was so he asked the young lady which paper she was representing.

'I'm from the Cheatham Star,' she answered hesitantly, 'but I'm not the regular scribe. I'm just standing in until we get our new editor. I'm afraid I'm just an assistant on the features,' she answered apologetically.

'Please don't apologise,' Cyril smiled, somewhat relieved that waste was not her area of expertise, 'afterall, we all have to start somewhere, my dear.' Cunningly Cyril recognised that here was the perfect chance to be nice and in doing so use his powers of persuasion to get Cheatham's new scheme reported in the most favourable of lights. He pinched the plate of biscuits away from Dingle and passed them to his new Australian friend and her colleagues who Cyril discovered were keen environmentalists and just as keen to recycle if they had the chance. Things were turning up trumps for Cyril; he could not quite believe his good luck. They all seemed to realise the predicament that the Council and the environment were in and how it was the duty of every local authority in the country to be take the lead. No pain, no gain, thought Cyril. They had grasped the message so without further ado he suggested they go outside and take some pictures of the bins. John's two little grandchildren were enlisted to gain the, *ah*, vote and the cameras started snapping as soon as they were positioned inside the bins.

That morning, back at the yard Micky was trying to manage with less staff than he needed and Alison from Must Work Ltd. was not helping much.

'Alison, Alison, what the bloody 'ell are you playing at? I asked you for four loaders. We booked them two weeks ago. I've got holidays this time of year what with the school kids being off. It's my worst time, so where are the men you promised me, eh?' Mick was not a happy bunny.

'Yeah, Mick, I'm sorry, honey,' she called back trying to sweeten the pill, 'the trouble is all councils are short at this time. The men can pick and choose where they go. I had ten men actually ask me to send them to Padwick this week and Padwick have asked to take five of them on permanently,' Alison said, lighting up a fag up in the yard.

'That ain't any good to me, Alison, my luv. You know we'll have to take on another agency if you can't provide,' Mickey explained. Alison ignored Micky's rant and left the yard to make her way back to her own offices in the High Street leaving him to stare after her.

Larry Wright arrived at the office yawning and looking as though he had just got out of bed, which was quite near to the truth since he lived within ten minutes walk from the depot.

'Are we keeping you up, Lal?' Micky laughed. Larry changed the subject ignoring the remark.

'Mick, have we had a medical certificate from Gazza O'Neill? He's been away for four days now. We should've heard from 'im by now shouldn't we?' Larry looked quizzically at Micky.

'He did phone a few days ago to say he'd been up all night with guts ache following a car accident, but yeah, you're right Lal, we should've had a certificate by now. Anyways, we won't pay 'im without one,' Mick said.

'The thing is, Mick, the Ice Man thought he'd seen him walking down the Dover Road only yesterday,' Larry revealed.

'Yeah, he probably did, Lal. On 'is way to the blinking pub, The Eagle, no doubt,' Micky had seen it all before, 'the bastard's probably doing a PJ,' Mick added. Larry looked mystified. 'PJ, you must 'ave heard that before? It means, private job! You ought to get out more, Lal,' he shook his head in disbelief, 'I suppose his absence is holding you up with your survey work?' He asked. Larry nodded whilst putting the kettle on and asking the whereabouts of the old man, referring to Reggie who was never known to be late when he was supposed to be on the early shift. 'That's no way to talk about your elders and betters,' Mick said, trying to be a bit funny, 'I don't know where Reg is. He's usually 'ere by 6.15 am; probably got a car problem,' Micky said, wondering himself now where Reg might have gotten to.

Gary Newton arrived at the office and with the crews now out on their rounds the three of them sat down in the relative peace to chat, mug of tea in hand, about any extra jobs that needed doing. The phone rang. Gary Newton took the call, bursting into laughter almost immediately.

'I don't believe what I'm hearing. Reg, have you been drinking? Alright, I believe you, thousands wouldn't. In a lot of pain, mm. Yeah we're OK. Mick's here. Wanna speak to him? OK I'll tell 'im. See you soon. OK mucker, you take care,' Gary put the phone down and broke the news to his colleagues. 'Reg's had an accident; only gone and broken his foot.' Gary paused.

'Gordon Bennett! I do hope it's not another blinking industrial. Our insurance premiums are rising by the bloody second. What's the silly bugger done now?' Micky asked.

'You won't believe this,' Gary said.

'Try us,' Micky suggested

'He's broken his foot falling over his boy's bike whilst chasing the cat, which was chasing a fox in his garden.' They were all laughing heartily. It was typical Reggie Turner, never there when you needed him, Micky thought.

One hour later at 8am, a sad figure approached the allocation office hopping along as best he could on crutches and fitted with a neck brace. It was not Reg Turner but Gazza O'Neill.

'Hi Mick, just thought I'd make the effort to come and let you know I won't be back for a few more days. I've got a bit of whip lash. The hospital's fitted me out with this stuff to stop me moving my neck around too much. Someone hit me car up the backside at the weekend. Sorry about not having a doctor's certificate and all that,' Gazza said, looking very apologetic, 'me girlfriend's waiting for me outside the gates so I'd better get on then,' Gazza added, hoping for a smattering of sympathy at least but no one seemed to be very sorry for his condition, 'I should be back in a couple of days, OK?' He asked, hoping for some sort of reaction but there was none to speak of, 'see you, then,' he called, hobbling away and then, 'oh yeah, I've finished with this newspaper. I'll leave it with you.' Gazza left a bedraggled copy of the Cheatham Star on the counter and made his way painfully to the depot gates.

'Do yer think Gazza's in agony?' Larry asked, watching him disappear through the gates.

'Get out of it,' Mick said, 'his girlfriend's a nurse at the Cheatham Royal Infirmary. She's probably dressed him up like that to get him off the hook,' Mick said, not looking pleased.

'Mick's right. Gazza has a reputation for fiddles of that kind and if Mick Davies saw him walking anywhere in the vicinity of the Eagle, you can rest assured that it was him and that was where he was going,' Gary Newton supported Mick. Being Gazza's manager he was well used to his ploys to get out of a hard days graft.

Micky Brown, now bored with the conversation about Gazza O'Neill and picked up the Cheatham Star lying where Gazza had left it. On the front page was a beautiful picture of two little boys standing inside wheeled bins and a smiling Cyril holding a pile of newspapers for recycling. The picture was good but the caption was not. *Cheatham kids pressed into helping the Council recycle.* Huckett was also reading the paper as he sat at home in his study, as was Sir David at the Civic Offices and neither were happy; the latter was kicking himself for not taking charge. Trusting others, he reminded himself, never seemed to work. In the next few days he could expect an avalanche of letters accusing the Council of anything from child labour atrocities to encouraging them to participate in dangerous stunts. The borough would no doubt be guilty of children dying by the bucket loads as they trapped themselves inside the new fangled wheelie bins, enduring long and agonising deaths
.

At the depot they had all had a little look-see at the photograph but the political fall out was lost on them. After just a few seconds they had moved on to discuss how Gary Biddle's hearing might go. It was scheduled for that afternoon and Kelly had taken annual leave since no one in the office seemed to have any sympathy with her plight and the dreadful insult she felt she had suffered literally at the hand of Biddles. All sympathy seemed to be with the immature and sexually inexperienced supervisor who in spite of his cocky bragging had barely left his mother's apron strings.

The Sexual Harassment Panel convened at 2pm on the Thursday to hear and deliberate on the behaviour of the Council's unfortunate waste supervisor in the case of Gary Biddles v Ms Kelly Dinhern & Cheatham Council. Cyril Huckett being the Lead Councillor for the department in which the accused worked was asked to chair the Panel. Poor old Cyril, he was never very good at remembering names and could not for the life of him remember which of the Garys, Gary Biddles was. He just hoped and prayed that *this* Gary would turn out to be anyone but the dolt he had seen crouching outside Edith's conservatory.

Along with Cyril on the panel was a female representative from the Personnel Section to ensure justice for the feminine view of things and an independent male adviser from another department to provide balance. The Panel took their seats and having read the case notes called for Gary Biddles and Kelly Dinhern to be ushered into the room. Cyril's worse nightmare had become a reality. One look and he realised that this silly sod was the one with the tattoos, the anorak and that bloody camera on which his eyes had focussed from inside Edith's greenhouse.
   'Oh my God, what shall I do,' Cyril mouthed without uttering a sound. He felt a real throbbing at the front of his head. The blood was simply gushing through his temples just as it had gushed around his projectory on the day of the conservatory faux pas. Cyril propped his elbow on the table and rested his head against it feeling decidedly sick whilst the Personnel panel member read out the charge.

Cyril decided to do his best in what was a very bad and compromising situation to find himself in.
   'Well, I must say, Gary, you weren't altogether acting in accordance with the true spirit of the Council's Equal Opportunities Policy, were you?' Cyril asked. Gary nodded in agreement, his head bent low. Cyril's mind was in a confused state. Equal Opportunities sounded alright to him but it was not good enough for the Personnel Officer, who nudged him. Whispering in Cyril's ear she reminded him that they should be discussing the appropriate aspect of the Sexual Harassment Policy. Panicked once more, Cyril apologised. 'I'm so sorry, Gary. I meant to say the Council's Sexual Harassment Policy.' Cyril was all of a dither and since Biddles was none the wiser which policy was relevant, he just stared blankly back at the Panel. Cyril continued, 'this policy is designed to make sure that both sexes are allowed to go about their work without fear of being offended or compromised because of their sexual gender. Do you understand?' Cyril looked directly at Gary hoping that a serious expression might frighten him into believing that Cyril's bite was indeed worse than his bark.

The moment he entered the room Gary knew he had Cyril on the run. He might be simple but he was not that simple. Right now all he wanted was to get out of this room with his job intact. Any revenge would come later. Biddles was invited to speak on his own behalf.

'I'd like to say Councillor that I'm very sorry that I upset Kelly, I never wanted to do that. We were always flirting and having a bit of a giggle and I didn't think she minded that sort of thing,' Gary said, looking penitently at Kelly and giving her one of his lovely smiles. Reluctantly at first, she smiled back.

'Kelly, I understand how you must have felt being pinched on the...,' Cyril hesitated, 'on a very private part of your body. This was an assault on your person and not to be taken lightly,' Cyril conceded, 'I hope that you'll consider that Gary made a genuine mistake and will never do it again?' Kelly nodded. She was filled with remorse and wished she hadn't been so quick to bring the case. Her friends had recommended Oil of Evening Primrose to off set the mood swings that preceded her PMT. How she wished she had listened to them.

'Do you have anything more you wish to say, Miss Dinhern?' Cyril asked. Kelly, gracious in defeat, did have something to say.

'Sirs and Madam,' she said in her squeaky high pitched little voice, 'I would just like to say that I'm grateful that the Council takes these things seriously. I know that Gary was probably just having a lark,' Kelly glanced at Gary and smiled at him again, 'but pinching a girl on her derriere is demeaning. Just because I wear short skirts doesn't mean that the lads can take advantage.' The Panel was nodding in certain agreement, 'I've suffered a lot of humiliation, (Kelly stuttered in an effort to pronounce the word, humiliation) in the office because I decided to bring this case and it has affected my health dramatically,' Kelly's eyes welled up and she clutched at her throat. Cyril was baffled. He could not quite work out how this business could have affected her throat. The silly girl must have a bloody good imagination, he concluded.

Cyril consulted in whispers with his colleagues before delivering the Panel's verdict on the affair.

'I propose to allow Gary to return to work tomorrow,' Cyril looked up to face Gary, 'there'll be no punishment this time but a record will be put on your personal file,' Cyril could feel another panic attack coming on. Not being well aquainted with digital cameras he just kept hoping that Gary had not had any film in the blasted thing or that the batteries had been flat or whatever could go wrong had gone wrong to stop this snotty nosed imp having any record of the last time they had come across each other. Cyril turned to Kelly, 'on behalf of the Council may I say Kelly, how truly sorry we are that you've had to endure such a humiliating experience,' he sympathised. 'I'm sure that Gary will be more careful and have more respect in the future,' Cyril paused and then turning to his colleagues on the Panel decided to cut through all the red tape, 'I think we're done here?' He suggested. They too were keen to get away as quickly as possible and nodded. Cyril wrapped up the proceedings, 'so I now declare this hearing closed,' a relieved Cyril put his pen away in his jacket pocket and rose to leave.

Gary and Kelly left together passing Cyril as they did so.

'Excuse me, Gary,' Cyril called. He had been focussing on Gary's hand for the last few minutes of the hearing and was reminded that he still did not understand the meaning of his tattoos. Defacing the human body always seemed a bit peculiar to Cyril, him being a believer in the wonder of its very being and a professor of things biological, 'I was just wondering what exactly that little tattoo on your finger represents?'

'Oh, that,' Gary replied, 'it's the Sword of Damocles,' Gary smirked, walking away. Cyril was suffering mental trauma. As he too left the mock tudor panelled room his brain was working overtime wondering what Gary proposed to do with those incriminating photos.

Kelly, however, for her part in the day's events was thinking she must play her relaxation tapes more often and pay attention to minimising her pre-menstrual tension whilst at the same time not giving up on the idea that her body was her temple. Gary, hands in pockets, slouching, looked up at the blue sky outside and reflected, *'I've let you get away this time Huckett but time is on my side'*.

The next morning Micky Brown et al were wondering how things had gone for Gary. The previous afternoon Personnel had relayed the important fact that he would be returning to work the next day so Mick was expecting him to turn up at any moment.

'He's a soppy halfpenny, probably short of the odd screw here and there but there's no harm inside 'im,' the fatherly Senior Supervisor conceded.

'Be careful, Micky, the word *screw* is probably not the best use of vocabulary in Gary's case. It's all he thinks about,' Gary Newton warned.

'Yeah, well as I said, it's all in his mind,' Micky said, braking off suddenly as subject of their discussion arrived. The supervisors greeted Biddles with a rapturous applause and he in turn saluted them. Amidst all the joyous shouting and laughter an impromptu sing song arose. "We are the Champions," rang out from the office, over and over again. Slump ran off to get the victor a coffee from the vending machine and after a lot of back slapping and questions about the hearing from Mick, Gary Newton, Gary Green, Larry, Slump and a couple of drivers who had called in to pick up more work, they left him alone to acclimatise. Micky resumed his conversation with Gary Newton.

'Right me old matey, what are we going to do about the survey work now Reg's off with a broken foot? He's supposed to be planning the work for Gazza and Larry. I haven't got much of a clue where they're supposed to be going, do you?' Micky asked whilst busying himself filling in overtime sheets from the previous day.

'I'm afraid not, Mick. Adrian may know the details. It would be a good thing if he had a bit more to do; he's always mincing about like his shit don't stink, if you'll pardon my lingo,' Gary Newton was considered to be the more refined of the supervisors so Micky was taken aback at this blatant use of bad language.

'If it will make you feel better Gar, I'll email Adrian and ask 'im to come down this afternoon so we can sort out a plan of action,' Micky humoured his pal.

A worried voice called through the office window and it sounded as though something needed immediate attention.

'Oy, Micky, where were the other fridge collection sheets? I had one and four but no sheet two and three,' the Ice Man had been prevented from finishing his daily fridge collections and it was approaching midday. He noticed Gary Biddles at the back of the office and waved to him.

'Didn't you see 'em?' Mick asked, 'they were on top of the photocopier. You must have passed them on your way out. I left them there with a big note attached saying, 'for the Ice Man'. It couldn't have been plainer, you silly twerp. Don't tell me you missed 'em?' Micky was not smiling. 'I told Kelly's agency stand in, what's her name, Jody something, to tell you they'd been found and were waiting for you there. It's always the bloody same, you just can't get the bloody staff!' The Ice Man was shrugging his shoulders as Micky rattled on, 'bloody roll on. Do I 'ave to do everyfink 'ere?' Micky shouted, clearly irritated.

With uncollected fridges and freezers Micky could expect more complaints from the public, which he could have done without
'You've got a radio, Mick, you could have asked couldn't yer?' He sounded all was lost.
'How did I know you'd found the bloody sheets? Whatta you want me to do look for ruddy smoke signals?' The Ice Man was not happy either but then climbing down off his high horse he decided to be helpful, 'look I'm sorry and don't worry Mick, I'll stay on and finish them if I can get overtime?' The Ice Man sounded apologetic and Micky who did not like to see grown men cry, smiled back at him,
'Yeah, go on then. We're not supposed to do overtime unless there's an emergency but if it means we don't get complaints then I consider that a very good use of public funds. Go on get out of here,' he said waving two sheets of paper around. The Ice Man snatched them from him and tried to lighten up the atmosphere with a bit of hilarity.
'Oy Mick, I've got a joke for yer.'
'Ice Man, you've got a joke for every occasion, mate. It's a pity it has to be the same one every time. Get out of here, will yer. You 'aven't got time for jokes, get on with that overtime,' a croaky Senior Supervisor shouted as the Ice Man departed.

The next challenge came over the radio from a sorry street cleansing driver.
'Hello! Gary Green are you there please?'
'No, GGs not but I'm here, Roger. Can I help?' Gary Newton replied, 'what's up mate?'
'God, I don't know how to tell you this, boss. Parking Services have only gone and clamped my lorry. I only went for a pee,' Roger the Bodger explained.
'I can't be hearing this. First Gazza O'Neill goes for a pee and allows his lorry to be stolen and now this,' Gary unburdened himself to those assembled in the office listening attentively to Roger's tale of woe, 'how much Roger?' Gary asked.
'They want ninety pounds in cash and they won't release it unless it's paid by 4pm this afternoon,' Roger explained.
'Right, Roger, stay with the vehicle. I'll get someone out to you asap,' Gary said, closing the call and looking blankly at his colleagues. 'Where can I get ninety quid in cash? It usually takes a month to get more than twenty five pounds out of petty cash let alone ninety quid,' a despairing Gary sighed.
'Try Dingle, that's all you can do, Gar,' Micky suggested, 'he's the only one who can authorise ninety quid in cash at a drop of a hat,' Micky added. Gary picked up the phone and spoke at length to their trouble-shooter, Dingle. The money in the form of a council guaranteed cheque was forthcoming, if perhaps reluctantly and the vehicle was released.

At the end of the day, the frazzled supervisors removed their yellow reflective jackets and chucked them in a heap on the office's old settee. As Micky locked the door behind them, he joked.
'Have a good evening fellas and shall we go again tomorrow?' They all laughed.

Elsewhere on Thursday in the Cheatham Council Empire, John Dingle had been discussing the first stage of the trial wheeled bin service with Adrian. Pamela Peters brought in the local papers.

'You won't like what's on page two of the Star,' she said in the usual brusque manner that was her norm. She dropped the Cheatham Star on the Executive Head's desk and departed. John liked the photo on the front page and although he was not all that keen on the heading, *Cheatham Kids Pressed into Helping the Council Recycle,* chose to ignore it for the minute in order to thumb through as fast as he could to see what dangers were lurking on page two. He found another large colour photograph of his grandchildren standing inside a couple of wheeled bins with the caption, *How Safe is This Council?* The article that followed whittered on about whether children should be put into wheeled bins for publicity stunts and a suggestion that giving everybody wheeled bins would lead to children using them as playthings and getting trapped. John Dingle was quiet. He knew he was a good and caring granddad and he did not like this at all.

The newspaper was casting aspersions and there were bound to be letters from the public about it. The local papers as usual had completely missed the salient points in favour of the shock horror headline grabbing propaganda. They had printed very little about the problem of landfills filling up, the toxic gases like methane and liquid leachates and all the other nasties that were pouring into the atmosphere. Dingle had gone to great pains to impress these facts upon them and they were missing. There was, however, a paragraph in bold print which described the breeding cycle of the fly and suggested that residents had read it here first. This was followed by a charming quote from an opposition councillor who termed the LIP a dire health and safety risk. *'Cheatham Council is doing more harm to the local environment than good. The LIP is forcing a recycling scheme on residents that they don't want. The LIPs are in short, as mad as a box of frocks.'* Things did not bode well and the wheeled bin trial had not even started.

'Damn and blast. We can expect several weeks of the *Letters Page* being full of rubbish about how the Council is setting a bad example to parents in the borough,' an angry Executive Head of Waste said to his Recycling Officer uncharacteristically raising his voice as his eyes rested on the name of the reporter at the bottom of the article, a Tim Baldwin. Would this be the same Tim Baldwin that recently left the Council following a strained relationship with Sir David? If so, that same Tim Baldwin was now Assistant Editor of the Cheatham Star and would undoubtedly be out for revenge. Cheatham Borough Council could expect a rough ride from now onwards. 'What was the point in having a so called Round Table discussion with the local Press? Huckett will be furious. Still, I suppose there was nothing we could've done to prevent this, eh?' John Dingle decided, 'get on to Russell in the Press Office and suggest he makes a formal complaint to the Star,' he requested of Adrian.

Succeeding with any policy was a real battle if the Press are not on your side. John needed this project to succeed with his early retirement only a year or two away. There were also bonuses to think about. It mattered not a jot to the likes of the youthful Adrian but Dingle knew only too well that his pension would be calculated on his final salary so the more now the merrier would be his pension later. Adrian did have a view, however, since he too needed his part in Cyril's pet project to succeed. His future career and reputation depended upon it. He left the Executive Head's office and drove to the depot to assist the supervisors in getting the wheelie bin survey underway. On arrival he laid out a large map of the borough on a nearby desk and using a yellow highlighter marked on the trial areas.

'These are the areas that Councillor Huckett wants covered first,' a rather brisk Recycling Officer said getting to grips with the little bit of power he had been entrusted with, 'I was thinking we might get Gazza to walk Area A, here,' Adrian indicated Area A by pointing his highlighter at the map and swirling it around a bit, 'and Larry Wright to cover Area B here,' another charismatic swirl of the highlighter, 'and when they've done those they can both cover Area C,' Adrian paused to allow feedback for his plan of action.

Micky Brown and Gary Newton were following Adrian's suggestions but made no comment. Adrian continued believing they were in awe of him.

'We need to make sure that we note where there are steps up to front doors, where there are no front gardens for bin storage and I suppose we need to know approximately how big the property is, whether it's likely to have a larger than usual family, in fact anything that will make a difference on whether we give them bins or sacks. Mind you, this won't happen automatically,' he looked up sensing that there were a few raised eyebrows, 'nothing to do with me you understand but you know how adamant Councillor Huckett is about that one. Residents will have to put a very good case to get a larger bin,' Adrian stood up slowly holding his back, 'too much cricket at the weekend,' he explained. Micky and Gary smiled meekly at Adrian and then threw each other mischievous looks suggesting too much leg over might be more likely.

Micky Brown who was older and wiser and understood all the ramifications of his job far better than some upstart college boy, had a question for Adrian.

'What about once we've given out the bins and they ring us up and ask for bigger bins?' Micky was a better judge of human nature than some of the councillors and knew what would happen for sure.

'The rules are quite simple, Mick. We do not give out the larger bins unless the household really makes a fuss and can prove that they really do have a big family,' Adrian looked at the disbelieving faces surrounding the map, 'sorry lads but that's what the councillor wants. No rule bending I'm afraid.' Adrian gave them one of his, *I'm better educated than you and therefore, I know what I'm talking about,* looks. Micky for one thing did not like being called a *lad* and had his own thinks on the matter of who gets what bin. What crap did they teach them at those colleges thesedays? Micky was sure it was nothing of any consequence. Gary was inclined towards the same conclusion.

The pre-bin arrival survey work began. Gazza and Larry walked their patches, recording any homes that might present difficulties for residents or collections crews. They noted the size of the properties and just how many there were in each road. The Council had never made a proper count of properties before which was probably why some crews were constantly complaining that they had too many houses for the number of hours they were expected to work. In the meantime, Adrian had printed up a letter from Sir David telling residents that they should feel honoured to have been chosen to be guinea pigs for the trial fortnightly rubbish collection. The 'F' word was left out of the publicity material as Dingle had advised weeks earlier. Along with the letter was a brightly coloured leaflet on which no expense had been spared in respect of the amount of colour or paper used, it being ten sides of information, diagrams and charts with the addition of a few quotes from various pieces of legislation. The leaflet, in spite of the pretty drawings was enough to persuade anyone except for the hardiest of environmentally friendly diehards to give up the will to live. Its only saving grace was that it was recyclable and indeed, had been printed on recyclable paper and as soon as the recycling bins were operational there was no doubting where they would all end up.

The next stage for Gazza and Larry was to retrace their steps quite literally and post the letters and the leaflets through doors on their respective patches. The leaflet also contained a contact telephone number for residents wanting to discuss the forthcoming trial with a council officer which resulted in a deluge of calls requesting a personal visit.

'How many calls is that this morning?' A less than happy Micky Brown asked Gary Green.

'I dunno. I haven't been counting but I know it's too many,' an even grumpier GG replied.

'I'm not putting up with this much longer. If they want to bloody well encourage residents to call, then they can blinking well employ someone to answer the bloody phone. We've taken umpteen calls this morning and it's only half past bloody ten! If we get a call from just about everybody on the so called trial, all five thousand of the buggers, we'll be here all bleeding night as well. How are we supposed to deal with our regular work?' Micky was venting his anger as only he knew how.

Micky hated the phone at the best of times and to be tied to the office was the worse possible scenario. It was time for some positive action.

'Hello, Mr Dingle,' Micky picked up the phone before it had the chance to ring again and using his best telephone manner let John know the true extent of their problem, 'its Micky Brown here. I was wondering if it would be possible to get some help with answering the phone down here at the depot. You see with the leaflets going out, we're inundated with enquiries and it's kind of drowning us. We're having trouble getting out to do our regular work and what with Kelly being on holiday and all...' Micky was perilously holding one of his roll your own fags, very thin and wiggly whilst scratching his head with the thumb nail on the same hand. He was not supposed to smoke in the office but he was being put in a very stressful position.

'Err, yes, I suppose that can be arranged,' Dingle was rather caught on the hop, 'I didn't realise we'd put your office phone on the leaflet. I thought all calls were being directed through the Civic Call Centre. I'm so sorry about that, Micky. I'll get Adrian to arrange something straightaway,' Dingle agreed without a fight, which surprised Micky no end.

As soon as Micky had finished his call to Dingle, the phone rang again. Micky snatched it up.

'Hello, Battersea bloody Dogs Home here. How can I help?' Micky, charming as ever was demonstrating his high level of frustration.

'Yes, I see,' said a surprised voice at the other end, 'I'm Sir David Hooper, Cheatham Borough Council and I'm so sorry to have bothered you. I thought I'd dialled our borough's waste depot. There must be a crossed line. Goodbye,' the caller put the phone down and Micky fell silent. The phone rang again just a couple of seconds later.

'Gary, get that would you?' Micky felt sure he knew who would be on the other end of the line. If Gary picked up the phone he thought his secret would be safe.

'Waste depot. How can I help you?' Gary was a little more courteous than his colleague.

'Ah yes. It's Sir David Hooper here. I've received a complaint from a resident in Bluebell Avenue about a concrete lamppost that was recently replaced. For the past few days it has been left lying on the grass verge. The dogs are having a wonderful time cocking their legs everytime they walk by. It apparently stinks of canine urine. Do your best to get the thing removed before all the dogs in the borough find their way there would you? I'd be so grateful. Oh, and while I've got you on the phone, can we have a few more dog bins outside Needham Junior School? I walked past there this morning and there was enough crap on the pavement to fuel that new incinerator in Deptford and while your at it, tell that friend of yours that when he answers the Council's phone, not to be such a complete arse. There is a correct way to speak to people and I expect all council officers to use it,' Councillor Hooper rang off. That was telling Micky and no mistake. Gary passed on the message with a smarmy smile.

As sanctioned by Mr Dingle, Adrian contacted Must Work Ltd. and within the hour a young male temp called Robin was standing at the office window eager to show everyone his credentials.

Gazza and Larry kept their appointments with the mothers of Cheatham to discuss the finer points of the wheelie bin scheme.

'How are you getting on, Lal?' Asked Micky Brown one morning as Larry popped in to pick up his list of appointments.

'Great. These old dears seem to really love me. I get invited in for a cup of tea and a chat about the new scheme, the weather and my holiday in Tenerife,' Larry explained. Micky stopped him in his tracks.

'Lucky bugger, are you sure you only go in for a chat and a cup of Rosy Lee?' Micky was winking at Larry.

'Mick, if you saw some of these women, you'd know for sure that I only go in for a cup of tea. Some of them are so pug ugly and talk about fat... ask Gazza, he's had the same trouble and he's foot loose and fancy free and looking for a soul mate but he's not been tempted,' Larry was using his fingers to make strange facial contortions to illustrate just how ugly some of the women had been and then he dropped a bombshell, 'actually Mick, I'm getting married,' he announced shyly. Gazza, who was also in the office stopped what he was doing and cheered. Mick was the first to speak.

'You kept that a secret, Lal. Comes to fink of it, I suppose I thought you were already hitched mate; still, I'm pleased to hear it. When's the big day then?' Mick asked looking pleased for his buddy.

'We're just setting the date. It'll probably be in the autumn when we've saved enough money!' Larry said looking serious.

'Cheer up mate. It's not a life sentence. You should be really happy about it especially as you'll be making the mother of your kiddies an honest woman after all these years,' Mick said slapping Larry on the back. Micky put an arm around his woeful colleague and called Gazza over to them. 'Lal's in need of a group hug,' he said sympathetically as Gazza put his arms around the two of them and squeezed. Larry picked up his paperwork and left the office for his van. 'Still looks like a condemned man, poor bloke,' Mick muttered as he watched his colleague go. Robin, the new temp had been listening into the conversation and eyeing Gazza up and down at the same time. He rather fancied him, being that he was that way inclined. It was the rough and ready look that attracted but sadly the chances were that Gazza would not return the compliment.

At the Civic Offices, Cyril, Marcus, Sir David, the Chief Executive and Edith met to discuss the roll out for the trial and generally chew over how things were progressing.

'How are we doing then, Cyril? When are the bins going out?' Sir David asked enthusiastically.

'This week, Leader. We've made contact with all the households in the trial areas and we've seen a considerable amount of interest. Two people have been assigned to get the message across to residents by meeting them on their doorsteps and answering their questions, that sort of thing. We believe that the majority of houses will be able to have wheeled bins, all four of them without any difficulties worth speaking about,' Cyril explained.

'That's good news. I'm kind of surprised that so many have room for all four bins though. Are we quite sure about this?' Sir David was fully aware of Cyril's desire for fame and his urge to get things done even if it meant riding rough shod over conventional methods of achieving his goal. Cyril, sensing distrust on the part of his political colleague made a guarded response.

'David, if you remember we settled on specific roads which we felt would be ideal for the trial. The four areas all have homes with large drives and a good amount of intellect amongst their residents and if I might add, and remember it must stay between these four walls, we deliberately left out those poor, wretched people on any of our council estates because of the trouble they usually cause us,' Cyril explained.

'Quite so,' was all Sir David would add.

Marcus and Edith had been listening quietly to the conversation going on between Cyril and Sir David and were not happy. A socialist at heart, the Mayor felt his heartstrings being tugged.

'I'm not sure that we should have left out those so called, poor and wretched people,' Marcus piped up as soon as there was a gap in the conversation, 'surely it would have been a good idea to have included those you perceive as downtrodden if only to see if it works for all classes?' Marcus may have been a diary salesman but he did have some scruples. Maisie was smiling lovingly across the table at the Mayor believing that only they recognised the mutual love that her smile conveyed. The true fact was that most on the Council had began to suspect that there was more than the usual boring professional relationship going on behind the smiles of Cheatham's first citizen and its first officer. Ignoring the knowing looks from her councillor colleagues, Maisie tried to soothe the Mayor's brow, metaphorically speaking.

'Marcus, if I might try to ease your conscience a little, I would like to remind you that we are about to begin one of the biggest regeneration programmes in the country and much of it is in your own ward. A lot of money is being sunk into new houses, playgrounds and shops and residents will be getting far more goodies financially than anyone else in Cheatham and if I might be so bold, most probably far more than they deserve,' Maisie's comments shocked Sir David whilst Marcus simply gazed into his lover's eyes knowingly prepared to accept just about anything that she uttered.

The meeting continued with Edith speaking next in her capacity as Cost Effectiveness and Best Value Champion.

'Cyril, I'm not yet convinced about the fortnightly waste collection or the need for each house to have four bins. Won't four bins make our roads look untidy?'

'No, I don't think so Edith. People will return them to their back gardens after emptying. Cheatham residents are good clean tidy people in the main and the majority have side gates leading to their back gardens. I can't envisage any great problem of that nature,' Cyril did not want negative comments.

'Nevertheless Cyril, Edith does have a point. Not everyone will be able to wheel them through a side gate,' In spite of Maisie's comforting words, Marcus was still unsure about many aspects of the new service, 'what about the few households where the surveys have discovered that they can't have four bins because of a lack of space? There must be some properties of this nature somewhere. What about Thatcher Road? That's in the middle of Trial Area A and their front doors face out straight onto the main road,' Marcus asked having paid attention to some things it would seem, much to Cyril's dismay.

Cyril was not to be deterred, becoming surly and gritting his teeth before doing his best to deflect the apprehension building up around the table.

'My dear friends let me put your minds at rest. We're trying to work on many levels here,' Cyril thought he would use the latest boardroom speak, 'we're not out to make life an absolute misery. We're working with people and we're listening to their concerns and we will, if we find the scheme doesn't work, be ready to make adjustments until people are happy. Let me also explain, which I forgot to do right at the beginning, where a property can't easily have wheeled bins, or, of course, residents opt not to have them and we fully accept that this is their right, there is absolutely no question at all that they may continue using black sacks for their waste. We'll insist that they have a pink sack for their dry recyclables but I'm happy to forget about the other bins in such instances,' Cyril said, putting on his most endearing look and wondering why Edith needed to be so difficult. The Mayor was a pain as well but a few drinks in the Civic Offices Social Club would soon sort him out.

Just to be a complete nuisance Edith had another bash at Cyril's fortnightly collection ideal.

'But Cyril, if some residents have sacks and they're on a fortnightly collection for all of their smelly waste, won't that cause them problems? Aren't they likely to stick it in their dry recyclable bin if they know it's the next bin to be emptied?' Edith's brow was furrowed which equally matched the one on Cyril's own brow.

'I don't think so,' Cyril bounced back, 'but as I said a few moments ago, we will monitor the trial areas and send out a questionnaire after three months asking all households to be quite frank and tell us what they think of it.' What Cyril was really thinking was unrepeatable but he was always so very good at whitewash. He also knew that he needed to keep Edith on his side since she would have the casting vote on the Scrutiny Committee. She also had the casting couch but that was quite another story. Cyril had to bite his lip to stop himself from smiling at his dirty thoughts.

Before the meeting could move on Sir David had just one other issue to raise.

'I've been thinking,' he paused for a second.

'Good gracious! I hope you don't do yourself any damage,' Edith muttered under her breath. Sir David didn't hear her remark and continued.

'I've been thinking that I should like to bring in that nice little lady from Aurelia Waste Handling. What was her name, Julia? I think we need someone of her calibre to help us mount a campaign to win over the hearts and minds in this great recycling drive of ours. Rather reminds me of the campaign the

Chinese wagered. I think it was called the Great Leap Forward; I read it in a book. It was when Mao decreed that China should make more steel. What happened was that everyone collected up unwanted metal objects and recycled them for the common good. That's what we have to do here in Cheatham,' Sir David said growing ruddier in the face than usual with the excitement of his own suggestion. His tubby little body was almost quivering with joyful tremors as he banged his fist on the table in sheer delight. Marcus could not quite get his head around the idea of a Chinese revolution in the London Borough of Cheatham and twiddling his moustache, glanced over at Edith with a look of utter dismay quite apparent on his long thin face.

Edith brought the conversation back to Sir David's much desired new recruit.

'Her name was Judy. Are you sure we can afford to employ another new face in the Communications Office? We have more staff in there now than in some of our front line areas. We're supposed to be introducing a moratorium on employment unless the post can be proved to be absolutely vital. Didn't we just agree this at full council?' Edith looked to her colleagues for confirmation.

'Edith's right,' Maisie confirmed, 'it was just last Friday that I sent round an email to all managers telling them that as from Monday all unfilled posts were frozen.' Sir David, ignoring Maisie's advice, pressed on regardless.

'This post is absolutely vital. All agreed?' He looked around for any dissenting hands but thankfully for Sir David, there were none. Returning to face the Chief Executive he gave her his order, 'Maisie, contact Judy immediately and see if she'll accept a principal officer graded post on forty four thousand pounds with a bonus of, lets say two thousand pounds if she starts in the next two weeks,' Sir David said. He was after all the Council's leader and there had to be some perks attached to the job.

Cyril had just one more item for, Any Other Business. He waved a piece of paper around in the air excitedly.

'I was just wondering whether we might like to go for this award. It's the Public Servant of The Year Award, what do you all think? I'm quite prepared to do the entry if you think it's worthwhile.' Cyril passed the sheet of paper around the table.

'How might we be justified in entering?' Edith was muddying the waters again for God's sake, that woman was driving Cyril mad. All he wanted to do was get himself a nice little award, a sort of precursor to getting his OBE in a year or two's time.

'Well, I was just thinking that if the scheme is successful and we increase our recycling rate dramatically to eighty five percent in one year or so...' Cyril was cut off sharply by Edith.

'But Cyril, we don't know yet whether the scheme will work,' she looked to the Chief Executive for support.

'Cyril, I think Edith's right. Perhaps we should just delay any award entries until we have some idea of whether we'll actually be adopting the new wheelie scheme for Cheatham boroughwide. Let's look at it again next year,' Maisie suggested. An unhappy Cyril put the sheet of paper on the table and childishly pushed it out into the middle in a fit of peak. The meeting finished and Maisie bade goodbye to each as they left her office. She then went back to the table and rescued the sheet of paper with the competition information. It might just be the thing she had been looking for. Marcus would make a wonderful Public Servant of The Year!

Chapter 12

Before you could say "Jack Robinson" or some other ridiculous phrase or saying that no one can remember the origins of, wheeled bins were arriving by the lorry load in all of the delectable colourways. Gazza and Larry had drawn up lists of households that wanted this and that and in particular those who had chosen to stay on sacks or felt the need to go on the infamous dead and dying list. Getting this list right had not been plain sailing. Following his earlier outburst on how to keep the d&d numbers to a minimum, Cyril had written specific instructions on how they should determine who was really needy. The memo had been marked private and confidential, which was just as well, because had it been leaked to the local newspapers they would have had a field day. The memo read thus.

'Team, please don't forget to get those applying for an exemption to supply a doctor's certificate and make sure that they get a visit from a supervisor before any decisions are made. Inspect them closely and be entirely satisfied that the bins are likely to cause them immense difficulties if not given assistance. We really do have to be selective, because as we've all seen, the Exempt List has suddenly exploded in length. Be aware of those jumping on the bandwagon!' Cyril warned.

During a break from the back breaking job of unloading and counting the new bins off the trucks, the Ice Man took the memo out of his trouser pocket and contemplated it, giving Larry the benefit of his wisdom.

'I don't know why CH doesn't just suggest the old dears keel over and have done with it really,' he said. Larry was not listening. He was trying to make sure the delivery note tallied with the sea of plastic bins, axles and wheels in front of, around and above their heads. There were five thousand in each of the four colours, black, brown, green and grey. They stacked them up as best they could against a wall although with so little spare space in the yard and some delivery vehicles still waiting to be unloaded, the yard was in utter chaos. The Cheatham refuse collection vehicles returning had severe difficulties getting into the yard and tempers were flaring and not only amongst the Council's collection staff.

'Oy, Davies, make sure they've delivered enough wheels for all those bins,' Micky blasted from the office doorway.

'I'm not counting every individual bloody wheel. If you want that done you'll have to do it yer self,' the Ice Man returned, exasperated and sweaty and looking thirty years older than when he'd started that morning.

The management of the bin delivery was down to Adrian who had booked agency guys to do the job. His refined college voice was at odds with the circle he was mixing with at the depot where the average reading age was around eleven.

'OK lads, first I want these sticky labels stuck under each lid,' Adrian demonstrated just how the labels were to be stuck on; 'the wheels and lids we'll attach once we're parked up in the roads. I also want you to post a set of these instructions with the calendar through each of the front doors as you go along.' He held up a set of leaflets for all to see, 'It's absolutely vital that you get this right otherwise we'll have the wrong bins out on collection days and that would be a complete disaster,' the Graduate Member of the Chartered Institution of Wastes Management informed. The bins began rolling out and Cyril's wild dream of recycling success came a step nearer.

Meanwhile at the Civic Press Office, Russell Webster greeted his newly poached Recycling Education Officer, Judy, on her first day with Cheatham. Sir David had been lucky to secure Judy on a secondment from Aurelia Waste Handling at short notice, although the substantial remuneration attached to the post possibly helped make up her mind. Aurelia said it would be pleased for her to gain experience in a different type of organisation and that they were particularly fond of helping councils. What they forgot to add was that they liked to help councils who may well have a contract to let at a later date. Russell, always the consummate professional welcomed Judy with open arms inspite of the unusual circumstances of her appointment and immediately put her to work on devising a programme that would raise awareness to recycling and explain CH's new service.

Judy had lots of questions on the service she had been employed to promote.

'How long is the trial supposed to run for?' She asked. Pragmatism was her strong point.

'Three months is what we've told residents but of course what usually happens in these cases is the Council can't make a decision on whether to expand, amend or cut altogether and the trial goes on seemingly for ever. I can't think that this trial will be any different to any of the others this council or any other I've ever worked for has run,' Russell enlightened, 'not being able to make a decision is one of this Council's particular fortes,' Russell smiled sarcastically at his new Recycling Education Officer. 'We need to put together a publicity programme and a questionnaire for each of the households on the trial. Naturally, we must carefully word the questions so that no matter what answers we get, they can be manipulated to provide the positive statistics that the Council craves. The scheme, you see, will most definitely go ahead. It's pre-ordained. They have to *consult* now as part of the Best Value Review process but there's plenty of scope for making sure that results reflect the overarching aim of the Council,' Russell beamed. Judy was spellbound. It had never entered her head that councils could be so dishonest. Her look of utter disbelief made Russell laugh.

'Don't worry, lovey, you'll soon get into the swing of things. It's only politics,' he consoled. Russell was thirty two years old and an extremely good looking six foot tall, flaxen haired gent and indeed most girls' idea of complete heaven. He looked at his watch, 'look, it's nearly midday; let's go down to the Social Club and have a drink. We can discuss wheelie bins further down there,' Russell said, ushering her towards the lift.

With Adrian at the distribution helm the bins were going out thick and fast. Ever efficient, he monitored each area's delivery closely to prevent slip ups and make sure that only a minority of homes were allocated a larger wheeled bin. For the grey and green bins on the alternate weekly collection only one vehicle was needed since they alternated so maximising use of the vehicle. Within a week of the service starting those having their rubbish collected on the second week were shouting for larger bins.

'Listen you moron,' was the charming greeting that Gary Newton received when he arrived for work one morning, 'I pay my Poll Tax etc.' Gary felt like correcting her by explaining that poll tax finished before it had even got started many years ago and it was now called Council Tax but on further reflection decided that the lady, if you could call her that, was probably not in the mood for a lesson in corporate financial history. The dear little voice at the other end of the phone came again. 'Listen you moron, can you still hear me or are you bloody deaf? I want a larger bin for my rubbish or you can have all these sodding bins back and you won't get any recycling out of my house. Do you hear me? I want a larger bin and I want it today,' Gary was polite, took notes and gently put the receiver down believing that here was a woman who knew what she wanted, a rarity.

Robin, the temp, was snowed under by requests for larger bins. John Dingle was asked to provide better guidelines on who should or should not be allowed to have them. He in turn thought it wise to consult with Cyril who drew up a crib sheet which was to be read out whenever a caller asked for a bigger grey bin for their non-recyclable rubbish. *To have a larger bin you must have six persons or more in your family. Do you have more than six persons in your family?* Cyril emailed this to Dingle who forwarded it onto Adrian who wrote it out in his very fine copperplate handwriting on an A4 piece of card. The card was laminated and passed to Robin and the other supervisors to use in battle with residents.

When Micky Brown saw the mandatory wording he was stunned as were the rest of the Waste Team
'I understand why the Council wants to keep down the number of large grey bins it gives out from the experience that Padwick had. When they went over to wheeled bins they gave everyone a large one just to get them on their side. Trouble was, have bin, will fill up. They ended up with double the usual amount of waste. I can't believe this though,' Mick said pointing at the prompt card, 'how on earth do they think that this is gonna stop people having a big bin? *Do you have six or more people in your family?* Anyone with any sense is just gonna say, yes, ain't they? I mean, people are gonna lie,' Micky looked at Gary Newton for support, 'how can they prove that someone hasn't got six or more living at their address? They're never gonna line them up and count them,' Micky was dumbfounded and was beginning to feel very old indeed. The conversation was interrupted by another telephone call from inside. Robin picked up the phone.
'What sort of cat madam? Just hold on, I'll look in the dead cat book for you,' Robin broke off and went to look through a hardbacked notebook lying on the counter, 'Yes, madam, we picked up a black cat with a red collar two days ago in Hamilton Road next to the chip shop. No, I'm afraid we can't return the body to you as it was thrown on the dust cart. It's long gone,' Robin held the handset away from his head as all hell broke loose at the other end.

Micky was beginning to despair as he listened to Robin's one sided conversation; first Slump and now this jerk. What was it with these youngsters? He took the phone and offered the resident the Council's apologies after which he engaged Robin on the finer points of misleading an unsuspecting caller in future.
'You see, son, you have to humour them. Tell them their pussy was humanely buried in a landfill site with pink roses between its paws if necessary,' Mick said smiling as Robin lapped it up, a bit like the residents' cat might have done a bowl of milk had it survived the rigours of Cheatham's main roads. Mick went out into the yard to have a smoke. Gary Newton having heard Micky's fatherly advice had a question of his own.
'Mick, how on earth can a pussy be humanely buried in a landfill site with a ten tonne diesel tractor running over it?' Mick leaned up against the office wall, shut his eyes and meditated. Gary winked at Robin through the office window.

The handsome Richard Holmes was the last to hand in his keys and work folder. He had been relaxing on holiday for two weeks and had spent the best part of it covered with sun tan oil, sunbathing on a sun drenched tropical beach. He handed his red ringed binder over to the chappie behind the counter. It was the first time he had met Robin and he was enchanted by what he saw. Robin, for his part, took one look at the handsome fella at the window and was overcome with embarrassment, alternating with giggles like a silly twelve year old schoolgirl. He watched Richard closely as he lingered longer than usual when finishing his shift and Richard likewisecould not take his eyes off the beautiful temp standing in front of him. The depot phone rang and reluctantly, Robin went to answer it.

'Yes madam, you can put all your plastic bottles in the green bin but only plastic bottles. I'm sorry, yoghurt pots are not plastic bottles nor are margarine tubs, meat trays or plastic carrier bags. We do understand that you would love to recycle these things but as I understand it, we don't have markets for other plastic items. Thank you for calling and supporting us,' Robin was becoming as depressed as the supervisors with these repetitive calls but seeing Richard still hanging about outside, he brightened. The attraction between these two men was mutual and immediate and you might even say love at first sight but that might be pushing it a wee bit.

'Hi, gorgeous and what are you doing here?' Richard asked, his normal tan had been seriously deepened by his Mediterranean holiday.

'I'm Robin and I'm just here for three months whilst the wheeled bins are being trialled,' he explained. His facial expression was a real give away. The bronzed godlike figure standing just a few feet away from him was truly to die for in his opinion.

'I'm famished. I could eat a horse,' Richard yawned, stretching his arms up above his head revealing as he did a bush of yellow hair nestling in his armpits.

'Yes me too,' Robin managed to find the strength to say, 'I forgot to bring my sandwiches with me today,' he emitted a nervous little laugh from his sweet effeminate mouth.

'I was thinking of having an Indian, why not join me?' Richard ventured.

Micky was spellbound. He and Gary Newton were just feet away and their ears pricked up listening to these two prospective love birds.

'Looks like its three in a bed now then,' Micky suggested sarcastically. Gary Newton looked surprised, 'didn't you hear? Richie said he fancied having an Indian and Robin, get it?' Gary wagged his finger at Micky. Meanwhile Richard and Robin were still engrossed as their eyes searched for knowing looks, the dilated pupils and the sense of sexual intoxication that pervades the atmosphere when those who are mutually attracted to each other are in close proximity.

'The Pearl of India is my favourite restaurant. You just turn left outside the depot and it's about two hundred metres. It stays open all day. Do you want to give it a whirl?' Richard asked his new fancy boy. The flushed young temp was hooked. He knew he was being lured to something much more than a curry but what the hell! You only live once.

'That would be great. I finish at four if you can wait a bit?' Robin asked.

'Yeah, sure. I'm gonna have a shower in the locker room so that'll take me half an hour. I'll see you there.'

Richard picked up his holdall and slung it over his shoulder and started walking backwards, keeping his eyes firmly focused on Robin. He stopped suddenly and walked back to the window and lowering his voice, which was rather annoying for Micky Brown who was straining to hear what was being said, whispered to Robin.

'If you've got a minute pop in to see me upstairs,' Richard pointed towards the crews' changing room. I'm the last in this afternoon so I can guarantee no interruptions,' he said, mouthing a kiss as Robin's face flushed pink, 'I'll see you in a bit then,' the bronzed god lured. He was sure he was about to make another conquest. The blonde bombshell danced off towards the showers, rocking his hips and snapping his fingers in his usual carefree manner. His first day back and he'd pulled. Jim Bowen need never know. Life was good to him, he thought.

Robin searched his brain for a reason to leave the office for a short time.

'Erm, Mick, would it be alright if I just go outside for some fresh air?'

'Yeah, go on. Don't be too long though,' Mick acknowledged. Robin made his way hastily to the men's changing room. As he entered his first sight was of a naked toned body blatantly soaping himself down without the comfort of a cubicle curtain. Robin could see instantly that he did have an appendage to be proud of. Richard smiled at him.

'Eight inches!' Richard exaggerated, 'come on, Robo, don't be shy, hop in, only take your clothes off first though,' he laughed. Such is the foolishness of youth that Robin did not need to be asked twice. He stripped off and dumping his clothes all over the floor, he was in the shower before you could say, *Oscar Wilde*. The tanned Tarzan began soaping Robin's little frame, massaging it well. 'My, my Robin, what a luminous little white body you've got,' he laughed, holding Robin tightly which resulted in them both having erections.

Shower time over, Richard dried Robin and then himself on his one towel. They gathered up their belongings, strewn all over the floor and walked towards the door.

'My close friends call me Richie,' he slapped Robin on the back. Robin was consumed by a feeling of guilt following his illicit liaison with someone he had known for less than an hour. Richie went to his car and Robin scurried back to the allocation office where Micky was waiting for him and looking at his watch and then at the temp noticing his dishevelled state.

'Your hair's all wet Robin. They said it might rain later today,' he said, tongue in cheek.

Reginald Turner's accident kept him off work for a couple of weeks. He returned just after the trial bin areas had taken delivery of their new bins and as he walked into the office, the first words that he heard were, *missed refuse*.

'Nothing ever changes around here,' he grumbled walking over to the kettle. Micky and Larry were discussing the rising number of complaints they were receiving from all over the borough and in particular, the new wheeled bin areas. 'You're not gonna tell me they can miss a bloody great wheeled bin?' Reg asked. Larry was nodding, 'come off it; that's flipping impossible. Those bins couldn't have been outside the properties at 7am in the morning. We've seen it all before. When everyone had black sacks they used to run out with their rubbish after the vehicle had been down the road and then phone us to say, *'they missed me, send them back,'* Reggie eyed the new temporary assistant, Robin, in a platonic way of course.

Reggie was already feeling exhausted after two weeks at home with his leg in plaster, unable to run quickly enough to avoid his Juney's amorous advances. Returning to the irritating missed bins saga was more than he could bear.

'We can't afford to keep going back just because the silly sods can't remember to put their blinking bins out at the right time,' Reggie said concerned about the amount of overtime the men were doing, 'we'll be over budget,' he added.

'Yep, you're absolutely right Reg,' Micky agreed, 'the men would have to be blind to miss a wheeled bin. It's just that Dingle has been breathing down our necks to make sure there aren't too many official complaints and then we've had Huckett, Merryweather and the Mayor ringing us every five minutes telling us to pull our fingers out and collect the missed bins that we know damn well weren't missed in the first place,' Micky described the regime that they had been forced to work under and in particular his dislike of giving preferential treatment to councillors who were not backwards in coming forwards when their own bins "were missed". Mick decided to allow Reg the pleasure of making the vital decision on the missed bins. 'What do you want us to do with today's missed bins then, Reg?' He asked.

'Give it to me. I'll have a tête-à-tête with Captain Waste if he's about. We must have support from them at the top of the tree if this is gonna work,' Reg said resting his foot on the office's dilapidated two seater settee. Micky thought Reg's words most profound for an ex-pikey and went to put the kettle on.

Reg drank his tea from a chipped enamel mug and realised something was wanting.

'Here, Mick, pass my cake tin over mate, will yer?' Reggie asked, pointing to a large tin with a picture of the Queen on the top. Mick did so. 'Here, try one of these,' Reggie handed round his biscuit tin that contained a batch of freshly baked butterfly cakes. Reggie licked his lips, his mouth full of cream and sponge cake, 'come on chaps, dig in,' he enthused, 'these cakes are out of this world even if I say so myself. It's a new recipe. I found it whilst kicking about the house when I was off sick,' he added as the cream oozed out of the sides of his mouth. Robin helped himself but Micky and Larry, who could not face such decadence so early in the day, politely refused. Micky returned to the subject of the missed bins.

'Dingle will not like it, Reg. I don't think you'll be flavour of the week and I'm not talking about your bloody cream cakes either,' Micky said with feeling.

'I don't give a shit,' replied a recalcitrant Reggie.

'Point taken,' agreed Micky.

'So you don't give a shit eh, Reg? You must have constipation as well as a broken foot,' Larry's attempt at being funny fell on deaf ears and he felt duty bound to make amends by propping Reg's damaged foot up on an office cushion.

Reggie, never known to be one of the shiny, happy people turned to Mick for a progress report on the wheelie bin trials.

'Larry's been out doing a wonderful job, Reg. He keeps all the residents happy, don't yer me lad?' Micky said. 'Larry can tell you about that himself in a minute. I'll just say that it was a really good idea to have someone making personal calls on residents. In fact, Larry has been calling on the persistent offenders as well. Those buggers that ring in every flipping week to say their bins haven't been emptied – well Larry diplomatically reminds them that their bloody bins need to be outside by 7am, don't yer mate?' Micky looked up at Larry who had perched himself on the allocation counter. They all waited for it to give way but when it held his weight they relaxed.

'Where's Gazza? I thought he was helping Larry on the wheeled bins?' Reg wanted a fag but he was supposed to stay indoors and keep the weight off his foot. He fumbled in his trouser pocket for his ciggys, 'do any of you mind if I just have a quick fag?' No one objected.

'Ah, Gazza, yes,' Micky started to explain, 'well Gazza went sick again, Reg. I told you about that the first time I popped round to see how you were; the car accident, yeah? Once again we've had no ruddy doctor's certificate,' Micky added, exasperated.

'When he gets back I wanna speak to him. Check with Personnel about sending him to see the Council's doctor. I bet he's bloody well living the life of Riley if the truth be known,' Reggie Turner was in a foul mood. Mick thought it was probably due to him being so immobile. A good patient, he was not!

'Oh yes, Reg, I forgot to tell you, Wright's getting married,' Mick announced.

'The poor sod!' Reg sympathised, casting a glance over at Larry who smiled lamely back. He expected some kind of sarcastic remark from his boss, 'can't someone put him off it before it's too late?' Reg added.

The allocation office was truly at the sharp end with the telephones, fax and radio all going at once. It was a cacophony of sound each vying for Kelly and Robin's attention. Residents who claimed that their bins had been missed just refused to cope with waiting another two weeks to have their rubbish collected. All over the borough they were going into purple frenzies and the depot's staff were bearing the brunt of a new concept called, *Rubbish Rage*. In addition, the new vehicles could not get into some of the narrow roads because they were much wider than usual and on top of this, they had repeated breakdowns. It seemed like residents all over the world were on the Cheatham warpath.

'Charlie Pratt's another one I want a word with,' Reggie moaned, 'you tell me how a puncture can be called *abusive damage*? This abusive damage category is costing us a mint each year and since I'm supposed to be managing the budget, I'm not bloody happy about it,' Reggie was definitely not a happy bunny.

Charlie Pratt walked in with a progress report on W23, a hired refuse vehicle in for servicing.

'Here he is,' shouted Micky Brown laughing, 'Pratt by name, Pratt by nature...' Micky was known for his caustic wit. 'Reg wants a word with you, Charlie,' he said heading over towards the kettle.

'Oh yeah, what can I do for you Reg? Good to see you back on your feet again, by the way,' he noticed Reggie's foot up on the chair opposite, 'whoops, not quite back on yer pins yet then,' he quipped.

'I'll have you know, Charlie that I'm in terrible pain but it won't be long before I'm back bothering you again. What's all this about abusive damage? A puncture can't be *abusive damage*! It should be part of the scheduled maintenance. How can you blame the men if some silly sod puts glass or tacks in the kerb? See this pile of workshop invoices?' Reg held up a bundle of papers, 'this is what I think of them,' and with a flourish he threw them in the bin with the ease of an Olympic shot-putter.

'So, you're not going to pay those invoices then, Reg?' A droll Transport Manager inquired.

'What do you think? I've got Dingle on my back asking me for ways of saving money; Cyril bleeding Huckett wants blood out of a stone and you're sending me stupid invoices for *abusive damage,* for problems which ain't anything like abusive damage,' Reggie said angrily and in doing so caused his leg to twitch. He yelped with pain.

'I'll take that as a negative then shall I?' Charlie Pratt said dispassionately adding as a passing shot, 'what if we were to change the abusive damage heading to *blameworthy damage?*' Reg tossed a phone book in Charlie's direction. Charlie made a timely duck, laughing like a drain.

As Charlie left the office he handed Micky Brown a piece of paper with a report on W23. A few seconds later Charlie was back.

'Oh, Reg, your van still needs its MOT done. It was actually booked in for today. Didn't anyone tell you?' Charlie didn't wait for an answer, 'never mind now though, it's too late. I've called something else in off its job. I will of course be billing you for not turning up at 8.30am. It wastes our time when people don't bring their vehicles into the workshop as scheduled. I'll get the invoice to you by this afternoon, OK, Reg?' Charlie always seemed to have the last laugh. Reggie was seething and Micky was rolling his eyes.

Cyril, too, began pressing for progress reports. Adrian met with Cyril, John, Reggie, Micky, Russell and Judy to discuss how the wheelie bin roll-out had gone. There was also the sensitive issue to discuss on how to tackle the promised questionnaire on residents' views. There was also the need for a publicity campaign for any future roll-outs, that is, should the Council decide that wheeled bins were the way to go. It was the only way they could go, thought Cyril and he would do everything to make sure that common sense prevailed. Adrian reported back to the meeting on the public's reaction to the trial so far.

'It would be fair to say that we've received a lot of phone calls. The switchboard has advised that over six thousand calls have been received but that's not always a bad sign,' Adrian added hastily, 'naturally, being such a revolutionary new service residents will get a little confused. Not everyone reads the leaflets, mores the pity.'

'But Adrian, six thousand calls? That's more than the total number of households on the trial isn't it?' Cyril asked anxiously, staggered by this admission. John Dingle came to the rescue.

'Ah! Yes, but Cyril, residents from outside the trial areas have seen the bins and they want to know whether they too will be lucky enough to have them. In short, they want to know when the scheme is coming to them,' John reassured.

'Is there any chance that we could get a breakdown of the types of call?' Cyril asked Adrian.

'I don't see why not, Councillor. Reg has a temp in the office helping on the telephones. I'm sure he could arrange something,' Adrian offered, looking over to Reggie for confirmation.

Adrian's job gave him access to councillors and the very seat of power or at least that was how he chose to view it. During a lull in the meeting he found himself day dreaming about his future professional plans. Mixing with the Council's hoy polloy would stand him in good stead. Thesedays it was all about whom you knew, other professionals called it, networking. Cyril, in turn, was having a few thoughts of his own. He liked having the serious and dedicated Adrian to call on. When Cyril said jump, Adrian said, how high? How many young men were like that? Most were diffident, hormone imbalanced and just plain rude half the time, Cyril reminded himself. After an interminable discussion on the reasons for residents' phone calls, Judy asked for some background information.

'Councillor, for my benefit, what were the reasons for introducing wheeled bins? It might just help me get the right perspective, hit the right spots with our propaganda, I mean publicity material,' Judy threw her hands up in front of her.

'Oh, I'm so sorry. Slip of the tongue. I didn't really mean propaganda,' she apologised. Cyril smiled in a sickly manner.

'Lovey, we could tell yer but then we'd have to kill yer!' Reggie joked. Judy laughed.

Dingle took it upon himself to get the meeting back on an even keel.

'There are several reasons,' he had been doodling on his pad but in this hour of need he sat upright, 'first, we think they're the only way that we can increase our recycling rate dramatically and climb swiftly to the top of the league tables, certainly the London league table that is. Wheeled bins are larger than any of the kerbside recycling boxes one can buy so we should be able to collect more in them. Secondly, we have to consider the health and safety of the men or women who work for us. It surprises people to know that our men do get injured from pieces of jagged glass left sticking out through the black sacks. Using wheelies also gives us the opportunity to reduce Repetitive Strain Injuries. It's quite easy for our crews to hurt their wrists and shoulders as they throw the sacks into the hoppers, you know,' Dingle explained. Micky and Reggie were sitting agog at these revelations. Never ever before had anyone said that Cheatham was adopting wheeled bins because they wanted to look after their dustmen? Life was full of surprises.

Dingle had more to say on the subject of wheeled bins.

'We have received endless numbers of letters from residents pleading for wheelie bins because of the large fox and rat population. What with all the fast food outlets, the number of foxes has exploded and black plastic sacks are easy pickings,' Dingle continued. The thought of foxes exploding was not a nice one, thought Micky. 'The foxes tear open the bags and leave a terrible mess on our pavements. It's then up to our hard working cleansing teams to clean up the mess. One last good reason for introducing wheelie is that they enable women to do the job,' Dingle finished and noted the anxious faces of his subordinates. Micky's head was suddenly full of an imaginary klaxon. He was truly shocked at this latest revelation.

'Women loaders!' The Senior Refuse Supervisor blasted, 'who are you trying to kid, Mr Dingle?' Micky had enough trouble with male loaders, the stropy lot. At least with male loaders you could rely on them being able to walk all day long and wait several hours for the toilet. Women would never cope with that, day in, day out. They had no muscles and no bottle for that sort of life.

Sensing unrest, Judy moved the conversation away from women refuse collectors.

'I come from a company that has a lot of strings to its bow. It doesn't rely on just one method of waste minimisation or disposal. How does this borough feel about incinerators?' A look of absolute horror swept across Cyril's face and Judy noticed it, 'I ask purely because if we are adamantly against it we can use it as a ploy to help residents accept a lesser danger such as your wheelie bins. If we suggest that these nasty, gigantic mass burn plants are dangerous to their health it could have the desired effect. Do you see what I'm getting at?' She asked, pushing her hair away from her face. Cyril was hanging on to Judy's every word. He was impressed by this young woman's display of knowledge and must remember to tell Sir David what a good choice he had made. 'There are other ways of reducing waste which are similar but not actually called incineration. Have you heard about Advanced Thermal Technologies?' She asked. Cyril, concerned that there was a gap in his knowledge, looked blankly back at her.

'Shall we keep to the trial for today?' John Dingle suggested, 'I have another meeting following on from this and we might run out of time,' he advised. There were just so many hours in a day that one could sit in a room with Cyril Huckett. Judy picked up the threads of the agenda once again.

'What I recommend is that we produce another leaflet and distribute it whilst the trial is underway. In this second leaflet we should thank residents for taking part, that's always appreciated. It doesn't do any harm to remind them that we're running out of landfill space either. I always find a picture of an enormous pile of rubbish has a good effect, usually causing a feeling of guilt. We should also tell them how many lorries drive through Cheatham full of rubbish enroute to landfill and make the connection between rubbish and the rise in children's asthma,' Judy's enthusiasm knew no bounds helped by the fact that each time she suggested something, everyone agreed.

Cyril listened thinking that Judy was like a breath of fresh air. Russell was not completely comfortable with Judy's suggestions as he hated cheating the public.

'Do we have a job finding landfill sites, John?' Cyril asked.

'No, I wouldn't say that. We have a contract for another ten years. We keep being told by the DWWW that the South will run out of landfill in the next few years but every contractor I've ever spoken to says that as fast as holes fill up, another is created elsewhere,' he explained.

'We mustn't let Cheatham residents get wind of what you've just told us, John, otherwise we're sunk,' Cyril spoke like a true politician and turning to Adrian he said, 'I think it would be a good idea if you work closely with Judy to design the leaflet along the lines of her suggestions. I will write a short letter to residents for the front page,' Cyril could not let the chance of some self publicity slip through his fingers and was aided and abetted by Russell at this point.

'Cyril, I'll get a press release into the local papers next week saying how well the trial is going. A picture of a nice friendly resident with their recycling bins would be nice. I wondered too, if perhaps you would like to be featured in that?' Cyril did not need asking twice, of course he wanted to be 'featured'.

Adrian had been doing a bit of research on the subject of publicity himself.

'Actually, I was wondering what you might think about having a video made about recycling?' He ventured. 'We could include a few pics of landfill sites and some really noxious waste being tipped. We could even get one of those out of work actors to do the voice over and talk about the environmental reasons for recycling,' he added.

'Yes. That's a splendid idea,' Judy agreed, 'I know just the person. I think I could get him cheap too. Actually, I've just had another super idea. Why not get a couple of residents to tip their rubbish out on their front drives and film a researcher going through the waste to see what else they might have recycled?' There were some apprehensive looks as Judy tried to elucidate. 'What I mean is, film someone putting paper in one pile, plastic bottles in another and so on,' she explained. 'I know it sounds daft but it would really push the message home in a very graphic way. Normally we avoid letting others see what's in our bins. Believe me, this idea will have an enormous impact,' she enthused.

Cyril suggested that there might be difficulties in finding volunteers but Judy was not to be beaten by such a trifle.

'That won't be a problem, Councillor. There are some real nutcases out there who are so focussed on environmental sustainability that they'll catch a train to a council thirty miles away just to recycle a carrier bag full of plastic bottles,' she emphasised. Dingle and Micky tittered, 'you laugh gentlemen, but believe me I kid you not! I'm confident we'll find a nutty eco-bore to help us raise the profile of recycling,' Judy added.

'Yes, yes. I like both these ideas very much. We need to think of a volunteer that we can rely upon and who is keen to do the Council's bidding,' Cyril said putting his thinking cap on. For a few seconds there was silence as they contemplated who might want to take on this project.

'Doesn't Councillor Dickopf live in one of the trial areas?' Adrian was having a brainwave.

'Eh, yes I do believe she does,' Edith's inamorato admitted.

'Good, all set then; we'll ask Edith Dickopf straightaway and get things moving,' Judy exclaimed.

A discussion of enormous proportions ensued at the depot.

'Are you going to the match tomorrow?' Micky asked Larry.

'Na; Kimberley's at the hairdressers and I've gotta look after the kids,' the disconsolate bridegroom replied.

'It won't be long before you'll be able to bring 'em with yer,' Micky said trying to look on the bright side.

'You're taking the piss mate,' Larry replied, somewhat surprised at Mick's remark, 'do you know how much it costs to take the whole family to a football match these days? You're OK; your kids are able to pay for themselves now,' Larry shouted, taking a piece of paper out of his pocket and studying the phone number written on it. It was Samantha's from his night of passion at the Pink Mojo Club but now that he was officially engaged to Kimberley, his long suffering partner of twelve years, he tossed it in the nearest bin.

'What about you, Reg?' Mick asked.

'Alas, my son, no,' Reg replied, 'June wants the hallway redecorated. Anyway, Larry's right; it costs an arm and a leg and I've got better things to spend my money on. How can they justify paying footballers so much money? You might be interested to know that there's a rumour that old Dingly Dell has a season ticket for Chelsea. I forget who told me now but you'd never take him for a football fan would you? He's kept it very quiet if you ask me; frightened to tell us no doubt just in case we ask to borrow it,' Reggie said searching the pockets of his dark green council issue bomber jacket for his fag packet.

Biddles was pondering the idea that Dingle might have a seat at one of the best clubs in London.

'I can't believe it! I bet he lends it to that poncey Pomfrey bloke,' he surmised. Micky was more concerned that some wives got ratty if their men went off to a match.

'It's the secret of a happy marriage, Mick. Keep the little woman happy and everything else will follow,' Reggie said, being a man who could speak from recent experience.

'I would never use the words, *happy* and *marriage* in the same sentence,' Micky chuckled and then changing the subject, 'has everyone had the new pay scales and the letter about the pay rise?' He asked.

'Yep, Mick. The crews have had their own individual letters. I gave them out at lunchtime as they returned to the office,' Slump explained as he sat down on one of the few chairs that would bear his weight. He overhung the sides with his excess fat and always looked decidedly unsafe. He took out his pay check and studied it whilst at the same time munching a cold hamburger with everything that could possibly ooze out of it, oozing out. Slump's fat tongue slobbered out of his mouth in an effort to catch the sauce dribbling down the sides of the bun and having curtailed the escape of the burger juices concentrated on his pay slip.

'Here, Micky, I'm not getting paid much more than when I was just an ordinary supervisor. Can that be right?' A concerned Acting Senior Supervisor for Toilets, Trade and Pest Control asked, ' I took on a lot more responsibility when I became Acting Senior Supervisor and I have to deal with a lot of moody bastards. I'm just getting an extra hundred pounds or so a month. I don't think it's enough,' Slump said unhappily.

'Oh my God, Slump. Think yourself lucky you've got one hundred pounds extra a month. It's better than a boot up the arse, my lad. How much do you think we earn?' Gary Newton asked as he arrived on the scene.

'A boot up the arse eh! I know some people who would actually like that. Richard Holmes is one and his friend, Jimbo Bowen another,' Mick Davies called and then lowering his voice to a whisper he added, 'and of course our new friend here...,' the Ice Man nodded in Robin's direction.

Robin was busy on the telephone and luckily did not hear the Ice Man's remarks.

'Anyway, talking about taking on responsibility Slump, you've taken on a lot of ballast recently,' The Ice Man sniggered, imitating Michelin Man as he walked around the office in an effort to copy Slump's rather cumbersome gait.

'I can't help it. I enjoy my food and I get hungry,' Slump said stubbornly finishing his burger. 'I've got a prayer hanging over my bedroom door, which reads, "Please God help me; Saturn wants me fat!' They all laughed until Reggie brought them back to reality.

'Talking about the pay deal, complicated letter wasn't it? Do you think the crews will understand it? Cos if they don't we'll get that blinking personnel manager down 'ere' to give 'em the idiots version,' he said determinedly.

'Well most of 'em don't know what the National Joint Council or the Greater London Provincial Council pay spines are in the first place. In fact, Reg, I'm not sure that I do and I've worked here over twenty five years,' Micky admitted.

'Right that's it. Get on that bloody blower and tell what 'is name in Human Resources to be down 'ere at 6.30am on Wednesday next. Personnel are not much bloody help to us at the best of times. How many times have we asked for their help with staffing problems?' Reggie said tersely turning to Gary Biddles, 'oh, and while I remember, Gary, Dingle wants some photographs of residents using their wheeled bins. Take the digital camera and meet Adrian one morning next week. I don't know where, you'll have to ring 'im and find out.'

The number of calls and complaints from residents increased still further and resulted in another member of staff joining Kelly and Robin from Must Work Ltd., a young lady called Janet. Some calls were nice but the majority were not at all nice. The new Customer Services Team was given rapid in-house training on how to manage conflict and deal with aggressive customers. The overall aim was to ensure that residents ringing the Council with gripes went away calm, happy and prepared to support the Council with its recycling policy in spite of any difficulties they might be experiencing. The shortage of room downstairs meant finding space upstairs for the new Customer Services Team or else ignite a bloody revolution amongst the allocation office staff.

'Yes madam, I do understand,' Janet answered, 'you say that someone in your small block of flats is contaminating the bins and it stinks? Yes, it must be awful for you. I see, yes I see, so you've tried leaving nice notices around saying what should go in the recycling bin and you are completely ignored? I do sympathise. I know people can be just so pig ignorant can't they? Would you like someone to visit her and explain what she's doing wrong? Oh, I do beg pardon; it's a man is it. Yes, you're quite right. It's a man thing. So unorganised aren't they, my boyfriend is just the same......' The conversation went on as did many others that followed. Downstairs in the allocation office the conversation was quite different.

'I wish those bloody Customer Services people would write down the correct details. It's always useful to have the correct house number if I'm supposed to go back and have a word with the resident,' Larry complained.

'You're dead right there. I think they spend all day having chit chats with 'em. Still I expect there's a satisfaction rating or a performance indicator for that an all now,' Micky Brown was feeling despondent.

'Be nice, Mick,' Reg said, putting an arm around his mate's shoulders, 'just remember not to shout at them, otherwise Personnel will have our guts for garters for verbal assault or something similar,' he sympathised.

Reggie's comment had been prompted by a leaflet accompanying his pay slip.

'I expect you've read the Council's new Harassment and Bullying Policy, eh? It apparently replaces the Council's Sexual Harassment Policy, kind of combines everything together, comprehendy?' he asked.

'Was that what that miserable little grey leaflet was about?' Micky asked, opening the leaflet and beginning to read, 'I 'aven't read the bloody thing yet. In any case, no one's allowed to harass anyone in this section except me and Reg, right Reg?' Mick winked across the room at Reggie who sighed heavily.

'Actually, Reg, I 'ave read the Council's new *Against Harassment and Bullying Policy* and if you ask me we're all being bullied,' Micky announced. He would have made a good candidate for speaker's corner, Reg thought. Once he got on his hobby horse there was usually no stopping him. 'This Council has deliberately set out to set targets which we'll never be able to meet. We've told them but we, the workers, have been completely ignored. That leaflet says we should write down exactly when and where we're bullied and that's just what I'm gonna do. I'm getting one of those A4 diaries, you know a page a day and everytime I fink we're being threatened by that Huckett bloke, I'm writing it down. This Council had better be afraid, very afraid,' Micky threatened, managing to send himself into a coughing fit.

'Mick, what's the matter? Get out of bed the wrong way did yer? Don't take it to heart, mate. You'll end up having a heart attack,' Reggie was genuinely concerned about his old buddy.

'I'm alright, just you mark my words,' Mick said, his coughing starting to die down, 'these bloody councillors are gonna catch a cold in the end with this blinking recycling malarkey. They've always got to be first. It wouldn't surprise me if all they were really interested in was getting some gong for themselves. Mark my words, Reg,' Mick predicted.

'Mick, the Council will always win. It's no good even thinking about it. Just keep your head down and get on with what you're paid to do. Keep your nose clean and get your money on payday. That's all we can do, mate,' Reggie advised as he left the office, shaking his head slowly and retrieving a half smoked cigarette from his pocket.

Gary Biddles rendezvoused with Adrian at the agreed time in Trial Area A on the outskirts of the borough. A very sedate road named after a previous alderman and mayor of the late fifties, Leoni Bridges Road, was chosen for the PR exercise.

'Micky Brown once told me a story about Alderman Bridges,' Gary tried to make friends with Adrian even though he felt there would probably never be a meeting of minds, 'yeah, apparently Alderman Bridges was ahead of his time. He understood Climate Change before the term had even been invented and had similar ideas on saving fossil fuels to our present Mayor. Alderman Bridges decided to ride his horse to official engagements and often rode it down the high street. The word, environment was probably first coined by followers of Mayor Bridges' horse,' Gary added. 'Mick says his mum and him use to run down the street after the horse scooping up the horse muck for their tomato plants,' Gary was in his element. Adrian listened and suddenly recalled seeing a picture hanging in the Leader's office. Sir David Hooper was an admirer of Mayor Bridges even though he had been a dyed in the wool Tory. Sir David had many photographs on his office walls including many associated with dogs' mess and the various means of dealing with it. Centre place, however, went to a beautifully framed photograph of Alderman Leoni Bridges and his horse captured on one cold winter's day, strutting down the high street with a pile of steaming horse shit erupting from his backside, the horse's, naturally.

Adrian humoured Gary for as long as he could muster.

'Have you brought the digital camera with you?' Adrian asked, unconvinced that Biddles was capable of remembering such a vital piece of equipment. Gary nodded pulling it out of his anorak pocket for Adrian to see. 'Good show. I want some pictures of the resident at number thirty nine. She's agreed to tip a mixed black sack of her own rubbish onto the front drive. I'll help her sort it into neat piles of recyclable and non-recyclable materials...' Adrian was galloping on whilst Gary was mocking him silently.

'Materials, materials, he calls them, *materials*. The rest of us call it rubbish. Call a spade a spade is what I say,' Gary muttered.

'I want you to take some pictures of me giving the resident some friendly advice. Can you do that?' Adrian was beginning to sound patronising.

'Piece of cake,' Gary conceded, worrying Adrian even more.

'Just make sure you get some good shots. Councillor Huckett wants to use them to publicise the wheeled bins,' Adrian explained. He would have taken them himself but for the fact that he wanted to be in them.

An elegant white haired elderly lady who was not Edith Dickopf but who nevertheless breathed public spirit opened her front door holding her black sack of rubbish. After thanking her on behalf of the Council for taking part, Adrian tipped the sack's contents onto the crazy paved front drive. Gary was ordered to take several pictures of Adrian chatting to the householder and then of him rifling through the rubbish, carefully choosing poses for each picture so that each shot told a story and captured his right side. He posed with a couple of newspapers and then a plastic milk bottle in each hand and then gaily held up a couple of green wine bottles, clanking them in the process.

Gary took to his David Bailey role easily and made some suggestions of his own.

'I don't think we want pictures of all those whiskey bottles,' he said pointing to a huddle of clear glass bottles in a cardboard box standing next to the neat piles of recyclables, 'they make this road look like it's full of drunks!' Biddles said speaking as he found. Adrian looked up at the resident who was not looking best pleased with Gary's insensitive remark. The Council had had the chance to get rid of this idiot only a few weeks ago, Adrian consoled himself, but instead it had decided for reasons that were unknown to the rest of humanity to give him the benefit of the doubt! Was there no justice in this world? Adrian wondered.

'Gary, are you intent on upsetting all and sundry?' Adrian asked at his earliest opportunity. As cross as he was, he did his best to control his frustration. An angry scene in front of the owner of number thirty nine would not have gone down well. 'If you haven't got anything useful to say, don't say anything. Understood?' On route to their next appointment, which was just at the end of the road, Gary found the courage to ask another simple but tongue in cheek question.

'Ady, are we gonna be asked to sort rubbish on everyone's front drive?'

'My name is Adrian, if you wouldn't mind Gary; and no, of course we're not planning to sort rubbish on everyone's front drive,' Adrian said, believing Gary to be a complete plonker.

Their next appointment was with Councillor Edith Dickopf. It was not until they were standing outside her front gate that Gary realised his dilemma. It was too late. He wondered if he might be excused because he felt he was about to be taken short? No, he would probably be told to use Edith's loo. Ah well, grin and bear it was the only thing he could do. Hopefully his face would not ring any bells. It was at this point that Gary remembered that he had not yet downloaded the pictures he had taken of the happy couple cavorting starkers in the conservatory, mainly because he did not know how to do it. Taking more pictures today would give him the perfect excuse to ask for help back at the office. Gary smiled to himself and thought retribution was on its way, yippee!

Gary had no real cause for concern because as luck would have it, with his hood pulled over his head, Edith did not recognise him. This merely served to impress upon Adrian even more that this oaf was more of an idiot than he had at first thought. Likewise, Edith concluded that Gary was part of the Council's plan to get mentally ill patients back to work and thought no more about it. He took many photographs of Edith's home, clicking here, there and everywhere closely directed by Adrian. He recorded where and how she stored her recyclables in the kitchen and garage before she put them in her wheeled bins. Back inside there were smaller bins in all of the rooms so that nothing escaped Edith's recycling mania. Biddles snapped away merrily as he was led from room to room. He saw the entrance to the conservatory looming ahead of him and felt hesitant. His thoughts shot back to that eventful day while on suspension. He even worried that Edith might just entice him into her den of iniquity to have her evil way with him. He did not fancy being eaten alive; the fate he had witnessed befall Cyril. He considered his appearance. He was a handsome young man with strapping muscles but eyeing Edith up and down he was sure of one thing, in a month of Sundays he could never fancy her; wrinklys were just not his scene.

Edith beckoned Gary into her tropical whorehouse and Gary, unable to refuse, followed. Adrian had temporarily disappeared to a call of nature, so Biddles was on his own. He amused himself by snapping pictures of Edith's cucumbers.

'They look nice and long,' he suggested to Edith waiting eagerly to see what she would say.

'Indeed and see how thick they are. I bet you've never see cucumbers like these before young man?' She purred, running her hands slowly up and down one of them making it quite shiny. Gary gulped. Adrian, meanwhile, having returned from the loo was looking around the lounge, tying to get some sort of impression of this typical resident. He thought it would help when he came to write up his thesis on, *Raising Public Awareness to Waste Minimisation* in his attempt at becoming a full Corporate Member of the CIWM. He could see why Edith had been chosen to head up the Cost Effectiveness Committee. She had boxes for this and that all over the place. He wondered if she might be waiting for a convenient sized box to turn up for her old dad, who was sleeping in a club chair in the lounge. Adrian regarded the décor and the sheer exuberance of the textiles, an eastern-oriental décor was manifest. He was a minimalist himself. Adrian sought out Biddles in the conservatory and saved him from being ravished by Edith's peaches. Their mission completed, they took their leave.

Calls to the depot were still flowing in and staff were feeling harassed.

'Micky would you take this call please. I just can't make this gentleman happy,' Robin's dulcet tones greeted Micky Brown from upstairs.

'There's a first time for everything then,' Micky mocked.

'I'm sorry, how do you mean?' Robin asked perplexed by Mick's reply.

'Never mind, what's the problem?'

'This man is very cross because he can't have large wheeled bins. We've been told up here that only families of eight or more can have them. This resident has six in his family and isn't happy,' Robin waited for Mick's reply.

'I didn't know we weren't giving out large bins unless there are at least eight in the family. When did that come about?' Micky was asking Gary Green and Mick Davies who both happened to be in the allocation office at the time. They hunched their shoulders and looked blankly back at him.

'OK, let me speak to Mr Miserable,' Micky said, taking the phone and adopting his most charming voice. 'Hello sir, how can I help you?' Micky asked. The unhappy caller set out his case for a second time that morning.

'I want large bins for both my refuse and recyclables. I'll do my bit to recycle in exchange for bins that will hold all my rubbish between collections. Do I make myself clear? I'm not even asking for a Council Tax rebate for recycling; all I want are bins that are big enough to safely contain my rubbish. And furthermore I don't want some buffoon telling me that half of my rubbish will go in the recycling bin and therefore I don't need a large bin for my other rubbish. I'm quite capable of being the judge of that,' the disgruntled resident said in well honed diction.

Micky was sympathetic. Here was a man after his own heart.

'Yes sir, I agree with you. I'm so sorry that you've been annoyed by what is obviously a new Council policy. I need to make some enquiries but in the mean time I will be arranging for you to receive some large bins. Leave the smaller versions outside this afternoon and we'll make the exchange today,' Micky agreed, replacing the receiver. Gary and Mick were agog.

'I hope you've made a wise decision there me old son,' Gary Green said.

'I've made an executive decision as well as a wise one. I sympathised with the poor bloke. How can we expect someone with a family of six to pack a fortnight's waste into one of those measly little bins? It's bloody ridiculous. If my memory serves me right that idiot Huckett wanted to collect refuse once a bloody month originally.' Micky did not have a university degree but he did have common sense, a commodity which seemed suddenly to be in short supply. Larry was called up on his radio and within half an hour two large wheelie bins had been delivered to a now satisfied customer.

Biddles arrived back at the depot clutching the digital camera.

'Anyone here know how to download this thing?' He asked, holding the camera aloof.

'Giss it here, I'll have a go,' offered Gary Green, 'I did it once before when we had to print off pictures of that big fly tip on the Beverly Estate. Mind you, I did need some help from IT,' he said glancing at his watch. He was babysitting. Gary caught sight of GG looking at the time and being aware of other explosive images which he knew to be captured and stored in the camera's memory, wisely decided that perhaps he should manage this exercise on his own.

'That's alright, Gary. Thanks for offering but I don't want you to be late for your wife's class again. You go. I'll get IT to talk me through it,' he explained.

Gary Biddles took himself upstairs, carefully checking through the glass door window before entering to make sure that Kelly had left for the day. He tried hard thesedays to avoid any further misunderstandings with his former opponent. Inside the office he settled in front of one of the Customer Support Unit's computers and then made an internal call to IT. Someone picked up the phone, which was a relief. He worked through the instructions as they were relayed down the phone line and hey presto, he was in business. He printed off all photographs so that Adrian could have copies for the Press Office and Gary could have his keepsakes from the Huckett – Dickopf Affair. He saved his own precious images on a memory stick and taking that and clutching his photographs in a crumpled brown envelope rescued from the waste paper basket he left feeling satisfied with life. Looking down at the used brown package he could not help thinking that reusing an envelope would please Huckett's waste minimisation objectives and at the same time Dickopf's cost effectiveness ideals.

Chapter 13

'Gentlemen, I thought it necessary to have another meeting to touch base with regard to the trial and make sure that we're all up to speed,' Cyril said addressing the Waste Minimisation Strategy Team to which Charlie Pratt had been invited along with golden girl, Judy Craig.

'John, perhaps we can start with your report?' CH suggested cheerily.

'Yes Councillor, of course. We have all five thousand hereditaments on wheeled bins with the exception of about five hundred in Area C, which is still awaiting delivery of the brown bins for garden waste. I believe we can expect these from Japan next week, am I right, Adrian?' John asked. Adrian confirmed that John's notion of things was correct.

Cyril wanted to know how residents had reacted to his waste revolution.

'I've received a few complaints through the councillor's mail service but not a lot yet,' he explained. Micky and Reg were still trying to work out the meaning of the word, *hereditaments* but so as not to miss the rest of the meeting they were forced to mentally put it to one side and move on. Whispering to one another, they wondered whether CH might like to come down to the depot and sit at one of the phones in the Customer Services Section for an hour or two. He would certainly find out what the public thought of his scheme there and learn some new words at the same time. And what was this about wheeled bins coming from Japan? Why was it, they wondered that Britain was no longer able to make a few plastic wheeled bins!

'Residents have taken relatively well to the bins especially the dry recyclables bin, that's the grey, eh no, it's the green bin; sorry about that,' Dingle laughed nervously at his own mistake.

'It's easily done, Mr Dingle. We do have several to choose from,' Micky supported Dingle in his hour of need. Pleased at Mick's intercession, Dingle went on.

'We're recovering some good tonnages from the green bin. Adrian has made some calculations and we achieved a massive fifty percent recycling rate overnight from the first week that residents had their bins,' Dingle knew what the Councillors wanted to hear.

'My goodness, fifty percent you say!' Cyril exclaimed. They were all relieved to hear their Lead Councillor so enthusiastic for once. 'You say we're only hitting fifty percent? That's simply not good enough, my friends,' Cyril wailed, 'I've pledged eighty five percent. We must get more out of those bins. John, I want you and the rest of your team to brainstorm this little problem and come up with a solution in the next few days,' and then changing the subject completely, 'where are we taking the materials for sorting?' he asked.

'Judy has persuaded Aurelia Waste Handling to take the stuff whilst we decide what to do with it long-term,' John explained. Cyril was at least satisfied with this answer and nodded a thank you to Judy whilst allowing his eyes to rest on her more than ample bosom, which he concluded were a fine size and not unlike Edith's pair of pomegranates, firm on the outside and nicely rounded. The thought made him feel quite randy.

Judy brought Cyril back to reality. Noticing that his gaze was focussed on her chest, she coyly returned his smile and coughed. Men, she thought, they are all the same, professors or the slimy jerks you meet at parties; they just want to get a handful of your tits! Dingle had also noticed Cyril noticing Judy's breasts and did his best to move the meeting swiftly onwards.

'Long term, Cyril, we need to build our own sorting plant or contract the job outside to another company. In fact, I'm glad you raised the question, because we'll need to make a recommendation to the Strategy Committee soon on whether to roll out the wheeled bins across the whole borough or abandon them altogether. If we go for the new system then we must decide how we'll deal with the recyclables. I've asked Adrian to cost out both options on current rates. Whatever we decide it won't be cheap,' Dingle warned.

'Cheap, who wants cheap?' Cyril raised his voice and brushed away his white flyaway hair at the same time, 'I want high spec, prestigious, state of the art paraphernalia. I want conveyors going left, right and centre; I want balers for every possible domestic container or package; I want bag splitters, trommels, shaking tables, lasers; I want the whole caboodle. I want, in short gentlemen, as I have mentioned before, a sorting plant better than the one which Greenhill Gardenville has, even if it was built with European money. Let me reassure you, I'm going to have the first plant of its kind in the country and possibly the European Union. I expect to spend at least two to three million pounds on this equipment, whatever it is we eventually settle on. I've already told Irene Bendover that we must have unlimited funds at the ready,' Cyril was almost spitting with a kind of tempered rage.

Irene Bendover had indeed been given Cyril's equipment wish list for developing Cheatham's recycling prowess. What Cyril had forgotten to relay to his team was her reply. Changing the subject slightly, Reggie Turner referred the meeting back to previous meetings where vehicles, their mechanical state and the need for a whole new fleet had been mentioned. Charlie Pratt sat upright at the mention of vehicles. He had just spent an enjoyable few minutes in the wonderland of his imagination reliving a jam session with his hero, Elvis in Memphis, Tennessee. He had read everything there was to read on The King of Rock and just looked forward to the day when he could afford a trip to America to see Gracelands in the flesh rather than stare at its picture on the internet.

'Didn't we get some secondhand vehicles recently?' Cyril asked as Charlie stretched his eyelids in an effort to get the blood flowing more quickly around his brain.

'Yes, Councillor we did get two W reg. freighters,' Charlie confirmed, 'we also had bin lifts fitted to them so we could use them for the wheeled bin trials. I am afraid though Councillor, if we roll out across the borough we will need to have another twenty five freighters. The old ones we're running with are knackered; Reggie and his team will back me up. I just can't keep them on the road for very long. They're always in the workshop, although I have to say that a lot of the faults are caused by abusive damage. It's all these agency drivers that Refuse keep using,' Charlie said. He could see Micky was irritated. 'My fitters just can't keep up with them. I've made some enquiries, as you asked me to do Councillor, regarding gas. It's possible but the Gas Board will need a lot of dosh up front before they'll consider sinking tanks and complicated filling station pipes and equipment,' Charlie handed Cyril a report he had written, which set out the costs and a schedule for implementation once the financial aspects had been agreed. Cyril thanked him for his work and wondered just how much he would need in total. Going cap in hand to Miss Bendover, the Vampire of Cheatham was not going to be a walk in the park.

'Councillor Huckett, I wonder if we might just spend a few minutes on the questionnaire for the trial areas?' Judy asked, 'I know we've only been running for a few weeks but time has a habit of flying past and before we know it the three months will be up and the whole world will be asking whether the scheme is to go boroughwide or not.' Judy was sitting pen poised to make notes. Russell was pleased that for once his PR sidekick was not being controversial.

'Yes, I think you're right,' Cyril agreed, 'we must give serious thought to this. Perhaps we can rough it out now and go over it in more detail in a couple of day's time. I'll come over to the Press Office and we'll finalise it there,' Cyril wanted to finalise it in private away from the rest of the Waste Management Strategy Team. Interference was not something he craved.

'Does anyone want to suggest relevant questions for the questionnaire? Cyril asked. Micky Brown was the first to speak.

'Ask 'em if they like the wheeled bins and whether they want to keep 'em,' a guttural Senior Supervisor suggested.

' That's a very good point,' Cyril agreed, 'and an important one as well. We don't want to be seen to be forcing the public to have a scheme they don't want, do we?' Cyril was smiling but his thoughts were more Machiavellian.

'Ask them if they've had any problem with smelly bins?' Reggie suggested, 'I've lost count of the number of calls from residents who have complained of stinking bins,' Reg admitted.

Judy made a note about the smelly bin problem whilst Adrian tried to be more positive.

'I think it's important to ask them if the bins have encouraged them to recycle more than before.' This suggestion from his favourite team member pleased him. He knew it was important for the survey to look genuine and this sort of stuff was basic common sense. Judy picked up on Adrian's suggestion.

'So, we could ask them for example, did you recycle paper, wood, rubble and so on before you had a special bin?'

'Yes, something like that,' Adrian agreed, 'you see, I think half of them will say that before wheeled bins they didn't recycle at all. So in that way the bins have been a resounding success,' Adrian suggested, jumping to a conclusion. Thank God for the pomposity and inexperience of youth, thought Cyril. Adrian, however, was thinking more on how the wheeled bin experience would help him get his corporate membership of the CIWM. He would also soon be in a position to start applying for jobs elsewhere; another rung up the professional waste ladder for sure.

'I've had another smashing idea, Councillor. What about combining the questionnaire with a leaflet to everyone on the trial using some analogies like, so far you've recycled the equivalent of ten elephants laid end to end, or, if we put all the plastic bottles in Cheatham end to end they would reach round the moon and back. Shall I put something together for when we meet in a couple of days? She asked. Cyril's increased libido made him feel randy most of the time now. He fancied Judy. Taking a swig of cold water he tried to think of more boring things like the chlorophyll making properties of the Holly leaf, all hardened and prickly with its nice red juicy berries... No, this just wasn't helping, he decided.

Whilst Cyril was busy deliberating on his recycling scheme, Marcus Bullman was enjoying some good press. Virginia, the Lady Mayoress was equally popular and now they had the use of a hired electric Bentley, the only electric model in the UK she was more often by his side on official engagements. The electric car had important environmental credentials beside the other attractions which included elegance and film star associations.

'Oh, Marcus, I feel so proud of you my darling and you do look so handsome in your mayoral get-up. I quite fancy you all over again,' Virginia said softly one morning. Marcus was perturbed by this suddenly more seductive Virginia. This could not be happening. He had Maisie to think about.

'Do you really think I look so attractive my dear?' He asked, his ego getting the better of him.

'Oh yes my darling,' she sighed in her silky, sultry voice as she moved closer to him and threw her arms around his neck. Just like the shameless hussy in her dreams she threw herself at him until both were overtaken by passion. They disengaged as the clock downstairs chimed 10am. 'Marcus my dearest husband did I satisfy your innermost desires?' Virginia asked, still feeling amorous and spreading herself over the bed. Marcus smiled and mustering the strength and resolution to get up, he cooed gently back as he pulled on his clothes.

'It was tip top, my love, tip top!' He glided over to the door and as he left glanced at himself in the mirror muttering, 'not bad for my age. A little bit of snow on top but that just serves to make me look distinguished.' He gave his remaining hair a quick comb before leaving for the Council.

Marcus skipped into the Civic Offices. Virginia was still quite a woman. Marcus had always had a hang up about the size of his penis believing it to be rather small for his height but the fact was, for the first time in his entire life he had two women falling at his feet wanting to tear his trousers off at every opportunity. Life was so exhilarating. You never could tell what was just around the corner. He wondered how that old dog, Cyril was getting along with his new bitch, Edith?

Marcus picked up a new leaflet lying on his desk which the Press Office had prepared for community groups who liked to visit the Mayor in his Parlour. It was entitled, The Mayor's Role. He wondered if it should have been called, The Mayor's Roll, in line with his new sexual energy, although he could see that this might not perhaps be quite in the public's interest. The Parlour door swung open. It was Maisie, clucking as she walked across to him, low neckline dress revealing an abundance of flesh, hands outstretched, ready. Was he up to another *fumble in the jungle* in the first three hours of the working day? A perplexed but excited Mayor rubbed his hands together. He would do his utmost to do his duty.

The Performance Committee met to hear how the wheeled bins were fairing. Chaired by Edith, she introduced the item on the agenda and indicated the Committee Clerk to start the ball rolling.

'Councillor Huckett,' the Clerk began, 'the Committee believes your written report on the trials is outstanding.' Cyril looked confused. He was pleased to receive such praise and adulation but was at a loss to understand how they could know its contents since he was still holding it in his hand. He had not given it to anyone yet, not even Edith. He smiled in any case and returned the compliment.

'Well thank you everyone for that glowing recommendation. Obviously, I've tried my best to report the trial in an honest light...' Now the Committee was looking vexed. Edith cut in.

'No Cyril. We haven't seen your report yet. Chance would've been a fine thing. When our Committee Clerk, Mr Pelham here,' and at this point Edith pointed to the balding gentleman sitting to her right, taking the notes and operating a tape recorder, 'says your report is outstanding, he means it was never received for the pre-agenda meeting in the first place and that we're still awaiting sight of it.' Edith looked around the room. It was a public meeting but unlike the full council meetings, it did not attract more than a handful. She spoke, in any case, as quietly as she could and then made light of it. The other LIP members maintained the illusion and laughed with her.

Cyril towered over everyone as he stood to speak.
'I have my report here,' he said waving a bunch of papers around, 'I will of course give it to Mr Pelham at the end of the meeting so he can get it copied,' Cyril then proceeded to speak from memory, 'the trial has been in place for six weeks and generally speaking are operating well. We've achieved a fifty percent recycling rate in every area. I'm delighted to say that even in the poverty zone known as Area D, the scheme is doing remarkably well. We've had a minor glitch in the form of a bit of contamination in Area D but nothing to worry about. Edith, you've had first hand experience of the scheme, perhaps you'd be kind enough to give the Committee the benefit of your experience?' Cyril winked at her and she allowed herself to be overcome managing in a silly girlish way to smile back at him.

Edith was more than happy to do her bit to help Cyril. She took a sip of water and once the room was quiet she began to elucidate on the experimental scheme.
'I live in Area C and have been using the bins since the trial began. I have to say that I've found them extremely useful and I've managed quite easily with the fortnightly collection for the general rubbish. I took the Council up on the offer of the free composter and I've been putting my leaves and food waste inside it. I've followed the instructions implicitly which means no meat and fish wastes. I'm convinced that the composter will be a wonderful way of helping me reduce my waste,' Edith said, satisfied that she had done right by Cyril with her glowing report. Cyril relaxed, believing Edith was proving to be a real credit to him.

Irene was sitting next to the Leader and on hearing Edith's praise of the free composter leant over and whispered something in his ear. The Leader then asked Edith a question.
'Edith you're a keen gardener aren't you?'
'I am indeed, Leader,' she answered gleefully.
'Didn't you already have a composter for your green waste?' He asked.
'Yes, of course but you can never have too many, especially if the Council is giving them out free of charge,' Edith laughed. Miss Bendover frowned as she thought of more of her money being wasted.
'So, I presume you haven't used the brown bin for any garden and kitchen food waste?' The Leader asked.
'Not yet. I like to compost my organic waste to make nourishing compost, Leader. Saves one from having to go and buy fertilisers and saves the peat heartlands too,' Edith said knowingly and wondering where this questioning was going. The Leader next turned his attention to Cyril.
'Cyril, if we're providing composters why the Dickens are we giving everyone a fortnightly collection for food and garden waste? We're not made of money!' The Leader said. The Chief Finance Officer had Cyril over a barrel on this one,

she felt sure. Here was an opportunity to pull back some of the shortfall on next year's budget. No other council she knew was stupid enough to give away free things like this one.

Marcus wanted to add his own two penny worth to the debate.

'I was wondering about home composters, Cyril. If people are composting just like Edith and your good self and the Council tells them to start putting it in the brown bin, isn't that a conflicting message?' Marcus asked. Cyril gave the academic's text book answer on the merits of home composting.

'Home composting keeps the waste within the household's own boundary. This means it doesn't enter the waste stream and the Council has no responsibilities for it. Providing composters encourages many who haven't come across this old fashioned idea to have a go at it. Our instruction leaflet is deliberately simple and explains how the compost produced will help nourish the soil and therein reduce the need for pesticides. We're committed to continue this work but...' Cyril was looking up at the ceiling as if to find inspiration, 'some residents feel their gardens just aren't big enough to have one of our composters,' Cyril said, not subscribing to this idea at all, 'and so we need to make provision for these residents as well. It's all about equality and diversity, which is why we recently appointed an Equalities Officer,' he knew they could not disagree with that.

With the recycling rate climbing Cyril visualised that this time next year Cheatham could be platinum winners in the Great Green UK Council Awards. He pictured himself standing on the podium under a grand chandelier thanking dignitaries and other competitors who had not made the grade. He described the riches that Cheatham would gain from beating their way to the top of the league tables and it seemed to do the trick. The Committee was quite overcome with excitement, including Marcus and agreed to recommend that the scheme be adopted boroughwide, subject to the results of the survey currently being organised by Judy. Irene's expression soured.

Miranda was not enjoying the same level of excitement, challenge and sense of fulfilment that Cyril was. The young nurse, Sadie, was still suffering from a complex set of anxieties and nervous disability. This was in spite of hypnotism and all the other therapies that Miranda had made available to her. Recognising a priority when she saw one and calculating that her husband's reputation was at stake here, she managed to get the nurse right to the top of the treatment list. It would not do her career any favours to be known as the psychiatrist friend of a debauched civic mayor. If the newspapers got hold of the story there was no telling where it would end. Marcus would be branded some kind of pervert for sure and since all councillors would be tarred with the same brush that meant Cyril too. The fall-out would not stop there either since she was married to Cyril and her own professional standing could be at risk; it was basically about self preservation.

Miranda did her best to put Sadie at her ease deciding to approach it from the motherly angle.

'Sadie, my dear, how nice to see you. My goodness, you have lost weight. That diet I put you on has worked wonders,' Miranda said, flattering her and thinking she might try the diet herself.

'Thank you, doctor. I've been eating a lot more cereals and fibre like you said; trouble is I keep farting. Some days I can't stop myself. I go off like a ruddy rocket and it's so whiffy,' she explained. Miranda covered her mouth with her hand desperately trying not to laugh. Fortunately Sadie changed the subject. 'I've got a new boyfriend. He works for Cheatham Council,' Miranda smiled, 'yeah, he's ever so nice, he's one of those HGV lorry drivers what drive the refuse lorries about,' Sadie said relaxing for the moment and putting her wind problem behind her literally.

'Well I'm delighted to hear you're feeling better apart from the flatulence problem you've described, which I'm sure will sort itself out in time,' Miranda reassured.

Miranda was still thinking about the new problem of Sadie's boyfriend. It is funny how the world seems to get smaller and smaller she thought. Why and how did she manage to get hitched up with a bloody Council rubbish cart driver? There must be millions of shelf stackers available in fact any job unconnected to the Council would have been just fine and dandy and then, oh my Godfathers, she's let off another stink bomb... Miranda searched for a handkerchief to cover her nose and minimise the impact of Sadie's fart.

'I have your notes here, Sadie and I understand that sadly you had a minor breakdown just after the last time I saw you?' Miranda looked over her glasses at Sadie and waited for confirmation. The unhappy nurse nodded. 'Would you like to tell me about that? It might just help you face up to things,' Miranda advised taking off her spectacles and allowing them to hang down against her chest on a silver chain. Sadie stared at her hands lying limply in her lap before answering.

'I feel a bit embarrassed about the whole thing now, doctor,' she started, 'you see I used to have an old Skoda car and before I met Gazza, that's my boyfriend, I was having real down in the dumps days. Well, you know after the shock of seeing that couple doing rude things I tried to end it all. Stupid, I know that now. I ran the exhaust round into the car and put the stereo up high and waited. The trouble was that the car had so many holes in it the exhaust was diluted and on top of that the stereo ran down the battery and the engine packed up. I was so hacked off about it I cried for days. That was when I met Gazza. My mate took me down the Eagle Pub on the Dover Road and there he was having a sicky from work. We've been together for several weeks now,' she said fondly.

'It seems to me that you are indeed on the mend,' Miranda said trying to sound upbeat, 'have you by any chance mentioned to Gazza what you think you saw in room twenty three?' Miranda asked in casual fashion.

'No, not at all, doctor. I thought he might just think I was a silly cow. Men run a mile if they think you have a mad streak in the family,' Sadie explained.

'Do they? I haven't heard that one before but I think you're quite wise. Somethings, as I said to you before are best left unsaid,' Miranda reminded her. Nervously, Sadie remembered that there was another important matter that she had wanted to ask Miranda about.

'Actually doctor, there is something that you might be able to do for me, if you don't mind of course?' An apologetic Sadie asked.

'Yes my dear, fire away, what is it?'

'I was thinking that a change is as good as a rest. That's what they say isn't it, doctor?' Miranda smiled back, 'well, I am thinking of applying for a job on Cupid Ward, which is part of the new Sexology Unit,' Sadie said giggling, 'the other doctor I saw when I was off with my breakdown suggested that I should face up to my worries. So I thought, well, if I actually worked in that area, it would help me come to terms with the incident in room twenty three?

Anyway, the new job is a grade up, which will come in very handy if Gazza and I decide to get spliced,' she added.

Sadie was tingling with delight at the prospect of marrying her new beau.

'Sadie, I would be delighted to provide a reference for you, if that's what you're about to ask? Your relationship with Gazza must be close?' Miranda cocked her head to one side in anticipation of Sadie's reply. She grinned broadly and mouthed the word, yes.

'If I can help you get settled and put this whole saga behind you, it'll be worth it,' Miranda said adding, 'I don't think we need any more of these counselling sessions, my dear. If you find that you need to talk to someone, I'll be more than happy to oblige. You're always welcome on Wednesday afternoons during my open door policy so just come along for a chat if you feel the need,' Miranda offered. As Sadie walked away down the corridor Miranda called to her, 'keep focussed my dear.' Miranda's voice made the nurse jump and then Miranda heard a distinct popping sound as Sadie farted yet again.

That same morning the conversation at the depot had been similarly depressing. Ending it all was the first subject of the day as the supervisors debated the psychology of throwing oneself off a high building. Gary Newton had been on duty first thing when Ernie Bradshaw, one of the beat sweepers came to collect the keys to his machine.

'Gary, you should have seen the mess at Cabul House last night,' Ernie was a bit of a drama queen, 'blood everywhere there was. Some guys in the late night coffee bar where I was taking my break couldn't eat their fish and chips because they said the blood and guts were curdling their stomachs,' Ernie explained.

'What happened at Cabul then? I heard there'd been some sort of incident. Fight was it?' Gary inquired. Ernie was shaking his head.

'Some old woman threw herself off the roof. I jetted the whole pavement and came back here for my break. Just as I gets all the way back here, I gets another call from the police telling me to come back, because I hadn't done the job properly. The old gel had hit the ground so hard that blood and guts had gone up the walls as well,' Ernie explained.

Gary was still wincing at Ernie's description of the previous night's activities when Slump and Micky arrived.

'Oy Slump, you keep fish don't yer?' Micky shouted.

'Yep, a few. Why?' Slump was putting his toast in the toaster and shoving a few slices of bacon in the microwave.

'My lad's away and he left me to look after 'is fish and snails. The bloody snails have only died on me. I want to get 'im some more before he gets home,' Micky lamented.

'Try the pet shop next to Arthur's green grocers in the high street. They had snails when I was there just last week,' Slump said whilst breakfasting on his toasted bacon sandwich.

'What do snails feed on then? I thought that you left them to eat all that green slime stuff that gets on the glass?' Micky asked.

'Well, you do have to give them something, Mick. Try flinging in a bit of lettuce every so often. That should do the trick,' Slump suggested.

'Lettuce? They're not bloody rabbits, mate,' Micky shouted in disbelief, 'maybe I should buy four snails instead of two. That way at least he'll have spares when they die off,' Micky reasoned.

Gary Newton could no longer stomach blood, guts, snails and green slime and went outside for some fresh air. The day drifted into being just another one of frustrations; men off sick, vehicles broken down or taken for their MOTs; residents complaining and to cap it all, Dingle on the phone every five minutes wanting this and that done and reports on the progress of the trial areas. The Ice Man walked in at 10 am, coffee break time having had two days off sick.

'Welcome back, Mick. What you had? We heard you'd had the runs?' Micky Brown asked.

'Was it a Ruby Murray, Curry?' Slump asked jovially.

'No it was just a stomach bug but boy did it clear me out. Talk about the eye of a needle and all that,' the Ice Man was used to their ribbing but Slump made out he did not understand. Gary Newton was looking even more off colour.

'You know, eye of a needle? It was like water running out of a tap, thin enough to go through the eye of a needle,' the Ice Man explained, 'I'm so blinking glad we've got a window in this office,' he joked, 'otherwise I'm telling yer, you'd all be gassed by the end of the day.' They all moved several paces away, screwing up their noses as they went.

'I hope you're not contributing to global warming,' Micky Brown asked, 'that Huckett bloke wants to reduce methane. Apparently, if you get everyone to compost you create carbon dioxide instead of methane, which is a bit better for the environment,' Micky gave them the benefit of his knowledge.

'That bloody silly arse Dingle wants a new data base set up. I've told 'im I ain't any good at computers so he's sending that Councillor Jimbo Bowen down 'ere this morning to help me. He's some kind of a computer wizard, apparently,' Mick said. At this point Gary Green arrived.

'Yeah, that's right. I met him when the new mobile library arrived and I had to show him around it, remember? He said he was interested in computers. I think he used to work with them but was made redundant,' Gary reminded. Micky was looking apprehensive.

'Don't worry Micky; he's in love with our Richie Holmes. He won't be looking at you, you silly old fag end,' Gary's choice of words did nothing to reassure Mick who counted himself as being a very regular man. Jimbo arrived at the depot dead on the stroke of 11am.

'Hi,' the councillor waved as he approached the office, 'if you're Micky Brown then we've got a date!' He was smiling broadly and waited outside the allocation window for a reply. Mick did not like the sound of being anyone's date let alone Jimbo's but decided he had better stay within the spirit of the Council's Equal Opportunities Policy and make the best of the bad situation he found himself in. He offered his new friend a cup of coffee before they settled down to work.

'I believe we need to create an Access database?' Jim asked. Micky nodded. He did not have a clue what Access was and was relying on the superior knowledge of this so called expert whom he hoped had talked it through with John Dingle beforehand. Councillor Bowen confidently set out the ground rules for setting up the new database.

'What we must do first is be absolutely clear about what outputs we want to achieve. That's the only way that we can be sure of choosing the right inputs,' Micky's eyes were already glazing over. The database was for recording customer complaints and telephone calls. Once it had been set up the new Customer Services Team would manage it for themselves. Mick listened carefully and followed Councillor Bowen's instructions as he attempted some simple exercises to help register the bones of the system in Mick's grey matter. Mick was looking as grey as his brain cells but his tormentor was still smiling.

'This is all going swimmingly, don't you think?' Jim asked Micky who was doing his best to stay awake. He needed a cigarette and badly. At Micky's instigation they broke for coffee and in Mick's case, a fag but all too soon they were back in front of Mick's computer again.

Councillor Bowen felt that this dinosaur was going to need a lot of patience.

'Just to get some practice at setting up a database, let's make up an imaginary table; let's have name, address, telephone numbers and date of birth, anything else?' Jim asked. Micky thought these sounded enough but alas Jim thought of another. 'I know, let's have sex,' he suggested and with such joy in his voice. Micky nearly fell off his chair. Speechless he stared at Jim Bowen. He thought gays were supposed to be forward but this took the biscuit. We've only just been introduced, he thought to himself. Jim awaited a response but since none came he passed a hand over the front of Micky's face in order to get his attention back. 'Wake up! I expect you started at 6am and are already feeling tired.' Jim was a considerate sort of person, no doubt about it. Mick had to hand it to him. 'If you're finding this difficult to comprehend at your age just be positive and keep saying, *I can do this,*' Jim reassured. Was he referring to the Access course or having sex? Mick wondered. Jim resumed the training session, 'we were going to make *sex* another field on the table, weren't we?' He said pointing to the next blank field. Relief swept over Micky as he began to type.

Micky fried up a nice greasy lunch to which he added a couple of doorstep wedges of white bread. Slump had just returned and was microwaving a lasagne lunch for his own dinner. Micky and Slump sat and chatted, the former holding his head in his hands each time he remembered that post lunch he must endure another session on the computer. He sat twiddling a banana and occasionally glanced out through the window to see if Jim was still sitting in his car eating his cottage cheese and fruit, the healthy option.

'You see this banana, Slump?' Slump looked up from gorging on his lasagne to gaze at Micky's banana. Micky went on, 'if it was loaded, it would be a lethal killer,' and with that he pointed his banana at the cause of his unhappiness and made a clicking noise with his tongue as he pretended to fire it at his human target. After lunch it was back to Access but by 3.30pm Micky had had as much as he could stand of information technology for one day. The supervisors were returning, curious to see what Micky and Jim had been up to. Councillor Bowen conceded that they had spent long enough for one day on the new system and packed away his manuals.

Judy was getting along like a house on fire with the Leader who seemed to really appreciate her talents. How nice it was to work somewhere that encouraged staff to blossom, she thought and Russell too, was quite fun to work with. The latter's public relations background and professional approach had been a great boost to her. Each time a resident threatened to go to the newspapers because of some trivial thing like the Council missing their bin for the fifth time or because a street sweeper had not been seen in a particular neighbourhood for at least a year, Russell kept calm and reassured her.

'Don't worry. You're new to public life I know; but just remember we've broad shoulders and we can ride out any storm,' he told her. It was some comfort to her as she preoccupied herself with getting to know the local newspaper editors. By getting friendly with them she thought she might be able to have some influence on how they wrote their reports, a suggestion that had come from Russell himself.

The Cheatham Star's Assistant Editor, Tim Baldwin was the first to respond to Judy's email officially introducing herself to him. He was keen to meet her although his motives might have been suspect. He invited her out for a Press lunch.

'Hello, how are you getting on?' Tim asked. Judy was reasonably pretty he thought as she shook his hand.

'Oh fine. I'm just getting my feet under the table, so to speak. It's hard going with so many residents calling all the time to ask about the new recycling services. I don't get much time to actually put a sentence together if you know what I mean,' Judy said. Tim was quick to pick up on the low note in her voice.

'I'm sure it's just beginner's nerves. There's bound to be a lot of interest from the public. Cheatham is trying to outdo all other councils in the country by meeting an eighty five percent recycling target. It's hardly surprising that residents are anxious,' Tim pandered to Judy's unease convincing her that he could not be more understanding, 'how are you getting on with the Leader, Councillor Hooper?' Tim could not help thinking, however, that this little darling would be a hard nut to crack. A major charm offensive might be needed to get her to spill the beans. A man's got to do what a man's got to do; and of course at the end of the day there might be promotion on the paper for a real scoop, Tim thought. As far as that bugger Hooper was concerned, he, Tim Baldwin, was definitely living to fight another day. He would do his best to befriend Judy, spend a few evenings with her...who knows where it might lead.

'Councillor Hooper? He's such a sweetie. It was he who approached me at Aurelia and asked if I might like to be seconded to Cheatham,' Judy explained, believing her first meeting with Tim had gone down well enough.

The next day Russell and Judy put their heads together and presented their ideas to Cyril for the wheelie bin trial questionnaire. The pair had worked hard to produce questions which they thought would provide the answers that Cyril was looking for but Cyril, being the perfectionist found fault and tweaked them to allow a more creative manipulation of the results. In his own view, there could only be one result; that the wheeled bins should go on being rolled out, all four of them per household.

Dear Resident, (Cyril's introductory letter began,)
I promised to seek your views on Cheatham's new quad wheeled bin service trial. Please complete the attached questionnaire and return it by October 23rd. Your views will be analysed fairly and used to help the Council make a decision on whether the wheeled bin service will be extended boroughwide. We really do want to include you in our decision making process. The Council doesn't want to force a scheme on residents that they blatantly don't want. So please do have your say and return your completed questionnaires as soon as possible.

As soon as the questionnaire went out, the complaints came rolling in. Residents were afraid the Council would do their own thing whatever the outcome of the questionnaire, which was rather a strange thing to believe when Cheatham had spent thousands of pounds in leaflets telling them the

Council valued their opinions. Residents were still reeling from the shock decisions on town centre parking. During another exercise in public consultation the Council had revealed its Community Strategy, which suggested that traffic in the town centre really got up the public's noses more than anything else, with the exception of dogs' muck. The Council presumed it was acceding to their wishes by implementing a town centre controlled parking zone that somehow ended up incorporating most of Cheatham. It resulted in the extraction of millions of pounds for the Cheatham coffers through the purchase of parking permits. Cheatham's Council Tax payers were up in arms but councillors blamed residents for saying that they had asked for it, perhaps inadvertently, but that's how the cookie crumbles. Who could argue with that?

The Customer Services Team struggled to cope with the number of enquiries. Frustrated residents took to writing to their MP, a Tory whose major concern was to cause as much discomfort as possible for the LIP Council with which he so often found himself at odds. Sir Geoffrey Lawrence MBE MP had formed his own secret Cheatham shadow cabinet which was meeting at his constituency flat in Tolpuddle Lane; a nice flat on the new Cheatham yuppy estate.

'We need to know exactly what this pie in the sky Council is doing. I want us to know what their next steps are before they do. We need spies, lots of them, both within the service and outside it and we want to encourage residents to tell us about any problems that arise from using these confounded wheelie bins,' Sir Geoffrey said. He had a nervous twitch, noticeable when he was cross and it began to make itself known now. The local Tory Party Chair, Henry Scott-Palmer spoke next.

'Geoff, can you get your parliamentary legal research assistant to look at whether David Hooper is acting within the law? Four wheelie bins for each house does seem a trifle over the top,'
Scott-Palmer suggested. The Chair's request was carried.

Two of Cheatham's Tory councillors were at the meeting, Sebastian Tetbury and Hannah Hanson. Sir Geoffrey Lawrence now addressed them.

'Seb, Hannah, there's a Council meeting next Tuesday night. It might be a good idea if you table some difficult questions to get the ball rolling. The local Press will be there and they'll be very quick to sense dissent and print it,' the experienced Sir Geoffrey said.

'You got it Geoff! Hannah and I will get together and come up with a few questions. I've also got a news sheet going out in my ward shortly. I'll make sure something goes in there to ruffle a few feathers too,' Sebastian offered.

'What about petitions?' Hannah chipped in. She was rather beautiful for a councillor but then Conservative ladies always did know how to groom themselves unlike their LIP counterparts who looked better with paper bags over their heads although some said this would be a misuse of paper.

'Petition is good. I think we should have a rosta for Saturday campaigning in the High Street. You know the sort of thing, clip boards and *Down with the Wheelie Bins* posters,' the Chair suggested, 'let's aim to get fifty thousand signatures. We'll go door to door if we have to,' he added. 'Now timescales...,' the meeting went on into the early hours. The Tory Party had nailed its colours to the wall.

The usual Tuesday full Council meeting met as scheduled. Several questions were tabled from the Tory Party.

'Councillor Huckett, would you please tell us why the wheelie bin questionnaire didn't include a section where residents could disagree with any of the statements made on that document?' There were some blank looks around the chamber so Councillor Seb Tetbury elaborated. 'Residents were asked to say what they thought about the new service by ticking one of several boxes. So against the statement, and I quote, *your wheeled bin for rubbish is adequate; indicate whether you strongly agree, agree or don't know on a scale of 1-5 where 5 is excellent.* What happened? I can only think that the Council's Propaganda Department must have prepared it. Shouldn't residents have been able to register their feelings if they felt that the size of their bins was, 'inadequate'? This could have been done by having an extra box saying, disagree strongly. Could you tell us, Councillor Huckett why this wasn't the case?' Seb asked, assertively.

'It was a slip up, I agree,' replied Cyril, hand on his heart for full effect as the penitent councillor, 'but we did correct it in the later edition,' Cyril said knowing that only two hundred out of five thousand questionnaires had indeed been changed, 'and we think we've enough information to judge fairly what residents would like us to do. Many of the completed questionnaires have been returned to us with additional comments. All of these are being analysed by the Council's policy officers,' Cyril spoke convincingly. Tim sat at the Press table making copious notes as did the young male reporter from the Cheatham Echo. Judy sat alongside them.

Councillor Hannah Hanson was up next with her question.

'My question is for the Leader. Sir David, would you please tell me what the result of the survey is? Will all residents be getting all four wheelie bins and a composter?' She asked. Sir David stood to answer.

'I believe the results are positive although we haven't fully analysed them as I understand it. Until that time, the Council will not be announcing its decision on whether it will expand the scheme, keep it as it is or change it altogether for something else. But, what you can depend upon is the fact that recycling is here to stay. It's now government policy and we do have statutory obligations to meet,' Sir David said, fearing that worse was to come especially as the Labour councillors hadn't even started yet. Before Sir David had a chance to put his backside back on his special Leader's chair with the padded arms Seb was asking his second question.

'Sir David, I've heard that the Council is planning to build a sorting plant of gigantic proportions on the industrial park north of the Beverly Estate. Can you confirm this? If this is the case, why is the Council making such plans behind closed doors when you've suggested that it hasn't yet made up its mind on the wheelie bin scheme?' Seb finished and as much as he felt elated the Leader felt winded. What was all this nonsense about a sorting plant? He had not heard of any such building. Cyril passed Sir David a note.

'There are no such plans for the type of sorting plant to which you allude. What we've done is merely make temporary processing arrangements for the materials that we're currently collecting from the trial areas. I think you'll agree that this is a sensible and logical step to take since to landfill the recyclables after residents have painstakingly separated them would be completely immoral,' Sir David read, glancing at Cyril who winked at him. They both felt relieved at being able to wriggle out of that one. Cyril's response seemed plausible and it did seem to quell the mounting pressure in the room. Tim was still writing his notes. He wanted to capture the true atmosphere created by what he saw as wayward politicians. After the meeting, Judy was persuaded to go for a drink with him in the Social Club bar.

'I do hope you'll write something that's fair?' She pleaded.

'Yes, of course, my dear. I'm always fair,' Tim reassured.

Two days later the front page of the Cheatham Star was emblazoned with a headline that was indeed fair, just not perhaps in the eyes of Cheatham's LIP Group. It read, *Council reneges on promise to local people*. The article went on to say that the wheelie bins were to be spread across the borough like a contagious disease at breakneck speed even though residents in the trial area had rejected the service outright. The whole consultation business had been a whitewash. It went on to say that the Council had lied to the public as a whole but this was to be expected, because after all said and done they were the LIES (Liberal, Independent and Environmental Party), although the newspaper diplomatically doubted that the Party was knowingly dishonest thus avoiding a libel action in the courts. The Echo's report was equally dismissive of Cyril's so called honest evaluation of the questionnaire. The newspapers begged all residents to stand up and be counted and so all in all it was not what you would call a Good Press. Russell and Judy were dismayed at their professional Press colleagues, the former suggesting that Judy should perhaps work even harder to persuade them to see the Council's viewpoint. Conscientious to the end, Judy was resigned to try her best.

The depot supervisors had also read the papers and found themselves agreeing with the sentiments expressed therein. Being at the sharp end they knew that a large number of the residents on the trial were just silly buggers and not using the service correctly. Adrian had staked his career on raising the recycling rate by forty percent within a few weeks providing the scheme went boroughwide and it was Adrian who calculated the recycling rate.

'Bloody liars those councillors,' Reggie Turner said, 'I wouldn't put it pass them to bring the scheme in by the back door. No one believes their bloody questionnaires will be taken seriously,' Reggie trusted Gary Newton with his personal view of things.

'I think your right Reg. I'm only glad I don't live in the borough. I wouldn't like to keep my waste for a fortnight, not with all those shitty nappies lying in the bin. My Brenda's childminding now and we get masses of the smelly things.

Gary Biddles walked into the office carrying a naughty catalogue and chuckling.

'Yes Sir! Gary look at these, my God, look at these big bristles. You've never seen any the size of these. They're bigger than Lolita's,' Biddles shouted. He had sent for a catalogue in a plain brown envelope of ladies ready to thrill on the phone. Some were also prepared to meet those interested for true friendship or so they said. The pictures held nothing back from the imagination. They were young and old alike, stripped naked and semi clothed. Gary held it open for Gary Newton and Reggie to have a butchers.

'No Gary, Reg can't look, his missus won't let him,' Gary Newton joked pushing the catalogue away from Reggie, who wandered off to complete some paperwork with the following parting remark.

'For God's sake don't let Kelly catch you with that in your hands. She'll think you're a potential rapist as well as a bum pincher,' he warned.

Gary Newton usually more noted for his stoical outlook on life and that of being a respectable married man put all this behind him for the next few minutes as he looked through the pages of Biddle's magazine and enjoyed the uninterrupted joy of letting his imagination run riot without Brenda knowing.

'Here, Reg, it gives their occupations,' Gary exclaimed excitedly, 'some of these birds are teachers, care workers and dinner ladies. They never looked like that when I went to school,' he drooled, 'yuck, what is the value in this one advertising? Look at the rolls of fat around her middle and boy is she ugly. You'd have to be really desperate for that or blind,' Gary added. 'For Christ sakes will you look at those?' Oh no! I don't believe it. This tart's supposed to be a councillor from Cheatham,' Gary shouted sounding shocked. Biddles and Reggie were there at once, searching the page at top speed for Cheatham's new starlet but Gary was pulling their legs, 'you pair of silly tarts,' he chided giving the paper back to Biddles.

Later that day Reggie arrived at the Civic Offices for a meeting with John Dingle. Adrian was late and whilst they waited for him the Executive Head waxed lyrical about a recent trip he had made to City Hall, the Greater London Authority's nerve centre.

'I've just been to see the London Mayor with Cyril Huckett. Well it was the Mayor's Waste Minimisation Working Party actually. The City Hall is quite fine you know. I just sat quietly in the foyer and feasted my eyes at the view across the river. I managed to pop in to see the Chamber too whilst I was there. The building reminded me of the Guggenheim Museum of Modern Art in New York, no stairs, just spirals which slowly walk you round until you get to the top, quite remarkable. Are you interested in architecture, Reggie?' Dingle asked.

'Not so much, John. I'm not keen on modern art neither come to that. Think it's a load of old rubbish. I've seen the City Hall on the TV though and you're quite right, it's quite different. The men in the yard were actually talking about it the other day,' Reg said, preferring not to repeat the men's actual comments.

Dingle was keen to pass on his total inspirational experience.

'There is a rather interesting building across the river from City Hall, which I believe Prince Charles described as a pineapple. I rather beg to differ and think it looks more like something else?' Dingle was hesitant.

'Penis, John? I think that's the word you might be looking for,' a devilish Reggie responded, 'I saw that building the other night on the telly as well. It was on the news,' Reggie pressed his lips together tightly recalling an incident a few months back when Dingle had only reluctantly torn himself away from explicit images of nubile young things cascading across Reggie's computer screen. 'If I'm honest, John, my view of politicians isn't any better than my view of modern art. You likened the City Hall to a modern art museum and I have to say that this nascent legislative building is similarly full of shit, about which the public is blissfully ignorant and if I had my way, both would be cleared out as soon as possible,' Reggie exclaimed, striking Dingle dumb. What was it, *nascent?* Was that the word he had used? John Dingle, king of the cryptic crossword, did not know what it meant and yet he had read the Daily Telegraph all his adult life. He was seeing Reggie in a different light. Beneath that simple exterior there lay hidden intelligence, an inner depth. The truth of the matter was that Reggie had read something similar in the Morning Star. A comparison between Parliament and something else but what the hell, it could be adapted for his own needs now. He was wondering himself what the word, n*ascent* meant.

Adrian arrived at the Civic Offices just in the nick of time to prevent Dingle from hyperventilating at the idea that Reggie might actually have a brain afterall.

'I wanted to discuss how we might go forward on Waste Minimisation,' John explained, 'by this I mean, waste prevention, rather than the end of pipe recycling that we usually do,' Dingle announced proudly, displaying the jargon he had picked up at his City Hall meeting, 'the GLA is keen to raise awareness to products with less packaging and home composting, which of course we're already encouraging. Other things that came up were, take back services for mobile phones and encouraging new mums to use cloth nappies.

'Part of my remit, Mr Dingle, is to educate residents on recycling and of course we now also have Judy's assistance. Together we're devising a programme along those very lines. It's more a question of how we deliver it to residents that is the real issue,' Adrian enlightened them.

'Exactly, Adrian and that's where you come in Reggie,' John enthused, 'I'm wondering whether your men would consider enriching their jobs by door knocking?' John asked.

Reggie made his two colleagues wait for his answer.

'John, I really don't think the men will be best pleased; they're at the end of their tethers. We've had new services to get our heads round and we still don't know if they're going boroughwide,' Reggie broke off for a second, 'and let me tell you, if they do go boroughwide, we're gonna need to double our resources. In addition, we've only got unreliable vehicles, which are always breaking down. The men are still working horrendous numbers of hours on overtime and to cap it all, you want me to ask them to deliver leaflets and knock on doors asking residents to buy things that have less packaging...,' Reggie tirade finished in mid air.

'Not a good idea then!' John commented. Reggie nodded. They broke for a cup of tea and in Reggie's case, a cigarette outside on the forecourt. Later Dingle recapped on the day's proceedings thus far.

'I understand Reggie's point about the crews being unable to help so we'll have to look elsewhere for this work,' Dingle was resigned to taking up Cyril's suggestion, which was to approach Miranda's Psychiatry Department in the hope that some of her day patients would like to engage in community therapy. There was also the Lower Lampney Litter Volunteers, a really super group of do-gooders who could always be counted on to help.

Dingle privately thought that Cyril's brain, like many of his depot colleagues' grey matter must be about the size of a pea. A rather apt analogy with CH being a horticulturist.

'I must inform you that I've a funny feeling Cyril's thinking of adopting another idea known as, *Zero Waste*. He thinks it could be a coup for Cheatham,' Dingle revealed. Zero waste did not register anywhere on Reg's radar, whilst Adrian was upset that he had omitted to come up with the idea himself. For Reggie's sake, John elucidated, 'the term, Zero Waste means that all waste is subjected to reuse, recycling, composting or energy recovery. If it can't be recycled then its burnt but only if it will provide heat and power. They're even digging up recyclables that were landfilled years back,' Dingle explained.

Reggie held off telling his staff about Cyril's latest wacky idea until his usual Friday afternoon team briefing session. This little chat before they all went home was to let the weekend staff know the current position with whatever had been going on during the week. The office was jammed packed with supervisors. The settee was occupied by Reggie and Micky on account of their age and apparent arthritis and it was now that Reggie felt he was able to reveal the latest to come out of the Cheatham Academy of Funny Walks.

'Right, the bad news is Cyril Huckett is putting a stop to waste altogether,' they all waited for an explanation, 'that's right, you all heard. He's single handedly going where no man in Britain has trod before. He wants us all to sign up to *Zero Waste*,' Reggie still wasn't exactly sure what he was talking about himself. It just seemed daft to him. The supervisors were now all wide awake.

'Zero Waste? What's he gonna do with it then Reg? Eat it,' Gary Biddles asked.

'I don't know. Crazy if you ask me. People will always have waste. There just ain't any way in my lifetime that even a green borough like Cheatham will have no waste,' Reggie moaned, 'that arsehole Adrian is looking into it,' Reggie was feeling harassed. It was the end of the week.

'Zero waste; that will mean we won't have any jobs won't it?' Biddles was thinking the process through.

'Gary, me old son, don't lose any sleep over it. The rest of us won't be having nightmares. I doubt very much if any of us are in danger of having to sign on at the Job Centre,' Micky Brown comforted the gullible Gary.

Gary Newton had a problem of his own to share with them. He held up a piece of paper introducing a new chemical company.

'They're starting on Street Cleansing now. I do wish they'd just leave us alone. We ran the Council far better before this LIP lot got such a massive majority. There's just no stopping them. Apparently, I've got to stop using the stuff that kills the weeds dead and instead use this silly stuff that just knocks them out for a day or two and then lets the buggers spring up again. It's that bloody stupid Huckett again. Just because he's a bloody professor! And, on top of that, I've got to use environmentally friendly cleaning products as well,' Gary was sounding hysterical. The other Gary in Cleansing added his own thoughts.

'We tried those years ago, Gar, don't you remember? It was part of the Estate Cleaning Contract? They didn't work. We had everyone complaining that we hadn't cleaned the floors in the communal areas,' Gary Green said.

'Exactly, Gar. What silly sod would introduce them again?' Gary Newton agreed.

'Phoenix Weeding and Cleaning Products,' Reggie read out, '*Phoenix cleansing products are kinder to the environment and to the user whilst remaining highly effective. They contain no phosphates, no nonyl phenol ethosylates, no optical brighteners, no chlorine bleaches, no enzymes, no EDTA, no isopropanol, no polycarbooxylates, no butyl glycols, no formaldehydes...*' Reggie read out the list.

'Bloody hell, do they have anything in 'em?' Slump shrieked.

'Well, Gary you will have to be like the Phoenix in those Greek legends and rise from the ashes,' Reg raised his arms in a victorious manner to illustrate his point, 'and retry these environmentally friendly cleaners all over again. No doubt this time next year, after all the complaints, you'll be allowed to slip back into your old anti-environmental ways once again, son,' Reg comforted his mate.

The others were getting restless, glancing at their watches, washing up their tea mugs.

'Right, it's Friday afternoon, Poets Day and I'm off to golf,' Micky Brown croaked.

'What does, Poets Day, mean Mick?' The Ice Man asked.

'Piss off Early, Tomorrow's Saturday!' Micky shouted as he walked out of the office.

'Gonna play with yer balls again then Mick?' Reggie quipped. Micky did not rise to the bait.

Chapter 14

Rosie's café on the Beverly Estate was a favourite rendezvous for crews. Slump and Larry had just arrived for their usual all day breakfast. The place was full to the gunwales and noisy with chatter and the clatter of crockery and cutlery. Most of the tables were occupied by refuse crews on their half hour break. Slump and Larry looked at their watches as they walked in and were greeted with a chorus of, *here comes Gary Glitter,* on account of Larry's quaffed greasy hair and earring. The troops could be very cruel but Larry was a hard nut to crack. Slump pointed Larry to a couple of seats near the back quite close to two pairs of familiar shoulders, obliviously sitting in front.

'Think about it, we could have more real fun,' one half of the pair suggested

'Yes, I would love that too but you know I can't. I've got my friend to think about,' returned the other.

'Just get rid of him, sweetheart. I can give you such a lot of good times eh?' The man with the blonde hair was very touchy, feely. Slump and Larry had difficulty averting their gaze. They caught the attention of Rosie as she waddled down the aisle and quietly gave her their order.

The two men continued with their intimate dialogue unaware of eavesdroppers.

'I want you, Jimmy and I want you now,' the blonde guy blurted.

'What here, no Richie you can't,' a concerned Councillor Bowen exclaimed.

'Stop it. I love you too. Just give me time. I'll sort something out. I'll ask Damien to leave but I must give him time to find somewhere else to go. I'd love you to move in with me, Rich. It would be a great opportunity for you to give up that seedy little flat of yours. Just be patient for a little longer,' the Council Member for Stonebridge Ward begged. Rich drank the last drop of coffee from his mug and picking up his Daily Mirror he mouthed a kiss at his lover and swaggered out of the café. Slump and Larry kept their heads well and truly down until it was safe to do otherwise and Richie's crew had followed the blonde bombshell outside. Moments later an anxious Jim Bowen also left.

'Blimey, did you see that bulge in Rich's trousers? Hung like a bleeding donkey that bloke is,' Larry commented.

'Absolutely,' Slump agreed, 'wonderful physique that man's got,' he added, jealously looking down at his own rolls of blubber. Rosie delivered their egg, bacon, sausage, beans, fried bread and large mugs of tea and they tucked in, forgetting about the trials and tribulations of gay drivers and wheeled bins for a while.

With Judy's help Cyril called in Aurelia Waste Handling Limited to find an answer to the sorting problem for the next few months. The trial areas were resulting in a massive tonnage of dry recyclables that had to go somewhere. Most of it in the early days had been landfilled but only because Cheatham was not fortunate enough to have a sorting plant of its own. It would only take a refuse collector with a grievance against the Council to spill the beans.

Augustus Aurelia, the French grandson of Antoine, the company's founder, attended Cyril's meeting. The company prided themselves on despatching their top brass to create a good impression when new business might be on offer.

'Now, Augustus, I'm so glad you could make it. I think Judy has explained our predicament. We're running some trials but we've nowhere to sort the materials. We're in what you might call a catch twenty two situation. We haven't had time to build a plant of our own and in any case until the Council decides whether or not to adopt the wheeled bins boroughwide, we haven't the political go ahead or the funding,' Cyril explained. Sir David was not completely at ease with Cyril's opening gambit and picked up the threads himself.

'Yes, Antoine, oh, I do beg your pardon, it's Augustus? Antoine was your father.' Sir David apologised. Augustus graciously bowed his head. 'Cyril hasn't quite filled you in. We're looking at letting a whole package that may well be available to your company later on subject to the normal bidding process,' Sir David added, 'I believe a twenty year contract is the norm thesedays and that's a lot of millions tied up in waste. We would have to advertise in the European Journal, of course, but there are ways and means,' Sir David winked at Augustus. 'All we're asking at this point is that you consider taking our recyclables and do so at a very cheap rate during our trial. This would help us balance the books for a while. Our accountant says we're heading for an overspend and with another five months to go we don't want to put our fledgling recycling service on the back boiler at such an early stage in its development,' Sir David succinctly wrapped up Cheatham's needs and waited for Augustus to reply. He was in no great hurry to do so having been here with other councils similarly short of the readies. They needed him so much more than he needed them, although for the sake of his new ten bedroom mansion, all with ensuite and with room for a yacht in the South of France, he was prepared to swallow his pride and pretend to be their servant in a crisis if need be.

Augustus thoughtfully placed his entwined hands on the table. *Yippee, it's show time!* Shouted a small voice from within, although he remained calm and collected on the outside.

'Councillors, I think I can see where you're coming from. Please let me reassure you at once that Aurelia Waste Handling is ready to formally receive your tonnages from your trial service. It would be our pleasure and indeed our privilege to help you in your hour of need. Aurelia Waste Handling prides itself on its recycling achievement. We recognised a couple of years ago that waste disposal wouldn't be the only option for much longer and that saving resources must be at the forefront of all waste disposal contractors' minds. Times change and so must the waste industry, and if I might make so bold, the whole of Britain knows of Cheatham's green credentials. We can't let the residents down, now can we? What is more important is that they get value for money. If you will forgive the pun, we can't have Cheatham's residents being cheated can we?' Augustus smiled patronisingly, leaving Sir David very unsure as to how he should take this remark. Cyril, on the other hand was pleased to hear that the whole of Britain was aware of Cheatham's sustainable policies. Augustus continued, 'why don't I meet with your Executive Head for Waste and take it from there? I'm sure we can have all your recyclables coming in to us within a few days. Shall we say first load in on Wednesday, how would that suit?'

Augustus was first and foremost a businessman. It was in his blood. He also had considerable charm and panache, which was enough to make Cheatham's Leader and recycling champion feel rather special, as if they were the only customers Aurelia had ever had. The fact that Aurelia was part of an expanding company which already had contracts with a sixth of London's businesses and on top of that another half dozen local government contracts almost in the bag had absolutely no effect on Augustus' determination to clinch even more deals. Augustus was a credit to his company and he knew it. 'How's my charming Judy doing here in Cheatham? I hope you're treating her well?' Augustus asked.

'Superb! She's very talented and we couldn't have done so much without her. Pretty too,' Sir David gushed.

Without delay, Pamela Peters arranged for Augustus to sit down with Dingle to schedule the loads into Aurelia's recycling plant poste haste.

'I will arrange for our bulkers to collect your dry recyclables from your transfer station. I haven't agreed a price yet but we're probably thinking of about twenty five pounds a tonne for the material. Does that sound about right for your budget?' Augustus was trying to be helpful. If he was awarded the contract at the end of the trial he could raise the price to something more realistic. Dingle accepted the offer and noticed Augustus' gold cufflinks, each one etched with the Aurelia crest. This reminded him suddenly of the bad taste he still had in his mouth from the Council's decision, only last year, to stop awarding gold watches for long service. It rankled largely because he had just missed getting one himself. This painful reminder brought other irritating thoughts flooding back to the forefront of his mind, like for instance the fact that there were no local government perks at all. He even had to pay full price to join the over fifties swim club at the local leisure centre. What really annoyed him was that he only swam to stave off the stress acquired from just doing his job. There would be no crocks of gold awaiting John Dingle when he retired, that was for sure.

Augustus returned to the Civic Offices a few weeks later for a contract monitoring meeting even though he had not seen anything remotely resembling a contract. He decided to introduce a few frighteners which might speed things up a bit.

'New legislation means that you'll need to consider the separate collection of BMW, that is, Biodegradable Municipal Waste or else build one of these new waste technologies that are appearing all over the place,' Augustus explained nonchalantly. There were blank looks from the Cheatham party so he put them out of their misery, 'I'm talking about garden and food waste, that sort of thing. You really should be doing this now otherwise you'll be heading for enormous government fines for missing your targets,' Augustus kept himself up to date with developments. Staying ahead meant staying in business; it was his commercial mantra. 'I'm sure that I don't need to tell you how important the Waste and Emissions Trading Act is for local councils.' Cyril and Dingle agreed, hesitantly, 'the aim is to reduce food waste from clogging up landfill sites and emitting methane. Global warming and all that sort of thing!' He waved his arm dismissively, 'I won't say anymore as I'll probably be boring you,' he finished. Dingle was not bored. He quietly took in Augustus' words and decided that he would be long gone before any fines of gargantuan proportions appeared on the horizon. Cyril however was feeling decidedly nervous.

As arranged every Wednesday and very shortly every Monday, Wednesday and Friday, Aurelia's bulkers were drawing up at Cheatham's transfer station. Everything went according to plan. It was the only part of the wheelie bin phenomenon to do so. The Performance Committee met a few weeks later to review the waste service and recommend next steps to the Strategy

Committee. Judy was there to advise on the survey as was Dingle and Adrian. Edith asked Cyril to report on the questionnaire.

'Thank you, Councillor. We delivered five thousand questionnaires and had a twenty three percent return, which is very high for such a survey. We asked users if they'd like to keep the wheelie bins and ninety percent said they would, because they were great at keeping the foxes at bay,' Cyril paused, noticing Marcus's eye twitching. He could not make out whether he was anxious or had new contact lenses.

'Councillor, can you tell us how many residents wanted to keep the fortnightly rubbish collection? It's just that I've been watching the newspaper coverage and it hasn't been all favourable. If I might add too, many of the residents in my own ward, Cheatham Heath, have written to me to say they like the bins but aren't at all happy with the frequency of collection. It's winter now but come next summer, frankly I'm concerned for the public's health,' Marcus finished speaking. Cyril was twitching himself now and even Sir David thought that Marcus was becoming a loose cannon.

Dingle sat quietly. He truly had sympathy with the Mayor's opinion and was glad that he did not live in Cheatham. There would be no summer pongs arising from rubbish bins in his town where the waste was still collected weekly. Cyril tried to appease Marcus.

'Mr Mayor, we did ask residents if they'd suffered any problems as a result of having the wheeled bins and the majority of those that did told us the problems would be solved if they had a bigger bin, which they have been promised,' Cyril explained. The Labour representative jumped in.

'So, there was no specific question on whether they wanted to keep a fortnightly collection for their rubbish?' A scruffy middle aged man with a bald head and bad breath asked.

'Not specifically,' Cyril returned swiftly. All this nit picking was very annoying; he looked askance at Dingle who waded in to try and smooth the waters on Cyril's behalf.

'If I might just add Councillors, Cheatham's residents are used to a good and reliable service and if it didn't meet their expectations they would be on the phone before you could say, *Wheeled Bin Trial*,' Dingle said. The fact was that residents *were* on the phones but as luck would have it, the new logging system had not yet been installed so there was no way that anyone could say for sure whether the calls were complaints about the collection frequency or just innocent enquiries about which day of the week their waste was collected. Dingle was not about to enlighten them.

Cyril gave the meeting details of the splendid deal they had struck with Aurelia Waste Handling Ltd., which was mostly for Edith's benefit since she would report to Strategy on how the trials were being funded. He also discussed at some length how they might take the scheme forward, should the Council choose to do so. Better deals, he advised, were possible for the purchase of wheeled bins if bigger orders were submitted.

'We'll need to tender for the bins, Councillor,' Edith reminded Cyril.

'Quite. I realise that and I've already chosen several preferred companies to invite to tender. We'll get some sample bins sent over and perhaps this Committee would like to help choose the company?' Hay-ho, Cyril thought, they are definitely coming round to my way of thinking. I'll have them eating out of the palm of my hand soon enough.

The Performance Committee recommended to Strategy Committee that the scheme be adopted boroughwide. The bins were to be rolled out in just under one year and Cyril was given permission to begin research on how and where to build Cheatham's very own recycling factory or Materials Recycling Facility or *MRF* in Augustus' jargon.

Chapter 15

The Tory's secret shadow cabinet was hell bent on turning public opinion against the LIP and that Party's dark green agenda and decided that the time had come to step up their battle campaign. They needed a name, an identity that residents would recognise and this new pressure group, decided to call themselves, *The Green Evangelists*. At the start of their crusade to rid Cheatham of the LIP's whimsical ideas they were meeting twice a week and communicated throughout the day by email but once they had gathered enough information in the form of idle tittle tattle from refuse collectors and local people they increased their activities and publicly launched their attack in the High Street and local newspapers. Their major aim was to make their peace with the public before there was any chance of them being misunderstood. Indeed, they went to great pains in a full page advertisement to point out that they were not against the wheeled bins per se, just the fortnightly collection of rubbish.

Tolpuddle Lane, a corner of Cheatham noted for its respectability soon became a hotbed of unrest and intrigue. Councillor Sebastian Tetbury, a lawyer by trade, which was bound to come in handy, opened their October 23rd meeting at 7.30pm sharp.

'Thanks for coming on such a dreadful night. They say we can expect gales later,' Seb began.

'Let's hope they blow away a few ruddy wheeled bins then,' Sir Geoffrey Lawrence, MBE MP, quipped. The reason that Sir Geoffrey had a flat in the borough was because he needed to comply with constituency rules. He was always in the borough on Tuesdays during the recesses and took every opportunity to get his face in the local paper just to prove to his electorate that he did spend time in Cheatham. He also kept his eyes and ears open for any LIP scandal that could be manipulated to give him the political advantage.

'I'd like to add my thanks to everyone for coming along tonight too,' Sir Geoffrey said nodding an 'hello' at the Party Chair, Henry Scott-Palmer, who had just arrived, 'might as well get some use out the place with all the rent I'm paying,' Sir Geoffrey added grumpily.

'Right, where are we?' Seb asked turning to Hannah Hanson. 'Hannah, tell us about your chats with the local rag,' Seb suggested.

'I didn't get very far with the Cheatham Echo. I did however have a very interesting conversation with the new Assistant Editor of The Cheatham Star, very interesting indeed. He had some valuable inside information on the Leader and that dictatorial, pompous arse of a councillor, Cyril Huckett. Tim Baldwin, that's the Assistant Editor's name and its the same Tim Baldwin who used to work for Cheatham Council. There was a falling out with Hooper and the usual skulduggery. The outcome was that Tim was forced to leave. I think he could be very useful to us and he's not averse to printing a few letters and articles with a bias against the LIP either,' Hannah paused allowing Seb to interject.

'Is there anything he can help us with immediately to get the ball rolling?'

'Yes, I do believe there is,' Hannah said, 'my next door neighbour is so fed up with having to ring the Council for a special collection every time her kids put recyclables in the non-recyclable bin that she's threatening to stop paying her Council Tax. Apparently the collection crews have been told not to empty the *rubbish* bins if they see newspapers inside. Trouble is, kids will be kids and she ends up not getting her bin emptied for weeks. You can imagine what it's like when the old spaghetti and curry leftovers start to stink. I have persuaded her to write to Tim and he's agreed to publish the letter in large print and in the middle of the page. Apparently he's had a whole post bag full of letters against the new scheme. Most, it seems, are just simply fed up with having to wait a fortnight to get their bins emptied,' Hannah said reaching down into her bag for a piece of paper from which she read the following.

Very Poor Standards Start Bin War.
  'I have been a resident for twenty five years and in all my life I've never known such low standards for waste collection as I have during the past three months. I used to be proud of our dustmen and the service they gave us. Not any more. My bin stinks which is not at all pleasant and it just isn't big enough for my family of six. Yesterday my youngest child saw a rat run across the front drive and I've had to call in Pest Control. What are we paying our council taxes for? The councillors should be tied together and horse whipped out of Cheatham for good. They're turning this green and pleasant borough into a rubbish dump, signed, Miserable of Needham, name and address withheld,' Hannah finished reading.

'That sounds really good. You say this Tim Baldwin fellow will put it in a prominent position?' Seb asked.
  'He certainly will,' Hannah said confidently.

The Green Evangelists agreed to meet with other members in the High Street accompanied by samples of the offending wheelie bins and several clip boards for taking signatures. All the Tory councillors for Cheatham who numbered only five would be there in turn throughout the busiest shopping day of the week. When the day came, it went well. It was fine and sunny and the signatures came rolling in so fast it was difficult to keep up with them. Residents who were afraid that they would be next for the deadly bins, queued up to find out how they might help in the war against the Council and its damn bins policy. Two young male Green Evangelists in their twenties held wheelie bin races up and down the High Street just for fun and these caused a fair bit of hilarity amongst the crowds. And so it went on throughout November and December with no let up for Christmas. As the Parliamentary Member for Cheatham, Sir Geoffrey Lawrence had suggested, they were truly at war.

For every pressure group against, there is usually another one in favour. And thus it was that a hearts and minds group, unrelated to the LIP but nevertheless believing passionately in recycling at any price, banded together to counterbalance what they saw as misinformation flowing from the pens of the Green Evangelists. The Cheatham Recycling Champions were born and soon set up their own web site. On this they posted pictures of wheelie bins and what should go into them. They also made bold statements on how Cheatham's residents could save the world's resources by recycling more. Save Resources Locally and You'll Save the World was their strap line. Most of this was lost on their potential readers who just wanted to get through their busy and complicated lives.

The Green Evangelists got wind of the Recycling Champions' web site and created their own. Being Tories they were not so strapped for cash and could also call on funds further afield. In addition, it turned out, the Cheatham Star had connections in all the right places too and an important link to the national Tory HQ. Once Tim had let his managers in on the Green Evangelists' agenda, support was forthcoming and finding money to print leaflets was no trouble for them at all. As the campaign grew fiercer and their resolve remained unbroken even Hannah could be heard reciting some of Churchill's well known sayings, *we must drive on to the end... we must do our duty,* as she made her way downstairs from Sir Geoffrey's flat after another of their strategy meetings.

There was one other group forming in the wings and this was the local Labour Group's Band of Brothers who also wanted their say on the LIP wheelie bin scheme. As with the Tories, their objection was to the fortnightly rubbish collections and not with recycling itself. The elected Labour councillors represented an area of the borough that was classed as being mainly below the poverty line. They lived on the Beverly Estate, a mix of high rise blocks and individual houses. Even the local Labour Party had to admit that here there was a preponderance of residents who would never cope with a complex wheelie bin system. Cheatham's waste staff were realising this fact too. It was households on the Beverly Estate that brought them their greatest challenge. What to do about recycling bins that contained low levels of recyclables but high levels of dead cats and dirty nappies was becoming a big problem.

The Band of Brothers met at Alfie Leadbetter's council house on the Beverly Estate with an aim to put together their own action plan.

The meeting was opened by Winston Clegg, a middle aged man in his fifties complete with a scruffy grey unwashed pony tail.
'Brothers, I would like to suggest that we keep up the pressure by asking follow up questions to those asked at the last Council meeting. The next meeting is in two weeks time and we should think strategically about the questions we wish to table,' the Labour Leader suggested.
'Cor blimey,' Alfie said, 'you should smell my next door neighbour's bin. I'm surprised it hasn't got up and walked away all on its own. It smells as though it's alive with something. Pigs they are next door. They'll never manage a bin system like the one we've got; black sacks is all they're ever gonna get their heads round,' Alfie finished speaking and started to laugh. The others looked at him expectantly, 'you know how people resemble their pets?' Alfie asked, 'well I think they often act like their names too. The woman living in the flat downstairs is a Mrs Crapp. That's CRAPP with two Ps. You should see her garden; I'm telling you, *Crapp* by name, crap by nature.

Winston brought the meeting to order and agreeing with Alfie asked for his suggestions. Alfie did not take long to consider this question.
'I think at Council we should mention that the thick bastards just can't get it right, only don't call them that of course. I suggest we stick to the *poor down trodden people* image. So deprived that they've more important things to worry about like where their next meal is coming from. Recycling isn't exactly at the front of their minds and they can't manage a fortnightly system, you know the sort of thing, really rub it in. Actually, all this talk about being deprived reminds me of a joke I once heard...One man says to another, I use to be a weak man and then the other one says, once a week is enough for any man! Ta boom! Get it?' Alfie looked around at his political colleagues but nobody could quite work out how the joke was relevant to the subject matter.

Back at the coal face, the Waste Management Team could relax for the moment because Aurelia was now taking all the waste away and the developing contamination problem no longer existed if they shut their eyes and thought of England. The Band of Brothers, however were not relaxing. They had arranged a meeting with a government minister for waste to interrogate her on whether Cheatham's new policy was legal. They enjoyed the trip to London and the chance to move in ministerial circles very much. Alas, it seemed that there was no law against the LIP scheme and they returned to Cheatham with their tails between their legs.

The Council's Strategy Committee had agreed to roll out the wheeled bins boroughwide and Cyril and his Team were hard at work dealing with this mammoth task which had to be completed within the short time-scale of just one year. The Customer Services Team had swelled to six and still they were unable to handle the number of complaints and enquiries pouring in within the accepted response times. The requests for bigger bins increased by the power of ten but there just were no bigger bins to be had. This was in spite of the Council stating publicly that they were there for the asking. Restive residents were caught stealing larger bins from neighbours who did meet the Council's strict criteria. Others became resourceful and proceeded in a more orderly fashion to their local hardware shop where they purchased their own large bins. Even more cunning, some drove up to Cheatham's Brookfields Civic Amenity Site and helped themselves to one or two of the larger bins lurking around the back of the site. These renegade bins were usually lying on their sides because they had no wheels but Cheatham's residents demonstrated their initiative by removing wheels from babies' pushchairs in an effort to make do or mend

Residents who had previously been house proud no longer cared if the front of their properties were littered with several wheeled bins; they would have their full entitlement to rubbish disposal. There were of course some unsavoury residents who, not being quite so resourceful or daring as those who crept unseen around the back of Brookfields, were more inclined to make little forays into the night, dumping their black sacks in someone else's bin or even worse in public litter bins or on street corners. The canny knew their rubbish would be easily spotted and picked up the next day by the litter bin crews. All in all, residents were digging in, preparing to do battle for some considerable time if necessary as battle lines were drawn up. It was scary; the Council may have made the rules but Cheatham's residents were prepared to break them.

Judy and Sir David met frequently to consider the Council's publicity needs.
'Sir David, I've been thinking about how much fun it would be to make a short film for showing to local groups. We could feature residents using their wheeled bins, the collection vehicles and a few shots of landfill sites; I'm sure you know the sort of thing? Aurelia made one for the DWWW about a year ago. It had some fantastic original music with a real fanfare at the beginning. Every time it played the audience started looking for their popcorn,' Judy said, whilst Sir David looked nonplussed by her words, 'the music made them think they were settling down to a good film!' Judy explained.
'What a good idea. How much will it cost to make?' He asked.
'I know a very good company who would knock one up as a goodwill gesture. Normally we'd be looking at fifteen thousand pounds for a film of

around seven minutes but I'm sure I can get it cheaper by calling in a favour of two,' Judy added chirpily.

'Oh, go on with you; get started on it and leave Cyril to me. As Leader of the Council I want a major role in this movie,' Sir David told her imagining himself as the star of the show, 'and lets include a bit about dogs' mess too,' Sir David called. Judy's smile left her temporarily as she pondered on the Leader's last request.

True to his word, Augustus continued to collect the loads on the prearranged days and deliver them to his recycling sorting plant in Middlesex. No mess or worries for Cheatham; it just could not have been easier. The waste being collected was muck of the nth degree and with such a cheap rate being offered by Aurelia, Cyril felt he had made a great deal for the Council and was exonerated. Besides it was only for the shortest of times until they had built their own Materials Recycling Facility.

'Oh bloody roll on,' Micky Brown cursed. He had just taken a telephone call from a member of the public who insisted on speaking to a manager. Micky pressed down the red button putting the caller on hold while he spoke privately to his colleagues, 'this old lady wants to know why she's not getting her clinical waste collected separately. Her husband's got a stoma bag,' Slump put a make-believe peg on his nose, 'this is bloody ridiculous,' Micky remarked angrily, 'just think about it, wheelie bins full of shitty stoma bags. What are they gonna be like after a fortnight?' He was grim faced and Larry Wright was pretending to vomit. 'I feel really sorry for anyone like this old dear,' Micky said, 'Biddles, get Littleton on the radio right now. He's out doing the missed bins but tell 'im I said he's to go to 19 Lark Way and empty the grey bin there. And tell 'im not to ask any stupid questions, right? I'm speaking to Dingle first thing in the morning. People like that should be treated with dignity,' Micky said getting down from his soapbox.

'You're going a bit soft in your old age Mick,' Biddles suggested eating an apple.

'No, I just think there are some things which need to be done more than once a bloody fortnight,' Micky answered.

'Yeah, I know, Mick and since we're talking about age, it's good news about young Dippy isn't it?' Biddles asked.

'Sure is,' Larry replied, 'I can't believe it and by all accounts neither can Dippy.'

'Probably hasn't sunk in yet,' Mick added.

'Funny old world isn't it?' Gary suggested. 'Who'd have thought his old uncle would die and leave him a fortune. Gazza says he's inherited over a million quid, a Merck and a detached house in Bournemouth all paid for with the profits from seaside slot machines,' Gary sighed dreamily.

'I don't suppose he'll be back at work will he Mick?' Biddles asked.

'It's not bloody likely, son. Same as me if I won a million; you wouldn't see my arse for dust,' Mick proffered.

A fax came through from the Customer Services Team upstairs.

'God Almighty! Gary Green will love this one,' Micky said exasperated and coughing from years of smoking. He called Gary up on his mobile phone.

'Gary, we've just had a fax from them upstairs. You'd think they could walk down those bleeding stairs wouldn't yer? A Mrs Stacy of Woodbridge Drive is complaining that you haven't swept up her leaves. Apparently there are still leaves falling from the trees and she hasn't seen a sweeper in her road for two months,' Micky read out the fax.

'The leaves weren't coming off the trees two months ago, Mick. We would've been wasting our time,' Gary jested.

'I think they believe we've got staff just sitting idly underneath all the trees just waiting for each leaf to come tumbling down. A lot of silly beggars these residents are. Autumn is like the spring with the blossom, a seasonal embarrassment to us but we get there in the end, don't we Mick?' Mick agreed. 'OK. I'll take a look and if necessary I'll get Team B out to clear,' Gary agreed, 'see yer later, and Mick, why don't you give up the fags and try those nicotine patches?' Gary Green did not like to hear his mate coughing up his lungs.

'Yeah, I know Gar. Trouble is those patches are buggers to light up!' Mick returned.

Reggie had paid a visit the previous night to the Royal Infirmary's Casualty Department and was now nursing a swollen and bandaged thumb.

'What the bloody hell have you been up to Reg,' Micky asked.

'You will not believe this. June ask me to put some bookshelves up last night. I was planning on leaving the job until Saturday but you know what these women are like, nag, nag, nag. I decided to put them up last night and to cut a long story short, cack handed Sam here managed to put the bloody drill through his thumb. Juney ran me up the hospital and they did this for me,' Reggie held up his plumply bandaged thumb for all to see. Still incapacitated from his foot injury, he hobbled over to the kettle, 'yeah, I know, I'm a fucking walking disaster,' he anticipated any funny remarks from his colleagues, 'June says I'm not allowed out after eight o'clock at night from now on,' he told them half laughing.

'Reg, on a more serious note, I've had a communication from our union brother, Bobby. He wants a word as soon as you can. Apparently some of the wheeled bin drivers and crews are not what you might call, enjoying life. They say they're working far too long on rounds which they say need adjusting. They want an extra crew put on or they'll jack it in. They liked it when they could get home at 3pm like the guys who are still on the black sack rounds. At the moment some of them are not finishing until six or seven at night and Larry and Slump are threatening to walk out too. They say they've had enough and want to get back to their own jobs not spend all day running round after new wheel bin crews,' Micky explained. Reggie listened and ignoring Mick went to go upstairs. 'Reggie, don't you forget to speak to Dalton when he finishes today will yer? I think they mean business me old mate and I think they want a pay rise an all,' Micky shouted up the stairs. They had been buddies for years and Mick knew that Reggie would put things off for as long as he could. As the solemn limping man climbed the stairs there was a howl of enormous proportions culminating in the cry of the walking wounded.

'What the fuck's coming next?' Reggie screamed as he stubbed his toe!

Informal talks with the Union did not go well. Reggie agreed to consider immediately how they could improve the wheeled bin round times and reminded Bobby that they were trying to get all houses on the wheeled bins by September next year, less than a year from now. By that time they would have more vehicles and more staff to operate them. Pay rates could also be part of future discussions. It was all to no avail. The Union called for one day strike action on Wednesday 27th November. This would be a difficult day because the Wednesday rounds yielded some of their best recycling tonnages and were also where the richest and better connected of Cheatham's residents lived. These were also the very residents who kicked up a fuss if their rubbish was not collected exactly when it was supposed to be collected, strike action or not. Reggie held urgent discussions with Dingle, Cyril and Miss Bendover to try and find a way forward.

'The Union is seeking a ten percent pay increase coupled with shorter working hours. The shortage of vehicles is causing them to stay out until after dark. If we had the new fleet and extra staff promised now we'd be able to spread the load more evenly. We've basically taken on too much, too soon,' John did his best to relay the Union's demands to his boss, 'you see, Councillor, wheeled bins take longer to empty because they have to be returned to their front drives. Black sacks can be thrown into the truck whilst it moves along. If we have a one-off strike we can handle it but if it escalates, what do we do?' Dingle was looking frayed at the edges as was Reggie at the prospect and he certainly had no intention of taking the blame for the consequences. Cyril did not relish strike action either and Irene was definitely not in favour of giving out anymore of her precious cash. It looked like stalemate.

Cyril tried to dismiss the grave situation but was quickly brought to see reality.
'We've got a couple of weeks left I suppose to make a decision?' Cyril clasped his chin with his hand, deep in thought and looked at Reggie whom he hoped would agree with him.
'They want an answer as soon as possible, Councillor. Delays will mean more strike action after November 27th,' he explained, wondering what planet these councillors lived on.
'Councillor, I think we have to think of the effects that long term strike action might have,' as though struck by some sort of divine intervention, Dingle added, 'just think what'll happen to the recycling rate which has been steadfastly rising over the past few weeks. The Minority Parties could well see industrial action as a feather in their caps and the local papers will absolutely slay us. They're simply bound to take the workers' side,' John Dingle somehow always managed to see situations more clearly.

The very idea that the new scheme's credibility and excellent recycling rate might be damaged was just too much to contemplate. Obviously Cyril must do something to stop the wheeled bins scheme going pear shaped. He glanced at Miss Bendover and instinctively, the words *hard-nosed cow* came to mind. Irene had no desire for Cyril to succeed. Indeed, her concern was always for Cheatham's financial well being, which needled Cyril no end.
'John, Reginald, tell the men that I'll personally take charge of their concerns,' Cyril said. Irene gloated. Cyril was getting no more cash until the next financial year no matter what he agreed with the workforce. She had already rubber stamped an extra two hundred thousand pounds on the Education Department for some stupid flavour of the month idea, setting up distance learning for the local travellers' site. How she hated anyone who sponged off the state. 'Reginald, please look carefully at the schedules to see how we can lighten the loads. Irene and I will discuss how we can bring forward the purchase of the new freighters,' he said as Irene gave him another one of her evil looks. 'Reginald have a word with the employment agency you use; get some extra drivers and loaders on a six month contract as quickly as

you can. We'll find the money somewhere, won't we, Irene,' Cyril said assertively.

'Councillor, the men are quite adamant about having an increase in their wages as well. The issue won't just disappear by getting a few more blokes in from the agency,' Reg warned.

Cyril's about turn came too late. The strike day arrived and the Council put out its usual bulletin reminding employees that if they had not already booked leave, no more would be allowed and if they were sick then they must obtain a doctor's certificate to ensure getting paid. The bulletin also suggested that the Council was working very hard to manage the situation but there was very little spare money to play with. In the meantime, Cyril had thought up a cunning plan, which involved his heart throb, Edith.

'Hello, my naughty little tease, you,' Cyril telephoned Edith. The line was silent. 'Edith is that you my love?' Cyril could feel sweat beads forming on his brow. It was bad enough that he had found himself speaking in this manner, which was quite unlike anything he had ever done before. But then of course no man speaks to his wife like that. Wives knew their place, washed shirts and darned socks, at least Miranda certainly did in their house. It would have been sheer indulgence to buy new socks whenever a small hole appeared. 'Edith, if you're there, please answer me, don't keep me in suspenders, I mean suspense,' Cyril was about to put down the receiver when sounds of life could be heard at the other end of the telephone.

'This is the Dickopf residence. How can I help you?' A frail old man asked. Cyril almost died as the voice continued, 'is it Edith that you want?'

'Yes, Mr Dickopf, it is Edith that I would dearly love to speak to if she's about,' Cyril suddenly felt sick. Did the old man realise who was asking for his daughter? If he did he must think Cyril a dirty old man.

'Edith's in the shower,' the voice faltered before being replaced with that of Edith's.

'Edith it's you!' Cyril shrieked joyously.

'Of course it's me, you daft halfpenny. I hope you didn't upset pops because he's been suffering from dizzy spells; something to do with his hearing, apparently. He's seeing the doctor tomorrow,' she explained. Cyril felt a tonne weight lifted from his shoulders. Mr Dickopf was deaf; what wonderful luck!

'Edith, I wondered if I might come round and spend a nice cosy evening with you. Miranda thinks I'm at that boring Education Truancy Subcommittee tonight and I do so miss you. Cyril said subconsciously clutching the front of his trousers; he was telling the truth.

'Why Cyril, you haven't contacted me for weeks. When last we met at the Performance Committee meeting you hardly acknowledged me. So what's changed?' Edith could smell a rat.

'I just miss you lots Edith. You give me what Miranda can't. Do I have to beg for it?'

Edith could just hear Cyril saying that his wife did not understand him. She had heard it all before from just about every married lover she had ever had. Cyril was rambling on.

'... and remember at the beginning it was you who made the first move. In fact, Edith my dearest bunikins, it was you who made all the moves and now I can't do without you. You are like a drug to me. Do let's get together tonight? I want to see the sun rise with you in my arms again, babe,' Cyril bleated. Edith laughed.

'Oh Please! Spare me the clap trap, Cyril. You'll hardly be able to do that. Miranda will wonder why on earth the Subcommittee needed to sit right through the night, although, I suppose one could say that you were playing truant!' Edith was taking the call wrapped in fluffy towels with her hair wrapped turban fashion. 'Dad will be going to bed about nine. Come round at half past. He's sure to be fast asleep by then. I'll be waiting for you,' she cooed. Cyril could hardly contain himself.

Cyril arrived on Edith's doorstep at the appointed time and pulled the Victorian gothic style knocker. The door opened and there stood Edith completely starkers except for little fluffy feathers on each nipple and a heart of fluffy white feathers covering her deeply private part. He was in for a good one. He could feel his virility building up as he stepped inside the dimly lit hallway and turned to take a peep back outside just to make sure that the house was not overlooked. Satisfied that his secret was safe he focussed on the business ahead of him, taking Edith in his arms and holding her close. He was tantalised by her perfume. Magnificent! He allowed his hands to slither all over her and then tugging gently at the little feathers he watched as they bounced back each time. Kissing her sensuously she responded by gently caressing him in all the right places. She led him upstairs to her bedroom and as they were making out beneath the bedclothes Cyril noticed framed pictures of prize bulls with enormous testicles on the wall above their heads making him feel quite inadequate and dousing his ardour somewhat.

They lounged about for sometime on Edith's opulent cerise silken sheets.
'I'm surprised at you, Edith, owning such glamorous sheets. I would never have guessed,' Cyril said shaking his head, 'they're quite sexy for a...' Cyril quickly changed tack. 'I was going to say, sexy for a councillor and a pillar of civic society,' he added smiling and giving her a soft dig in the ribs.
'I know what you were about to say, Cyril. You think that for a middle aged maiden lady like me they're a bit bold. Mutton dressed up as lamb, I shouldn't wonder?' Edith said rather tersely. She ran her hand over the silky sheet, 'you think I'm out of my mind don't you? Well, Cyril, women like me are not all lesbians you know. We have inner desires and needs just like married women. It's just that I've never managed to find Mr Right,' a tear began to roll down her cheek and Cyril was overcome with affection and pity. Holding her tightly he found himself having another erection and they felt the earth move for a second time that night. Afterwards Cyril wondered how he could bring himself to mention the subject that was burning in his brain just as hotly as a part of his anatomy had been burning not that long before.

For the first time in his life, Cyril felt a cad. He had truly enjoyed his evening of passion and it was going to be so difficult to expose the real reason for his visit. He must bring it up somehow. Edith was still wittering on, although, having got bored with politics she had moved the conversation onto the realms of love and marriage.
'Cyril, my dearest love, do you think you will always be married to Miranda?' The question really threw Cyril off his guard. It was one thing to have sex and whisper sweet nothings but did he want to marry Edith? He thought not but how to impart this sensitive information? What about his political career and his standing in Cheatham and status in the wider world? Did men who left their wives for a bit of fluff ever get the civic honours they so desired? He thought probably not.

'Difficult question that Edith. Miranda is the mother of my children. I love her in some strange way and I don't suppose I'll ever leave her. I enjoy seeing you so very much and if we'd met earlier, (about thirty years earlier, Cyril was thinking), we might have gotten together and things might have been completely different. It's called, I think, the luck of the draw,' Cyril explained hoping his little speech was enough to stop her dwelling on the concept of marriage. Edith made as if she was disappointed but said nothing. It was close to midnight and Cyril still had not broached the ultimate reason for his visit.

Cyril prepared to leave and as they stood in the hall he grasped the mettle whilst at the same time noticing more rosette covered photographs of well hung Charolais winding their way up the stairs as well as over the bed.

'Edith my sweet, what do you think about this strike action? I think it could harm the Council. My recycling dreams could suffer a heavy blow,' Cyril was frowning, making the lines on his brow stand out. Edith, however, was still feeling jaded from Cyril's obvious disinterest in their romantic entanglement

'Yes, I've been following it closely. The newspapers haven't been kind to you,' Edith said, 'is there anything that I can do to help make life easier?' She asked. Cyril could not believe his luck; she was like putty in his hands. He must visit her more often when he needed her help.

Edith was not as simple as she would have Cyril believe. She knew he needed her as much as she needed him but perhaps for different reasons. She would never really chastise Cyril for keeping her a hidden part of his life. Maybe Mr Right had not come her way but she was used to being on her own and she liked it. She had the freedom to come and go whenever and wherever she wanted and no way was she looking for someone to clip her wings in her middle years. Good God No! All she wanted was for Cyril to keep her sexually fulfilled. In fact, she prayed that he stayed with Miranda. Men, she had found, performed more effectively when they were married to someone else and especially when they had been in that state for about thirty years. They seem to find a new lease of life.

'Edith, I want you to do your best to intercede on my behalf with Irene. Persuade her that the Council must do all it can to avert any further strike action. This would mean finding money up front, I'm afraid. It's the only way of baling the Waste Management Division out and getting everyone back to work. As Chair of the Cost Effectiveness Committee you have the perfect cover to make a stand for industrial harmony,' Cyril pleaded, 'you're a woman and in the perfect position to have a friendly chat with Irene and help her see the error of her ways,' Cyril rubbed it in a bit more.

'I suppose you're right,' Edith said yawning, 'being two maiden ladies, I suppose I could go one further and invite her for a gay romp in my emperor sized bed?' Edith watched Cyril's face as it dropped, 'it's alright, Cyril. No need to get your knickers in a twist,' she teased, 'I'm no dyke!'

Chapter 16

It was far too late for any Council initiative to stop the first strike and it went off as planned. Micky Brown turned up for work because as a Senior Supervisor he felt he had to take the management's side. He busied himself making a list of all those who had obeyed the Union's request not to turn up, which happened to be most of the workforce and then he set about rescheduling the missed collections for later in the week. The men would lose a day's pay but Mick knew they would all be screaming for overtime after the strike to make up their wages. The quality of the recycling materials was his major concern as the strike, he knew for sure, would make some residents retaliate by throwing their food waste in their recycling bins.

Aurelia's Quality Control Manager phoned about the state of recent deliveries to its plant.

'What's this muck you're sending us?' The plant manager asked.

'It's the same muck we sent you the day before yesterday and exactly the same as we will be sending you tomorrow,' Mick shouted down the phone knowing there was nothing he could do about the so called, recyclables, which were not going to improve in a month of Sundays. Reg sighed and took the phone apologising for Mick and explaining that they were about to embark on a highly visible education campaign that would change behaviour all round. Mick was staring up into the ether; another campaign he was not aware of.

Throughout the day of the strike frantic footsteps were heard running up and downstairs as Robin and the other agency temps tried to keep up with avalanche of calls about uncollected rubbish.

'Micky, what's an Applied Sweeper?' Robin shouted. The office temps and the agency drivers and loaders were not Union members so at least they could be relied upon to turn up, Micky contemplated, even if some of them were as bent as a nine bob note, he smiled as he glanced at Robin.

'It's those bloody mean green machines that the Cleansing guys push up and down Cheatham High Street all day long, sucking up cigarette ends and all the other muck. Why d'yer wanna know?' Micky asked wondering why so many gay men seemed to be crawling out of the wood work. What happened to men who liked to work on engines and go fishing? Such a load of namby-pambies they were all becoming. There must be something in the drinking water or perhaps it really was something to do with the gels used in the disposable nappies.

Robin's camp voice brought Mick back to the current topic of conversation.

'I've just taken a call from Gary Green,' Robin said filling Micky in on why he needed to know this vital piece of information, 'he's out in Needham High Street with one of the agency guys trying to keep the main street swept but he's saying the brush head on the Applied has had it and there aren't any left in the Stores. He wondered if you knew whether there were any stashed away elsewhere? He tried your mobile and the radio but couldn't get any answer,' Robin advised.

'Oh bugger, he's right,' Mick remembered, 'I forgot to put my phone on charge last night and the radio wasn't working first thing this morning. I think the strikers have jinxed it. No worries, I'll get back to Gary and thanks Robin, me old son,' Micky said trying to override the feelings of hopelessness sweeping over him and make it sound like he was in control of his destiny.

'Howdy partner' Mick radioed Gary Green, 'what's this about needing brush heads for the Applied Sweeper?'

'Yeah, tell me why is it we always buy such bloody shoddy goods? If we bought the more expensive ones they'd last a lot longer,' Gary moaned, 'the ones Dingle insists we buy only last for four weeks and then they're absolutely knackered. Those Applied Sweepers go up and down the bloody street for thirteen hours a day and we need to buy longer lasting brushes. Anyway, there are none to be had in the Council's Stores and if Dingle lets me order some now, it's gonna take two weeks before they arrive. I'm telling you, unless I find some brush heads somewhere quick, we ain't gonna have the high streets cleaned for over a bloody fortnight,' Gary wailed.

'So you do the roads every fortnight do you, bruv?' Mick asked, putting Gary's immediate problem to one side. Gary was taken by surprise at Mick's sudden interest in the street cleaning frequency and grimacing, nodded a reply. 'Well bugger me that explains it!' Mick went on, 'no wonder we have so many bloody complaints. I tell everyone you do them weekly!' Mick laughed and then returning to the subject of broom heads, 'I've got a mate in Padwick, Gar, who I think might be able to help us. They use the same models as we do so I'll give him a ring and see if he has any in his Stores. They might be able to let us have a couple to keep us going,' Micky had a knack knowing people in the right places and he picked up the telephone. 'Right Gar, its all sorted mate. Get that van of yours down to Padwick's Julian Road and there you will find Padwick's Stores. My mate has squared it for you to take five brush heads. Just sign a billet-doux for them and when our new ones come in we'll replace theirs,' Micky explained. Gary was pleased. At a stroke, Mick had saved Cheatham from sinking into an abyss of dirt and muck.

Edith averted any further strike action by having words in the right ear. Money was found to pay for overtime at quadruple rates appeasing the wheeled bin crews and getting everyone back to work. This extra funding also covered the cost of an additional supervisor and an advert was drafted for the local newspapers. As a result of this four people were short listed for interview. Reggie could not get involved because one of the candidates was his own wife, June. He made no apologies for this fact and since he was related to one of the candidates he asked Slump and Micky Brown if they would interview on his behalf. Micky went through the application forms. June had written a good one. The English was of a high standard and according to the job application she had had relevant supervisory experience some years earlier. Micky knew he must be fair but he felt uneasy about having the governor's wife on board and discussed the situation with Personnel.

'The situation is this, Micky,' the Personnel Manager explained, 'the Council is looking at putting a stop to having husbands and wives working in situations where one could be the line manager of the other. Unfortunately, they haven't decided when it will come into force, so, I'm afraid at this time if you find she meets the criteria then we must give her a chance.' Micky followed the rules and invited June Turner for interview.

The interviews progressed and June answered the questions well. There was one other candidate, Warren Taylor, who shone just that little bit brighter and when they came to tot up the marks, luckily for Micky, Warren beat June by one point and was duly appointed. As fate will intervene a few days later Warren wrote to say that he had been offered another job and was therefore unable to accept the Cheatham post. John Dingle could not face anymore staffing difficulties and he would not have any more spokes in his freighters' wheels. He wanted normal service resumed at any cost. Personnel were instructed to offer June the post, whether or not Micky had reservations or not. In any case, Dingle thought, it would be good to have a woman on board in what had been considered traditionally men's work. The Council's new Equalities Manager would think very highly of him for making this appointment. He made a mental note to mention it at the next Departmental Management Group Meeting. All this fuss about the new post made him think about his own re-evaluation. His final pension would be calculated from his best salary years. He wasted no time in approaching Human Resources about an upgrade, warranted on account of the increased stress levels he was now suffering.

By the time June Turner had given in her notice and started at the depot, Christmas was upon them. Micky welcomed her to their happy mob and was soon finding her a force to be reckoned with. At the same time, Kelly was planning the Christmas party and the usual fun.

'I want you all to bring in a picture of yourselves when you were babies,' she told everyone excitedly. With her head full of Christmas shopping and Peace on Earth and Goodwill to All Mankind, Kelly was once more her bubbly self and her friendship with Biddles was beginning to blossom again too. 'We'll have some nibbles in the office the day before our Christmas lunch on the 22 December as well,' she babbled on, 'and that reminds me, don't forget I need your money for the lunch. I've booked that really nice room upstairs in the Eagle on the Dover Road. I'll send round the menu so you can decide what you want before we go,' she was speaking to the supervisors assembled in the allocation office.

'How much is it again my darling?' Slump asked.

'Fifteen quid to you Slump. It's good value too. You get little mints and one free glass of wine with your lunch and there's a disco until 5.30 pm,' Kelly told him excitedly.

'I'll come if I get to snog you, gorgeous,' Slump called and then remembering the Biddles saga wondered if he should have said it.

'You cheeky monkey, Slump,' Kelly replied happily. No one else said anything. They left to go on their rounds, leaving her looking more than a little disappointed with the lack of enthusiasm for her festive lunch plan.

'Don't you worry, gel,' Micky Brown comforted, 'some of 'em will come but you 'ave to remember some of 'em have trouble making ends meet, lovey. Fifteen quid spent on a dinner just for them is hard to find. Have you thought of asking that lot in Transport? They would plug any holes in the numbers, I'm sure, deary. I know they like a drink or two. You've only got to see how well they repair our bleeding freighters to see that,' Micky laughed.

On 22 December there were forty five hungry horses from Waste Management, Transport and a few from the Highways Section all dressed up in their glad rags as the Eagle Christmas lunch beckoned. At 11.30 am they had downed tools and left a skeleton staff behind them as they made their way to what they all hoped would be a boozy party. The Refuse crews attending the festivities had been allowed to start at 6am instead of 7am so they could finish in time for lunch. Similarly, some of the sweepers had made special arrangements or agreed to make up time on the Saturday. The workforce lunch delegation showered and changed their shirts at the depot before rushing to the Eagle. Alfie Littleton and his own little group arrived at the pub first and went straight to the bar followed in quick succession by the rest of the manual workers. Whilst they were propping up the bar two temporary clerical dolly birds from the Transport Workshop arrived and ordered high powered alcoholic drinks. The Cheatham workforce eyed the girls closely. One had spiky blonde hair and wore a short skirt and see through lace top with a little gold necklace adorning her neck proclaiming that her name was, Tracey. The other, Annie, had short spikey black hair and modelled an interesting black leather trouser suit which was very tight around her backside, a fact that was noted by Micky Brown in particular.

Kelly ushered the high spirited Christmas lunchers upstairs to their private room and after several attempts managed to get them seated. Their next taxing task was to override the effects of the alcohol and remember what it was they had each pre-ordered.

'It's a pity Reg wasn't allowed to come, isn't it?' Biddles commented, 'when I get married, I won't let my wife tell me I can't go to things,' he said loudly, trying to speak above the general din.

'God help us when June really gets her claws into us. She keeps her 'usband well under her thumb,' a rather gloomy sounding Micky Brown said managing to spear a sprout onto his fork, 'these caterers are 'aving a laugh, aren't they? Why are these sprouts so bloody hard? They always give us frozen vegetables. You'd think for the bloody price we're paying they could rustle up a few fresh sprouts from Cheatham Market, wouldn't you? They have a stall right outside this bloody pub on Thursdays,' Micky agonised.

'Yeah, Mick. My mum says exactly the same. It doesn't take long to prepare a few fresh vegetables. And did you know they're so much better for you. Lots of vitamin B, my mum says so,' Biddles explained. Micky smiled wanly and continued his struggle to get through his Christmas lunch.

To wash down the food they ordered jugs of beer from the bar. Alfie Littleton was getting the worse for wear,

'I'm going away for Christmas, Mick,' Alfie's speech was already sounding slurred.

'Where are you off to then, Alfie?' Micky asked.

'Needham,' Alfie said laughing.

'But you only live on the Beverly Estate, Alf. Needham's all of two miles from your 'ouse, mate,' Micky chuckled.

'Yeah, but it's still going away isn't it?' Alfie slurred, 'me daughter lives in Needham and me and the missus are going there on Christmas Eve and we're not coming 'ome until Boxing Day night. I'm gonna put me feet up and just play with the kiddies whilst the ladies cook me a lovely Christmas dinner,' Alfie took another gulp of his beer.

The disco started up as soon as the meal was over and those that were well plastered but still able to stand allowed themselves to be urged by Kelly onto the dance floor. The two clerical chicks from the Transport Workshop did not need much encouragement and were soon up and providing a floor show as they twirled and rolled their hips in a seductive manner to the beat of the music.

Richie Holmes joined the milieu on the dance floor. He was dressed in his macho combats consisting of khaki t-shirt and baggy camouflage trousers with a thick leather belt slung around his hips. His arm muscles looked permanently flexed and glistened as the disco lights caught them. Moving towards the girls he gyrated his hips. They adored him and within seconds they were positioning themselves as best they could to dance as close as possible to him, ever hopeful that the music would change to a sloppy romantic ballad. When the chance finally came it was Tracey with the short skirt and the white lacy blouse that got her claws into Richard. Smooching around the pub's party room oblivious of anyone else and under the protection of the dimmed lighting, their hands wandered. It was only 4.30 pm but their lips met in a passionate kiss. It was not too long before he was kissing her ear lobes, bare shoulders and in fact anywhere that he could decently get away with in a public place.

Most of the party guests had had a skinful by 5pm. If they were not dancing, they were sitting around watching every move that Tracey and Richard made. It was as good as sex itself for those who usually got so drunk at weekends that conjugal relationships were never high on their agendas. Micky Brown and Gary Newton were older, wiser and visibly more sober.
'I thought our Rich was gay?' Micky asked, smoking a cigarillo.
'Apparently he's bi,' Gary explained.
'What exactly is bi?' Mick asked.
'Bi, as I understand it, is when they don't care whether it's male or female. They'll sleep with it whatever it looks like,' Gary informed his naïve mate.
'Alright for some ain't it,' said Micky
'Why d'yer fancy having sex with a man then?' Gary teased. Micky shuddered.
'No Gar, I don't fancy sex with a bloody poofter,' he said unequivocally.

Twenty minutes later the disco began winding down. There were a few more slow dances before the run up to the final rowdy Christmas songs, a ploy used to wake everyone up before they ran for the bus home. A few taxi drivers were arriving to collect those that had pre-booked knowing that they would be, without a doubt, well and truly sloshed. A young man in his thirties with a slight hook to his nose and ginger hair came into the room and stood behind the taxi drivers waiting patiently for their customers. It was a very unhappy Jim Bowen who watched in agony as the nubile dancers on the polished floor carried on regardless. His gaze was fixed steadfastly on Richard and Tracey with the occasional glance at Annie in her tight, seductive leather trousers as she circumnavigated the horny pair. The heat generated by the leather had caused her to discard her leather jacket and undo her blouse until it was gaping dangerously, displaying her wares. The music, 'Nobody does it better,' from the James Bond film was intoxicating and Richard and Tracey moved in unison to it. Richard was loving every minute; he now had two ready and willing girls hanging on his every move, après party fun would be even better!

Jim had seen enough. He was livid and his only thought was to make it all stop. He walked swiftly up to the disco DJ and remonstrated with him to stop the music. The DJ wanted an easy life and since he had been paid in advance did as he was asked. Jim took the microphone and in the sudden silence bellowed at the three dancers in the middle of the dance floor.
'What the hell do you think you're playing at Richard Holmes? Strutting about like the bleeding dog's danglies? You slut! What do you think you're playing at with those cheap tarts? Richard just stared. Annie and Tracey moved swiftly back to their table and made haste to the exit. The realisation that this guy was gay did nothing for their libidos. The lights were turned up

so that everyone could find their belongings and leave. Micky and the gang watched the fun. It was just like East Enders on the telly.

Richard picked his khaki jacket up from the floor.

'Jim, let's talk outside,' he suggested. Once outside Richard embraced Jim. 'Please let me explain; it was just me showing off, like I do. I'd no intention of doing anything with those two girls,' Richard pleaded, 'believe me, you're the one true love of my life,' Richard promised him. Micky and the lads looked on and changing the subject, he told his spellbound colleagues a joke.

'How do you know when someone is really posh?' Mick took a drag on his ciggy while he waited for an answer, which didn't come, 'someone who has fruit in the 'ouse when nobody is actually sick,' he told them. The only person to titter was a passer-by. Mick's little group made its way to the next pub.

'And that was that, was it? Reggie asked the following day at the depot.

'It certainly, bloody was. You can't say we don't see life 'ere on the dust mate can yer?' Micky Brown was describing the turn of events at the party to his colleague.

'So we think Jimbo's still living with our Rich then?' Reg asked.

'Who bloody knows and who bloody cares at the end of the day,' Micky spoke with a certain amount of indifference, 'did you know that Holmes' is supposed to be bi?' Micky asked.

'Bi?' Reg was not sure what it meant either.

'Yeah, bi. It means he's bi-sexual, likes men and women,' Micky was beginning to think of himself as an expert.

'Well I should hope so if what you've said is true about the Christmas party, Tracey, Annie et all,' Reggie said laughing, 'and by the way, Mick, more bad news I'm afraid, Councillor Fuck it, excuse my little joke, and the duo Adrian and Judy are coming over this afternoon.'

Reggie looked around the office to mentally register the state of it before his guests arrived. He took a few deep breaths and wrinkled up his nose in horror.

'Oh my God; I hope they don't catch a whiff of the air freshener we seem to be using here today. How many sprouts did you lot get through yesterday? There's enough flatulence in the air to power all the high rise blocks on the Beverly Estate. Open that bloody door and let some fresh air in,' Reggie shrieked. Micky Brown did as he was bid. 'I'm sorry Mick but Dingle and the rest of his lot are coming over to discuss tactics for the final part of the roll out. It seems that Marcus Bullman is on the verge of taking sides with the Tories. Have you ever heard of the Mayor of the Party in power taking sides against his own kind before? I think we can expect some fireworks soon enough,' Reggie said, picking up a leaflet lying on the table.

'What's this then, *Noodles to Go*?' Reg asked.

'Oh, it's just a new takeaway place on the Dover Road. Slump was thinking of ordering some for lunch one day after Christmas; they deliver it,' Micky explained. Reggie read the menu and then tried his hand at cheering Mick up.

'There are a few dishes here that Richard Holmes would love: shredded ginger beef; sweet willy chicken, oops, I should have said, sweet chilli chicken; Mick smiled and Reg threw the leaflet down on the counter, 'Oh, Mick, I almost forgot to tell you, I had another shot at a Victoria Sponge last night whilst you were all enjoying yourselves down the pub. I used Irish butter this time and organic flour,' Reg pulled out a cake tin from his cloth bag, opened it, took out the cake and proceeded to cut it up for later. Micky took a piece and found it surprisingly good.

Chapter 17

Cyril et all arrived at the depot for their meeting with Reggie who had roped in a reluctant Micky Brown for support.

'Before we begin,' Cyril settled his large frame in one of Reggie's uncomfortable office chairs and pushed his fingers through his white hair, 'is everything under control for the Christmas holiday collections?' Cyril raised an eyebrow in Reggie's direction.

'We're as ready as we'll ever be, Councillor,' Reggie reassured.

'We need to ratchet up the roll out after Christmas,' Cyril announced, 'I want all the rounds out by Easter at the very latest. We're getting rather concerned that the opposition parties are conspiring to plot against us. The more quickly we get the whole borough on the bins the better,' Cyril advised. They were all wondering who the 'we' in Cyril's little speech were.

'Councillor, if I might make so bold as to say that it's a bit unsettling for the crews to keep reading in the local newspapers that residents don't want the scheme,' Reggie said.

'Quite right, Reginald, we don't want that at all, do we?' Cyril agreed and not waiting for an answer said, 'so you can see why we must speed up the programme.' Reggie did not see at all. What he knew for sure was that if they put the whole borough on the service before they had ironed out the problems, they could look forward to a doubling of their present number of complaints to say nothing about contamination or the stress levels amongst the staff.

'Reggie, map out the new rounds as soon as you can and let me see them,' John Dingle requested, 'we want a quick turnaround so get at least eight street surveyors in. I know it sounds like overkill but it will allow us to swamp the new rounds by door knocking and find out exactly what we'll need in the way of bins. By doing that we can order exactly what we need reducing the number of exchanges we need to do later on,' Dingle explained knowing that Reggie was already worried about the depot looking like a graveyard for unwanted wheelie bins as more and more residents exchanged the smaller ones for a bin size that would actually contain their waste. This did not go down well with Cyril.

'Mr Dingle, Ehm John, I think you've misunderstood me. I don't want residents to have large bins just because they think they'd like to have a large bin. Large bins lead to more waste. Adrian will agree with me, won't you Adrian?' Cyril looked for Adrian for support.

'The Councillor's right. Every council in Britain that has issued large bins, like Padwick next door, have lived to regret it. Residents put rubble, garage waste and even whole car engines in them,' Adrian informed. Micky sat quietly looking at his finger nails thinking unkind thoughts about college blokes.

Judy listened thoughtfully to the interesting discussion on wheeled bin sizes going on around her. She had an equally interesting idea to share with them.

'Councillor, I believe a well designed communications campaign that educates residents in the most efficient use of their bins will assist us. I have drafted a leaflet reminding residents what can and can't go in their recycling bins. The collection crews are reporting an increase in contamination,' Judy glanced at Reggie and Micky for confirmation; they agreed by nodding, 'I think if we give residents a simple reminder we will also reduce the number of households wanting the larger bins because they will realise just how much they can recycle. If they find they have less non-recyclable waste as a result of recycling more they will cope adequately with a smaller bin,' Judy waited for Cyril to reply.

'Judy, I think that's a splendid idea but I don't agree with your belief that contamination is getting worse. Have we had any feedback from Aurelia's Middlesex sorting plant? Cyril looked at John for an answer. It was slow in coming.

'I would have to say, no, to that, Cyril. We've had the odd phone call but no official written communication from Aurelia, although the crews are reporting smelly recycling bins and I'm very much afraid that it may not be very long before Aurelia sends us a detrimental report,' John Dingle could feel his muscles tense up. This would not be what Cyril was hoping to hear.

Dingle's frank admission did take the wind out of Cyril's sails for a second and he remained silent whilst he pondered his Executive Head of Waste's wise words.

'It doesn't matter,' a bullish Cyril Huckett replied in the end, 'the scheme is new and it will take people some time to get into the swing of things. I think we ignore any contamination problems for the moment,' Cyril said, 'Judy, I want you to get your leaflet printed and we'll get those community people, The Lampney Litter Pickers or whatever they call themselves, to deliver them to every house already on the scheme as well as those still to go on. We'll pay them of course, fifteen pence per door, that should make them get out and deliver them quick enough. John, make sure they're tied to a time schedule so they don't fall behind. I know sometimes you can't trust these so called, community groups,' Cyril humbugged.

'They're called the Lower Lampney Litter Volunteers, Cyril. And if I might just say, I think fifteen pence per door is a little excessive. That would cost us in excess of twelve thousand pounds just to deliver one leaflet. We just don't have the money in the budget and I'm sure Miss Bendover would suffer apoplexy at such expenditure,' Dingle thought Cyril was losing his grip of reality.

'Look I don't want to get into an argument on how much we pay to get the leaflets delivered. Just get the job done and as quickly as you can and leave Miss Bendover to me,' Cyril said tersely. He had come a long way and had no intention of falling at the last hurdle. Adrian was beginning to see another side to his all conquering hero.

Cyril's desire for a flexible recycling programme led him onto the next item on his agenda.

'Now, what I want to know is why we're not taking plastic washing up bowls and plastic carrier bags in our wheelie bins; Adrian, why not?' Cyril regarded Adrian as the oracle. In any case he was responsible for setting up contracts for selling Cheatham's recycling materials.

'Well sir, there just isn't a market for that type of plastic. The only place I know of is Crappendale and the City's project with the plastic tree making,' Adrian explained, 'up until now all the materials have been given to Aurelia Waste Handling Ltd. and they've sold on what they could, if any, given the rising level of contamination. Unfortunately, those materials don't include plastic carrier bags or the plastic that washing up bowls are made of,' Adrian explained.

'I'm rather surprised that after such a successful visit up north we haven't done anything about sending our plastics to Crappendale? I was most impressed by their plastic tree project and I'd sincerely hoped that we might have some here in Cheatham. I know the Leader is keen as well,' Cyril admonished. 'Adrian, I want you to contact Crappendale ASAP and get us some sample trees. It's the tree planting season!' Cyril laughed, as plastic trees could of course be planted at any time of year, 'I'll have some in my Stonebridge Ward. Rowans would be nice providing they've perfected the red berry look,' Cyril said thoughtfully.

'Judy, I want you to revise your leaflet telling residents they can put all plastics in their bins. Adrian will find us a market, won't you Adrian?' Adrian felt a hot flush of anxiety coming on. 'Once we've got our Beverly Estate sorting plant we'll want to have robust contracts in place for the materials. I'm leaving that matter in your capable hands, my boy, so get cracking straight away. We've no time to waste,' Cyril said causing Adrian to wince. The suggestion that he might be considered Cyril's boy filled him with horror. John, Reg, Mick and Judy were deep in thought considering Cyril's remark about a sorting plant on the Beverly Estate. What sorting plant on the Beverly Estate? They had never heard of any such plans. Cyril knew that he had dropped a clangour. Only he and the Chief Planner had discussed locations for the plant and it was of course, subject to planning permissions but since these were granted by the Council's own people, it just had to be in the bag, as they say.

The Beverly Estate was part of a multi million pound regeneration programme and a waste factory would provide much needed employment and for this reason alone win the LIP many votes. All those residents on the dole would soon be meaningfully employed sorting other residents' rubbish. It would be just like the old days of the Mudlarks on the Thames beaches only they would be paid for their time. Cheatham might even get some council taxes out of them or even their back dated rents. It sounded like an excellent strategy. John and his colleagues, however, felt mutually apprehensive as they visualised a tsunami wave of opposition coming from those living on the Beverly Estate to any such plans.

Irene Bendover invited Cyril to attend an emergency meeting with the Leader and the Head of Planning.

'Councillors, after many attempts to balance the books with the proposed recycling plans, I've come to the conclusion that it just can't be done. Rather than a decrease in waste brought about by increased recycling, I understand from Mr Dingle that our waste tonnages to landfill have actually increased. The whole situation is getting out of control,' she warned. The dark rings underneath her eyes were darker than usual and she spoke as if she had just downed a whole bottle or two of wine. Her clothes looked dishevelled and her hair was in need of a comb.

'Irene, Irene, it will be alright. As you know we'd intended to roll out the service over several years but we've found, following thorough investigations that we'll get better value for money if we speed it all up and do it in a year,' Cyril cajoled.

'Professor Huckett, it's not the purchase of the bins and vehicles that's the problem; they can be purchased from capital and we can borrow money until it's coming out of our ears. It's the revenue costs that are really bothering me and the cost of building your so called sorting plant,' she said, her eyes resting on the Head of Planning whose stutter prevented him from engaging in conversation at that point, 'Cyril, I'm concerned about the running costs. How will we afford to run the damn thing? Have you even considered this problem?' She asked hoping he would tell her she was wrong.

The Leader could see the advantages of having the factory built on the Beverly and came to Cyril's rescue.

'I do assure you Irene that we've given the matter serious thought,' he lied, 'do you remember, Cyril, you were only saying yesterday that you must put the proposal in writing as soon as possible for the benefit of the Finance Department?' The Leader supported him.

'Yes indeed, David. Irene you need have no fears on that account. You'll have something on paper by the end of the week,' Cyril promised.

'Well that is good to hear. I do have a suggestion that you may wish to think about,' Irene hesitated. Her suggestion would not go down well she knew, because it would be coming from a mere woman who knew nothing about waste management. Nevertheless, she was not known for her reluctance to come forward and in any case, she would never have got to where she was today without making her thoughts known to those who really did not want to hear them.

'Gentlemen, I would like to suggest that Cheatham invites a partner to work with it, perhaps another local council? I've heard that Padwick has a new Director of Environmental Services who is keen to give recycling a bit of a shove up the backside, pardon my French,' she laughed. Had she been drinking? Cyril and the Leader were wondering. Irene was suddenly giggling but although she appeared slightly sozzled she was still coherent. This woman clearly had no idea what she was talking about. Cheatham, enter a partnership with Padwick, their neighbouring council? How ridiculous. Cheatham could never share the glory of a successful recycling initiative. Neither uttered a word.

Cyril had no wish to sound churlish or to dismiss Irene's partnership idea out of hand, so he made some attempt at pretending he would consider her option seriously.

'Irene, partnership working sounds interesting but I really don't think that we want to be held back by the likes of Padwick. In any case the partnership idea is becoming rather blasé.' Cyril stopped when he could see Sir David was eager to add his own thoughts on the subject.

'Yes, yes, quite right Cyril. My dearest Irene,' Sir David adopted the fatherly figure approach, which did nothing for Irene, 'my dear, in the past there have been many occasions when we've invited Padwick to join us on all kinds of projects, haven't there Bob?' Sir David sought support from the Head of Planning but remembering his stutter went on before he could reply, 'yes Irene, there have been so many occasions and suffice it to say, the idea didn't work. I don't wish to go into any details but generally speaking Padwick's commitment was somewhat lacking. We can't jeopardise our recycling targets; you do see that don't you, dear? And lets remind ourselves that we now also have government targets to meet,' Sir David prattled.

'Sir David, I understand completely the need to meet targets, indeed, I have targets to meet too. Working with a partner will half our capital and revenue expenditure and reduce our risk. I have spoken to Adrian Moses-Pomfrey and I also understand that selling the recycled materials is another risky business because of yo-yo markets. We can't rely on such an irregular return on our investment to fund this *MRF* thing,' she concluded leaving them to think more on the issue.

Cyril had been considering the need to save money and wanted to show solidarity with Irene.

'Let me tell you how I propose to reduce our waste tonnages,' he began. Irene was keen to hear Cyril's pearls of wisdom. 'I'm thinking of shutting our Brookfields Civic Amenity site for three days each week, which will cut our waste down substantially,' Cyril announced. Dingle was all ears now since this was another piece of news to him. What was the dolt talking about? Now Huckett had announced it, Irene would hold him to it. The borough would be full of flytips by usually law abiding residents frustrated at getting to the site with their cars loaded just to find the place locked, barred and shuttered. Dingle's head was getting sore. Irene was smiling one of her, I'm gonna get you Huckett smiles, as she thanked Cyril for taking her concerns seriously before leaving for another meeting with the Social Services Department. Sir David watched her leave.

'I heard a new saying the other day, *lateral arabesque,* it's synonymous with a sideways move in an organisation's hierarchy. Apparently every employee tends to rise to his level of incompetence except where an employee is subject to a lateral arabesque. In this case the employee or the incompetent gets a new title and a job which doesn't have as much clout as perhaps the employee might have had previously,' Sir David said, tucking his hands inside the pockets of his check waistcoat and nodding in Irene's direction.

Bob Mason, Head of Planning was keen to get a word in.

'With rega-rrrr-d to planning permi-ssss-ion, Irene has a pppp-oint. We expect it to ggggg-o to a ppp-public inquiry. Pppp-utting it anywhere on The Beverly Estate will cause u-ppp-roar amongst the co-mmmm-unity. It will be such a dog to get through!' Bob Mason's short speech completed, he relaxed back into his chair. His debilitating stutter had come on in recent years. His doctors put it down to stress caused by working for the Council with all its stops, starts and U-turns. Bob's last words about dogs got Sir David thinking. Residents were not supposed to keep dogs on the estate and yet he was always getting complaints about dog shit on the pavements and in the children's playground. This needed more thought.

The Mayor was looking forward to a night of alternative civic duties with his loveable dumpling.

'What excuse are you making tonight Marcus?' The sexy black Chief Executive asked him.

'Oh usual thing, I shouldn't wonder; late night working party,' Marcus replied.

'You know where the key is, don't you, babe? Just come straight in,' Maisie invited. It sounded like an offer he simply could not refuse.

'See you about eight then my sweet little black pudding,' Marcus called as he put away his mobile phone, straightened his tie and admired himself in his bedroom mirror. Virginia was out at some women's meeting so he was free to splash on some expensive after shave without arousing any suspicion.

Marcus arrived at Maisie's door at the allotted time and let himself in. Before he had managed to close the door, she was slapping lots of big kisses all over his face and as soon as she had tired of that, she led him to her lounge where the lights were dimmed.

'What no sensual music tonight?' Marcus smiled, showing off his stained teeth.

'Marcus, please don't take offence but I thought with your recent little problem, and I know that it is only a temporary problem, my sweetie and happens quite often to men of your age,' she said hesitantly, 'I mean people of our age do sometimes experience problems, don't they?' Maisie sympathised. 'To cut a long story short, Marcus, I have something so much better than music for us tonight, my dearest lover. I've got something that is going to make every hair on your body tingle and every muscle throb with sheer delight. Tonight, we're going to enter the world of ecstasy,' Maisie promised.

Marcus looked vague but excited. He also thought that she must be on something as he had never seen her this intoxicated before. And another thing, all this talk about *ecstasy* worried him somewhat. He did not want to get busted for drugs. Adultery he could cope with, but narcotics were a whole different ball game. He dwelt for a second on the possible headlines, *Mayor banged up for drug offences.* This could never be but whilst he allowed his mind to wander, Maisie was disrobing and was already down to her suspenders, which were attached to an extra large suspender belt made especially for her by the larger woman shop in the high street. White lacy stockings were pinned to her belt and there were no knickers. She popped on a kimono and started to undress Marcus who was now entering into the full spirit of the game with gay abandon.

Maisie pressed play on the dvd player and settled down with Marcus in his jockey shorts to watch a sexy film that did the trick. Afterwards they talked about wheeled bins.

'Did you know Cyril's plan is that only families of six or eight will be allowed to have a large wheeled bin? He's a complete arsehole,' Marcus commented.

'Marcus, stop thinking shop and don't mention those ugly bins when you're here with me. I'm not the slightest bit interested in big bins,' Maisie told him. Wheeled bins were not the usual post coital conversation that she was used to.

As Marcus prepared to leave Maisie's flat he caught sight of his figure in Maisie's mirror for the second time that day and admired his physique. His recent sexual rebirth had caused him to suffer a sudden rush of narcissism. For a pensioner he could not help but praise himself for being in spectacular shape. A little skinny perhaps but hell, he was sure he could still give many of the young blokes at the Civic Offices a good run for their money. He finished dressing and went to the front door with Maisie following closely behind clad only in her black silk kimono.

'Goodnight my roly poly, darling. See you again soon I hope,' he said feeling relaxed and happy, 'tip top, Maisie my love, tip top,' he called as he slipped away down the stairs.

Chapter 18

Cyril's absurd mania to push Cheatham to the top of the recycling league tables was growing manic by the day.

'What's our recycling rate doing at the moment?' Cyril asked Adrian.

'It's excellent, Councillor. We're achieving a fifty one percent recycling rate in the trial areas,' Adrian reported coolly.

'It's good, but it's not good enough, I'm afraid,' Cyril said shaking his head.

'It's early days yet. We'll have the whole borough on the scheme within the next four or five months and the recycling rate will go sky high, I'm sure of it. You can't fail to have your eighty five percent recycling rate by the summer months,' Adrian explained. Cyril was thinking more deeply.

'Adrian, how do we calculate the recycling rate?' Cyril asked.

'I take the total amount of waste we send to landfill excluding trade waste, naturally. I add this to the amount we recycle such as the dry recyclables, the recycling banks and of course the garden waste and then I work out the recyclables as a percentage of the whole lot,' Adrian said making it sound a straightforward calculation.

'So what if you forgot to include some waste? Would that bump up the recycling figures? What if we then included the abandoned car and road planning tonnages?' Cyril was visibly sweating as he contemplated skulduggery and his devious plan to increase the recycling rate.

'Well Sir, I don't think it's usual to add those other categories into the equation. Wouldn't it be cheating?' Adrian suggested.

Adrian had his Corporate Membership of the Chartered Institution of Wastes Management to consider. It would do his career absolutely no good at all to be dishonoured in this way.

'Cheating! Good Lord, Adrian. What do you take me for? I'm a respected LIP councillor for a London borough. I'm not representing one of those Labour dens of iniquity up north. I should make you go and wash your mouth out, son,' Cyril retorted.

'Councillor, I'm really not sure about not following the government's guidance on how to calculate a recycling rate? What about external auditors like the Audit Commission?' Adrian was worried about his own reputation.

'Well OK. There must be some other way of keeping the waste figures down. I'll think on that one for a bit,' Cyril acceded.

'I'll work on recalculating the rate including the other things that you suggest just so you can see what it would work out but I don't recommend that you use it on any official forms,' Adrian advised. Adrian trusted Cyril not to submit his recalculations as he was after all a respectable public servant and if anything should go wrong with that theory, Cyril, he believed would naturally put his hands up and take the blame squarely on his own shoulders.

Cyril was thinking about creative accounting.

'Can we include something for home composting?' He asked feeling desperate.

'I'm afraid not, Councillor. You see it can't be measured so it's not included in the formula,' Adrian explained.

'For God's sake!' Cyril blasphemed. He was tired of being told what he could and could not include by just a bit of a boy. It was simply ridiculous. 'Look, I don't want any more nonsense. Add in half a tonne for every household we've issued a composter to,' he demanded. Adrian was gobsmacked. Half a tonne in just kitchen waste? He was wondering where the councillor's grasp of common sense had gone. The recycling rate was fast becoming just a figment of Cyril's vivid imagination and totally unrelated to the facts. 'Thirty thousand composters at half a tonne each gives us another fifteen thousand tonnes to play with. I'll get the coffees whilst you, Adrian, redo the sums using the extra tonnages we've just been discussing. I'll be back in two ticks,' Cyril searched his back pocket for coins and taking an empty stationery box lid to use as a tray, popped outside to the vending machine.

Adrian re-calculated the recycling rate and was able to inform Cyril on his return that they had now achieved a fifty five percent recycling rate. Cyril was relieved to hear it but was still not satisfied.

'Hmm. I'll have to give this recycling rate malarkey a bit more thought,' he told Adrian. 'I want a report on our recycling performance so that I can present it to the Performance Committee in a couple of weeks' time. Get on with it will you. Make sure you give it to Mr Dingle to peruse before the final edition, and thank you for all your work. You've been extremely helpful,' Cyril extolled. Adrian, he believed, was indeed a real asset and one that could be easily moulded at that. 'Adrian, there's something else. What about if we were to close the civic amenity site on two or three days a week? If we stop residents taking their waste up there that would reduce our tonnage figures wouldn't it?' Cyril asked.

'Waste has to go somewhere, Councillor. If people can't take it to the site, where will they take it?' Adrian was only pointing out the obvious.

'Obviously, they'll keep it in their garages a bit longer and soon enough they'll get the waste minimisation message,' Cyril answered. Adrian wondered if this man was living on the same planet as everyone else.

'Sir, if I might just say that what I think will actually happen is that we'll end up sending our cleansing teams out to pick up more fly tips,' Adrian said having a brave moment.

'Good point there, Adrian. Let's look again at just omitting the tonnages in the first place. Blow the government's guidance. We'll cope with any questions if they arise,' Cyril said, throwing caution to the wind.

The contamination reports for the recycling wheeled bin rounds were arriving thick and fast and Cyril was forced to meet with John Dingle and Adrian to see what could be done about it. Even Cyril had noticed the problem on recycling days in his own ward. As he walked along the road to the bus stop the stench emanating from the bins was disgusting. John had written to Cyril to say that Aurelia Waste Handling Ltd. was strongly suggesting that the material being delivered to their Middlesex plant was plain muck.

'I'm afraid, Cyril, it's not good news. For the time being at least Aurelia has agreed to go on taking the stuff because they say they want to be helpful and they realise that Cheatham's residents are still getting used to the new scheme. Unfortunately, the only option open to them for the waste is to either landfill it or burn it,' Dingle revealed.

Dingle placed Aurelia's letter on the table in front of Cyril but his thoughts were elsewhere.

'I don't care where the bloody stuff ends up. It can go to Timbuktu as far as I'm concerned, just as long as Adrian remembers to add it into the recycling rate calculation. It'll be our little secret. No one need ever find out,' Cyril whispered manically. Adrian and John were staggered by the depth to which Cyril was prepared to plummet.

'John, how many enforcement officers do we have?' Cyril asked.

'The last enforcement officer we had went to Padwick and we haven't had the funding to replace him. The Council introduced a moratorium and the post was frozen,' Dingle explained.

'We must do something about that. We must somehow employ a whole string of enforcement officers to talk to residents and make them use their bins properly,' Cyril insisted getting back on track.

'We could really do with some joined up enforcement,' Dingle admitted, 'we have problems in other areas too, like street cleaning and of course there is the Leader's pet subject, dog fouling. But how do we go about employing them when we've no money allocated in the budget?' Dingle asked. *Joined up enforcement*, Cyril liked the sound of that.

There had been a lot of talk about *joined up* everything in recent months. They called them, cross cutting services and the experts had been banging on about this idea at the last Strategy Committee. *Joined up enforcement* with the Waste Management Team? He doubted whether they knew how to do joined up writing but still it would sound very good to the policy writers.

'Get on to one of your employment agencies as quick as you can and take on enough enforcement officers to look after the new wheeled bin rounds,' Cyril insisted as he wondered how on earth he would persuade Irene that he needed even more money than the six million he had been allocated. It was time to crack open another bottle of home-made dandelion wine before he broached that one, he decided.

Unaware of the impending recycling rate storm, Gary Newton, the intellectual, was reading things. The latest issue of *Sweeping and Refuse Collection News* carried an article that could have major repercussions for the services. At the very least it would provide fertile ground for a bed of unrest at the depot, Gary considered.

'You wanna read this Mick and Reg. It says that wheelie bins and dustmans' lungs do not go together. They're saying that some study carried out in Scandinavia found that dustmen are more likely to have chest infections. They're at risk of *respiratory tract inflammation,* is what it says. It's the organic waste which is the worst, apparently. Well, they say it's a real health hazard. It's because we only collect it fortnightly, you see. It has time to degrade, they call it, *putrefaction.* It gives it time to release potentially harmful discharges and when the dustmen go to empty the bins and they open the lids, the *bio aerosols* fly out and the men breathe them in,' Gary explained, completely wrapped up in his reporting, 'it's true alright Mick. I'm only glad I'm with Street Cleansing. They tested their sputum, Reg. That's how they knew all this,' Gary explained.

'Do you mind, Gar? We're trying to drink our coffee. Why d'yer 'ave to mention spit for?' Reg shouted almost spilling his drink.

'I'm just telling you because the article says that dustmen suffer long term respiratory illnesses from collecting rubbish and recyclables as well.

'But Gary there is nothing we can do about it apart from making them all wear masks and that will just scare the living daylights out of the residents. Change the subject for Christ sakes,' screamed Reggie as Bobby Dalton came to the allocation window, 'or we'll have a strike on our hands and right now that's the last thing we need,' Reg finished just in time.

'Hello Bobby. What can we do for you mate?' Micky Brown asked.

'I've just had a call on my mobile from Brewer. He's smashed his leg getting out of the cab and says he tried to get through on the radio but couldn't and the phones were engaged as well. One of the crew has called an ambulance. I'm finished so if you like I'll go and finish his round for him?'

'Thanks Bobby, that would be decent of you,' Mick said turning to Larry, 'Larry get over to Brewer and wait with 'im and Bobby until the ambulance gets there. You'd better go with 'im to the 'ospital too. Make sure he gets a proper check. Don't let 'im discharge 'imself without seeing a doctor,' Mick knew the drivers better than they knew themselves, 'oh, and Larry, we'll need an accident report form filled in,' Mick shouted as Larry hurried out of the office. Mick turned back again to Gary Newton. 'You see, Gary, the crews have enough trouble as it is without them having to worry about bio aerosols in their bleeding sputum as well,' Micky explained.

Chapter 19

The whole recycling gambit had become a political game with several main players. These were the Council, the Council's Officers, the three pressure groups and Cheatham's residents who were awarded little bit parts and might be considered as extras as in the film industry.

Labour's Band of Brothers were still holding their meetings at Alfie Leadbetter's house on the Beverly Estate and as luck would have it, Alfie picked up on a give-away remark by one of the Planners at the Development Control Committee he sat on that the Beverly was to be the location for the new Recycling Factory. This was an unbeknown banana skin for the LIP and the Band of Brothers excitedly discussed how they might best drop the bad news on the Beverly's residents. The fact that fifty jobs overall would be created for the unemployed on the beleaguered estate was brushed aside as the thought of all that pollution from proposed industrial processes was too good an opportunity to miss. Alfie hatched his plan for the benefit of the brotherhood.

'I say we contact the Cheatham Star,' Alfie began, 'that Tim fellow, what's 'is name, Tim Bevin? Alfie paused for a second, 'd'yer think he was related to Ernest?' Alfie could not contain his glee.
'I think, Alfie, the newspaper man to whom you allude is called, *Baldwin*,' the Labour Party
Leader corrected.
'Well, whatever it is I suppose I'd have to concede that *Baldwin* is an acceptable name
even if it is from Tory stock,' he twittered. 'Anyway, as I was saying Clegg, why don't you contact Tim whatever 'is name is and tell him you've heard that the LIP are up to something. Explain they're scheming to pass planning consent for a recycling factory without consulting the public. Just say you've grave concerns about the dust and noise that such a factory will bring with it. I want you to really lay it on with a trowel by suggesting that it will blight the lives of those poor unfortunate residents who being on low incomes won't be able to up sticks and move away and escape the polluted environment that the factory will produce. You could also mention something about the LIP ideals, about them claiming to be greener than green and yet don't care when it comes to poor disadvantaged folk. Meet Timmy in person, don't be satisfied with his secretary,' Alfie was emphatic, 'and Clegg, remember Sweeney Todd the Demon Barber! Use your thespian skills from your wartime dalliance in amateur dramatics to get your point across. Who knows perhaps at the end of this little campaign of ours we'll have a lot of LIP meat pies to sell off!' Alfie said feeling the battle was already won.

Clegg, along with others in the room felt they really needed to reflect on the bigger picture.
'I'll contact Tim Baldwin but most of us think that a better approach would be to show
integrity, or at least make it look as though we have some,' the Chair remarked, 'we must
somehow get across to the Press that we're not just gung-ho but do in fact have some
convictions,' the Chair chewed his lip and waited for a response. Alfie laughed out loud.

'Do yer mean convictions like our ex-member Ruben Butler? He had a conviction for bootlegging booze from the Calais hypermarket,' Alfie squealed. Clegg quickly put an end to the eschewing laughter.

'You see Alfie, please don't take this as a put down but we want the support of Cheatham's residents from all wards, not just the Beverly Estate. We want everyone to see us as potential leaders at the next election. We want to appeal to all and we want them to have respect for our Party,' the others were nodding at this picture of morality and complete honesty that Clegg was painting, 'the residents of Stonebridge Ward won't exactly thank us for only taking the helm
on behalf of the Beverly residents, will they? I've a jolly good idea that residents in other wards wouldn't care twopence what went up on the Beverly Estate. The LIP could build a fully fledged incinerator there and we wouldn't hear a murmur from the rest of the borough,' Clegg maintained.

Alfie Leadbetter was not as white as the driven snow and thought a bit of moral turpitude went a long way at times. He genuinely had his misgivings about the new waste services but he had discovered a loop hole that might well furnish his own bank account with a golden nest egg. If his little scam paid off, it would allow him to retire gracefully and even to give up being a councillor. The down side to this would be giving up the ten thousand pounds he received each year for just being elected. There was, shall we say, just a little bit of the rogue in Councillor Alfie Leadbetter.

As a member of the Area Planning Committee for the Beverly Ward and past experience of the building trade, Alfie knew a few tricks of the trade. His niece had married into the industry and now had a double barrelled surname. She had hitched her wagon to a well respected building firm with a good track record but Alfie knew there was always a few bob to be had for tipping the wink in the case of building contracts. What harm did it do? The customers achieved their buildings at a good price and some lucky people like himself also received a slice of the cake. What was it his mother used to say? Alfie pondered, as he stepped out of his bath and pulled a fluffy environmentally friendly green towel around him, God helps them who helps themselves, that was it right enough, that was what she used to spell out to him.

The next day Alfie telephoned his niece and nephew, Stella and Mark Denton-Beckett inviting them to have lunch with him at the Cheatham Hilton. This would set him back a few bob he considered but it was good to keep up family relationships. Stella had just had a birthday so he had the perfect reason for contacting them. There is no such thing as a free lunch, Alfie toyed. You have to speculate to accumulate, he reminded himself. The lunch went well and Mark Denton-Beckett was fascinated to hear Alfie outline the Council's plans and the possibility of a new contract for what would be a state of the art recycling factory and more to the point, a potential contract for Denton-Beckett Partnerships. Mark and Alfie spoke the same language. They both believed whole heatedly in the Adam Smith, *invisible hand theory,* that self interest is the way forward. Or, in other words, keep your eyes glued on getting new contracts and the world will look after itself.

Alfie filled Mark in on the usual rounds that applications must take and on the budgetary constraints that Cheatham was facing. It was expected that the application, filed conveniently by Cheatham's own Planning Department would pass through all of its stages with scant interest paid to any of the usual planning conditions. A contractor would then be appointed and naturally, the Council would need to be seen to be taking note of any European competition rules and advertising in the European Journal, but hey, worst things have happened! At Alfie's suggestion, Mark started work straight away on architectural plans for a revolutionary new Materials Recycling Facility. It was only when Alfie mentioned the idea during their Hilton lunch date that Mark had ever heard of such a thing as a MRF before. Still, no problem, stranger contracts had come his way and recycling was certainly topical.

The next step was to cold call on Cheatham Council and send in some company literature. Alfie had told Mark of Cyril's obsession with size. That the plant must be bigger and better than the one built in Garden Greenville. Mark made detailed investigations sending his minions far and wide to research any new developments. Representatives of Denton-Beckett Partnerships flew to the USA and Canada to see what was flavour of the month in New York and Toronto. He sent others to Europe to find out what the Austrians, Germans and Italians were up to and he could not believe the number of technological advances for waste treatment facilities that came back to him.

Mark put his most experienced engineers on the job of designing a recycling factory using all the latest ideas. The result was a sorting plant that was fit for a king or at the very least a London council that wanted to be at the cutting edge of the waste industry. All these ideas were incorporated into glossy, full colour literature. He even had a film made with sexy artistic impressions using the latest in graphics to promote Denton-Beckett Partnership's MRF design. All in all, it was just about the best promotional campaign for a MRF and a MRF builder that you could ever hope to see. To top it all the company adopted a new strap line, *Respect for Recycling! Pick the Best.*

Cyril met with Bob Mason to discuss planning consent tactics for the MRF. The very suggestion that the LIP would pull a fast one and try to squeeze through a planning application without fully consulting the electorate was preposterous. Cyril had heard the rumours too and he knew he must prevent them from getting to the ears of the local newspapers. His dilemma was complicated further by the need to move his programme forward or else be out of step with his timetable.

'Bob, I want to scotch these silly tales about us not consulting with residents on whether they would like to have a sorting plant built on their doorsteps; as if we'd do such a thing?' Cyril glanced at Bob who frowned in sympathy. 'It's daft really. If they'd thought about it sensibly they'd realise that the recycling factory will provide so much employment. They should be jumping at the chance,' Cyril went on. Bob was afraid that he would be jettisoned into an explosion of stuttering if he tried to answer so he merely nodded in the affirmative. 'What are we to do Bob? We've surveyed the wheeled bin trial areas and that has indicated a resounding *yes* to our new service. I don't want to end up having a public enquiry because some stupid busy body living on the dole with all the time in the world objects to my scheme and thereby ruins the chance of permanent employment for everyone else,' Cyril explained having forgotten about his moral stance just a few seconds earlier. Bob racked his brains for a solution.

The speech challenged Chief Planner came up with a cunning plan literally speaking.

'Cyril,' Bob began, stuttering whilst unfurling a outline drawing of the Beverly Estate. The plan showed the footprint and dimensions of the site to scale showing all the houses and blocks on the Beverly Estate, 'you'll see thththat the site is on the boundddary and lies close to park landddd used by the estate's residddddents. I would like to ppppropose that we build the plant on the pppark landdd and release the land from the old laundry and coke store for reinstatement into a park. We can dress it up with the promise of a new swimming ppppool and even skating rink for residents use only,' Bob relaxed, exhausted. Cyril was smiling. There was more to Bob than met the eye. What a cracking idea; swimming pools and skating rinks. Cyril thought if would do the trick. Residents would not be able to turn down such wonderful new facilities. The local residents' group had been crying out for better recreational facilities for the kids.

'What Joy! We offer them a piece of land which is nearer to them and in turn makes it easier for them to watch the kids,' Cyril winked at Bob Mason, 'meanwhile we get the present parkland category changed to Light Industrial Class B and Bob's your Uncle, if you will pardon the expression,' Cyril chuckled. 'We can build on the industrial land without having to invite everyone to comment. Naturally, if residents want to come along to your offices, Bob and see the plan, they'll be entitled to do so, won't they?' Cyril asked. Bob nodded.

Bob had something else to say and was struggling to drum up the effort to begin.

'I've checked with the Mayor of Londdddon's Waste Strategy Ddddepppartment and they tell me that sites earmarked for recycling will get support from the Mayor because such developments are not considered to be *bad neighbours*. It's unlikely that the Mayor would object to plans for new sorting facilities. He actually wants more processing facilities not less and he wants waste treated within the borough in which it arises,' Bob managed, now feeling relaxed, knowing that Cyril would be very pleased to hear he would be in the Mayor's good books.

'Oh how marvellous, Bob. You are indeed a sly old fox,' Cyril congratulated him and telling him to start straight away on getting his henchmen to draw up plans for the new park and sporting features and to announce them omitting all mention of the proposed new recycling factory on the adjacent land. As Cyril left the meeting he did just wonder how on earth a bloke with such a dreadful stutter managed to get an executive head's job that entailed public speaking? Life was so baffling.

Cyril next arranged a meeting with Sir David and invited Russell Webster along.

'This is kind of difficult,' he began, causing a sense of unease to pervade the room, 'we're all aware of the challenges we're facing at the moment which are nothing, might I add, that we can't cope with. We're still in the trial stages of a revolutionary new way of doing things which is bound to bring with it a certain amount of teething problems. Be assured gentlemen, we will solve them,' Cyril paused and as he did so Sir David and Russell took the opportunity to glance at each other. They did not need Cyril to remind them of the so called teething problems. The daily post and high street demonstrations did that. The Leader did not like Cyril's use of the word 'we' either because he had no intention of putting his own head on the block should Cyril's teething problems cause the nasty brown stuff to eventually hit the fan. Russell had his own concerns, since he had heard that the Tory Group had joined forces with the Cheatham Recycling Champions, local 'do-gooders' with lots of time on their hands for any noble cause that came their way.

Sir David who had other more sporty things on his mind hurried Cyril along.
'The bowls club beckons old man, hurry up,' the Leader encouraged. Cyril continued.
'We're getting some negative reports from Aurelia Waste Handling. Apparently the materials we're sending are, if I might use their own phraseology, pure and unadulterated muck. Well of course they're being totally unreasonable. It really can't be as bad as all that. Cheatham residents' have consistently told us, and you know this as well as I do David, that they want more recycling so why would they cock it up by contaminating it? It has to be a fault at Aurelia's end; their equipment I should think is faulty or more likely Aurelia has been approached by another council keen to sign a contract with them and ruin Cheatham's chances of success. Aurelia is also trying to get us to sign up to a thirty year contract before we've had time to really think it through,' Cyril announced.

The Leader liked Aurelia Waste Handling Ltd. The company had come to his rescue once and as a result he had the delightful Judy Craig working wonders in Cheatham's schools and assisting his every need although he had not asked her make the ultimate sacrifice and was unlikely to do so, it just was not his style. Even so, he cherished having her around the place and was adamant that Cyril would not frighten her off.
'What does John Dingle have to say about Aurelia's comments and this new contract?' The Leader asked.
'Dingle has concerns too. Aurelia has landfilled so many of our loads because it says it just can't risk putting the stuff through its nice new machinery, which is a bit of a change to when they first tried to convince us they were the answer to all our prayers, eh?' Cyril smirked, conveniently forgetting to mention that Dingle had no idea about the contract.

Russell Webster was bored and was wondering what his part in this meeting might be.
'Councillor, what is it that you propose to do to improve the situation?' He asked.
'Business tycoons like Augustus Aurelia are only interested in us for one reason and for one reason only, money making! I would like to propose that we look further afield and to a different kind of company. One in which we can be a full partner and have total control of our affairs. I have invited Crappendale City's own arms length commercial company, Crappendale Associates, to come to Cheatham as soon as possible and give us a presentation on what they can do for us. I've also ordered a selection of plastic trees which I know you are keen on David, especially the palm trees. I've seen them in their sales catalogue lit up with gorgeous red and gold fairy lights. Magnificent they look. I've instructed Mr Cherry in the Parks Department to install them in Cheatham High Street. You see you have to install a plastic tree, not like real trees which you plant,' Cyril prattled on whilst Russell was still unclear as to why he had been summoned to the meeting.

'Councillor, what about these dreadful rumours I've been hearing about a recycling sorting facility on the Beverly Estate?' Russell asked, feeling he needed some answers if he was to get on and do his job properly.

'Oh yes, quite,' an apprehensive Cyril replied, 'you won't have to worry about that anymore. I've sorted that with Bob Mason.' Sir David looked surprised as he had only recently heard the suggestion himself and now it would seem the ink was already dry. 'Yes indeed, it's all in hand. There'll be no more problems with the Beverly residents; I can assure you on that score. We're going to give them a splendid new leisure centre complete with skating rink and a brand new park right on their doorstep. No need for them to trek over the muddy field to the swings any more. We're getting estimates as I speak and Russell, if you would speak to Bob Mason, difficult, I know with that confounded stutter of his, but try anyway and get a press release out ASAP. I've already spoken to the Estate's committee. They're absolutely crazy about the idea and agree residents will be over the moon with the plans.' Cyril was swallowing glasses of water like they expected a drought.

'Ehm, Cyril,' began Sir David, who was somewhat shocked at the pace Cyril seemed to be moving and in the manner he appeared to be seizing power, 'what about the Council's committees and the usual channels through which these kinds of decisions are normally taken? How can you make such drastic decisions without consulting your colleagues on the Strategy and Scrutiny Committees to say nothing of the electorate?' Sir David was restrained by the fact that Russell was sitting with them. He wished that Cyril had spoken to him privately first. Russell took the hint and left the room to organise some hot beverages.

'David, think about the future. I've had to work fast to stave off any counter attack by the Tories and that hopeless Band of Brothers. We do have a problem with contamination, I just didn't want to admit to it in front of Russell but if we control it by putting it through our own sorting plant we can keep it under wraps and can win through, I'm sure of it. We can keep it a secret and nobody need know the true extent of the problem; what do you think?' Cyril said wondering why he was having to explain himself to Sir David whom he knew wanted fame and glory as much as he did himself. 'The new MRF can be built at the same time as the new leisure centre. I have a contractor waiting in the wings, it's a company called Denton Beckett Partnerships. They appear to be the best in the country and their literature is very appealing. I haven't shown the plan to Russell or Judy yet, for obvious reasons,' Cyril uncharacteristically winked at Sir David.

Sir David was beginning to see that Cyril might be right and there could well be some mileage in Cyril's plan. It certainly would not be good for the papers to pick up any signs of discontent amongst the LIP as they would have a field day and the opposition would rip them to pieces. Cyril was right. The LIP had made their bed and now they must lie on it. They must cover up their mistakes as best they could and stick to their manifesto.

'Just one thing, Cyril,' the Leader said, 'if all the recycling materials are being landfilled, how is our recycling rate doing? Are we going to meet our own ambitious targets?' Sir David asked as
Russell eased his way back into the room, shoulder to the door carrying three vending cups of hot coffee.

'Oh yes, yes, yes. What we do is we turn a blind eye to the contaminated materials and count everything that comes out of the recycling bins as if it's being sorted for recycling. No one will ever know the difference unless you tell them, will they?' Cyril was looking directly at Russell who, although wearing a look of utter disbelief thought it better to agree at this stage and think of the consequences later.

Sir David, realising the trouble they might incur if this strategy escaped into the wrong hands came to the rescue.

'Eh, Russell, you and your team have been doing a splendid job on the communications front. The Council thinks that you should get some sort of extra remuneration. I have given it some thought and I think another three thousand pounds on your salary might just about cover it. How does that sound?' Russell, struck dumb by this generous announcement managed a nod. 'Good,' replied the Leader, 'I'll speak to the Head of Human Resources and arrange an honorarium straight away.' Russell brightened as the day suddenly got better.

The three of them hatched a plan to appease the rest of the LIP members. They needed to find a way of getting the necessary stamps on all the statutory pieces of paper confirming that the decisions had been discussed properly and that the normal democratic process had been adhered to. There were ways and means and Sir David knew of a few of them. There were emergency orders for one thing and he intended to study the Cerise Book of Council Rules as soon as he got back to his office. Cyril was feeling more confident now that he had Sir David on his side and as he made his way home the final words of Lord Horatio Nelson drifted through his head, *now I am satisfied. Thank God, I have done my duty.* Unfortunately Cyril had forgotten the circumstances in which Nelson uttered those fateful words, his deathbed following a sniper's bullet and history often repeats itself.

Aurelia Waste Handling Ltd. was told that its services would no longer be required once the new Cheatham MRF was built which would be at breakneck speed. Planning Permission went through without a hitch as the Beverly residents were too busy watching the development of their new leisure facilities and arguing about the colour of the walls and whether the crèche would be dirt cheap or not. Mark Denton-Beckett told his wife to start looking for a bigger house and Alfie Leadbetter began eating in Cheatham's best restaurants and look for somewhere more up market to live, somewhere well away from the Beverly Estate and more fitting to his new bank balance. Judy decided to extend her secondment to Cheatham which pleased Sir David. He had no idea that his protege was growing fonder as the days grew longer of Tim Baldwin, the enemy editor of the Cheatham Star.

Chapter 20

Winter at the depot was such a miserable time of year. Gary Biddles was glad of his anorak which was once again firmly in place on his back. June Turner, complete with alluring off the shoulder skimpy tops and dangly earrings was making her mark as a supervisor and strongly resisting the chance to make the tea insisting that she did plenty of that at home. Reggie kept out of June's way except when a dispute arose and he was required to play Solomon and make a judgement.

'Micky, I don't care what you think, my June is not doing the early shift and that's final. How are we gonna get our kids to school?' Reggie asked a desperate Micky faced once again with staff shortages.

'Fairs fair, Reg, how can I face the blokes? I can't keep asking them to come in early when one of the supervisors isn't pulling her weight, now can I? Juney should do the same shifts as everyone else. We can't have favouritism, mate,' Micky was ground down by the wheeled bin problems and added to that now was the inter-supervisor fighting caused mainly by the fact that the Refuse Manager's wife was getting preferential treatment, 'anyway Reg, your kids are old enough to get themselves off to school now. They're all at secondary schools aren't they?' Micky asked.

Micky Brown was suffering from battle fatigue. The gradual degeneration in his health was beginning to tell on his face where more ingrained lines than before the wheeled bin saga were appearing. His cigarette habit had increased and he spent more and more time standing in the yard smoking his fags, polishing his MK 3 and wondering what he would do with all the lotto money he was going to win.

It had rained for days. The yard was flooded and even this place of refuge had ceased to be such an escape from the fax, radio and telephone. It was not a pleasant place to be. The drains were blocked and a backwash from the sewerage works down the road was definitely a health hazard.

'What the fucking hell are we doing 'ere?' Mick complained to Slump as they tried in vain to sweep the acrid waters away from the office doors and out onto the main road.

'I keep asking meself the same question, Mick. Sometimes I feel like a bloody mushroom.' Slump looked over at Micky who had momentarily stopped swirling the waters with his broom and stood staring at Slump, waiting for an explanation, 'you know, like a mushroom, kept in the dark and fed on shit,' Slump explained.

Micky was thoughtful. Slump was quite right; they were never told exactly what was going on.

'All those bloody meetings,' Micky said despairingly, 'at first I thought the Council was entering into the spirit of consultation with us but I was dead wrong. All those meetings with *Cyril bleeding Huckett* were just an exercise so the Council could tick all the right boxes. At one point I thought of putting up a sign saying, "are you feeling lonely? If the answer's yes, why not call a meeting..." Micky clasped the top of his broom with both hands and rested his head on top before continuing. 'We run round like blue arse flies to make everyfink look hunk bloody dory when those blinking stupid inspectors come round for their coveted Investors in People Award and all the time we're just covering up. You know what I mean?' Mick searched for his ciggys and lit one up, 'yer see, Slump, them meetings was just for bloody show, mate. It was the powers that be just going through the motions, pretending to take us into their confidence by asking for our opinions.'

Micky was stressed out and Slump tried a bit of humour to lighten his mood.

'Yeah, yer right, Mick. IIP should stand for Investors in Paper not Investors in People. Now all they got are complaints from residents and even more complaints from some of them snooty Councillors themselves,' Slump said scratching his blubbery belly.

'We've always had complaints and we've always had missed bags of rubbish but nowadays, nine times out of ten it's because they've forgotten to put their bloody stupid bins out at the right time,' Mick said, 'in the past it didn't matter because we'd enough men or resources, as that idiot wanker likes to call 'em, to just go out and pick the bloody stuff up, didn't we Slump?' Micky looked to his buddy for confirmation and Slump obliged by smiling back at him, 'now though, at the first hint of a missed bin, straightaway it's the Refuse Section's fault. Even if the resident has made a genuine mistake and admitted it, those stupid pricks that calls themselves councillors want me to send a crew out straight away to collect it,' a melancholy Micky Brown frowned as he placed his cigarette back in his mouth and motioned Slump to get swirling again.

The buzz of the radio called Micky inside to take a call.

'Yeah, Mick 'ere. Wheeled bin five, please go ahead,' he answered.

'Mick, Tony here. We've got a problem. We've just left Clover Drive and there's one very angry woman at number twenty-three. You can expect a call. I've given her your details.'

'Nice one, Tony,' Mick answered sarcastically thinking, oh God what now? 'What's the problem?'

'We collected a load of boxes stacked around her green bin. We all thought they were just a load of old cardboard boxes for recycling but turns out one of them had the kid's hibernating tortoise inside. Now how were we to bloody well know that? We're not blinking psychic are we, Mick?' A distraught HGV driver cried across the radio waves.

'Oh bloody roll on,' Mick replied, already visualising the newspaper headings; *callous council crushes boy's pet tortoise on unwanted wheeled bin scheme*. Huckett would come down on them like a tonne of bricks.

Sure enough an irate mother phoned and Micky had the unenviable task of trying to calm her down. There was no way he could magic the tortoise out of the freighter, not in one piece at any rate.

'Madam, we're really sorry about your son's tortoise. The Council can't apologise enough. The crew are very sorry too but I know it won't bring Maximillian back,' Mick grimaced at the posh name, 'we would like to make amends and were wondering if you would like us to get your son a replacement tortoise when they are available? A colleague has been in touch with a breeder and we think we can get one later on,' Mick explained.

The mishap had been passed to Adrian to sort out and he had turned up trumps by finding a tortoise breeder on the internet. College educated recycling officers sometimes had their uses, Mick acquiesced, however, Micky's peacemaking efforts were to no avail, because 'angry mother' went straight to the Cheatham Star and the following week there were photographs of a sad seven year old boy crying his eyes out for the benefit of the newspaper reporter, his mother standing next to him with her wheeled bin, the deep rooted cause of all the trouble. The next edition of the newspaper showed a smiling, grovelling Councillor Huckett handing over a brand new bicycle as well as the promise of a replacement tortoise in the late summer. Mick read the report and wondered wistfully whether he was likely to live as long as the average pet tortoise with all their escalating troubles!

Publicly, Cyril put on a brave face but in private he sulked and worried about the progress of his new scheme. On top of the wheeled bin problems, the Council was proposing more changes to the way it did business. If Micky Brown was feeling low, then Cyril was enveloped in a cloud of doom and gloom and sat reading through the latest document on local government reform. Cheatham had not long taken itself through the process which had resulted in the Strategy, Scrutiny and Performance Committees and the honary mayor and chief executive model that they had got used to. What now? This had to be Sir David's doing. It was all just at the wrong time. If only the Leader would just leave things alone until Cyril's wheeled bin revolution was complete. Residents would just find even more to complain about and all complaints thesedays ended up with a dig at the refuse and recycling services.

The government report was long and the diatribe could only be described as tedious, if it was anything. On the Leader's instruction, Maisie Atichitawomba had brought in consultants at nine hundred pounds a day to draft plans for a Cabinet styled government should the Council decide to go down that route. This could mean an elected mayor with a salary to equal that of Maisie's, if not more. Padwick had recently introduced a similar system, Cyril recalled, and their new mayor was romping all the way to the bank. Sir David, Cyril knew, would not stand for any dissent having made it crystal clear that he was only behind Cyril's wheeled bin scheme to a point. He was prepared to bathe in any sweet waters of success alongside Cyril should the Council reach the adopted and ambitious eighty five per cent recycling rate but he would not be taking the blame for any catastrophes attributable to Cyril's new recycling revolution.

Cyril read very little before he was snoozing in his favourite armchair, the local government reform report slithering to his feet whilst he dreamt. His dream was jumbled. He pictured Sir David getting a standing ovation as he set out his reasons for changing Cheatham's governmental regime. In the dream, the Leader reported on the intrinsic value of Cabinet styled government and he was going on about microeconomic theories of principal-agent relations in production teams. It was monotonous in the extreme but in spite of this everyone clapped heartily. Cyril moaned and shuddered in his sleep, his muscles moving involuntarily like a dog having a nightmare. His spirits were raised momentarily when he dreamt of meeting the Queen at Buckingham Palace at an honours ceremony. Unfortunately for Cyril these nice thoughts were dashed when the person receiving the honour revealed himself to be the Leader rather than Cyril. Cyril woke up sweating profusely and concerned that his glory days might be over before they had had a chance to get started. He needed something to cheer himself up and his thoughts turned to Edith.

Cyril was gleeful by the time he arrived at Edith's front door. He knew where the spare key was hidden and found her seated in her lounge surrounded by perfumed candles. There were incense sticks burning in three or four well chosen places around the room and the curtains were pulled together leaving just a slight gap for the daylight to peep through. Edith had furnished this room with oriental and Indian fabrics such as voluminous throws showing exotic birds and beautiful blossom covered trees, none of which grew in our own temperate climate. There were Persian rugs on the floor and giant scatter cushions covered in mysterious oriental patterns arranged around the feet of her three-piece suite. Cyril glanced upwards to see a wooden effigy of Ganesh, the Elephant God perched upon a little shelf. Edith offered Cyril an explanation.

'Ganesh is the Hindu God of prosperity. I like to have him up there just to bring me good luck,' she advised. Cyril nodded politely. Luck was not something that Edith usually relied upon. When it came to taking off her clothes and enjoying a bit of rumpy-pumpy, Edith was an expert.

'I could do with a little bit of good luck or even God luck,' Cyril laughed. He had not spent any length of time inside this room before and it suddenly dawned on him that it resembled a shrine. The relaxed atmosphere subdued him, making him ready for whatever was coming next.

Edith's house was a rambling Victorian gothic pile and for all Cyril knew, she had half a dozen other rooms each devoted to a different God. He was just beginning to see how chameleon like she was and he could not help wondering if she was thinking of donating her home to the National Trust on her death.

'Cyril, why don't you take off your tie? You don't usually wear a tie my darling do you?' Edith, the temptress, seductively tugged at Cyril's tie before she slunk down onto the floor. For the first time since entering the room, Cyril concentrated on Edith's dress. She was, like the room, hot, in a sensual sort of way, dressed head to toe in a flowing organdie robe of a pretty red shade. The robe was delightfully see-through and Cyril could see something beneath which he presumed was her underwear. Being the typical husband he was ill at ease in the Women's Wear Department. Edith motioned for Cyril to undress and whilst trying to decide what he should take off at this early stage of events, he concentrated on Edith's organdie robe satisfying himself at last that she was not wearing any underwear at all or if she was, it was extremely brief.

Whilst Cyril procrastinated on his striptease routine, Edith was wriggling about on the floor cushions, trying to get into a more comfortable pose. He decided to remove his old cord jacket for starters and then prudishly unzipped the flies of his battered gardening trousers, lowering them slowly and feeling like a West End actor, nervous before giving his performance. As he undressed, his eyes were focussed on the pulsating flesh that lay beneath Edith's flowing garment as she rolled over and picked up the hi-fi's remote control. The CD player burst into life with romantic Indian music causing Cyril to imagine himself the master of his own harem. He allowed himself to sink into the soft cushions and breathed in the intoxicating and soporific fumes of burning incense sticks.

Edith helped Cyril relax by caressing him in places that imparted such unimaginable joy, suddenly flinging herself upon him and guiding his hand to her own body.

'My darling Cyril,' she cried out happily, 'please touch me here, my love,' she whispered, placing his hand carefully on her secret place. 'Darling, have you ever read the Kama Sutra?' Edith asked in her most sultry manner. Before Cyril could answer, she continued, 'sweetheart, I have studied the Sutra but you're the first person that I've trusted enough to share it with. I bless the day you came along, my dear,' she said blowing him a kiss as she slipped her hand beneath a cushion and pulled out a version of the book of sexual pleasure complete with illustrations both uninhibited and brightly coloured. 'The Kama Sutra is such a wonderful book, Cyril. It sets out the act of love in every form,' Edith explained as she enjoyed Cyril's rough gardener's hands running all over her. The smell of incense and the Eastern aura surrounding them caused a certain intoxication, heightening the pleasures felt by both as they performed the sexual rituals in Edith's little book of love.

Tired and exhausted, they slipped into a trance from which they did not emerge for over an hour and still they yearned for more. Cyril had quite got into the swing of things and the biologist inside him was as keen as mustard to try out several more of the positions in order to derive as the book suggested, *optimum sexual pleasure.* The book was full of fighting talk and just reading it made them want to dabble again. It talked of Edith in the heat of passion, coiling herself around Cyril and absorbing his strikes readily. It talked of licking and sucking and all manner of activities that would lead them to the ultimate sexual pleasure.

They tried all the little book's positions until they were well and truly sated. Once their passions were spent, Cyril relaxed by flicking through the rest of the book reading out loud a section that he knew would galvanise the feminist in Edith.

'It says that the woman always concedes to any posture her male proposes to be in,' he waited for a reaction. She would not like the idea that she was totally subjugated to any man, Kama Sutra or not. Edith responded. Life is full of surprises. Her answer was not quite what Cyril expected.

'Now, Cyril that little book is so right. My libido and sense of satisfaction have reached zenith heights this afternoon. Now that could not have happened if I, as a woman, had objected to what many ignoraminouses outside refer to unnatural positions. You see, this is the whole point about the Kama Sutra. It sets the human spirit free. It takes away all the conditioning that we're normally subjected to. It puts the sensual urge uppermost.' As she finished her outburst she reached for Cyril's *langam,* the male instrument of love. Cyril did not have any views on whether his conditioning had been set free. He was overjoyed that at his age and by four o'clock in the afternoon he had managed to come three times and that was worth celebrating with another bash at *sexual congress,* as it said in the book.

It was dark by the time the amorous couple, de coupled and sat relaxed in Edith's kitchen drinking Indian tea, the natural beverage to round off their afternoon of divine unity. Cyril's thoughts drifted back to the new style of Cabinet government that Sir David was planning.

'Edith, poppet, what do you think about David's ideas on the Cabinet system?' Cyril asked

'Well Cyril, I have read up on it you know and the idea is that Cabinet members make decisions collectively. That means, my dear, that they'll share the credits and of course, the blame, when policies don't exactly go according to plan. No one person takes the blame, do you see? That has to be a good thing doesn't it especially when councils' thesedays have to make some very unpleasant decisions, like your wheeled bins Cyril? Now suppose that was to go dreadfully wrong,' Cyril looked aghast, 'only suggesting my love,' Edith added hastily, 'if we'd had a Cabinet style administration, we'd share the blame and take the consequences which would probably mean we'd get voted out at the next election,' she giggled.

Cyril smiled although his brain was racing wondering where the praise would be directed if his recycling service proved to be really successful. He believed that it might well manifest itself in another New Year's Honour for Sir David Hooper; another bloody gong to go with the one he already had, probably making him a Lord.

Edith deliberated over the assortment of chocolates in the box lying on the table, finally helping herself to a plain chocolate orange cream. The chocolates were a Christmas gift from a resident she had helped to the top of the Council's housing list, a genuine case. Edith had no hidden agendas unlike many of her colleagues and she included Sir David Hooper here. Somehow, Sir David had worked his magic for the sorting plant allowing the plans for the MRF to sail through the Area Planning Committee. The Scrutiny Committee had supported the plan for Cheatham to have its own MRF and the Strategy Committee had studied the plan in camera with only superficial discussion in public. Despite all committees being cross party, Sir David had achieved a miracle.

Edith was well aware that something was not quite kosher in the way that such plans had been passed but she was a senior LIP member and knew she had better toe the line. She kept her comments simple and revealed nothing of her true fears.
  'Cyril, with such a landslide victory and so many members who'd undoubtedly go with the flow and the general wish for change, you can be sure that the Cabinet system will win. I think it would be best to adopt the, *If you can't beat the blighters, then join them,* approach, don't you?' They kissed each other goodbye and Cyril walked home to his wife and their cold but economical house in Stonebridge.

In the Chief Executive's office alarm bells were ringing for a similar reason. Any new Cabinet system would make Maisie redundant. The whole point was that the elected mayor took over and ran the Council and its employees. Either Maisie would have to take early retirement or accept a post on a lower grade. The true fact of the matter was that if she stayed on she would have to take a back seat even though she had been reassured that her current salary would be protected for at least five years. These things happened to other staff not Chief Executives, Maisie thought. She poured out her troubles to Marcus.
  'Do you think that David will push this Cabinet idea of his through?' She was feeling fragile. 'I believe he needs to have some sort of referendum on the matter before he can go any further doesn't he, Marcus?' A small tear appeared in the corner of her eye. It was close to that time of the month when

women feel weepy at the drop of a hat. Marcus understood and put his arm around her bulky form as best he could.

'Now, now, don't get all upset. Nothing's happened yet and in any case what if it does? You my dear have so many talents. You would come out of it smelling of roses, my little treasure,' Marcus cuddled his lover finding his senses reacting to her perfume, 'the Council would have to pay you a handsome redundancy sum or failing that you would get a very good early retirement settlement,' he consoled her.

Marcus watched longingly as Maisie's breasts rose and fell, the spirit was willing but alas the body was weak. He had not been to Maisie's flat to partake of any intimate ding dong for a while now having succumbed to what is commonly known as erectile dysfunction. On the last occasion Maisie had attempted to arouse his vital organ by using all manner of toys and it was only after several attempts that Marcus had managed to rise to the occasion. His was only a temporary setback, he was sure. In his pocket he concealed a prescription for Sildenafil, more commonly known as Viagra. He had read up on his problem on the internet before getting up enough courage to visit his doctor.

Marcus was having difficulty finding the courage to discuss his problem fully with Maisie since she was still moaning about her possible future or lack of it within the Council.

'What sort of talents do you think I possess, Marcus?' She asked. The Mayor pulled a fine white cotton handkerchief from his trouser pocket and as he did so the prescription dropped to the floor. He hastened to pick it up but Maisie got there first. She unfurled it whilst Marcus spoke.

'Well my dear, you are very good on committees and working parties and you've had some very good experience running a local council. The government is always looking for people like you to chair quasi-governmental bodies. I heard only yesterday about a Chief Executive of a northern council who'd been employed to lead an electoral monitoring party to one of the African countries. You could do that. It would be right up your street,' the Mayor reassured her. Marcus was suddenly aware that Maisie had closed her office door tight shut and was using her free hand to re-kindle desire in her man. In her other hand she wildly waved the dropped prescription. He snatched it back from her.

'Marcus, you naughty man! Do you think it will work?' Maisie asked, having forgotten all about her fears of redundancy.

'I do hope so my love. I've read that over twenty million prescriptions for Viagra have been issued world-wide since the stuff came on the market in 1998 so it must be good stuff,' Marcus surmised.

'You do hear of some very funny stories, Marcus,' Maisie began, 'there was one I heard about a man who took too much Viagra and couldn't get it down.' Maisie was laughing but stopped suddenly, 'the chemist is just down the road, Marcus. Pop down there right now and meet me at my flat in about an hour,' she said excitedly, shutting down her computer. Marcus not being one to disappoint rushed next door to his Parlour shouting at Mrs Carter that he had just remembered a dental appointment. Strange, thought Mrs Carter, I thought he had false teeth.

Marcus arrived panting at Maisie's block of flats having shackled his bicycle to a dustbin in the bin store. He pushed her door bell and awaited a reply stamping his feet on the ice to keep warm. It seemed like an eternity before he heard Maisie's voice on the security entry phone. She released the door lock to the communal front door letting him in. Marcus raced upstairs, whipped off his overcoat and scarf dislodging fluffy flakes of snow as he did so. 'Now Marcus, where are those magic pills? Come on, be quick, lets read the instructions. I do hope we won't have to wait too long. I'm so excited. Come to me, my little Munchkin,' Maisie stretched out her arms and beckoned Marcus over to the kitchen sink, where he handed over his prize pot of pills. Maisie reached up and took a glass out of the kitchen cupboard and filled it with water. 'It says it needs about one hour to take effect. I do hope you haven't eaten, because it says action may be delayed if taken with food,' Maisie prattled as she prepared mentally for what was going to be a physically challenging couple of hours, she felt sure.

Time seemed to be on a go-slow but eventually Marcus rose to the occasion and it was a case of, chocks away.

'My dearest Maisie, do you know I sometimes have naughty thoughts about you being my sex slave?' Marcus spoke with difficulty between hastily taken breaths and thrusts. Maisie was enjoying every second. She moaned, sighed and listened to Marcus's revelations.

'Sweetie, I am your sex slave,' she said softly, blowing into his ear, 'your wish is my command,' Maisie was quite the woman of the world. Marcus was left in no doubt when she reached her pinnacle. The sweet moment was heralded by a sheer scream of delight. The Viagra was doing its stuff and although Marcus was tiring, his erection was still there proving a source of endless enjoyment for both of them. It was only then that Maisie realised that something was wrong with Marcus.

The Mayor was motionless and still rigid. How could he fall asleep at a time like this? He was just so much the typical man, Maisie sighed. Time was getting on and they simply could not afford to lie there for too much longer as she had a council working party to attend. She nudged Marcus. It was dark outside although it was only 5pm. Marcus did not move and yet he was still as hard as a rock. She nudged him again, still nothing.

'My God he might be dead!' she whimpered until she noticed he was still breathing.

All the worries she had about being made redundant were history now. She was surely for the chop on the grounds of indecent behaviour or some other similarly silly charge. She managed to push Marcus away and with difficulty manoeuvred herself out from beneath him and dressing him as best she could, reluctantly called an ambulance. The Viagra was still working and Marcus's lunch box was still showing signs of recent use. Even with trousers covering his private parts there was evidence of a substantial bulge. Maisie was forced to leave his flies' semi open although she had managed to tie the belt loosely at the top. She sat with her head in her hands and waited for help. It was just as the door bell rang that she thought she sensed movement in Marcus. The erection had begun to subside and Marcus was breathing more normally.

Maisie let the medics in and feeling completely humiliated explained the sorry tale. Accompanied by Maisie, Marcus was taken to the Cheatham Royal Infirmary and during the journey they colluded on the story that Marcus had wanted to surprise his wife, Virginia and so had taken the drug to see how quickly it would work. There was no need for this connivance as far as the casualty doctor was concerned because he had heard it all before. The strong smell of semen on the Mayor's legs gave the game away. The doctor suggested that Marcus stay overnight, just to be on the safe side. Virginia would have to know and he would give her the excuse that he and Maisie had concocted earlier.

The doctor phoned up to the ward and called for a nurse and a wheelchair. Maisie and Marcus fussed over each as they waited and Maisie delivered a sloppy kiss just as the door swung open and a wheelchair appeared. Behind it stood a pretty little nurse called, Sadie. The colour drained from Sadie's face. This was another of her bad dreams. This just could not be happening to her again. In front of her stood a fat black woman who was bending over a thin old man lying in the bed. Was this deja vu? No of course not, the time before it had been the fat black woman in the bed and the thin old man bending over her. What was happening to her? The nurse was totally thrown into confusion.

'Am I going mad?' Sadie screamed as she fled the room. The casualty nurse came running to see what was up. Apologising profusely for the nurse's behaviour, she called a porter to take Marcus up to the Sexology Ward. This was all too much for Marcus and Maisie and whilst awaiting the porter's arrival the lovebirds fled, jumping into a taxi on the hospital forecourt. Maisie continued on to the Civic Offices for her evening meeting, a discussion on proposed changes to the Council's Disciplinary Procedure.

Chapter 21

The weather still had something of a chill about it and there was a fresh fall of snow in the yard. Micky Brown arrived at the crack of dawn as always and with extra electric heaters he was as snug as he was likely to be for the rest of the day. At 6.30am the virginal snow would be subjected to what would amount to gang rape as over one hundred feet clad in steel capped boots stomped through the gates. Deep breaths, the doctor had told Micky to take. *When you feel stressed or anxious about your work, take several deep breaths.* The stress indeed was beginning to tell on him. The wheeled bins were all out, ahead of time he might add, but this had only fuelled the fire of complaints and things that had gone wrong. In fact, anything that could go wrong, he thought, had gone wrong. It was Sod's Law.

Bobby Dalton arrived early in the hope that he might be able to finish on time and get away to do a little bit of moonlighting on his painting and decorating jobs. Job and finish was what he was paid for and no more unless double time was on offer.

'You know what they say, Mick?' Bobby joked, 'first sign of madness is talking to yourself, mate,' Bobby ribbed him and he listened to Mick murmuring to himself.

'No Bobby; the time to worry is when I start answering me bloody self,' Mick returned, 'anyways, if I did answer meself, I'd get a lot more sense than if I let any of you lot advise me and as for that doctor of mine, he's got something to answer for; *refocus your mind* indeed!' Micky unburdened himself on his captive audience, '*recall a calming image in your mind or a past success until your breathing returns to normal.* I haven't had any past successes,' Micky chuckled, 'unless of course you count that nice little woman who used to make the tea and cheese rolls when we had such little luxuries. You must remember her, Bobby? It must have been, oh, what, twenty five years ago,' Micky reminisced as he put the work folders in order ready for the crews, 'mind you, nothing happened between me and Cecilia, I think that was her name. We were innocents compared to thesedays but we did enjoy our little bit of slap and tickle. If I'd wanted to go further she would definitely have been game, though,' Mick concluded dreamily.

The crews jostled beneath the shelter for the warmest spot, closest to the building. Micky slid open the glass window.

'Oy you lot out there, shut up! I can't hear meself fink,' he admonished. Before long the radio was alive with fretful HGV drivers fighting to negotiate icy roads. Littleton was first to hog the airwaves.

'Mick, I'm slipping and sliding all over the place; me wheels are spinning. This ice is scaring the living daylights out of me,' he yelped. Micky wondered momentarily if he should give him the name of his doctor and then trying to retain an atmosphere of calm he started singing, *four wheels on my wagon,* receiving the sharp end of Littleton's tongue.

'OK, only pulling yer leg, Littleton. Do what you can to keep everyone safe. That's all any of you can do today, mate; just radio in the list of roads that you can't get to. Robin will make up a list for the Missed Bin Round which we'll run as the weather improves. Let's hope for some sunshine to melt this bleeding lot, alright mate?' Mick said, settling Littleton's nerves.

'Thanks Mick. I'm sure the residents will understand if their bins don't get done today,' Littleton replied. Mick was not so sure about that.

As the morning progressed there were several reports of freighters colliding with parked cars and brick walls and Micky reached into a drawer and pulled out a book titled, Stress Busters. He opened it at page twenty six and started to read, *stress is quite natural. It becomes dangerous when it starts to take over the whole day and begins to impair performance and prevents rational thinking.* What followed was a list of all the ways that he could reduce stress such as *cutting out coffee, tea and alcohol.*

'Not bloody likely,' Mick mumbled, 'what else have I got if I take away my few comforts? *Know the signs. List changes in your language, behaviour or health.* There haven't been any changes in my behaviour,' Micky recalled, forgetting that he had recently told Cyril to *bog off,* although luckily the councillor had not heard. He read on, *'ask a friend or mentor to help you put together a management diary...,'* now this piece of advice was worth noting.

Mick considered sharing his problems with Reggie Turner but thought better of it since Reggie never seemed to be around when he was wanted. Ever since Juney started working as a supervisor Reg was ominously never in the office. There was always a good excuse for his absence; a problem at another of the Council's depots or the need to visit a resident or go to some seminar on say, W*orking Practices for Waste Managers.* He had also embarked on a course that would lead to him qualifying as a Competent Person in Charge of Cheatham's civic amenity site.

'Fat chance!' Mick chuckled. It was no good employing an ex-dustman of Reggie Turner's calibre. No amount of courses would turn him into a Competent Person, Micky thought. He laughed his dry croaky laugh thinking, 'who needs enemies when you can have a friend like me?'

Alison from Must Work Ltd. was outside in the yard talking to Gary Green. Micky invited her into the warmth of the office for a coffee.

'Thanks Mick,' Alison coughed and spluttered, 'I'm so sorry, Mick. I've picked up a dreadful cold. I didn't get a wink of sleep last night and I think it's going to me chest,' she said, patting it and making herself cough again.

'It's your lucky day then my love. What you need is to have your chest rubbed with Vic. My middle name just happens to be Victor!' Mick winked and Alison smiled back wanly.

'Thanks for the offer, Mick. I really appreciate it and it's hard to resist but resist I must!' She said laughing and coughing at the same time. Mick looked hurt just for a second.

'Alison, we need some more of those little booklets you usually give out to the agency guys. Sometimes they claim they haven't been given one,' Micky rasped, his chest was playing him up as well. It was the damp. The doctor and everyone else knew it was the smoking but apart from the doctor, no one was brave enough to say anything.

'Yeah, sure Mick,' Alison snapped. She was eager to please because she and Must Work Ltd. were well aware of the new agency that had just opened its doors in Cheatham High Street. Must Work Ltd. could ill afford to lose business to anyone just now. 'Actually Mick, I was wondering if we might go through the booklet together and see if there are any points that need updating? I think we might need to update the working hours information with Single Status on its way in,' she added.

Alison took out her cigarettes and remembering that smoking was no longer allowed on Council premises, put them away again. It's bloody cold outside today Mick, d'yer fink I might just have a quick drag on a fag in 'ere?' She begged. Mick shrugged his shoulders but seeing Slump, who was a non-smoker on his way over to the office, left it for Slump to decide.

'Ask Slump when he gets 'ere. If he's OK about it then I don't mind just this once, in fact I might join you. Mind you love, the state you're in a fag probably isn't the best idea,' he added.

'Mick, that's the pot calling the kettle black, if ever I heard it. Are you alright? You seem down in the dumps today, mate,' Alison said stating the obvious.

'Yeah, down in the dumps, that's a good one since I work in one,' Micky almost chortled, 'draw up a pew, Ali, my love. We'll go through your booklet now whilst the channels of communication seem a bit quiet shall we?' Mick put the kettle on.

With Slump authorising their indoor fag break the two of them lit up as Mick explained the ins and outs of Single Status and what should go into the new booklets. Slump was unaware of the impending changes and made the mistake of asking Micky how Single Status would affect them at the depot.

'Well for one thing Slump, the men will work the same hours as the office workers, which means the whole service will cost the Council more. I think even you can work out what that's likely to mean. The Council will think it can provide a cheaper service by putting it out to the highest bidder,' Micky said handing round the coffees.

Slump took his coffee from the tray and went into contemplative mood pondering the dilemma that Mick had just drawn to his attention and then changed tack.

'You know, Mick, I've just read that more than three coffees a day kills off bone cells and makes you more susceptible to osteoporosis later in life,' Slump took a slurp of his coffee.

'That, my little ray of Sunshine, is probably the least of our problems. If they put the service out to one of those big waste companies we'll all know what's hit us soon enough. If they do that, the pay will be lousy, the conditions crap and God only knows how many of us will still be working 'ere within six months; TUPE's not the same as it use to be,' Micky warned, wiping his brow with the palm of his hand, a cigarette sticking out between his fingers and mug of coffee in the other. Slump looked blank; after Micky's explanation, he was none the wiser.

'TUPE,' Alison began to explain, 'it stands for Transfer of Undertakings. Mick, can you remember what the rest of it stands for?' She asked. Slump was still looking baffled.

'Basically, Slump, it used to mean that when a company took over a public organisation's workforce, they undertook to keep all staff employed for at least six months,' Mick enlightened in the most lacklustre way.

Slump having become bored with the TUPE discussion went back to sipping his coffee and allowing Alison and Mick to continue with their booklet discussion.

'Are the hours due to change, Mick?' Alison asked.

'Well, yes. They're looking at making everyone work thirty seven hours. At the moment the men are supposed to work thirty nine hours. That's already three hour less than they used to do. I have to pay them overtime if they go over the thirty nine. It's costing us a fortune now. I hate to think what the consequences will be if the hours are cut again to thirty six. The white collar workers are not best pleased about it either. They work thirty six hours now and say there is no way they'll increase their hours to thirty seven to match the manual workers, if that's what the Council decides,' Mick explained, 'I'll tell you what Alison, I'll draft something and get Mr Dingle's approval before you print it, because there'll be ructions if I get it wrong,' Mick assured her.

Micky was getting more and more depressed as the minutes ticked by.

'I don't want anymore complaints from them upstairs. I'll tell you one thing, Ali, this Council is a bugger to work for. All it bloody thinks about is recycling figures and being top; always looking for another gong to hang up in the Civic Offices. They don't use common sense. I mean they keep going on about cutting costs and then they go and announce that they're adopting the Single Status Code of Practice. At the moment the men only get paid if they're off sick after three days. I'll tell you what, it don't arf cut down on the sickness and as you know we've enough of that already. Moonlighting they are. They get a nice cushy job laying a carpet and they're off. We don't see them for a couple of days. If they get sick pay when they're pulling a fast one where's that gonna leave us? I'll be tearing me hair out if I should be lucky enough to live that long,' Micky said pouring out his worries.

Alison agreed with Mick her commercial good sense was proverbially rubbing its hands together thinking about all the extra business for Must Work Ltd. Lots more agency guys would be needed to undertake the extra hours necessary to get the job done to say nothing about all the planned sickness the men were bound to take now that they would get paid for being sick.

'Mick, for God's sake cheer up mate. Otherwise you'll be six feet down under before your time. You might as well start thinking about your epitaph,' Alison said trying to get Mick to look on the bright side.

'Ali, my love,' Mick rallied, 'I have already chosen my plot at Cheatham's cemetery and when I'm dead and gone, on my gravestone will be written thus, Michael Brown, a man who had truly *bin* there and done that!' Alison could not help but burst into laughter. She picked up her paperwork which had been lying on the settee and left Micky with his thoughts on death and Single Status passing a breathless Ice Man as she left the office.

'Mick, I think we might have a problem,' the Ice Man gasped.

'OK, just the one is it?' Mick had returned to being his old sarcastic self, 'why are you out of breath, Ice Man? Where's yer van?' Mick asked.

'I've parked it outside. It's a bit slippery in the yard and I thought it might be safer, after all Mick, I wouldn't like to bump into your beloved Ford Cortina Mk 3,' the Ice Man said smiling.

'Bloody right an all,' Mick shot back, 'I'd have your guts for bloody garters if you touch me bleeding car. Antique that is. I've just managed to get hold of some authentic alloy slot rims for that baby of mine. Did I tell yer, I took her to the twenty fifth anniversary rally of the Cortina Marque last summer?' Mick asked. The Ice Man was nodding appreciatively; Mick had bored the pants off them many times before. 'Bloody good meeting an all, it was,' Micky said as he reflected on his happy years driving around in his pale green thirteen hundred litre beauty that he affectionately called, Audrey, after his screen idol, Audrey

Hepburn. Mick was never happier than when he had the chance to talk about his Cortina and his retirement plans to renovate her from tip to toe.

Mick, the Ice Man, Davies explained his breathlessness to Micky Brown.
'There's a problem with the bulky household,' he began.
'I know, you've already said there's a problem. So what is it? Come on, I haven't got all day,' Micky groaned.
'Mick, I don't know how to tell you this but a resident in Stonebridge has suggested that yesterday one of our blokes held his hand out for a tip when collecting a settee. Apparently the resident felt so threatened that she gave the crew ten quid to share out between them,' Mick frowned and then trying to make light of it, turned it into a joke.
'Only ten quid? That wouldn't have gone far between the four of them would it?' The Iceman looked dumbfounded.
'You know whose ward it is, don't you? It's that idiot Cyril Huckett's,' the Ice Man revealed as Micky lost his jovial spirit and sighed a long deep sigh.
'Ask Robin to find out who was collecting bulky household up there when it happened. We'll pull the whole crew in and see what they have to say for themselves. Let me know what you find out. Thanks mate,' Micky decided he had better toe the Council line and use the disciplinary procedures.

Micky, for all his wackiness and apparent hardness, hated confrontation. He would have to tell Reggie about this incident and that would mean that Juney would get to hear. He dreaded this more than anything else because Juney was the supervisor controlling the bulky household crew. Micky could just hear her giving Reg a headache over the issue.
'Suspend them Reg. You can't have people who let you down like that. If one lot gets away with it, they'll all do it. The next thing you'll know, it'll be you in the dock for letting them get away with murder.' Juney was quite right of course but men usually took a different view somehow, which made it difficult for Micky to carry out his own duties as Senior Supervisor. Luckily she did not like sharing the office much with the other grubby supervisors and finished most of her paperwork at home. Micky rang Reggie on his mobile; there was no answer as per usual, he was probably having a cup of tea in some cosy café with Juney. Mick decided to leave the bad news until the next day. It was time to turn his attention to the next problem manifesting itself in the form of the local newspaper.

Gary Green was showing Micky an article on the front page of the local rag. *Council at it again!* Read the headline in the Cheatham Star. Micky read it out loud.
'*Is this Council heading for disaster? Following the issue of wheeled bins to all houses for the Council's revolutionary Quadruple Wheeled Bin Scheme it now insists that residents can only have a small bin for non-recyclable rubbish. It is only families that can prove they have eight or more persons living in the house that will be allowed to have a larger bin from now onwards. This is a major service change; at the start, the LIP promised that all residents would be able to have exactly what they needed to contain their waste. This administration has failed to keep its promise. Just a couple of months ago they were saying that families of six or more could have the larger bins. Insisting that large bins are only available for families of eight or more is shameful.*' The quote was from Winston Clegg, the local Labour Leader.

A quote by Sebastian Tetbury from the Tory opposition followed. Micky continued to read out loud.

'This is preposterous. What will the Council do next? What about all those residents that already have large wheeled bins? Will they dare to take them back and replace them with small bins? Residents, if I were you, I would chain down your bins in between collections and watch them like hawks just in case the Council decides to whisk them away from you...'

Looking mystified, Micky handed the newspaper back to Gary.

'Why is it we always have to read about these things in the bloody newspapers? Whatever happened to communication?' Micky shouted, feeling disconsolate.

'Someone needs a cuddle!' Gary laughed. Micky continued with his rant, 'I didn't know about this. I wonder when they were gonna tell us about this new rule?'

Slump, just like Biddles was often thought of being a sandwich short of a picnic.

'Why can't they have larger bins Mick?' He asked.

'Because Huckett and...,' at the mention of Cyril's name Slump thrust his fist into the air, not dissimilar to the pictures of a well known caped crusader and shouted...

'Captain Waste, to the rescue!' Micky was startled.

'I suspect Adrian ponce-face Moses-Pomfrey has told him that if he only gives out small bins he'll keep the waste tonnages down and the blessed recycling rate up. Mick was exasperated. 'Yup, I can see we can expect even more contamination now; as if we haven't got enough already. They must be barking mad,' Micky suggested working him up into froth.

Gary Green entered the fray.

'And that Pooper Hooper, he's barking mad as well. Do you know what I've been doing this afternoon?' Gary asked.

'No, go on surprise me,' a glum Micky replied.

'I've been walking the length and breadth of Cheatham High Street organising Tiddler, the old sweeper bloke, to take a brush, a bucket of soapy water and a strong disinfectant to scrub down those bleeding artificial plastic palm trees that Huckett's had erected to please the Leader. Apparently, Hooper has spotted dogs using 'em as urinals and he says they stink; says they remind 'im of the Cheatham sewage works. Apparently, little puddles, he says keep forming around the bases of 'em. So instead of basal growth as in the old fashioned real trees, we now have piss to clear away. Old Pooper wants us to send a special patrol down the High Street twice a day to keep 'em clean and sweet smelling. Where am I gonna find another set of men (or women come to that now the Equality Officer is in place?)' Gary asked, smirking at the thought of equality being taken seriously at the Depot, 'where am I gonna find a spare team to keep this bloody new patrol staffed?' Gary looked as drained as Micky.

Micky was overcome by an urge to go outside for a ciggy and a think. He did not have the courage to tell them that Sir David had also suggested that the refuse and cleansing crews should be *empowered,* that's right, the word was, *empowered.* He wanted them to have the power to fine people if they saw them throwing litter on the ground. Something to do with some new *Statutory Instrument* the memo had said and *delegated powers.* They had enough problems with residents without risking a swipe round the lughole for trying to wring money out of them in the middle of emptying their bloody dustbins or sweeping the street, he thought.

The final hitch of the day was a call from the Chief Executive in person. Maisie's block of flats had missed its collection and she wanted it done immediately. Micky sent a crew out of its way to deal with it. They reported back that they had had to leave one bin because it was chained to a bicycle. Micky telephoned the CE's office with his report and then shutting up the office, he headed for home, gingerly, so as not to skid on the ice and damage his beloved Ford Cortina, circa 1972.

Chapter 22

The Materials Recycling Facility sorting plant development was racing ahead and Cyril was keeping a close eye on it. John Dingle was meeting with contractors, Denton Beckett at frequent intervals so he could report all new stages to his Lead Councillor with the portfolio for Waste Management as fast as they occurred and Reggie was despatched to complete his Competent Person's Technical Certificate which meant that once the site opened for business, he would be the main man on whose shoulders any blame would fall should there be any accidents.

The land was cleared, the perimeter walls were constructed and within a large shed rose menacingly. John applied to the Environment Agency for a Waste Management Licence which would allow Cheatham Council to operate the site within environmental health and safety requirements. Denton Beckett suggested several specialist contractors who turned up one by one to screw together bits of kit in Meccano like fashion. It was all rather colourful; the framework enclosing the conveyors was bright blue, the hoppers were bright eggy yellow and other bits of metal were crimson red or lime green, an absolute feast of colour. Cyril liked the MRF idea very much and behaved like a kid with a new toy and just like a kid, wanted it to be the envy of surrounding councils. Just for now though, he decided to settle for his Cheatham colleagues.

'Adrian, ring round a few of our friendly councillors will you and invite them along to see how the MRF is developing. See if you can get four or five along next Thursday afternoon and let Russell know so he can invite the Press along. We should have a nice picture in the local. I'm sure it will create a lot of interest,' Cyril said hoping the event would achieve a double page spread on the swash buckling Cyril Huckett himself.

A few photographers arrived on the scheduled topping out day but Cyril's fellow council members were noticeable by their absence.

'Typical!' Cyril grumbled to Adrian and Dingle who were waiting patiently inside the warehouse like structure. The latter now had a roof but was still without a decent set of shutters letting in a dreadful February gale.

'Brass Monkeys!' Dingle muttered turning his back to the open gateway to protect his manhood from freezing.

'Well, let's get on with it,' Cyril called tersely, being a little miffed that his colleagues had decided not to support him probably for something as trifling as the weather. Then again, it might not be so bad. At least there was more chance that he would take centre stage in the photographs. Cyril talked to the photographers and the reporters in turn, pointing to this and that piece of equipment and giving them complicated explanations of what each piece of kit did. He took great pains to use technical terms from the manufacturer's literature which he had studied in bed the night before. The reporters did their best to write down Cyril's flowing discourse. Being an academic he went into overdrive as easy as pie, explaining the mysterious workings of this new concept, the sorting plant.

'From this hopper the materials, because we regard them as a resource, not a waste,' he humoured, 'will pass along this conveyor to the first of the cabins for pre-sorting. Any larger unwanted items entering the rest of the plant will be taken out here,' Cyril said pointing here and there, 'they will then pass onto a sort of shaking table and through another exciting piece of equipment known as a trommel. This revolves and as it does so, loosens the compacted waste,' Cyril was flamboyant in his delivery, if he was anything.

'Blimey, who's this old codger then? Fancy getting excited about a few bits of metal,' a reporter was overheard saying to another member of the Press.

'That's Cyril Huckett, the world's one and only recycling champion,' came the answer from the Press attaché, sniggering.

'What's the matter with these council blokes? Why don't they get a life?' Another whispered. Before long, Cyril was being snapped by photographers in front of the plastic bottle balers, the magnetic steel can separator and just to show that he was not averse to getting his hands dirty and grafting like the common man, he donned a high visibility vest and posed broom in hand beside one of the mechanical shovels. The publicity stunt over, Russell ushered the Press away. Cyril had a final look around the spanking new shed and smiled approvingly.

'This is all mine, he muttered contentedly underneath his breath, 'all mine!'

Reggie Turner, having become a competent person was considering staffing levels for the sorting plant. He telephoned Crappendale City for advice and also sought the intelligence of Judy who of course had previously worked for Aurelia Waste Handling and knew something about how they had staffed their Trashnox Separating System. Judy had settled into Cheatham and she was now getting on very nicely with Tim Baldwin at the Cheatham Star. Unbeknown to Sir David Hooper, Augustus had offered her a bonus to return to Aurelia but she had declined, for the moment at least. Augustus was not too troubled by this. She could be very useful to him where she was and he did have a score to settle with Pooper Hooper; was that really how people referred to him behind his back? And that dick of a Lead Councillor for Waste, Cyril Huckett, he had heard some interesting rumours linking him to a councillor controlling the Council's purse strings.

Reggie invited Judy to meet him in the Civic Offices Social Club bar so he could pick her brains.

'Reggie, this is what I gather is the best scenario for a MRF taking thirty thousand tonnes each year and running one shift. You will need at least ten sorters for the paper and six on the plastic bottles. It would be best to have a couple taking off any rubbish that gets through the pre-sort and you will need a couple at the front-end where the vehicles tip. One of these should be an experienced mechanical shovel driver and the other one capable of driving a forklift,' Judy stopped for breath and then added, 'sorry, Reggie, I've missed out the supervisors. You'll need two or three of them to make sure there's always someone to crack the whip. In each of the cabins it would probably be wise to have a team leader, someone who sets the pace and I'm afraid there is also the pre-sort cabin to consider. You'll likely need another two in there to take out the plastic carrier bags, the cassette tapes and the coat hangers and all the old rubbish that just fouls up the equipment otherwise,' Judy explained.

Reggie was spaced out at the thought of having to explain to Cyril that they would need to increase the staff budget by at least twenty five persons.

'I can't get enough drivers for the services we run now let alone the thought of having to find all these sorting staff,' he croaked, twiddling his gold earring, a birthday present from June, between his fingers, something he did when he was anxious, 'I can't see this Council agreeing to all these extra staff. What about the budget cuts? I have just been told by Dingle to seek out areas where we can cut back,' a stunned Reggie said.

'I might be able to help you there,' Judy said, 'if the Council thinks it's likely to be criticised for building a white elephant, it'll soon find the money to pay for the right level of staff. In any case Reggie, how can't it? Cheatham must have somewhere to sort its recyclables because as we have seen, no one else will touch them. The so called recycling materials are, if you will forgive my French, a load of shit,' she concluded. Reggie shuddered on hearing Judy's choice of words but nodded nevertheless because he knew she was right.

'I wish you wouldn't mention elephants,' Reggie winced, 'if I have the likes of Cyril Huckett fighting the rest of the Council over staffing costs with me in the middle, it'll be like that old saying,' Reggie said. Judy looked mystified. They say that when two elephants fight, the ants suffer. Well, I'm gonna feel like one of those bloody ants, pummelled into the ground, good and proper,' he explained with feeling.

Judy pondered Reggie's words before coming to his rescue with a clever plan.

'Reggie, I might be able to help by using my Press contacts. What if I was to make sure that the Press Office puts out a really good release about how Cheatham is moving ahead of the times and will be taking in excess of twenty five people off the unemployment register once the new recycling factory is finished? My good friend Tim on the Star will run the story, I'm sure of it. The LIP won't make a fuss, I promise you,' Judy said having seen a way to kill two birds with one stone and help Reggie and Tim at the same time. Judy dropped another bombshell, 'sorry again, Reggie but you might need someone extra to co-ordinate the paperwork at the MRF and to look after recruitment. In my experience these MRFs have a high turnover of staff,' Judy advised. Reggie nearly keeled over at the thought of yet another member of staff to recruit but then his expression brightened. Could there be a chance here for his delectable wife, Juncy? It would be nice to have a bit more money now the kids expected foreign holidays every year. It might not be such a bad idea this MRF business after all

Cyril met up with Marcus in the LIP Group Room at the Mayor's request.

'Cyril what the devil do you think you're playing at? Are you deliberately trying to mess up the waste service single handedly? I'm tired of reading in the newspapers every single week about more changes to the service and, I might add, never, in my opinion are they changes for the better. I want to see more recycling like everyone else but not at any price! What on earth is all this nonsense about not letting people put out extra black sacks of waste? Only houses with more than eight persons are eligible for larger wheeled bins? Have you gone completely off your head, Cyril?' The Mayor said angrily, 'the idea is political suicide!' Cheatham's first citizen added.

'Marcus, it hasn't been fully decided yet but don't you see, it's a splendid way of driving down the waste and increasing the recycling rate at the same time? I know it'll be an inconvenience for some but people get used to change soon enough. What they had before will shortly be a distant memory,' Cyril said attempting to change the Mayor's view of things.

Marcus stood his ground. He had his foibles but underneath he was one of the few senior politicians on the Council with any common sense.

'Cyril Huckett, I've known you for many years and I just can't believe that you're the same person anymore. What has got into you? David is not much better. We seem to have become a Party obsessed with statistics and league tables and before you say another word, I do appreciate that we've legal obligations in some areas such as your beloved recycling rate but we're public servants and as such we should be putting the public first. We should be about providing services that our tax payers want and are satisfied with. Just because you won't be satisfied unless we achieve an eighty five percent recycling rate doesn't mean the whole of Cheatham feels the same way,' Marcus exploded. He was definitely not happy.

Cyril folded his arms in defiant mood and stood leaning up against a pillar in the middle of the room whilst waiting for the Mayor's rant to finish.

'Marcus, I hear what you're saying. We've a Scrutiny Committee meeting next week and perhaps we should discuss the minimum of eight persons per household issue then. Perhaps we might have a little pre-meeting just for the LIP committee members where we can get some idea how the voting will go in public?' Cyril suggested.

'I think that would be a step in the right direction, Cyril. However, I don't see how we're going to tackle the contamination problem in the recycling bins unless we make sure that every household has the right sized bin for their needs. It shouldn't be down to what the Council believes they need. I don't support fortnightly waste collections. I think the whole business is a health hazard and we haven't yet witnessed a full summer with the whole borough on the bins. I haven't heard you mention Climate Change either. How will a fortnightly food waste collection fair in fifty degrees centigrade? Have you thought of that? I think that you and the Party are heading down a one way street,' Marcus said, helping himself to coffee from a flask on the table.

There was a slight lull in the proceedings whilst Cyril thought of the best way to pick up on the Mayor's use of the word, fortnightly.

'Marcus we don't use the F word you know. We explain to residents that the collections are regular, which is in line with the Environmental Protection Act. It's just that we collect different bits of their waste on different weeks with the non-recyclable bits on alternate weeks,' Cyril advised.

'Cyril, I'm not just a resident. I'm the Mayor, OK? Don't try pulling the wool over my eyes. The waste is being collected fortnightly and if I want to use the F word I bloody well will! I'm sorry but I'm so disappointed in you, Cyril. You, of all people have always advocated that honesty is the best policy,' Marcus swallowed his coffee and in a fit of pique threw the empty plastic cup into the waste bin deliberately missing the dedicated vending cup recycling bank to annoy his colleague, 'Cyril, I insist in my role as Mayor that you write to the local newspaper and state unequivocally that Cheatham Council has not made any decision on the so called, more than eight persons rule or the banning of black sacks. If I have anything to do with it the Council will not be making a decision until both issues have been fully debated. Do we understand each other?' Marcus demanded.

'Of course we do Marcus, of course. We shouldn't fall out over this. We are after all batting on the same side,' a rather disgruntled Cyril reminded the Mayor.

'Good. I'll expect to see something in the next Cheatham Star then shall I? I will let David know about our little chat,' Marcus said sweeping out of the room allowing the door to bang shut.

Cyril, in all honesty was somewhat taken aback by Marcus' attack on him and having given it some thought decided it might be wise to reduce any more flack to an absolute minimum and concede victory to the Mayor. Cyril wrote the denial to the Press entitled, *'No decision on black sacks'* followed by, *'Residents of Cheatham, the Council has no wish to make rubbish collection an inconvenience. We pride ourselves on doing whatever we can to meet your requirements and demands. The suggestions reported in the newspaper last week were merely ideas put forward by our Waste Management Officers for consideration. If we reduce our waste, we will increase our recycling rate and that will help us reach the exacting targets set by government.*

I would also like to make it quite clear that the Council has made no plans whatsoever to restrict the amount of rubbish that residents may put out. Our aim is, as it always has been, to provide residents with enough space in their wheeled bins for all of their non-recyclable waste. The recent survey that we undertook at the start of our wheeled bin trial told us that ninety percent of you wanted to keep the wheeled bins. This and subsequent internal survey work, (Cyril could not for the life of him think of any but it sounded good and it was unlikely that he would ever be challenged), *has provided additional proof that wheeled bins are the neatest and most efficient way to go.*

Cheatham Council is not laying down the law by saying residents can't put out extra black sacks or that they must use a wheeled bin. We are fully aware that sacks are preferable for some households who have narrow frontages or no front gardens and of course in many cases for the elderly. (It was always a good idea to slip in something to do with pensioners, Cyril remembered). *So let me repeat once more that no decision on black sacks or larger bins has been taken nor will be until we have the results of a full and frank study.'*

Cyril finished his letter and read it through several times checking it over for plain English and was particularly pleased with his suggestion that the ugly rumour had been circulated by Waste Management Officers. It would at least deflect some of the missiles from himself and the rest of the Council. Cyril sent his letter to Russell, who in turn emailed it to the Cheatham Star and Tim Baldwin for printing in the next edition. Judy too, was at work writing an article on the advantages of having a Council owned and run Materials Recycling Facility. She visited the Beverly Estate's Job Club and interviewed several job seekers attending classes there. Some of the quotes she managed to record on her dictaphone she believed would come in useful.

'Yes, I would love to work locally, I'm a single mother and it would be a great opportunity to get myself off the unemployment list and do something really worthwhile at the same time,' said one interviewee.

'I'm disabled and there are so many jobs I can't do but I could work at the recycling factory and what's more it's just a few yards down the road from my specially adapted flat,' said another.

'I'm a keen recycler and I've always wanted to do something to help the Council achieve it's environmental goals and help the planet at the same time. When I'm working at the recycling factory I'll be able to fulfil all of my dreams,' said the idealist who had not paid her Council rent or tax for several months.

Judy wrote her column recording verbatim the tear jerking things that the Beverly residents had said to her and Tim published it. The article made the Council seem all heart. Judy sent a copy to John Dingle who had been nonplussed by Cyril's own letter to the Press. In particular he was outraged by the suggestion that *Waste Management Officers* were guilty of suggesting black sacks be banned. The only officer that this would reflect on was himself. His early retirement pension seemed to be drifting further away at every encounter with his lunatic Lead Councillor. On top of this he now had to contend with the high numbers of staff that Reggie insisted he would need to operate the MRF.

'Reggie, this list is as long as my arm. How will we afford all these?' Dingle was a worried man and did not cherish asking Cyril to go cap in hand to that old witch Bendover yet again.

'It's *horses for courses*, Mr Dingle. We'll sell our recycling materials to the highest bidder; sign up some really good contracts and hey presto! We should make a healthy profit to cover all of our staffing costs,' Reggie explained, convinced his argument was watertight.

'If only life was that simple, Reggie,' Dingle lamented. It was all becoming too much, following the threat of the ban on black sacks and the suggestion that large bins would not be made available to households of less than eight persons or was it six? He was slowly getting to the end of his tether.

Dingle went to see Cyril whom he found to be surprisingly unconcerned by all the troubles. Cyril wanted first and foremost a well run recycling factory and if this meant a large amount of additional staff then so be it. One of the Council's Core Values was about staff being an asset and all that mumbo jumbo but sometimes a man's got to do what a man's got to do. These things were dictated by the needs of the moment. The Council had to consider the path that benefited the majority and in this case this was the electorate and, if he might fly his own flag, certain leading councillors who had pulled out all the stops to make Cheatham a place to take pride in.

Cyril went to see Irene Bendover taking Sir David and Edith along with him for support. Sir David outlined an idea for restructuring the Council's Finance Section and therein Irene's empire. As planned, Irene felt pressured and miraculously found powers under the relevant emergency funding procedures to move things along quickly. She addressed the Emergency Finance Committee in camera reminding them of the public relations problems the Council had recently faced and finishing with a plea for common sense. The Committee's decision would be somewhat irrelevant since she had taken it upon herself to release the money in any case. For the sombre occasion the Head of Finance was dressed from top to toe in black with the usual dark splurges beneath her eyes. The latter attracted the gaze of all who came into contact with her. Were the patches of dark pigment makeup applied lackadaisically or were they indeed caused by decadent living? It was always something to dwell on when meetings became tiresome and ran on far too long. On this occasion, however, she was wearing a new lipstick called Pink Haze rather than her more usual colour, Frosty Orange. The change was by more of a celebration because unbeknown to Cyril et al, on that very morning Irene had received a letter of appointment to Padwick Borough Council as their new Chief Executive. She would be leaving Cheatham in three months time and underneath her austere exterior she was feeling ebullient and indifferent to the Council's whimsical spending sprees. Soon she would be free.

Irene read out her statement from the Pink Book of Emergency Finance Rules to the Emergency Finance Committee.

'The Council cannot allow itself to be branded heartless. If the Council doesn't find the funds to employ the Beverly Estate residents it will be sending out the wrong message.' The Emergency Finance Committee were staggered by Irene's apparent Road to Damascus life embracing attitude change and granted the funding. Reggie celebrated by having another fag.

Over the next month nothing about the service improved except the excitement and anticipation of Cyril Huckett. Once the MRF had been completed the machinery was put through two weeks of commissioning before being handed over to the Council.

'We must have a grand opening,' Cyril announced to his colleagues on the Performance and Strategy Committees. Grand, was precisely the right word to use for the ensuing event. The guest list became longer as did the days approaching the Spring Equinox.

'Adrian my good man, I want you to invite the waste managers from the London councils and the committee chairs from the LIP administration both in London and the Home Counties. Can you think of anyone else we should invite?' Cyril asked, his brow furrowed as he thought deeply about this wonderful chance at showing Cheatham off to the world. 'We want to project Cheatham as a leading light; as a Council full of forward thinkers and of course, one which gets on with things and doesn't just talk about it. D'you see what I'm getting at, Ady?' Cyril smiled the sort of smile one would imagine a pervert hanging around a public toilet might smile, friendly and interested looking.

'No one calls me Ady, Sir. I prefer Adrian,' the Recycling Officer retorted. Cyril was taken aback.

'I do apologise,' he said shocked by Adrian's mild retribution, 'I don't like it when people shorten my name to Cy. I can't think what came over me,' Cyril admitted, inwardly chastising himself for forgetting the need for propriety and distance between councillor and council officer. Adrian went to the coffee machine.

Adrian returned with two steaming plastic cups of white coffee and along with his hot beverage he offered Cyril his thoughts on the MRF opening.

'Councillor, I think we should invite our contractors, (any that are still talking to us, he privately thought), and a few senior officers from Cheatham's other departments such as Social Services. I think we should also make sure we invite the Crappendale City Council officers and their lead councillors,' Adrian added.

'Good idea Adrian. I think too, that an absolute must is the new London Mayor and his merry men and naturally the Waste Recycling Section at the DWWW,' Cyril was away with the fairies again, 'actually, Adrian, remind me what the DWWW stands for? They keep changing the blinking departments; it's difficult to keep up with them,' Cyril said.

'It's the Department of Wind, Water and Waste, Councillor,' a woeful Adrian replied.

'Damn good that one. I bet there's enough wind in those Westminster offices to run turbines to power most of London,' Cyril laughed.

Adrian smiled for Cyril's sake but secretly was wondering if perhaps now was a good time to be looking for a job in the commercial world. You could have enough of political gerrymandering, undertones and just sheer self indulgence and a serious lack of general knowledge.

'I think it might be time to get out of Dodge,' Adrian whispered to himself. Cyril's brain was elsewhere and did not catch Adrian's words of desperation. 'Eh, what was that Ady, beg pardon, I mean Adrian? Cyril returned, innocently.

'I was just saying such a glamorous launch will cost such a wadge,' It sounded plausible.

'Now don't you worry about funding,' Cyril explained, 'just leave that to me and Irene Bendover, and I think you mean, 'wedge' not wadge,' Cyril corrected.

Cyril and Adrian drank their coffees whilst the former meditated and Adrian made a few phone calls trying to get hold of the relevant contact lists.

'Let's get this show on the road by the first week of April and make sure that it looks good. I want proper cups and saucers, white table cloths and let's have a glass of champagne for when the ribbon is cut,' Cyril said, rubbing his hands together with glee whilst Adrian felt the strain of pandering to this geriatric politician.

'Who will be cutting what ribbon?' Adrian asked. Cyril was surprised that Adrian had any need to ask this question. There might have been some discussion over where the ribbon should be positioned in readiness for cutting but not about who would actually cut it.

'Well, I thought I might do the honours,' Cyril said.

'Far be it for me to interfere sir, but I wonder whether we should think about asking the Mayor to do something? After all he is Cheatham's first citizen,' Adrian acknowledged. Cyril was seized by a minor panic attack. Ask Marcus? After all the rows they had had about the contamination? In public they were polite to each other but privately Marcus constantly harangued Cyril on the issue of larger bins and bringing back the weekly collection for general rubbish.

Cyril thought quickly. It would be difficult to leave out the Mayor; it would be considered a slight of enormous proportions unless it was possible to wheel in a different bigwig, someone who was thought to be of even greater standing than the Mayor. Cyril rubbed his neck and then his eyes whilst Adrian sat and twiddled his pencil. Various possibilities ran through his mind as Cyril toyed with various names. There was the Tory MP for Cheatham, Sir Geoffrey Lawrence MBE but he would be unthinkable. Cyril's colleagues would think he had taken leave of his senses. Then there was the London Mayor himself although he was likely to deflect attention from himself and it would be just as unthinkable to allow the London Mayor to be associated with Cheatham's recycling achievements as it would be to invite a Tory to launch the MRF.

Cyril was going from the sublime to the ridiculous. What about the Queen herself or Prince Charles who was always banging on about being green. The thought of Her Majesty stomping around gantries in a high visibility jacket, helmet and steel capped boots looking at conveyors full of dusty paper, smelly soiled nappies and all the other contaminants they were getting in the recyclables just didn't seem right so he dismissed that idea straight away. There just must be others who had sufficient standing in the industry and government circles to be considered a good choice, but who? Cyril racked his brain for a suitable celebrity. He fancied that big breasted slut he had drooled over on the front of the local paper, her name he recalled was something like Lolita? Local girl made good. She would certainly be a hit but then he supposed he had better keep it clean.

'Who's at the top of the DWWW tree, Adrian?' Cyril was thinking a government department official might be a safer bet. Cheatham was sure to get a good amount of publicity in government circles as a result.
'Erm, I think the person that would be of most interest to you would be Sonia Chang, the Head of Waste Policy,' Adrian waited for a reply; there was a noticeable pause. Cyril was wondering how a person called Chang could conceivably be the head of a British Government Civil Service section and one as important as Waste at the DWWW and a woman as well. Still, he supposed she might be the answer. Women were not usually remembered for long, the exception to the rule being Maggie Thatcher of course, Cyril thought. With a name like Chang, this woman was sure to be forgotten in a trice. It was the strong alpha male who succeeded everytime. Cyril, the chauvinist piggy, believed he would be perceived as the stronger character and without a doubt it would be his picture published in the professional journals. It would be his own name that would be remembered in those inner circles, he had no doubt.
'What a great idea, Adrian. Let's invite Sonia Chang. Keep me informed. I'm happy to write a letter to Ms Chang if you think that an official letter from me, being that I'm a councillor, might help. Give her a ring first just to see if she's available and ask her if she'd like to make a speech on Cheatham's behalf,' Cyril felt satisfied with his choice; he would have to invite the Chief Executive and of course there would be some questions about the ceremony. He must prepare his answers carefully.

The new MRF would be the crowning glory to his revolutionary new service. Adrian was already dialling more numbers on his mobile as Cyril made his excuses and left reciting a quote from the bible, Proverbs 17:22, *a merry heart doeth good like a medicine.* Cyril made his way to the Chief Executives office.
'Hello Cyril, what can I do you for?' A jovial Maisie Atichitawomba asked as she flicked through a pile of committee reports stacked high on her desk.
'I thought I'd update you on the MRF's progress. I've been discussing an opening ceremony with Adrian Moses-Pomfrey, good lad that one. I expect good things of him,' Cyril praised. He believed the best policy was to let people think that you did at least have the best interests of your staff at heart.
'Yes, Maisie,' Cyril went on, 'we've been planning a grand opening day to launch the plant and we've chosen the first week in April. Adrian is finding out which day is best for the Head of Waste Policy at the DWWW to cut the ribbon or what ever happens at these events,' Cyril was deliberately dismissive to make it sound like it was not such a big deal.

Maisie listened thoughtfully to Cyril's ramblings but had a few thoughts of her own.

'The Mayor will be interested to know what part you'd like him to play in your big day, Cyril.' Maisie was never backwards in coming forwards but then that's how Chief Executive's became Chief Executives, Cyril supposed. Cyril stood with his hands casually in his corduroy trouser pockets, swivelling his right foot around on the carpet.

'Absolutely! I quite agree Maisie. I had thought that perhaps it would be a better idea to have someone from the Civil Service and government circles to do the honours on this occasion. You know, get us a good report with the Minister and perhaps some extra grant funding?' Cyril was looking up at the ceiling.

'Well Cyril, I understand your desire for Cheatham to gain as much clout in the corridors of power as possible but don't you think that Cheatham's own Mayor should be seen to have an important part in any opening ceremony?' Maisie was wearing two hats; one as the Chief Executive and the other as Marcus Bullman's lover.

Maisie called Mrs Carter who was cleaning the Mayor's mace in a large walk in cupboard off the corridor just outside the Mayor's parlour.

'Mrs Carter, please ask the Mayor to step into my office as soon as his engagement with the Tenth Stonebridge Girl Guides is over,' Maisie requested. An obedient and dour Mrs Carter went straight into the Parlour. The Mayor had just presented community service awards to a handful of Guides and was now chatting and taking tea with them. He had never fancied young girls and this lot reminded him of just why that was. They were just plain ugly, all spots and greasy skins. He sat at his desk, coaxing them to sign his visitors' book. It was all part of the accepted way of doing things. One Girl Guide had given his pen back to him saying there was a problem with it. Marcus took the pen and unscrewed it. The Guides looked closely at his lap where he was fiddling with the pen.

'What are you all looking at?' Marcus, asked jokingly, feeling somewhat embarrassed at having five pairs of female eyes staring intently at his flies. There was a sudden popping noise, 'oh, now look what I've done. I've shot my pen top off right under the table,' he shouted without thinking.

'Is that what you call it?' One of the Guides piped up as they all fell about laughing. It was at this point that Mrs Carter rescued the red faced Marcus, who courteously offered his goodbyes and left at top speed for Maisie's office.

'Well Cyril, I would very much like to be involved with your event. Maisie's quite right, as Mayor it's only right and proper that I should be. I'm the first citizen of Cheatham and unless a member of Her Majesty's family or indeed her own good self attends, I'm your man!' Marcus felt he was being undervalued. Maisie had also called Russell from the Press Office for his views on the subject. You could have cut the air with a knife never mind ribbons at an opening ceremony. Russell tried to ease what he sensed was a difficult situation by introducing what he felt might be the diplomatic answer.

'I wonder if we might combine the opening paraphernalia by having one person cut a ribbon and another to press a button and start up the machinery or whatever is appropriate? We could have speeches from more than one person couldn't we? I'll arrange for a plaque to be made up with both names on it. How does that sound?' Russell asked enthusiastically. It did not sound at all good to Cyril because a plaque with two names, namely those of Sonia Chang and Marcus Bullman would not include that of Cyril Huckett. Could they have three names on a plaque? He wondered.

'Marcus, perhaps we should restrict the dignitaries performing any official duties to members of Cheatham Council? I might have been a bit hasty in thinking we should invite an outsider. In any case, Sonia Chang is likely to be here today and gone tomorrow,' Cyril said cheerily, back to Hong Kong with a bit of luck. How did they all get in? The xenophobic councillor wondered. 'Perhaps we should do it ourselves?' Cyril hoped for a positive response from his colleagues. Marcus was perfectly aware that he had Cyril on the run and he was not about to give in now.

'Cyril, it was a fabulous idea to bring in a government representative. We'll need to campaign for more money for Social Services and I'm sure that if we show the DWWW that we want to be recycling flag bearers we're far more likely to be seen as a council that delivers. I say we stick to your original plan,' Marcus smiled one of his conciliatory smiles; Maisie agreed with Marcus. Cyril could feel his neck aching; it always did when he was frustrated. He rubbed it and was resigned to suffering defeat. Just at that point Sir David Hooper arrived to say that he was available should there be anything required of him at the opening ceremony.

The Launch plans proceeded but now under the watchful eye of the Chief Executive and the Head of Communications. On the grand day Marcus, surrounded by about fifty guests cut a green ribbon in front of the MRF's control panel and then pushed a large green button causing the conveyors and other bits of kit to explode into life. Paper, plastic bottles and cans previously loaded into the hopper started to flow through the veins of the plant. The noise was deafening. There were tin cans clattering against each other and the noise of balers squashing bottles. Sonia, the Head of Waste Policy at the DWWW tried to deliver her speech but struggled with the high noise levels. Councillor Bowen, the technical whiz kid bounced across to the public address system and turned up the volume thus drowning out the crashes and bangs of the machinery. Sonia Chang continued with her message on the importance of getting to grips with waste, how important it was for all councils to meet government targets and make determined efforts to minimise damage to the environment. In line with the printed order of the event, the Mayor also said a few words in Cheatham's favour. The photographers took several shots of Marcus and Sonia. They were snapped standing on bales of plastic bottles, piles of waste papers and peering over the sides of conveyors; Cyril just looked on and smiled. The day was a runaway success with many guests from other authorities looking on with envy at Cheatham's new toy.

Reggie stood at the back ensuring that all of his new sorting staff were in the right place, at the right time and wearing their sparklingly clean new uniforms. They looked very smart indeed surpassed only by the machinery, which looked absolutely gorgeous all spanking new and brightly painted with no sign of dust anywhere. Running this MRF was going to be a doddle, Reggie believed as he joined the invited guests munching chicken wings and smoked salmon canapés. The Press attaché collared Cyril for a few vital questions to fill out their reports.

'How many tonnes can this MRF process each year, Councillor Huckett?'

'What materials can it deal with?'

'I thought I saw sorting staff with learning disabilities? This particular question was asked by Tim Baldwin himself.

'Yes, you're quite right,' Cyril replied, 'we've employed some people from a local mental health charity. We like to provide work for those who may not be able to work in more traditional work placements,' Cyril explained. Luckily he was called away just in the nick of time to say farewell to Sonia Chang. Unfortunately for Cyril, the Press had not finished asking their questions and whilst Cyril was otherwise employed they latched on to the new MRF manager, Reggie Turner.

The next edition of the Cheatham Star featured a very nice selection of photographs taken inside the MRF some of which Cyril had managed to squeeze into. These were accompanied by an article on how the new recycling factory would help to save the earth and a short piece about the staff working at the site.

Twenty five staff with learning difficulties are employed at the site; I witnessed them sorting the materials. It looked as if many were confused and unsure of what to do. A chat with the MRF Manager, Reginald Turner revealed to me that these folk are being paid a pittance, only a fraction of what able bodied persons would be paid to do the same job. Where is the justice here? It was signed the Editor.

Cyril could not be consoled; his grief at such a report was immense. He rang Reggie.
'What the bloody hell have you told these irresponsible wordsmiths?' Cyril screamed.
'Councillor, I didn't say those things. All I said was that we pay them an agreed rate which would top up their government benefits. In return, I said that we've agreed to train them in preparation for going out into the wider world of work, when they're ready,' Reg defended himself.
'How many do we have with learning difficulties? Cyril asked, utterly distraught.
'There are just two, Councillor. The rest are able bodied,' Reggie replied, feeling distinctly uneasy with just a few days as MRF manager under his belt. Cyril contacted Russell and commanded him to put together a rebuttal of the lies featured in the Star. That same day, Tim received a request from the Council's Head of Communications to print a more honest piece on how the MRF was staffed. The carefully prepared Council press release read:

Cheatham wishes it to be known that it does have a policy to employ, where practicable, those with learning difficulties but not in areas where they will be in danger or unable to manage. These particular staff members have been taken on to help their rehabilitation into the world of work. They will be trained so that they can move on to other more appropriate work when they are ready. The Council in no way exploits those with learning difficulties, in fact, it is providing all the necessary support in the way of transport to and from work, personnel to assess progress and plenty of supervisors to oversee them during working hours and ensure their safety.

The Council's reply was published but not before the workers at the MRF, the remaining twenty three able bodied staff had contacted their Union. They voiced their unhappiness at the Press's article.
'This is ridiculous,' ranted Cyril to Sir David Hooper on receiving a critical letter from the Union's steward, Bobby Dalton.

'Cyril, we can't afford any more cock ups. The Tories are on our tails. It's one thing to have a scheme which is suffering severe problems but on top of that we now have the Press picking on us for exploiting the disabled who can't look out for themselves. And, if that's not enough, the rest of the staff are calling for strike action and we've only been open for one week; it's the last straw, it really is. Just fix it Cyril, otherwise I will be forced to ask for your resignation,' Sir David blurted. He would not be taking any blame for this latest crazy mishap of Cyril's.

It was a few seconds before Cyril found the strength to speak.

'David, what shall I do? I've issued another press release with Russell's help stating that the number of staff with learning disabilities is only two. It should be in the paper the day after tomorrow, Thursday. Is there anything else I can do?' Cyril was mortified at the prospect of having to resign. This just could not be happening to him. Sir David ignoring Cyril's pleas for mercy recalled a joke which he began telling Russell, rubbing salt into Cyril's fresh wounds.

'Have you heard the joke about the three envelopes?' Sir David asked Russell who shook his head. Sir David was enjoying himself, 'there was a government minister who had to resign because of some scandal. As the new minister arrived he took the opportunity to ask the outgoing minister for advice. He said, I've already thought about that. In your desk, you'll find three envelopes. Open the first at the first crisis, the second at the second crisis and so on. The new minister started his job. When the first crisis occurred he took out the first envelope and it said, *blame the out going minister.* The new minister then made a statement to the Press saying, *I apologise for this fiasco, it was ordered by my predecessor. I'm taking steps to rectify the situation and will make sure it cannot happen again.* When the second crisis occurred, the new minister reached for the second envelope. It read, *blame the staff.* The new minister made a statement to the Press saying, *I apologise for this complete and utter foul up, I truly had no idea that it was happening. I will be holding an enquiry and procedures will be tightened so that it can't happen again.* The minister had saved his own skin but when the third crisis erupted, he reached once more into the drawer and pulled out the final envelope. It read, *write three envelopes.*' Sir David was in stitches at his own joke. Russell laughed in sympathy whilst Cyril felt more miserable than ever.

A doleful Cyril asked Reggie to drive him to the MRF. Outside the building they found an angry mob massing and chanting. Cyril managed to read a placard which said, *workers rubbished!* Cyril sunk down in the car seat hiding as best he could from the crowd as Reggie drove round the back to his parking space. Inside the plant nothing was happening; it was quiet. There were no conveyors running, no giant shovels waltzing around dropping waste into hoppers. It was eerily silent except for the incoming waste, which was still being delivered by refuse freighters directly from their rounds.

'Oh, my God, Reginald,' Cyril suddenly felt religious, 'how are we going to cope? What will we do when the bays get full? Can't you get them working again?' Cyril could see the growing mountain of waste and he could smell the stench of what appeared to be rotting food in amongst the recyclables. Reggie had noticed it too. The puke making stink was difficult to ignore.

'Councillor, I've tried talking to them but it's you they want an apology from. I understand that the supervisors and Bobby Dalton would like to speak to you privately at your earliest convenience, like today,' Reggie explained, quietly enjoying Cyril's discomfort.

Reggie ushered Cyril into a room that the staff used as a canteen and dumped him there whilst he went to find Bobby and the supervisors. Cyril took several deep breaths and desperately tried to re-group his thoughts and regain a little confidence before Reggie returned with the war party. Cyril was as ready for them as he could be. He could do this! He would say whatever they wanted to hear if it saved his skin and got the plant working again.

'Please sit down,' Cyril motioned to the Union representatives to sit on the benches arranged along the length of the room and then wringing his hands he spoke to them in his most conciliatory manner, 'now, please understand this, I want you to know that I have a high regard for you all and am really grateful for your hard work and conscientious attitude,' Cyril said, knowing full well they had not been there long enough to show any kind of commitment but then he considered that since none of them were out of the Einstein stable they would most probably lap it up, 'the Press are not exactly our bosom buddies at the moment and they're pouncing on anything that they think they can make a meal out of. The Council values you and we're proud to have you working for us in our technological masterpiece, this MRF,' Cyril explained. Dalton asked for a chance to speak to the supervisors in private.

The union representative and his stony faced brothers returned in just a short while and Dalton addressed Cyril on their behalf.

'Councillor, my colleagues here are pleased to tell you that they'll be returning to work this afternoon. They're satisfied with your apology and hope that in the future they'll be consulted before any more press releases relating directly to themselves are given out.' Cyril breathed a sigh of relief as the supervisors trooped outside to tell the workforce to prepare for their shift. Cyril wondered how such a fiasco could have occurred in the first place. How could such mountains out of molehills be created? He felt in need of a little relaxation and asked Reggie to drop him off on the corner of Leoni Bridges Road saying he would walk the two miles home. Cyril struck out for Edith Dickopf's house and Nirvana.

Chapter 23

Work at the MRF resumed but not until a minor contractual clause had been agreed, namely the free provision of workforce refreshments at tea breaks. The materials delivered to the MRF were as mucky as ever and as the weather warmed up so did the general odour clinging to the dusty air. Reggie made an appearance several times a day to make sure that the chief supervisor was coping. Back at the depot, the Waste Management Team watched developments with consternation as the green wheeled bin crews returned each day to the allocation office reporting vociferously that their loads had been full of food waste and were simply not worth unloading into the MRF.

Reg tried extremely hard not to hear the constant whinging about the contaminated loads.

'But Reg, it's muck. You've never see such a load of shit; I'm telling yer mate! They don't like us dropping it in the MRF. That poor bloke with the pony tail who works at the front end keeps telling us to take it to landfill,' HGV driver Brewer shrieked.

'Never you mind what they say, Brew. You just keep taking it to the MRF. I'm in charge of that place and if councillors want it all recycled, it'll all be recycled,' Reg replied wearily.

'But Reg, that's just it, it's not being recycled. The whole lots going to the dump,' Brewer said to his chagrin.

'Oy Reg, what part of SHIT don't you understand?' Another crew member shouted from outside.

'We'll have the Health and Safety Executive shutting the place down,' Richard Holmes, temporarily transferred to domestic collections, added. Reggie had heard them right enough and was trying very hard not to get worked up about it. *Stay calm,* whispered an inner voice; he consoled himself by lighting up another fag.

Reggie received another minor irritation in the form of a phone call from the Mayor's office. Mrs Carter who often doubled up as the Mayor's secretary to save money was on the phone.

'The Mayor wishes me to point out that the plaque erected at the plant doesn't record his OBE. He's rather disappointed by this and would be extremely grateful if the plaque could be redone,'

'It certainly can, Mrs Carter. Tell the Mayor he can rely on me. I'll get it redone asap; just fax me the correct wording if you wouldn't mind and it shall be done. Thanks for letting me know,' Reggie said. Richard Holmes was asked to call at the engraver's shop on his way home and order a new plaque. True to his word two days later Reggie put up the revised plaque and that same day he received another phone call this time from Sir David Hooper's secretary, Pamela Peters.

'Reggie, Sir David was down at the MRF with Cyril earlier today and he noticed that his name isn't on the plaque. He did say a few words of congratulations on the day and he's wondering if it would be possible to get his name put on under that of the Mayor's and before that of Miss Chang?' The Leader's PA asked.

'Yes, I don't see why not, Mrs Peters. Tell the Leader I will personally arrange for the plaque to be redone as soon as possible,' Reggie agreed, forlornly.

'Thank you so much, Reggie. Please make sure you get his title correct. Sir David's a bit of a stickler for titles,' Pamela Peters advised.

Reggie recounted the plaque tale to his Senior Supervisor.

'Mick they treat me as though I'm some sort of lacky,' Reggie groaned, 'do you have any idea how much this simple plaque has cost? All I need now is old Huckett to come strutting in and flipping well asking for his name to go on it as well. This plaque will be as big as a house before long,' Reg said making the Ice Man and Gary Newton laugh. Mick just kept his head down; he really did not want anything to do with the MRF. He had enough to deal with just getting the muck collected. Coffee break time arrived and Reg opened a large cake tin.

'Here, 'ave some of this chaps. It's a new recipe I'm trying for chocolate fudge cake. Its beautiful, so soft and moist. Come on just 'ave a bit,' Reggie nudged the tin under Micky's nose.

'No thanks, Reg. I don't usually eat chocolate,' Mick said still feeling miserable.

'I'll have a bit, Reg,' Gary Biddles called looking up from his tabloid crossword.

'I wouldn't if I was you. Look at that rich dark brown colour. With Reg working down that MRF you can't be sure what's in it,' laughed Gary Newton who then took a bit and crammed it into his cakehole.

'Oh blimey Biddles, you're not trying to do the crossword are you?' Micky Brown asked.

'My mum says one should always try and improve oneself,' Biddles retaliated and then, 'Mick, what does the word, xenophobia mean.'

'It means a fear of foreigners, me old mate,' Mick explained.

'My mum was telling me about something peculiar at her work recently. I think it must have been xenophobia, Mick,' Gary said, 'the workers had a collection for a lady who was leaving whose mum was German and one of the ladies refused to put any money in the collection, because her granddad had been killed in the war,' Gary explained.

'Gary, that's not xenophobia. That's just plain stupid. I bet if you looked into it, you'd find the lady who wouldn't put any money in the collection was just a mean old git. She's just using the war as an excuse. It's like religion..., at this point Gary Newton and the Ice Man suddenly remembered that they had jobs to do elsewhere and left the office.

About lunchtime the radio started to warm up. Gary Newton was managing the office allowing Micky to go out on a mission. Littleton called in.

'Gary, I think Mick's gonna get a complaint from some old bag. I've just had a bit of a run in with her in Wales Road, big tits,' Littleton was singing down the radio.

'Littleton, you know the rules, no swearing and no obscene language on the radio. Now what's the problem with this lady?' Gary asked.

'For starters, Gar, she used a few choice words. We'd never heard half of 'em before. She's behind us, right? I've stopped so the boys can empty the bins in Wales Road, a few minutes that's all we were. She's honking and screaming out of her car window for us to get out of her way but Gar, there was just no way I could have moved, honest,' Gary was shaking his head. They could expect a complaint for sure and it arrived dead on cue. The complaint came within the hour redirected from the Chief Executive's Office. The complainant felt insulted as though her privacy had been invaded by the rude and uncouth language the crew had used. Gary asked Kelly to use her most beguiling telephone manner to ring the lady back and apologise. Richard Holmes was just going off duty and was asked to buy her a large bunch of flowers.

The bouquet of mixed flowers hid Richard initially from the gaze of the offended lady of Powys Court. The flowers were plucked from the strong arms of Waste Management's bearer of gifts by the so called old bag who on seeing the face of this golden Adonis was struck as if by lightning and suffered a weakening of the knees spurring Richard to catch her as she fell.

'Oh, I'm so sorry. I must have caught my heel in the rug,' she cooed before asking him in for a cup of tea. Richie was keen to show that Cheatham Council wanted to make amends and was Mr Charm himself. Lolita and Richie made a lovely pair both tanned and beautiful.

'I'm bi sweetie. How do you swing?' Richie asked.

'I'm Lolita,' she replied giggling. As the evening beckoned they sipped pink champagne and Richie cast his eyes around Lolita's apartment. He liked what he saw and she would make a great room mate now that he was technically homeless having been thrown out by Councillor Jim. Living with Lolita was a bearable possibility, he considered.

The temperature at the depot had risen as rapidly as it had in Wales Avenue. The radio was saturated with strained voices trying to get through to someone in authority and Micky, now back at the depot had picked up a call from an unhappy customer.

'Oh yes madam,' Micky listened to the tale of woe. Gary Newton and Slump listened to the one sided conversation. 'I don't know Madam but just hold on, I'll ask,' Micky said turning to Gary Newton, 'Gary, the resident wants to know if we've a Mr Jobsworth working 'ere, mate?' Sniggers broke out at the back of the office. Micky smiled and returned to his caller, 'no, I'm sorry there's no one of that name working 'ere,' Mick said, replacing the receiver and deciding it had been another trying day.

The following day was not much better. A medical appointment meant Micky needed to leave early and the Ice Man had agreed to cover but forgot and went home. Two crews were still out battling against the elements, high winds and torrential rain to get their loads in. Recycling Three had broken down earlier and as was usual another crew namely Recycling Six, had gone to help them out. They were running very late and were in danger of arriving at the MRF after lights out. The driver of Recycling Three tried several numbers he could think of but no one answered. He rang the Civic Offices and was put through to the Call Centre.

'Hi luv, I'm one of the refuse truck drivers. Put me through to Mr Dingle will yer luv. Yes it's urgent my sweet, ta,' Recycling Three's driver went back to chewing his gum whilst at the same time keeping an eye on the back of the wagon as his team moved along the street from bin to bin.

Mr Dingle was not best pleased about being called to the phone. He was taking a few minutes out of his busy day to read a few pages of his latest find in the Cheatham Antique Bookshop. He had a beloved collection of Dandy and Beano albums but he had been missing the 1984 issue of the Dandy until that very morning. Various chuckles emanated from his office as he flicked through Desperate Dan, The Odd-Job Man, Bully Beef and Chips and Harry and His Hippo. He was having such fun and had quite forgotten about his dream of early retirement and the traumas of Cheatham's Waste Management Section. The phone brought him back to reality.

'What is it?' Dingle used his barkiest voice, which was not very barky at all more strained and ineffectual.

'Sorry to bother you, Sir, but I'm still out with Recycling Six and we'll be out for a bit longer yet. We don't know what to do with our loads. What time does the MRF shut? Health and Safety says we can't leave anything on the back of our vehicles overnight,' explained Recycling Three's driver

'Well, why are you telling me? Contact Reggie Turner or Michael Brown for goodness sake man,' he made an attempt at sounding authoritarian.

'Sorry Sir but we've tried that. There's no one's at the depot and we don't know the phone number of the MRF,' an apologetic driver answered.

Dingle huffed and puffed and bellowed in his thin little voice for Adrian's assistance. Adrian came running thinking the place must be on fire.

'Call the MRF and say that two of our recycling crews have been delayed and won't be there until at least 5pm. They must stay open until those two vehicles have tipped,' Dingle insisted and then giving Adrian time to make his vital telephone call challenged him to find out where the hell the supervisors were. 'Anything could have happened to those crews. I want an explanation ASAP and Adrian, let Reggie know I want a word with him as soon as he gets in tomorrow,' Dingle said, concerned that he might have to supervise manual workers on a regular basis if this lackadaisical attitude was allowed to continue.

The delayed crews drove through the MRF gates at 5.20pm to find the tipping hall locked tight. The crews were wet, tired and just about knackered and they still had to take the vehicles back to the yard for garaging. They looked hard at metal shutters barring their way; the workers were just going home and were simply not prepared to stay even one minute longer than necessary.

'Sorry mate, we only gets paid until five o' clock,' shouted one bloke defiantly as he skipped out through the main gate.

'Sorry fellas, it's the Union you see. They won't like it if we break the rules for you lot,' called another, 'we'll be here again at 7am tomorrow and we'll make sure you're first in. See yer.' The MRF workers continued their march towards the gates. Red faced and about to explode, Recycling Three's driver reversed his vehicle up to the MRF shutters and tipped his load hard up against them. Recycling Six did the same and hit the building's metal uprights at the same time bending them substantially and splitting the bumper on his freighter. They drove back to the depot, parked up, filled out their daily log and went home. The duty supervisor bringing up the rear and in charge of locking the gates just stared in astonishment as the crews drove out leaving their loads behind them.

The next morning was mayhem at the MRF. The tipped rubbish was strewn everywhere as a result of the forceful wind that had got up during the night. The yard stank and there were plastic bags and bottles all over the place with rats frolicking amongst the bits of uneaten pizza. The rain had turned the yard into a quagmire in which an orangy coloured mud seemed to predominate. This had been made up largely from a mixture of tinned spaghetti and baked beans or what ever else had been on a buy one get one free offer at Sainsbury's the day before. It was sick making and Reggie found himself retching.

'God, what a mess,' he was heard mumbling piteously as he got his mobile out and phoned his pals in Cleansing.

Gary Newton was just making a cappuccino with liberal sprinklings of chocolate powder on the top just as he received Reggie's cry for help. Ever since Micky Brown had introduced them to the delights of cappuccino, he had developed a craving for it.

'Yeah, what's up, Reg?' Gary asked, puckering his lips at the prospect of his smooth Italian beverage.

'I need your help urgently. You should see the mess here and I've got Padwick Council coming for a visit in three hours time. Get everyone down here quick and tell 'em to bring sacks, brooms and every bloody thing they've got,' Reg cried in desperation, 'oh, and Gary, they need bloody face masks an all,' Reggie added feeling sick as the nauseous smell overpowered him yet again.

Mick Brown came over to see the damage. He was dumbfounded.

'Charlie Pratt's taken the damaged vehicle into the workshop for repair. Neither of those bastards have come in today, Reg. I doubt we'll see them again. The only trouble is it means we're two drivers and one vehicle down. Alison's trying to get replacements for me. They were both agency drivers you know, Reg. That Must Work Ltd. lot have a few questions to answer. I've told Larry to try that new agency in the High Street, can't be any worse can they?' Mick was speaking to himself since Reg was walking away trying to put as much distance between himself and the stench as possible and have a fag to aid his recovery. Mick walked after him.

The yard was filling up with an army of cleansing personnel dressed in protective overalls and gloves. They scurried around the yard holding litter pickers, brooms and shovels and everywhere you looked there was a human sea of green reinforced cotton stretching out here and bending down there to recover the escaping waste. The screams and squeals of cleansing staff slipping over in the mire were clearly heard followed by sightings of a dripping mass of green cotton overalls surfacing and looking like the monster from the deep.

'It's a good bloody job they've got showers here somewhere,' said one who had just traversed the yard on his backside. The rushed attempt at a clean up went well and not much remained of the slurry after it had been hosed away except the lingering pungent odour that even strong disinfectant could not remove.

The Padwick delegation arrived at the allotted hour and Reg kitted them out with yellow vests, a colour that reminded him of the morning's activity and turned his stomach over. There was a load of fresh waste inside the factory waiting to be processed and Reg did his level best to steer his visitors away from the storage bays, avoiding any close inspection. From a distance it looked as though it might pass as decent recyclable material, he thought. As luck would have it a mechanical shovel was working in the delivery area which provided him with a very good excuse to keep them well away from the danger zone. Health and safety, he told them, he could not take the risk of getting them run over. He swept them on towards the conveyors.

Unfortunately, Padwick's staff had heard the rumours circulating about the contamination and were hell bent on asking some pertinent questions.

'Reggie, I thought I noticed quite a bit of food waste down the other end. Will that affect the quality of your materials?' Padwick's Recycling Manager asked innocently.

'No, not at all, James. We do get a little bit of contamination, about ten percent but that's all. It's not a major problem. The stuff you saw down the end was from one of our council estates. We'll have to do some monitoring and enforcement there shortly to get them up to speed with the rest of the borough, that's all,' Reggie fibbed his way through the interrogation. The Council's problems were fast becoming his and he felt guilty about clouding the issue but then it was hardly his fault if the bins were full of rubbish. Reggie consoled himself with this thought as he ushered his party over to the bales of plastic bottles awaiting despatch.

'I would like to extend a welcome to anyone who'd like to return at a later date to have a look at our planned Education Centre once it's built,' Reggie said, thankful that he had got to the end of the tour without putting his foot in it.

The day finished on an upbeat note when the sun finally showed itself.

'There you see,' Reg remarked to Micky Brown when he returned to the depot, 'they say that every cloud has a silver lining,' Reggie said pointing at the blue sky.

'Yeah Reg, but It's also true to say that every sliver lining has a cloud, mate,' Micky replied, holding out a photograph that had been taken from the top floor of the nearest block of Beverly Estate flats. It clearly showed a heap of dishevelled rubbish, food and rats within the yard.

'It was sent in by an anonymous resident. There was a note about more of them being sent to the Press and I should think the opposition just for good measure,' Mick said. Reginald Turner could feel a headache coming on.

'Bastard, whoever it is,' Reggie shrieked, 'I'd better speak to that showbiz comedy duo, Dingle and Huckett, and quick too,' Reggie cried as he reached for the telephone.

'Ah yes! I forgot to tell you mate, Dingle wants to know why the office was empty at 5pm yesterday,' Mick added for good measure.

'Was it empty?' Reggie asked, 'anyway, what's that to do with me? You're the Senior Supervisor.'

'Quite right Reg but if you remember, I told you I'd a hospital appointment and you agreed to cover for me?'

'Bollocks!!' Reg swore as he dialled Dingle's number.

Lunchtime approached and Dingle decided to claim something of the day for himself. Having been interrupted the day before, he took his Dandy album to the local park café to enjoy over a pot of tea and an all day breakfast. Arriving just before midday there were plenty of free seats and he plonked himself down by the window which overlooked a bed of daffodils and hyacinths. The sun was warm and it was truly spring like, the ideal morning for unwinding before the rest of the day kicked in. The café filled up as Dingle became engulfed by his comic strip heroes. As his eyes wandered across the pages his mouth moved silently from *EEK, YIKE, ZONK, ZOW or GAWSH*. Suddenly Dingle was aware that he was surrounded by other noisy customers although he was the only person in a suit. The remainder of the customers were dressed in green cotton trousers and jackets with yellow high visibility vests on. The back of each vest read, *Cheatham Waste Services*. He slowly raised his book and hid behind a comic strip of Korky the Cat although his concentration had been ruined and all he could do was listen to the conversations flowing around him.

'Oy Spinks, leave me chips alone,' yelled one annoyed loader.

'Sorry Gazza, only I know you're supposed to be on a diet. I thought I'd help you out. How's your Sadie thesedays? Still got you eating all those grains and cereals? She'll have you looking like a hamster before long,' Spinks replied.

'Sadie, no she's back on the chips, thank the Lord. She's a lot better although she still has the occasional nightmare,' Gazza said eating his breakfast. Another loader wearing a silver cross around his neck with a matching earring, asked for more details.

'What's up with Sadie then Gazza?'

'It's ridiculous really,' Gazza began, 'she works at the Cheatham Royal and a few months ago she walked into a room to find some bloke in fancy dress. Dressed up to look like the Mayor he was. Anyway he was committing what they call, *a sexual act* with some fat black woman patient lying in the bed. Sadie got really upset about it. Well you know she's had a strict Baptist upbringing and all that. Understandable I suppose,' Gazza identified with Sadie's emotional state.

The men went on eating their meals until 'silver crosses' barracked Gazza for more information.

'Yeah, so what were they actually doing then Gaz?'

'I don't know exactly. Sadie gets upset when anyone asks her to talk about it but I believe a plastic penis was involved,' Gazza explained as his colleagues collapsed with laughter. The worrying bit was that recently she was transferred to work on a new specialist ward for sexual problems. They said it would help her get over her hang ups. Well, to cut a long story short she goes to collect a patient from casualty and what did she find but the same dirty old man, only this time he's in the bed and the black woman's bending over 'im. Sadie thinks they were about to have another go. She didn't wait to find out and screaming her 'ead off she ran out of the 'ospital,' Gazza continued with Sadie's story as more laughter followed. He waited for the noise to subside before finishing his story, 'she's working at the Crest Home for the Elderly now and is as happy as a lamb,' Gazza smiled affectionately and shoved another forkful of fried bread and black pudding into his mouth.

'Lucky buggers. When I went in to have my appendix out I couldn't get my Linda to give me anything except a bunch of grapes and a bottle of blackcurrant juice,' Spinks said.

A second crew, enjoying their dinner near by were straining to hear Gazza's revelations. Dingle, meanwhile was feeling the strain of trying to remain concealed. He was sure that unless he could get to the counter to order another pot of tea, the waitress would clear his plates and he would be left looking guilty sitting an empty table. The waitress passed by and he tactfully touched her on the arm and requested in a whisper another pot of tea. His ears were beginning to ache with the juicy titbits he was party to and then an Irish loader with the second crew began spilling the beans about an even greater scandal.

'Biddles had a funny experience a few months ago. Do you all remember when he was suspended for getting inside Kelly's drawers?' There was a wave of laughter at Irish's choice of vocabulary, 'OK, when he tweaked her bum. Well, he was telling me something which I swore I wouldn't tell anyone, so it doesn't go any further than these walls, right?' He warned. Everyone nodded in agreement. 'Biddles was doing a bit of moonlighting and he'd been sent to cut the grass at the 'ouse next door to that German councillor woman, Edith somefink? I'll spare you all the details but that slap head Biddles looked through the conservatory of the house next door and what d'yer think he saw?' The Irish driver hesitated for a second and then put them out of their misery, 'there they both were, Edith Dick somefink and that stupid bloke who says he doesn't have any waste, Councillor bleeding Huckett,' Irish revealed.

Everyone took gulps of their tea or shoved food into their gobs until Silver Crosses spoke up.

'Is that it? What were they doing, Irish. Don't leave us in suspenders mate,' he yelled from the next table.

'They were in the nude and he was all over 'er like a rash. Biddles says they'd obviously had *intimate* relations. That Edith woman apparently had very red cheeks and Huckett was, well, looked as though he'd been well satisfied. Biddles says they looked like Adam and Eve in amongst all the tropical climbers. He's got pictures as well because he just happened to have a digital camera with 'im didn't he!' Irish added looking flushed from having gorged himself on his Bob the Builder breakfast and large mug of tea.

'Blimey, what you've told us is hot property, Irish,' someone commented.

'Yeah, and if any of you say anything to anyone about what I've just told you, I'll break your flipping legs, OK? That poor bugger Biddles has had enough trouble,' Gazza reminded them all.

John Dingle was never so relieved to see people leave as he was then. He had come out for a quiet cup of tea and a spot of lunch and was returning an expert on *council affairs*! He could not suppress a broad smile as he made his way back to the car park. Marcus Bullman and Maisie Atichitawomba using sex toys, Incredible! Cyril Huckett and that fellow Pareto's greatest follower, Edith Dickopf having carnal relations in a conservatory, Priceless! He was wondering about several other councillors, Sir David Hooper for instance. Who might he be shagging? Blackmail was an ugly word but Dingle was feeling fairly confident that should it be necessary.... all's fair in war and peace, especially when one wanted early retirement. He felt sure that when the time came, the Council would look favourably on any request he might make for a good lump sum and perhaps a bonus in there somewhere for a good job done over many years. He returned to his office in a mood that most would have associated with the regular Friday lunch-time piss ups in the Eagle. His cheeks were crimson.

Chapter 24

An anonymous package arrived at the local paper's offices marked for the attention of Tim Baldwin. He opened it and studied the contents for sometime hardly believing his luck. The package contained some still photographs and an amateur video clearly showing a recycling factory out of control. He would publish and be damned and with a few other snippets supplied by Judy, he put together a thought provoking article which he knew would stir the emotions. The community groups opposing the alternative weekly collections, otherwise known as the enemy to LIP Councillors, would also find Tim's revelations interesting. The video was an absolute masterpiece showing the true reality of the ugly mess; plastic bottles and papers were being blown by the wind sky high and over the fence. Men wearing high visibility vests were flying around on the slippery ground and copious thick black clouds of diesel smoke filled the air from the mechanical shovel's exhaust. This enormous beast was working flat out in the yard, pushing up the waste so that it could be lifted into an articulated lorry at break neck speed. There did not appear to be anything sustainable about Cyril's waste revolution.

Tim's article read thus: *Lifting the lid on the Council's new recycling factory. Residents should feel worried about the condition in which the Council manages its new recycling facility on the Beverly Estate. As readers can see from the photographs accompanying this article, rubbish meant for recycling is allowed to blow around and litter the surrounding estate. An ex-Cheatham employee says that the risk of infection should be taken seriously as food waste outweighs the so called recyclables in every load delivered and this will undoubtedly harbour pathogens, that's germs to you and me! Parents with children should make sure they keep them well away from the area surrounding the factory. The Star has made some enquiries about the other great cause for concern, the breeding of maggots in the coming summer months. Readers suffering any problems with their fortnightly waste collection should contact the Star. We will monitor your complaints and take up any issues with the Council. Watch this space.*

The letters came rolling in and the Leadership Office was also flooded with them. Sir David was not at all pleased with this adverse publicity and instructed Judy to organise group visits for residents to the factory so that they could see for themselves that there was absolutely nothing to fear. Judy advertised the visits but those that booked were not just interested locals. Unbeknown to the Council, several members of the various pressure groups put their names down for an information gathering trip round the MRF.

The Tory Group, the Green Evangelists led by Sebastian Tetbury was still meeting in the High Street gathering shoppers' signatures.

'Our petition has grown to fifteen thousand names. I've persuaded ten of our supporters to start cold calling door to door and they'll begin that tomorrow. I'll soon have this petition up to thirty thousand signatures. Let them simply dismiss that in a hurry,' Sebastian confidently remarked. Over their High Street stall hung a hoarding inciting residents to dump their rubbish at the Council's front door. *Bring back our weekly collection! What do we want? We want a weekly collection and we want it now!* This was the chorus that greeted residents out shopping each Saturday and without hesitation they showed their approval by cheering them on.

One Saturday, Sir Geoffrey was on duty in the High Street and was impatient to reveal to Seb a trick he had up his sleeve.

'The Central Conservative Party Office can help us. They have access to some pretty powerful people who could put across the health risks in an eloquent and authoritative manner. That fellow from the World Health Organisation who was here last year to speak on disease and childhood poverty would be quite a scoop,' Sir Geoffrey suggested, 'let's challenge the LIP Group to a public debate inviting the WHO expert to speak for us?' Seb listened to Sir Geoffrey and agreed to sound out the idea. Tim Baldwin and the other members liked the idea and it was decided that the Cheatham Star would invite the Council to field appropriate personnel for a debate on the whole issue of the fortnightly collection.

The Cheatham Recycling Champions were invited to take part in the public debate and specifically to put up a display to illustrate the serious health consequences resulting from the continuation of the fortnightly waste collection. The Cheatham Recycling Champions had been doing some homework of their own. One of their members, Matthew Corbet, a PhD. student and member of the local Friends of the Earth Group had been studying the recycling figures of other London boroughs and trying somehow to make a comparison with those that Cheatham had announced. At the Recycling Champions' next evening meeting, the latest Cheatham Press Office bulletin was circulated.

Cheatham reaches over fifty five percent recycling. The Council announced today that its fortnightly rubbish collection has encouraged residents to recycle so much that the recycling bins are full to overflowing. The Council is on schedule to reach its own eighty five percent recycling rate during the coming twelve months.

There was a look of disbelief on the faces of this local pressure group. If this was true they were failing in their mission to change the course of Cheatham's history and reverse the Council's decision to keep fortnightly collections. Matthew relieved them of some of their concerns and set the Cheatham record straight.

'Now, don't be downhearted. I've received a document from the DWWW and it clearly sets out the formula that should be used by every council in the country to calculate a recycling rate. I managed to get Cheatham's tonnages for the individual materials from an old friend of mine called Adrian Moses-Pomfrey. Adrian's the Council's Recycling Officer and it just so happens Adrian and I met at uni a few years ago. Anyway, the figures are supposed to be public knowledge, it's just that usually you can't get the latest figures until they're published by the Audit Commission two years late,' Matthew explained with a glint in his eye.

The Cheatham Recycling Champions eagerly awaited Matthew's pearls of wisdom. He took a sip of his coffee before enlightening them.

'Cheatham Council claims to have reached a fifty five percent recycling rate. I've recalculated the figures according to the correct formula without home composting and certain other categories that should most definitely be excluded and I only make it thirty five percent. Strange isn't it? Something is very wrong somewhere. I don't think it would do us any harm if we challenged the Council on its figures. How we do it though is a mystery at the moment,' Matthew said furrowing his brow. He would need to arrange a meeting with his old friend Adrian that was for sure.

'But Matthew, thirty five percent is still very good isn't it?' Hannah Hanson asked. Hannah had been nominated the Green Evangelist's representative on the Recycling Champions' Committee.

'Yes, it certainly is but with all the materials they say they are getting, it should be much, much higher,' Matthew commented, 'we keep hearing vague things about massive contamination levels and if that's true then it should be going to landfill. The landfill figures don't match up to those you'd expect to see for so much contamination. It's all very odd,' he declared, shaking his head. Matthew worked freelance as an environmental auditor for a well known consulting firm in the City. The inability to understand the figures was worrying him and he put together a few questions that the others could ask at the debate.

The Star's report on the MRF incident had left Cyril reeling once again. At the same time he had received a letter from Augustus Aurelia suggesting that the company was considering legal action because in the opinion of its lawyers, Cheatham had reneged on a promised contract for Aurelia to process the recycling materials. Aurelia Waste Handling Ltd., Augustus argued, had invested thousands of pounds preparing to receive Cheatham's waste. In good faith his company had taken the contents of its wheeled bins even though they had not been up to much and were so contaminated that landfilling was the only viable option. Augustus' letter reminded Cyril that his company was at the forefront of innovation and that they had installed emerging technologies in a bid to help Cheatham, a council they had thought was an organisation after their own hearts. With this in mind they had laboured for months under the impression that Cheatham would keep its promise and sign a lengthy contract with them. Cyril had not expected Aurelia's reaction, in fact he had banked on the idea that since no contract had been signed he was in the clear.

'But Cyril, there is such a thing as trust and you know what they say in the City, don't you?' Sir David asked sporting his usual florid complexion which seemed to be redder than ever today.

Cyril, bemused, stared at his colleague and awaited his pronouncement on the subject. 'My word is my bond, Cyril. You academic types don't know much about the real world do you? Of course for myself, I'm used to mixing with big business; it's in my blood,' Sir David said sighing, as he looked out of the window. He would have to find a way of appeasing Aurelia Waste Handling Ltd. and he was getting rather fed up with having to get Cyril off the hook time and time again.

Matthew Corbet lost no time in tying up with Tim Baldwin who in turn was delighting in the idea of tying up Judy but contented himself with an entente cordial over bottles of wine at a local Greek Taverna. He had become genuinely fond of Judy and she felt likewise and he agonised over whether to involve her directly in undercover work. Before he had fallen for her charms it had not been an issue but things had changed. Industrial espionage is what it was boiling down to and the dilemma facing Tim was that Judy was the ideal, if not the only person to whom he could turn. Through her relationship, latent or otherwise with Augustus Aurelia, she had access to normally restricted information, the very facts and figures that were needed to calculate the recycling rate. Tim thought about the problem deeply over another glass of Chardonnay. Frankly, he surmised, if she felt the same way about him she would not balk at helping and he would broach the subject after dessert and during liqueurs. Why not? All's fair in love and war, he considered.

Tim and Judy felt relaxed after their second bottle of wine.

'Judy, I need you to use your feminine charms,' Tim said once she was appropriately sozzled.

'Just how many of my feminine charms do you need?' She giggled hoping he wanted to take advantage of her; she was definitely ready for him. Truth was she had been ready for bloody months and she was beginning to think that there must be something wrong with her charms.

'Darling,' good start thought Tim, 'I don't want to get you into trouble but you know how much I think of you don't you?' Judy nodded and hiccuped. She knew there was no chance of him getting her into trouble because she was on the pill. Tim continued, 'you're very good friends with Augustus Aurelia,' Tim suggested. Judy was horrified.

'I swear to you on the holy book, Tim, we're just good friends,' she insisted. Tim nodded.

'Oh, yes I know that, I didn't suspect anything more. That's how you can help the cause. There's a service that only you can render,' Tim said immediately regretting his choice of words and moving on quickly, 'you know that Matthew, the student who works with the Cheatham's Recycling Champions?' Judy nodded feeling rather disappointed with the way the conversation was going, 'well, he needs some information and you, my darling, could get that from your friend Augustus,' Tim explained, taking her hand and sending tingles down her spine. She was glowing, partly from the alcohol and partly from the intoxication brought on by Tim's tender caressing of her hand. 'I might be persuaded,' Judy admitted, 'I'm sure you'd like to come back to mine tonight?' She had him at last. Tim went like a lamb to the slaughter and they were like two kindred spirits, the night was still young and it was Saturday tomorrow so there was no need to be up with the lark.

Judy wanted Tim and if it meant a spying assignment with old friends, what the hell.

'How are you Judy my love? Want your old job back?' Augustus teased when Judy visited him a few days later, looking her up and down to see if the goods had been damaged.

'Gus, I'd love to come back but not quite yet, however, I do need your help. You can't be very happy with the way Cheatham has treated you, can you?' She posed the question but went on before Augustus could answer. 'I shouldn't be here but I might be able to help you get your own back in some small way,' Judy said, her opening gambit getting Augustus' undivided attention, 'a friend of mine Tim Baldwin, an editor on the Cheatham Star is researching the degree of contamination. Would you be able to supply him with the necessary figures? I shouldn't ask but some people feel that there's a cover up going on,' Judy explained feeling every bit the traitor as a picture of Russell flitted through her mind.

'All in the name of love then is it?' Augustus asked recognising the glint in her eye and offering her a second glass of Moet. Judy declined the drink and then coming up very close to him whispered in his ear.

'Gus, we had such a good time together once but you're much too old for me, granddad,' she said laughing in an inoffensive way. Augustus slapped her bottom and laughed with her. The Aurelia patriarch held her tight for a moment and then with some regret, released her.

Augustus took Judy's hand and leading her to some comfy chairs, beckoned her to have a seat.

'Judy, you old slapper, you still have the same good sense of humour, the Aurelia Waste Handling sense of humour, I think. Yes my dear, of course I can get you the figures for the period Cheatham's waste came into us. I can tell you now actually, it's ingrained on my mind; ninety percent of it was going to landfill. We did inform Councillor Huckett of course so I know full well that he was well aware that very little of the stuff was being reclaimed. In fact, we were just about to pull the plug on Cheatham and lock them out of our sorting plant when they told us we weren't needed anymore,' he explained. He contemplated life for a moment or two before deciding to ask something of Judy in return for the information that she sought. 'We've been investigating the commercial history of Denton Beckett Partnerships. They've put out such a load of old twaddle about their contracts overseas most of which no one has ever heard of. They're swindlers, we're convinced of it. They've never built a recycling plant before. Still that's not what we're challenging. There's a man named Albert Leadbetter on Denton Beckett's regional board and a Labour ward councillor for Cheatham. We believe that he may be related to Mark Denton Beckett, one of the managing directors. If this is true we're interested in whether Cllr. Alfred Leadbetter declared a pecuniary interest in the contract and stepped aside while the Committee deliberated on the contract's benefits. We believe that Cllr. Leadbetter might have received a financial incentive to push the contract with Denton Beckett through as quickly as possible,' Augustus revealed. Judy was struck dumb for several seconds.

'Yes, you're right. Albert Leadbetter is a Labour councillor but I've no idea who he's related to. I do happen to know though that he recently moved out of his council house. He's bought one of those smart new houses on one of the borough's new estates. Someone said they'd recently seen him driving around in a brand new four wheel drive car as well, cherished number plate and all,' Judy added.

Augustus looked pleased with this vital information. He would get his revenge on Cheatham Council one way or another.

'Thank you very much. It's something to give the police to be going on with,' Augustus said winking. Judy suddenly had the urge to get back to Tim and tell of Augustus' fears. Kissing him on the cheek, she said her goodbyes and left. She had the figures and she had something even more explosive to share with Tim. It had nothing to do with the LIP this time but certainly something that would rock the local Labour Party and any shock waves at all were very likely to impact on the politics of the new Materials Recycling Facility. The breaking rumours about Councillor Alfie Leadbetter and his abuse of Council Standing Orders were in the papers before you could say, Jumping Jack Flash.

Miranda cradled Cyril's head in her lap and stroked it as he wept, keeping an eye on the clock at the same time. Her yoga class beckoned and not being known for her sympathetic nature she suggested he take a pill and get some sleep. Her philosophy was quite simple, if you play at politics then you must be ready to suffer the criticism and the pitfalls when they arise.

'Cyril sweetheart, you simply must set the record straight. Write to the local paper and insist they report the truth. It was nothing to do with the LIP was it? You cannot answer for Labour's antics, my dear. It was Alfie Leadbetter who got his fingers caught in the till not you my love,' Miranda reassured Cyril as she regarded her own threadbare carpet. If only Cyril's fingers could have been caught in the till, she thought wistfully. She would have new carpets throughout the house like a shot but then she remembered it was not all about money. It was Cyril's stubbornness and resistance to change in his private life that was their problem. She wanted a pink bathroom with pretty tiles and fluffy towels; she wanted one of those new vacuum cleaners that sucks up the dirt without a bag and she wanted a leather settee with deep seats that one could laze about on. How to get them without suffering a divorce though? It was a headache just thinking about it.

The anti-fortnightly collection campaigners stepped up their actions whilst the Press were more than eager to cover their antics. The month of May arrived and still the contamination level rose. As per usual May was followed by June, a flaming June in fact which brought with it a dramatic increase in the number of complaints about maggots. The Star set up Maggot Watch, a special page in the newspaper where reports of maggots were recorded and highlighted in a special box. *Nine hundred complaints this week,* read the Maggot Watch box. The borough began to suffer, *Maggot Rage.* Horror stories about maggots flooded the local papers and some residents took their maggot ridden extra sacks of rubbish to the Civic Offices and dumped them at reception. The blue bottle fly population in Cheatham rose dramatically and one mum wrote to the Star about how her pet guinea pig had died as a result of being attacked by a cloud of flies. A new illness started to strike pets of all kinds in the borough. It was given the name of Fly-Strike by some professor at the London School of Tropical Medicine. Apparently it had only been seen in the African Congo before its debut in Cheatham.

Cheatham was beginning to feel the strain. Cyril's migraines were becoming more frequent as the recyclable materials became nothing more than pure and unadulterated muck. As the maggot frenzy reached dizzy heights residents who had previously behaved themselves started to change their habits by putting their meat waste, cat litter, doggy poos and anything else that would rot and stink to high heaven in their recycling bins instead of their rubbish bins. Residents developed an overwhelming urge to get rid of any putrescible waste they had on a weekly basis, regardless of which bin was due for collection effectively awarding themselves a weekly service. The letters to the editor of the Star were rolling in again.

Dear Editor
Has this Council gone stark raving mad? Cheatham has regressed to the days of Queen Victoria when rubbish was thrown out into the street and people died of cholera and typhus. What the hell are our environmental health officers thinking about? They should all be lined up against a wall and shot. This Council calls itself green and forward thinking, they couldn't negotiate their way out of a paper bag. It was signed, Angry of Needham.

Dear Editor

I've had recurring maggots in my rubbish bins and since I work in the field of food technology, I thought I would give you the benefit of my experience. Councillor Huckett seems to find the whole subject of maggots something to laugh about. I have reason to believe that it's a serious matter and the Council should be taking action now to prevent an outbreak of some ugly and devastating disease. As everyone knows the maggot develops from the egg of the house fly, blue bottle and blow fly. As a larva it then feeds on decaying matter like rotting food in our bins. They walk over anything, one minute they're on dogs' mess and the next they're on a tasty pork chop or sugary doughnut in your kitchen. The result could be dysentery or typhoid. The maggots in our bins are there because the waste is only collected once a fortnight. When will the Council stand up and be counted and honestly admit that there is a health problem? Name and address withheld.

Sir David Hooper responded to the irate letters received at the Cheatham Star's offices.

Dear Editor
The LIP is committed to promoting a community that is environmentally aware and efficient. We are investing in the future of the planet and Cheatham. Our aim is to make Cheatham a clean, green and safe place to live. I don't believe that anyone who cares about our planet would disagree with this sentiment. We also need to meet government targets on recycling. If we don't, the government will be within its right to fine the borough for not meeting its legal obligation. A heavy fine can only impact on other services and perhaps leave the less well off and those needing Social Services such as day centres and meals on wheels, in a worse position. It was signed, The Leader of the Council, Sir David Hooper.

Mentioning Social Services it was thought, would bring the public into line. No such luck. It set neighbour against neighbour and minor skirmishes along pleasant tree lined roads became the norm. Decadent residents purposely contaminating their recyclables with smelly food remains were admonished by their keen recycling neighbours whilst the not-so-keen recyclers, did not take too well to being dictated to by a load of do-gooders. The massing crowd were baying for blood along with a weekly rubbish collection. Cyril would need a magic wand to get out of this one. As ever, the local newspaper captured the increasing discontent on its letters pages.

Dear Editor
Unhappy Mum of Cheatham
I'm a mum of three small children and I've waited months to get a larger bin. The small bin was simply too small for all my disposable nappies and the amount of waste that one gets with small children. I spoke to someone at the Council many weeks ago and was told that I would be able to get a larger bin when the next batch arrived from the manufacturers. It didn't arrive. After contacting the Star who took it up on my behalf, I now have two large bins, one for waste and one for recycling. I fill these bins to the top and I can't imagine how a family of seven will manage under the new rule that only families of eight will be able to have large bins in the future. Fiona Chapman, Stonebridge.

Dear Editor
Clean up this borough now!

I live on the Beverly Estate and I'm proud to live there. Your paper prints so many derogatory stories about residents living on the Beverly and the good things are missed. Most of my neighbours are good, honest, clean living people who want to recycle, want to help the environment, but where is their incentive? I looked out of my window a couple of weeks ago and all I could see was muck and waste blowing around from the new recycling factory. Why was it built in an area that already has so many social problems? This white elephant is just adding to our health problems. I know we need the jobs but couldn't it have been built a bit further away? Does the Council care about us or are we, the Forgotten of Cheatham? I also want to ask the Council why we don't have any recycling facilities of our own? Most of us can't have the wheelie bins but would like to do our bit. Delroy Jones, Tintagel House

A disgruntled Leader contacted Cyril.

'Tell me Cyril what was the result of your enquiry into that debacle at the MRF a couple of weeks ago?' Sir David asked

'Oh, that. Well it seems we had a couple of belligerent agency drivers who were at the root of the problem. Dropped their loads in a fit of pique as I understand it and just went home and left it there to blow around,' Cyril explained.

'Who was in charge of the drivers?' Sir David asked.

'Well, I suppose I'd have to say it would be Reginald Turner, Refuse Manager,' Cyril was hesitant about dropping Reggie in it but then that's life!

'And who, Cyril, was in charge of the MRF?' Sir David inquired further.

'Um, well that would be Reginald Turner too since he holds the competent person's certificate,' Cyril explained.

'Are we sure that this Turner chappie is up to the job? It caused us a lot of grief and judging by the local rag's letters, it's not over yet. The name Turner sounds familiar. Don't I remember something about a disciplinary hearing and a rather attractive woman called Turner accused of something indecent; worked for Education didn't she? It was about a year ago?' Sir David recalled.

'That was June, Reginald's wife. She's actually working for Waste Management now and just about to move from being a supervisor to being the Administration Officer for the MRF,' Cyril suddenly felt ineffectual and waited for the pregnant pause to pass.

'Let me get this straight. Reginald Turner and his wife are now virtually running the Waste Management Section single handed and the wife now reports directly to him as MRF Manager? Oh please, Cyril, don't tell me this is the case,' Sir David begged to be wrong. The Lead Councillor for Waste was feeling rather silly.

'David, first of all, June Turner was let off. It was deemed that since it was a first offence and unlikely to happen again that a lenient approach would be the right one to take. Marcus was on the panel and they don't come more full of common sense than our Marcus do they?' Cyril went on, 'secondly, the Council has no policy which says that a husband and wife can't work together. I know that it has talked about introducing one but no decision has ever been agreed. I took advice from Human Resources,' Cyril defended himself.

'Who interviewed June Turner for the job?' Sir David asked. Cyril scratched his head; he was feeling inadequate

'I would think it was Dingle,' Cyril said rather hopefully. The Leader allowed the subject to drop and moved on to suggest that Cyril write again to the local paper and apologise at least for the mess on the Beverly Estate.

Dear Editor

The Council apologises to residents on the Beverly Estate for the mess caused at the recycling factory on the morning of the twenty sixth which was due to a timetabling dispute between management and drivers. The dispute coupled with the strong wind and rain during the night unfortunately made the incident a graver problem than it should have been. The Council wants to ensure that nothing like it ever happens again and has ordered a full inquiry. We are a caring Council and will do whatever is needed to keep the Beverly clean, tidy and free from any health risks. In answer to your reader last week I will be personally looking into how we can improve recycling facilities on the estate. It was signed Cyril Huckett, Lead Councillor for Waste.

'Why haven't we got recycling facilities on the Beverly?' Cyril asked Adrian a few days later, annoyed that he had been forced to even consider having such a conversation.

'We've tried Councillor but the bins are either continuously filled with non-recyclables or the kids take the glass and smash it on the parked cars,' Adrian warned, hoping that Cyril was not going to suggest trying again.

'Adrian, I want residents to think we care about them. A resident has written to the local paper suggesting that we've blatantly ignored the Beverly Estate's residents' rights to recycling banks. It's just the sort of rubbish that ends up at the European Court of Human Rights. I want you to put in as many sets of glass and paper banks as you can and ASAP,' Cyril insisted matter of factly not prepared to argue over the finer points. Adrian was aghast and feared for the worse wondering why councillors were so stupid as to ignore their expert and professional staff like himself. The likes of Adrian had been there and worn the t-shirt and knew the pitfalls. He felt a gloomy cloud descend around him.

John Dingle often ruminated along the same lines as Adrian; his almost fixed frown thesedays said it all. There would be no compromising with Cyril and so he told Adrian to make a start to look for suitable sites on the estate. Placing banks where residents would still get a good night's sleep away from the noise of smashing glass or where the kids would not regard paper banks as a fire lighting challenge would be nigh on impossible but try they must. Avoiding cars parked in the cramped parking areas and finding places where collection vehicles could get near enough to service the banks would not be easy either. Adrian forced himself to identify six potential sites on the estate. He sent the list to Cyril suggesting that it might be a good idea to consult with the tenants association beforehand. Cyril, as always, wanted the job done yesterday and gave strict orders to install the banks straight away. Of Adrian's six sites, three were brand new and three were sites which had been tried previously but had been closed down because of constant vandalism. Within a week Adrian's worse fears were being realised. There was broken glass all over the pavements and the paper bins were either set on fire or filled with builders' rubble.

Residents were up in arms about the debris and to add to the catalogue of problems the glass collection vehicle reversed out of one access road ripping off the bumper and several other bits and pieces from an old car parked along its route. The Council always encouraged its drivers to acknowledge any accidents they might have, so the driver, Brewer, left an apologetic note on the windscreen.

'Do you recognise that car, Stan?' Brewer asked his loader.

'Yeah, it does look kinda familiar, Brew. It looks a lot like that one Micky Brown drives, in it?' Stan answered. Silence followed. They knew Micky lived somewhere on the Beverly. They looked at one another.

'He wasn't in the allocation office this morning,' Brewer said sheepishly.

'Yeah, your right, Brew,' Stan said, looking grim faced in sympathy with the driver who was now feeling as sick as a parrot.

Brewer sat in silence for a couple of minutes while Stan jumped out and smoked a fag and inspected the damage. Brewer decided he must contact the depot and took the courage to radio in.

'Hello. Larry Wright please come in,' Brewer called urgently with a distinct hint of panic in his voice.

'Hi Brewer, go ahead.'

'Larry, is Micky Brown in today?' Brewer asked.

'No mate. He's taken a day's holiday. Why, anything I can help you with?'

'Only if you know where I can get a bumper for a Ford Cortina Mk 3? I think I've just hit Mick's car on the Beverly. You wouldn't happen to know what Mick's registration number is would yer?' Brewer asked, feeling a large lump in his throat. He knew how much Micky doted on his car.

'Dunno mate. Tell you what, I'll ring 'im and ask 'im,' Larry suggested.
Oh, Christ, was the only words that Brewer could find the strength to utter. Larry telephoned Micky. This was not going to be easy.

'Hi Mick. Would you mind checking your car for us, pal. Brewer thinks he's just taken yer bumper off collecting glass from your block,' Larry just told it how it was. He had never understood the nature of the love between a man and his classic car. Micky on the other hand was beside himself with worry.

'This is a joke, Larry?' Micky asked with a cigarette in his mouth, 'I'm standing 'ere in towels, I've just had a bleeding bath. I'm supposed to be taking it easy today. You know, getting up late and relaxing? If you're having a joke at my expense, I'll have your guts when I get back tomorrow, Wright.' There followed a cloud of black and blue words. Micky was not happy and dressing as quickly as he could rushed down to inspect his car.

There was no doubting it. The bumper was lying in the gutter and there was a nice dent in the wheel arch. Mick went back to his flat and made some phone calls. One call was to the Council's insurance department; he reported the damage. They knew Mick well and accepted his word. Micky reminded them that he needed his car to get to work for his early shifts. They understood. The waste must get through!

'Get it into a garage and we'll put a claim in for you, Mick,' the Council's Insurance Manager told him. It was just the reply Micky was hoping for and by midday the car was being towed away to the nearest Ford Cortina workshop.

'What the hell is this, Micky?' Reggie asked one week later when the invoice arrived, 'half of this stuff is engine parts,' Reggie scratched his head as he studied the bill.

'Yeah well, when the cullet lorry hit the car it did some other damage. It somehow damaged the steering linkages causing them to weaken,' Micky explained.

'And the new cylinder head?' Reggie was intrigued.

'Ah well it's an old motor you see and the knock caused it to crack,' Micky explained avoiding Reg's gaze.

'And I suppose the new tyres to the front of the car were necessary because the glass punctured them?' Reggie had caught on but Mick was an old friend so he authorised the invoice for payment. Mick was very pleased particularly since he had been unable to drive the car for a couple of weeks prior to the accident because of a failed MOT.

In the meantime, the Star was full of letters from residents on the Beverly.

Dear Editor,
I want to complain about this Council's determination to ruin our lives. I live on the Beverly and do shift work. Every Tuesday I'm woken up by glass being emptied into a Council lorry. It's such a shattering noise and it's causing me distress. Why do we have to have these things right under our windows? I was quite happy taking my bottles to Sainsbury's recycling centre in the High Street,' signed, Annoyed of The Beverly Estate.

Dear Editor,
My life is being made hell. As if we don't have enough problems living on this God forsaken estate. Every night just as I get my kids off to sleep some idiot comes along and throws bottles into the banks underneath my flat. Why do we have to put up with this nonsense? The Council is wrecking my life. Please help us, begged Ruby, a single parent of two under five on the Beverly Estate.

Dear Editor,
Please tell this stupid Council that we don't want recycling shoved down our throats. The kids nearly burnt down my place last night. They set fire to the paper banks and the fire brigade were called out. If they're not burning them they're climbing on the bins. Some kid is going to have a nasty accident. The Council will be sorry then. Cheatham Council take these banks out now! Anonymous of the Beverly Estate

Dear Councillor Huckett
I'm writing to let you know that my son, Danny aged ten years old fell off one of your recycling banks last night. He was rushed into Cheatham Infirmary and is now awaiting an operation to reshape and stitch his scrotum. The doctors are not sure yet whether he'll be able to lead a normal life when he grows up. I will be suing the Council. Mrs Kathleen O'Connor, resident on the Beverly Estate

Cyril was mortified. The Beverly recycling banks were a total failure and with most of it going up in smoke it had produced little in the way of recycling tonnage.

'What am I to do now?' Cyril whimpered to himself as he telephoned Adrian, 'take out all the banks from the Beverly today,' he ordered Adrian not having a clue about the degree of coordination necessary to achieve such a request at short notice.

'But Councillor, we don't have a tail-lift vehicle available to do it today. The tail-lift is out picking up fridges,' Adrian explained.

'Stop the fridge collection and get those damn banks off the Beverly Estate today. I'm fed up with the wretched people complaining all the time,' Cyril shouted. Adrian managed to refrain from saying, *I told you so* and contacted Micky Brown, who called the Ice Man on the radio and told him to stop collecting fridges, pick up one of the loaders from Wheeled Bin Round Two and go and sort out the Beverly. Peace returned once more to the walkways of the Beverly Estate and Cyril positively looked forward to the local newspaper and a Letters Page which he anticipated would be of a less troublesome nature than in previous weeks.

Dear Editor,
I want to know why the Council takes my money for a fridge collection and then doesn't collect my fridge. I paid thirty pounds to have my fridge collected on a particular day and one week later it's still standing in my front garden. I have a small child and I'm terrified that she'll climb inside and die a horrid death through asphyxiation.
Mr Tom Johnson, Lower Lampney.

With no end to the misery in sight, Cyril felt he could do with some professional help from his wife. The weather was getting hotter as indeed were the sorting staff at the MRF as they battled to overcome their nausea, a result of the stinking food waste. Everything was covered in slushy, slimy food dregs. It was rank. Cyril received a detrimental report from the paper mill threatening nasty things like a total ban on Cheatham's paper until the Council had cleaned up its act. Most of the loads were being rejected and returned to the MRF for further sorting which in turn caused a log jam as the daily loads continued to arrive from residents' wheelie bins. Reggie was tearing his greasy hair out and Adrian was called in to find another outlet for the so called, recycled materials.

In the midst of this emergency Sir David Hooper phoned Cyril.
'I was walking along the High Street this morning and as I passed those new plastic palm trees we bought from Crappendale, I, ehm, noticed a funny smell coming from them,' Sir David said. Cyril was finding it hard to concentrate on the Leader's problem.
'David, I've already asked the Street Cleansing Team to clean the base of the trees of dog pee for you, what more do you expect?' Cyril was not in one of his more relaxed moods.
'Cyril it's not urine. The smell is more like plastic melting slowly in the summer heat. I'll leave you to investigate. Catch you later,' Sir David said putting the phone down. Cyril started mumbling to himself.
'Here I am, trying my best to keep Cheatham from being hauled through the courts by our paper merchant for supplying smelly paper whilst at the same time fighting to keep the workers working and educate the public not to foul their wheeled bins. I'm entering the heart attack zone and all David's interested in is his bloody plastic trees!' Cyril cried. A rage was building up inside his large frame, a rare occurrence in academics but there it was most definitely a rage. This MRF business had definitely got his goat. He needed some tender loving care and thoughts about asking for professional help from his wife quickly faded away. He was in need of something more satisfying even naughtier perhaps. 'Sod Miranda and her stupid psychiatric therapies, I bloody well need Edith,' he muttered to himself, picking up the phone. Edith did not answer and so he strode steadfastly towards the LIP Group Room to see if she was there.

There were a couple of Councillors chatting in the LIP Group Room but no Edith so Cyril caught the bus to Leoni Bridges Road and found her just returned from shopping. Cyril received his sexual gratification in the hallway from an Edith still wearing her precautionary raincoat; it had threatened to spit earlier in the day. With Edith always saying how she preferred spontaneity it came as quite a surprise to Cyril when afterwards she berated him.

'That was a lacklustre performance if ever I saw one. I give you four out of ten for that,' Edith barracked. Cyril could not believe his ears. He had come to be relieved of his anxieties not get criticised for not reaching the right grade. At least Miranda would have made him a cup of tea. She might be a doctor but she knew her place was in the kitchen looking after her man right enough, Cyril admitted. He had trained her well and he knew, even though she had her little jokes occasionally about being independent and walking out on him that she would never leave him. Then another thought entered his head. Could Edith have grown tired of him? Could she have found someone else? No, of course not; Edith was just an old unattractive spinster, Cyril laughed inwardly at his ludicrous thoughts.

Edith's reaction to Cyril's love making performance still rankled and he searched his brain for an answer. Perhaps she did not appreciate being tied to the hall table although she had seemed to like it at the time and they had done something similar before using the bed headboard. Sometimes he had used four scarves, one for each appendage as being completely helpless was all part of the fun. It had been Edith's idea. Cyril walked home thinking of the saucy Edith manacled to her bed which brought on another erection. His house was in sight and he just hoped it was empty because he would need to go straight up to the bathroom deal with it. Miranda was home as it was her early day and as Cyril approached the front drive he could see her car sitting there. He cursed her and opening the front door ran upstairs. He shouted to her in the kitchen saying that he needed the bathroom in a hurry. He was all fingers and thumbs, his zipper was stuck and he cursed his charity shop trousers! He felt ready to explode. Miranda was standing in the bathroom wiping her face with a piece of cotton wool and was rendered speechless. Cyril had never lunged at her in a month of Sundays and feeling rakish she made the most of it.

Chapter 25

Augustus Aurelia's clandestine investigation into the relationship between Alfie Leadbetter and Denton Bennett Partnerships led to Alfie being thrown out of the Labour Party and declared unfit to be a town councillor. The publicity surrounding this made it difficult for the Band of Brothers to continue with their dastardly task of discrediting the LIP wheeled bin scheme. They slipped away quietly into the background, believing that perhaps it was better to lie low for a few months. The Green Evangelists, however, were keener than ever to unfrock the LIP and to get the weekly refuse collection re-instated. The Great Rubbish Debate initiated by the Green Evangelists was arranged to take place at a local theatre and the Press and the local radio station, Green Waves, had been invited. The latter offered to act as a referee and master of ceremonies should it be necessary and promised to broadcast the debate the following day on the internet. Speakers were chosen to support the Council and since no councillor felt any great urge to stand up and be counted, an unsure John Dingle was put forward as the Council's representative. The Green Evangelists wheeled out their expert witness from the World Health Organisation and Dingle dragged along under duress, one of the Council's Environmental Health Officers.

A nondescript LIP councillor, the only one they could find without an allegedly urgent meeting to attend, welcomed all to the debate and tried to break the icy atmosphere by making light of the usual housekeeping notices.

'In the event of a fire we are required to make our way through the doors at the back of the hall and to meet up by the dustbins in the car park,' he read from a sheet of paper, 'I don't think you should worry too much about there being a fire tonight though. Twice in one week would be unfortunate!' He waited for a general titter but apart from the lady giving out the agendas who seemed to find it extremely funny, there was none. This did not bode well for the rest of the evening. Mr Dingle was asked to come up to the microphone and pronounce first in favour of the alternate weekly wheeled bin scheme.

Dingle stumbled over his words and sensing that he must be sounding much like that poor old sod Bob Mason, the Head of Planning, took a deep breath and concentrated hard on what he was trying to say.

'We have incredibly high government targets to meet and I argue that we need to increase recycling quickly if we are to meet these and satisfy Whitehall. As a local authority we need to show commitment and leadership so that commercial companies like the one set up by Crappendale City Council know we mean business. It's only when this is obvious to industry that they too will invest in machinery and ways of dealing with the recyclates we collect. If we show that we're serious about recycling, industry will develop markets for all the materials that we collect and all the silly suggestions about green glass mountains shooting up because the stuff can't be reused, will fade away. If I may, I would like to use Crappendale City Council as a good example of a company marching ahead with market development. The wonderful plastic trees that we now have gracing our High Street all year round...' Dingle went on for ages, spelling out the *heart and minds* argument for recycling.

As Dingle's stance pushed the audience towards their boredom thresholds fidgeting broke out. *'What the hell has all this sentimentality to do with wheeled bins and fortnightly collections?'* They were whispering to each other. Dingle, feeling the unease in the room, changed tack.

'And, I expect you're all wondering what all this has to do with wheeled bins? Well, I will tell you!' Dingle said stubbornly.

'Thank goodness for that,' an elderly gentleman called followed by sniggers towards the back.

'Economics! This is what it's all about.The wheeled bins scheme works by alternating collections and because of this it can be provided at half the cost of a weekly waste and fortnightly recycling service. It is ingenuous. We only need one set of vehicles,' Dingle paused for effect before going on, 'I would like to remind everyone that Cheatham has a lot of problems with foxes ripping open the black sacks leaving rubbish strewn along the roads. The wheeled bins are making Cheatham a cleaner place to live,' Dingle explained, being interrupted again by more heckling and seeing this as an opportune moment to bring in his own expert witness, the Environmental Health Officer, he did so.

Following John's presentation the officious and now ever so slightly scared, dark suited young man stood up and started speaking into the microphone.

'I would like to convince you all that the alternate weekly scheme is safe and not a health risk. I understand from the local newspapers that many have concerns that the wheeled bin scheme is unhealthy. In particular, I believe many of these anxieties are rooted in the breeding cycle of the fly. Let me state unequivocally that it takes two weeks from egg to fly so if the bins are collected every fourteen days there shouldn't be any problems. If everyone wraps up their smelly, mucky, food waste really well, the flies won't get inside the bins in the first place,' the *eager beaver* Environmental Health Officer said and turning to the screen behind him showed various pictures of flies in all their developmental stages and especially that of the maggot. The Tories found the presentation tiresome and not at all convincing and from somewhere in the audience came a cry of, *what a load of rubbish* bringing more sniggering and a *bollocks,* from someone in the back row.

Just as the heckling died down a small voice came from the middle of the audience. Heads turned to see who was speaking and an elderly, grey haired woman going through her beige phase stood and repeated her words of wisdom.

'Mr Dingle, it's no good keep telling us that flies won't get at our rubbish if we wrap it well. What about the holes in the back of the bins? The flies get in through those don't they?' The room was silent. Dingle looked confused. What holes in the back of the bins? He was unaware of any holes. He begged for clarification and wished that Adrian was there. Why were these young people never around when you needed them? He was probably in bed with some girl when he should have been supporting his executive head at this wretched event. No commitment these youngsters, he thought, panicking. 'Where the handle joins the back of the bin there is a gap, Sir,' the old dear shouted, 'and on the bigger bins there is another gap under the lip which I presume is there for ventilation. My bin is full of flies all the time and I'm one of the few who always wraps my food waste well,' she explained. Dingle was speechless and it was a few seconds before he could find the stamina to reply. The audience started to chat amongst itself until Dingle raised his arm for quiet.

'Madam, all I can say is that I'll look into the matter. I wasn't aware of any such holes in the bins,' he replied, feeling overcome by a sick feeling deep down in his stomach. The Executive Head of Waste Management was considering self harm and had quite forgotten about early retirement.

The Tories were up next with their World Health high ranking scientist, Professor Pierre-Henri Allain who took the podium and began his more technical presentation in his delectable French accent.

'The House Fly, Musca domestica feeds by mopping up semi-liquid foods. To ingest solid food it must soften it. It does this by expelling saliva over it first. These fluids, which contain the semi digested liquid food, are then sucked back up into the crop. It is this alternation between vomiting and sucking which makes the House Fly so dangerous to our health. Any disease it has picked up on one piece of food is then passed onto its next bit of food. House Flies are well known to cause infections of the gut. The fly lays its eggs in batches of about one hundred and fifty and in totals of around one thousand. They have a preference for horse dung as a breeding medium but they'll thrive in most decaying materials associated with animals.'

The WHO speaker waited patiently for a lull in the background noise before continuing.

'I beg to differ with the earlier speaker since it's generally known in scientific circles that the life cycle of the fly is shorter than fourteen days. In any case the maggot stage comes before the fly and it's that which most object to. There are very sound reasons for collecting the waste weekly. However, I must say that the WHO has always campaigned for a collection which is *regular and appropriate* across the world. This means that in some parts of Southern Europe, the waste is collected twice a week or even daily. It's not for the WHO to dictate frequency but it would encourage, for the sake of health, a collection that maximises the chance of improving health rather than resulting in a population which is always on the brink of one epidemic or another, which we tend to see in the poorer countries of the world.' Professor Allain, who had about sixteen letters after his name, illustrated his talk with pictures of diseases caused by the fly and its habit of secreting juices all over our food in order to digest it more easily. A young pregnant woman struggled to get to the end of her row and then made a beeline for the toilets; someone else was seen holding her stomach and overheard to say that she wished she had forgone dinner before attending the debate.

Questions followed with Sam, the Green Waves representative acting as Chairman. A Labour councillor raised his hand. The Band of Brothers may have disbanded but as individuals and elected members, they believed they still had a right protect the public.

'Mr Dingle, don't you think that the contamination in the wheeled bins is enough to cause disease? Isn't the food waste in the bins a threat to the health of the people who have to sort the stuff? I've spoken to dustmen and they tell me that the material in the bins is so badly contaminated that most of it has to be landfilled. Is it fair that we should expect people to touch the muck that is being sent to the MRF?' Dingle was wishing that exclusion orders preventing attendance at the debate had been enforced on certain councillors. Life was so unfair. He attempted to answer the question.

'Councillor, let me correct you on a couple of points. Most of the materials entering the MRF are not sent to landfill and secondly, if the materials were so bad that they could be credited with the description, muck, I would be the first person to do something about it. To answer your other point about the food waste in the recycling bins being a threat to health, I would have to say that it is not. You've heard what the Council's own Environmental Health expert has said, that flies cause no problems worth mentioning. I can personally assure you that the level of contamination is under control. When such incidents do occur, and these are rare indeed, it's possible to isolate the unsuitable materials and discard them before they ruin the remaining high quality recyclables and that is what we most certainly do,' John insisted although his real thoughts on the subject were quite different. Most of the materials he knew to be so bad that it would be truer to say that they were nearer one hundred percent rubbish. But how could he reveal that?

Dingle waited anxiously for the next question and just as he feared the next was for him too. An elderly lady with white straggly hair and dressed bizarrely in a multi coloured caftan and weird peacock feathered minimalist hat put her question to John Dingle.

'I'd like to ask what the Council proposes to do about those rare households that do contaminate their bins?' She asked. Dingle recognised her at once as the mother of the local MP, Sir Geoffrey Lawrence. Mrs Lawrence had always been known as a bit of an eccentric.

'Madam, I'm in the process of appointing two Enforcement Officers whose job it will be to call on residents who put the wrong things in their bins. This will clarify the situation for those who are confused by the scheme. I feel confident that it will be enough to resolve the situation and lead to only first rate quality materials entering the MRF at all times,' Dingle announced, his heart pounding in his breast. He was thinking on the hoof. Enforcement Officers were a brilliant idea why had he not thought of them before? He would speak to Personnel tomorrow.

Mrs Lawrence, who in spite of her years had an agile mind was within moments waving her hand in the air for a follow up question.

'Mr Dingle, is it really possible to achieve a recycling rate of eighty five percent? Recycling should be such an easy concept but Cheatham seems to have turned it into a marathon of difficulties. People can't remember what to put in their bins. If they're putting the wrong materials in it's because they're making an honest mistake. Should the Council aggravate residents by sending an Enforcement Officer to harass them?' Dingle was hoping his wife had recorded his favourite BBC police series. He wanted to be at home with his TV supper rather than in the middle of this public discontent. His thoughts were interrupted from the back.

'Excuse me, but I have a family of four children and all I'm allowed are the small bins for both my recyclables and my rubbish and we manage,' shouted the shrill voice. Was this really happening? Dingle wondered. Was someone actually speaking up for the Council? Dingle breathed a sigh of relief feeling someone must be looking down on him from above. A wheeled bin supporter, hip hip hoorah! The young mum went on, 'we recycle everything we can and I compost my vegetable waste. I always have plenty of room in my bins because I recycle. I'm a busy mum and if I'm capable of putting the right things in the bin then everyone else can do it too. That's all I wanted to say. Oh, and thanks Mr Dingle for having this debate so that everyone can air their views,' purred the mum of four. Dingle smiled. A paid up member of the LIP no doubt but hell, who's counting?

Sam, the Green Waves compere allowed a few more questions and then looking at the clock, brought the proceedings to and end. John Dingle was exhausted and limped home thinking how good his job would be if there were no residents and no politicians. He was quite clear about another thing too; when he retired he would go nowhere near a council building, become a councillor or ever recycle his own waste again. Familiarity breeds contempt, he thought, as he stopped on his way home at the local chippy to get himself some junk food therapy.

At the depot the following morning another great debate was underway. Gary Green was agonising over having to get in an agency chap to clean the plastic trees in the High Street.

'We're already overspent on our agency budget for this quarter. Why should I have to take someone on just to keep those silly arse trees clean of dogs' dirt and urine? It's ridiculous. I feel like asking the silly bugger for a cost code, let him bleeding well pay for it out of his own budget. What do you think, Mick?'

'It's not what I think, Gar, it's what Pooper Hooper wants. Hooper is king, remember?' Micky said sarcastically.

'I fought he was God,' the Ice Man chipped in.

'Look at it another way, Gary, if they were real trees you'd have to take on more than one man because we'd be having to do leafing like we used to. You know what the public are like, if just one leaf falls on the ground they want to know why Street Cleansing hasn't picked it up within five minutes of it landing there,' Micky said.

'Oh no, Mick, I'm afraid you've got it all wrong. If they were real leaves, it would be Refuse's responsibility to collect them because the service would constitute a kerbside collection like what the wheeled bins are,' Gary Green congratulated himself on such a cunning shot.

'No Gary, you're barking up the wrong tree, if you'll excuse the pun, because when leaves are picked out of the gutter the job becomes part of Street Cleaning's duties, matey; anyone can see that,' Mick did not like to lose an argument. The Ice Man came up with a middle way.

'Look you two morons, the best thing would be to give the job to the Parks Service and their Grounds Maintenance Team. They could take them back to the Parks' depot and compost them and that way we'd please Huckett as well because we'd be recycling them. End of story.' Mick smiled back at his colleague and went back to putting his head in the daily tabloid as the other two got on with their paper work.

Reggie Turner called in at the depot but was in a frightful hurry to get to the Civic Offices.

'Sorry lads, must dash. Cyril Huckett's wife, Dr Miranda, is giving a lecture at Civic. It's on the Management of Change and how we deliver it to our customers,' Reg said.

'It's a bit late for that isn't it? The wheeled bins are already in place,' Larry commented.

'Yeah, your right but it's all about occupational therapy and industrial psychology now. Apparently Dr Huckett's quite an expert in that sort of stuff,' Reggie explained as he raced out into the yard leaving his colleagues staring after him.

'Reg seems to have gone up in the world?' Larry Wright asked Mick.

'No Lal, he just thinks he has. Don't you worry mate he'll come a cropper especially with that blonde bombshell of a wife of 'is helping. Just you wait and see. It'll all end in tears, mark my words,' Mick reassured.

Biddles had been listening to his colleagues and had a burning issue of his own.

'Mick, what's E-government?' He asked whilst reading the staff news sheet.

'I think it's to do with using e-mail and stuff like that, you know to save paper. The Council is also putting in some computerised customer enquiry system. It's supposed to make sure that when a resident rings the Council their call is recorded and can be tracked to see where the query has got to at any one time. Reg was telling me about it. It's another one of those courses he went on,' Micky explained as best he could picking up a load of printed e-mails that were lying on the table and proceeding to read them. Biddles nodded.

'If we're supposed to be saving paper why have you printed out that lot?' Biddles asked.

'Biddles please do as I say and not as I do,' Mick suggested, 'and don't forget this afternoon at 3pm the crews will be coming back for their celebration buffet although why the bloody 'ell Cyril Huckett is calling it a celebration, beats me. I doubt very much if they see the completion of the wheeled bin rollout and a fifty percent recycling rate as anyfink to celebrate. More money in their pay packets is what they would like to see,' Micky moaned.

Dr Miranda's delegates were gathering eagerly for her seminar. The Leader of the Council was particularly keen to hear her speak as he had long held an interest in the psychology of the mind. He was, therefore, somewhat surprised when she began her lecture by talking about a part of the anatomy that was a long way from the head. She started her talk with the topic of Anal Retention and how to unzip and encourage growth. Sir David sat upright in his chair and was all ears as was Councillor Jim Bowen who had crept in at the back and was beguiled by both suggestions especially Miranda's last remark about the degree of workforce penetration that would be necessary to muster change.

Miranda went on with her talk, speaking in her beautiful middle class, privately educated voice.

'Workers suffering from stress may present many symptoms that are not easily recognised as attributable to stress. Constipation is one of these. In the trade we refer to it as, Anal Retention. Freud studied bowel movements in children. He found that when children were worried they became constipated. They also became obsessively tidy and preoccupied with minute details. The same happens to adults in stressful situations such as excessive change. Every team has an anal retentive amongst its number,' Miranda glanced around the room; she knew Cyril was not a sufferer because he was not at all tidy that was for sure. Cyril in turn regarded John Dingle whom he knew to be obsessively tidy and wondered whether he might be the anal retentive on the Waste Management Team. Was he a liability? He had heard that his performance at the 'debate' had been mediocre. The local newspaper reports were awaited with some trepidation. Perhaps Dingle could be a risk to the stability of the service?

John Dingle, unaware of Cyril's stare was also surreptitiously surveying the gathered clan. His eyes settled on the Mayor. Dingle was privy to both Huckett and Bullmans' dirty little secrets; he ruminated, wondering what part public service stress had played in causing these pillars of Cheatham society to wander from the straight and narrow? He took a long hard look at the Mayor. He always walked as though he was holding both cheeks tightly together, Dingle smiled quietly to himself. As for Cyril Huckett, he could not possibly be afflicted because he was always lecturing on the need to eat more fresh vegetables and fibre. As Dingle's thoughts flashed from Cyril to the Mayor and back again, Sir David was sitting quietly wondering if dogs might suffer from stress and anal retentiveness too and if so, should it be encouraged? Just think of all the Street Cleaning cost savings to be made in that neck of the woods! Anal Retention would be the answer to the prayers of anyone who had ever stepped in their mess. With her audience focussed on her every word, Miranda went into the second part of her lecture entitled, How to Loosen up. Everyone was agog.

The workforce's wheeled bin celebrations beckoned and Reggie, Dingle and Cyril drove back to the depot together to thank the crews for their hard work over the previous few months. A sincere Cyril invited them to tuck in to the mouth watering spread he had requested for them. They swept over to the table, removed the cling film and jostled to get to the paper plates. The rowdy voices subsided and there was a lull in the proceedings as they stared at the array of food laid out before them. There were tiny sausages on sticks, canapés with thinly sliced cucumber and all kinds of cocktail finger buffet foods. Cyril caught sight of these large, muscle bound men trying to work out how to eat such dainty foodstuffs. One man was trying to stuff as much as he could on a biscuit; another was wrapping a great wedge of food in a slice of ham and eating it like a sandwich. It was a pitiful sight to see. Had no one in Waste Management any manners or idea about etiquette?

Adrian Moses-Pomfrey arrived and straight away realised there had been a terrible mistake. He phoned the caterers.

'I ordered baguettes, so where are they?' He asked brusquely, 'I've got forty dustmen here about to lynch me because they were expecting a bean feast and what they've got is canapés,' Adrian screamed down the phone, 'well make sure you get them here pronto. I'm not paying for this lot,' he said, putting his mobile phone away and then turning to the crews, 'I'm so sorry chaps. The caterers have delivered the buffet meant for the Townswomen's Guild. Some proper food will be here in a jiffy; just be patient,' he begged them. The token bean feast had improved Cyril's relationship with the workforce but the Great Wheelie Bin Debate debacle was far from over and very soon reared its ugly head again. Tim Baldwin had attended the debate and had a few points to share with his readers on the matter.

Contamination or no contamination that is the question? The Star's headline read. *A senior Council Officer told the Great Wheelie Bin Debate last Thursday that there is no contamination in the wheelie bins. The Cheatham Star has proof that this is not true. Workers at the MRF have complained of sore throats and respiratory illnesses caused by the dust and pathogens emitted from the rubbish or so called recyclables. John Dingle, Waste Management's Executive Head, is recorded as saying that the level of contamination is under control.*

What does that mean? The Star also has information from one of the Council's reprocessors claiming that the paper is well below an acceptable grade and that it's considering turning the Council's lorries away if it doesn't clean up its act. And that's not all! Astonishingly, it turns out there are actually holes at the back of the bins where the flies can waltz in without any trouble at all. So much for the Council's pep talk on how the little blighters won't get in if residents take care! For more on the Great Wheelie Bin Debate, look at our web-site and the link to the Green Waves Radio Station, where you can listen to the debate itself. Keep your letters coming. We will dedicate a whole page to them next week. As requested, the letters rolled in.

Dear Editor,
I heard the Great Rubbish Debate on the Green Waves Radio Station and was horrified to hear the WHO expert talk about possible diseases that Cheatham's residents might contract from their wheelie bins. I was so scared by this that I checked out the Musca Domestica and residents may be interested in what I found. More than one hundred pathogens are associated with the house fly. These include typhoid, cholera, bacillary, dysentery, tuberculosis, anthrax, ophthalmia and infantile diarrhoea, as well as parasitic worms. These organisms are picked up from sources of filth including our rubbish. I've noticed a vast increase in the number of bluebottles in my house this summer; in fact, I've been unable to open my windows, because as soon as I do my kitchen is swarming with them. What do other residents say?
Fly Blown of Needham.

This was one of several hundred letters received by the Star. There were so many that they were forced to post them on their web-site for all to look through at their leisure. The newspaper reminded residents about its *Maggot Watch* page, where residents were invited to write in if they found maggots in their bins. In the first week nine hundred maggot sightings were reported and the following week this figure rose to over two thousand incidents of maggots. A special section of the paper was put aside especially for the fun with a squishy maggot called, *Legless Lilly, the Lava Lovely.* Legless Lilly sported a bashful smile which made everyone chuckle. Cyril tried to ignore the newspapers. The Cheatham Star campaign gathered such momentum that Russell was told to contact the Star and beg them to report the issue more seriously and even to give up reporting it at all. For Tim, who was just warming up, this was just like a red rag to a bull.

Augustus Aurelia was just getting his own game plan moving having met up with Tim to discuss tactics for issues which he believed were in the public interest.
'You know, Tim, I'm just a public servant really not unlike those elected councillors. I like to see the public get value for money. It's just not fair that residents pay such exorbitant rates of council tax and get nothing back for it,' Augustus sounded earnest, a knack he had developed over his years in business. Tim recorded his words of wisdom for use later on. 'Yes Tim, I'm afraid through sheer incompetence, I've seen councils sign contracts which have squeezed their authorities dry. Talk about legal departments supposedly knowing their stuff, they're so very often incompetent idiots. I'm not saying that this applies to Cheatham's legal department or indeed its councillors but I've seen some pretty awful deals go through. At the end of the day, it's the

poor council tax payer who has to foot the bill. At Aurelia Waste Handling, we've tried to be honest. We're a commercial company sure enough but we always try to be helpful and have the local tax payer at the centre of our thoughts,' Augustus said thoughtfully. This was all very interesting but Tim needed something a bit meatier.

'Augustus, how did Cheatham perform against those other council's that you've dealt with?' Tim was hoping to get some hard facts.

'Let me tell you Tim, my friend, we took all the waste from their recycling bins and we did it in good faith. But Tim, we were being harassed by the Environment Agency. They inspected us every week as a rule but once they got wind of the Cheatham recyclables, so called, they just happened to drop in every day, twice sometimes to catch us unawares. They threatened us with closure if WE didn't clean up OUR operation. Can you believe that? But really, Tim, the stuff was awful. You wouldn't have wanted your dog to go anywhere near it let alone men and women who were supposed to sort that dirt,' Augustus paused whilst Tim popped a new tape in his recording machine; he could not afford to miss anything.

'So, Augustus, what happened next?' Tim asked excitedly. He was looking for that sting in the tail that he could use to his advantage and Augustus knowing full well he had Tim's undivided attention gave him precisely what he wanted.

'I had several talks with that Huckett bloke and some for good measure with that Hooper chappie. I tried to make them aware that the recyclates were not valuable materials at all but stinking crap. We had no other option but to send it to one of our landfill sites. We even sent that Councillor Huckett the tonnages so he could subtract them from the recycled tonnages and make sure the recycling rate was accurate. But alas, I guess he was just another dishonest councillor like so many others. In reality, he was just another town clerk looking for a gong. I understand that the recycling rate is still shooting up?' Augustus looked to Tim for acknowledgement, Tim nodded, 'well, I'm pleased of course for Cheatham but extremely surprised. It wouldn't do any harm to get hold of the figures and check them out, would it?' Augustus suggested with a wicked twinkle in his eye.

'Well, as it happens, Augustus, I do have the figures and we'll be looking at them closely after what you've just told me. I think that there may be a few more questions for Professor Huckett,' Tim sighed.

Tim visualised the headline for the next edition, *Cheating Cheatham! Recycling Rate Rogues.*

The Star has uncovered the Council's recycling ruse. It has misled the public about its recycling rate. Cheatham Council has regularly insisted in recent weeks that it is recycling fifty five percent of its waste. The Star has evidence that this is a figment of someone's vivid imagination and that the true recycling rate is more like fifteen percent. The Star has recovered photographs which prove that the waste in the recycling bins is completely unusable and has to be dumped; and it doesn't look like it will get any better. The Star invites Cyril Huckett, the Council's Lead Councillor for Waste to clear both his own and his Council's name.

The Green Evangelists were shocked by the revelations and they redoubled their efforts to discredit the LIP. They now had over thirty thousand signatures on their petition and it was ever growing as they trudged the streets every night knocking on doors. Residents were shocked too. They were even more shocked when little wrist slapping notices came through their letter boxes telling them they had in error put something as inconsequential as a crisp packet in their recycling bins. This latest act of Big Brother was one of sheer desperation initiated by Cyril to reduce the contamination. Residents saw red on receiving the little correctional notes and put more than a crisp packet in their recycling bins the following week.

The cumulative effect was like an avalanche with residents showing their grim distain for the new recycling service by purposely contaminating their bins. The Council's accountant was pulling his hair out as the operating costs for the recycling factory soared. An emergency meeting with Dingle was called.

'Mr Dingle, I feel I must discuss the Waste Management budget with you because we are definitely heading for an enormous overspend. We sent three hundred tonnes of materials into the MRF in June and we brought two hundred and ninety tonnes out again, which went to landfill. How can this be when the recycling rate was still said to be fifty five percent? Amazingly, it increased again last week as I understand it to fifty six percent and that's not all; the price of sending a tonne into the MRF is sixty pounds and if it goes to landfill we have to pay the waste disposal contractor another fifty pounds per tonne. This means that we're paying one hundred and ten pounds for every tonne we collect in the recycling bins,' the accountant stated his case.

The accountant was a youngish man who was already balding with the stress of trying to manage Cheatham's Waste Management finances. He had recently become a father and had yet to enjoy an uninterrupted night's sleep; he rubbed his neck to relieve the stress.

'We expect to have a minimum of twenty thousand tonnes through the MRF and if we carry on like we are, Mr Dingle, we'll be paying over two million pounds for this waste. We should only be paying just over a million pounds. It would be cheaper to landfill it all instead. A million pounds Mr Dingle! That buys a lot of Social Services for the needy,' the bullish Council Officer reminded him.

'Yes, Bruce,' Dingle said, being a few grades above the accountant he felt he could call him by his first name, 'the contract was pushed through by the Head of Legal without proper scrutiny. I think Huckett was behind it. Trouble is we're now well and truly stuck with it. You see, although we own the MRF and the staff are ours, the capital repayments on the building are very high and we are unfortunately locked into the Denton Beckett contract for many years to come,' Dingle explained feeling rather depressed and mightily bored with the subject. He sensed the game was almost up for him even though the mess was not of his doing and as Bruce left he re-started his letter requesting early retirement.

Chapter 26

John Dingle wasted no time in sending his request for early retirement to Maisie Atichitawomba. She read it thoughtfully and passed it to the Leader for comments. Sir David called in Cyril and together they discussed their Executive Head of Waste's letter.

'Bloody cheek if you ask me and in our hour of need as well? I should cocoa. What does he think he's playing at? Cheatham residents are rioting in the streets and the man in charge of the army wants to bow out. I've never heard anything like it. A man of Dingle's seniority should be prepared to go down with his ship,' the Leader proclaimed.

'You're quite right of course,' Cyril said, 'if Dingle goes now, we'll have no one to blame and dismiss later on. Better keep him here for a while until we see which way the wind blows. Anyway, in spite of that dung cow Bendover leaving next week, I doubt very much whether she'd agree to another early retirement. I don't even know how old the beggar is. Does it say in his letter?' Cyril asked.

'Ehm, my age, I think Cyril,' the Leader replied, stroking his goatee beard and taking a seat at his desk so as not to draw attention to his short stature. He often did this when finding himself standing next to those rather taller than himself such as the likes of Cyril Huckett.

'Even more reason to make him stay on. If we can stand the heat then he jolly well will have to be there with us,' Cyril concluded.

Dingle waited and waited for a reply. It was a bit like waiting for the second coming, he thought. Every day as the internal post arrived he was just like the proverbial birthday boy scampering out to see if any cards had arrived. Sadly, he was always disappointed. He was constantly making plans for how he would spend his retirement days. He dreamed of relaxed weekends allowing him to make better use of his Chelsea season ticket or fishing along tranquil river banks. Instead he spent his Saturdays catching up with paperwork. A mean spirited public constantly harassing him by telephone and letter made his desire to escape the Council's clutches ever more determined. Nothing was going to keep him in his Cheatham Council hot seat for too much longer. He telephoned Maisie to see where his request had got to.

'Good Morning, John. How are you?' Maisie asked kindly.

'Oh I'm fine, Maisie. I was just wondering if you'd had time to consider my request for early retirement,' he asked.

'Do you mean to tell me no one has got back to you? I'm so sorry, John. I did have a word with the Leader and I believe he has spoken to Councillor Huckett and I'm afraid they're not at all keen to let you go just at the moment. They feel that you are absolutely vital to them with the wheeled bin problems and all that dreadful business. I'm sure if you were prepared to wait say another six months the situation would be quite different,' Maisie said reassuringly. John Dingle had other ideas. He would be leaving Cheatham to start his early retirement in just a matter of weeks. Nobody was going to put anything in his way. He began to plan his exit strategy with cunning precision.

A few days after Maisie had delivered the devastating news, Dingle invited Cyril to meet him in his office for a chat about how they might tackle the continuing wheeled bin uprising. The contamination levels were at their highest and as if that was not enough, the gas fuelled refuse collection vehicles were exploding all over town creating scenes that resembled guerrilla warfare. As a result of these horrendous breakdowns residents were not getting their rubbish collected. Sometimes bins remained uncollected for several days and the Council's switchboard was jammed from 8am until the time the telephone operators went home at 5.30pm.

'Come in Councillor, come in. Can I get you some coffee?' Dingle asked Cyril cheerily.

'Thank you, John. I would prefer tea if you have it. An unsuspecting Lead Councillor for Waste replied, 'I read in one of those sustainable food magazines that tea is actually very good for you. It apparently builds up the immune system, creates antibodies, protects against some tumours too,' Cyril enlightened. Dingle was listening to a point.

'Councillor, why don't you make yourself comfortable over there in my chair? You get a nice view of the Civic Offices' rose beds. You, being a gardener, I think you'll appreciate them,' John suggested as he fished around for a tea bag. Cyril slid down into Dingle's comfy leather chair whilst looking out at the roses.

Dingle poured the teas and placed them on the desk in front of Cyril. The Lead Councillor swung his chair back round to face the desk and as he did so stretched out to take his tea. To do this it was necessary to glance downwards and what he saw sent shock horror waves through his body. A set of full colour photographs showing two people completely starkers, cavorting around a glass conservatory stared back at him. Convulsed, the colour drained from his cheeks.

'Shit!' Cyril shrieked. John wanted to laugh but quickly his sense of occasion took over and he felt sorry for this professor of learning who was sitting in some discomfort on the other side of the desk. It was such a shame that it had had to come to this. Dingle's game plan had no get out clause for Cyril and at this moment he chose to ignore his dilemma.

'Councillor, we need to resolve the vehicle problems or we will be in dreadful trouble. We must hire in diesel freighters immediately to replace our useless gas freighters,' Dingle prattled. The very sight of the pictures, he knew, would be enough to get his real message home. 'Please don't let your tea go cold, Councillor. You really want to make the most of any antibodies therein,' Dingle reminded him. They talked for about ten minutes and then Cyril told him to book whatever transport he needed and he would square it with the Finance Department. They appeared to have reached a mutual understanding.

'John, I understand from Maisie that you'd like early retirement,' Cyril began. Dingle sat expressionless, his hands folded in his lap, 'I'll speak to Maisie and my colleagues on the Council to get a speedy settlement for you,' Cyril said staring down at the photographs. Dingle smiled back at him.

'Don't worry about those, Cyril. They'll remain under lock and key and will be destroyed at the appropriate time; trust me,' Dingle said sincerely. Cyril gulped his tea and left, leaving Dingle listening to his hurried footsteps going full pelt down the stairs. Dingle felt sure Cyril was taking the steps three at a time! Blackmail was an ugly word Dingle admitted to himself. How fortuitous it had been, finding those old photographs filed away on the H drive labelled, Biddles Pics, he thought to himself. He was, however, realistic enough to know that his retirement may not be quite in the bag. Maisie could be difficult especially if she was unable to understand Cyril's sudden change of mind. Dingle, Cyril convinced himself, had not been all that bad. He worked hard and on many an occasion had helped him out of some very tight corners. Surely, early retirement at this time, even if it might not be the optimum as far as the service was concerned, would not be that inconvenient? Afterall there was that Reginald Turner chappie running the MRF who could take some of the flack, perhaps? And Russell was on hand to help fend off the Press.

Cyril approached Sir David's office suite and as he did so put on his serious academic face, the one that suggested he was a world renowned expert. Pamela Peters sat at her desk in front of Sir David's inner sanctum and looked up as Cyril's mighty shadow loomed over her.

'Hello Cyril, do you have an appointment as the Leader is fairly stretched today?' She asked. Cyril raised his eyebrows. How could she talk to the Lead Councillor for Waste in this way?

'No appointment, I'm afraid Pamela but I must see the Leader about an urgent matter right now, it just won't wait. Please let him know I'm here,' Cyril insisted.

'Actually Cyril, between you and me, he's a bit upset. He's lost his favourite photograph of Tweetie Pie. He had it in the drawer until we moved his office furniture around. I can't seem to console him,' she admitted. Cyril was nonplussed. He had the world tumbling around his ears and David was crying in his tea because he had lost a photograph of some slapper, he supposed.

Pamela waited for words of condolence from Cyril.

'Sly old dog,' Cyril uttered, 'I'd never have guessed it. So David's at it too is he?' There was a look of indignation and absolute horror as Pamela realised Cyril's misinterpretation of the situation.

'Cyril Huckett, *sly old dog*? What are you talking about? I hardly think that you can imply such disgusting assignations about the Leader,' Pamela was noted for her staunch defence of her boss, Cyril remembered. Perhaps she was right, calling him a sly old dog was probably the wrong phrase to use, especially since he hated them so much. Pamela went on to clarify the situation. 'Councillor, you certainly have a way with words. Tweetie Pie was Sir David's budgerigar, a beautiful green and yellow bird which suffered a catastrophic accident a couple of months ago when he flew out of Sir David's kitchen window straight into the jaws of his neighbour's cat. When you speak to Sir David, it might be as well not to mention it,' she suggested brusquely, nodding towards the Leader's door. Cyril re-armed himself and lost no time in putting all his cards on Sir David's table. He poured out his sorry tale but there was little reaction from Sir David who could not quite take it all in especially following the loss of his Tweetie Pie memento.

A more hopeful Cyril called on Maisie next.

'Hi Cyril, I believe you've come to talk about Dingle's dosh? I can't think for the life of me why because I thought we'd decided that it wasn't quite the right time. He's pretty much the rock of the establishment when it comes to Waste Management, so tell me Cyril why the change of heart?' Maisie was sitting at her computer keying in characters using her two index fingers. Cyril chose his words carefully so as not to arouse suspicions.

'Maisie, I've given it much thought and you know old Dingle, he's not such a bad old stick. He has his shortcomings...' Maisie found the use of the word, shortcomings funny and laughed. It reminded her of something Marcus had said to her just the night before when he had ejaculated far too early and without warning describing it as a *shortcoming* of his own. 'On reflection,' Cyril explained, 'I just think this whole business with the wheeled bins has been rather stressful and well, poor old Dingle, he's not getting any younger, is he?' He added.

'I think it's often a mistake to change a joint decision unless of course there are additional reasons for it,' Maisie answered. Cyril was getting nowhere and feeling even more depressed than ever, he left to re-think his strategy.

Cyril looked up Dingle's private telephone number on the Council's Emergency Call-Out list.

'Hello John, how are you?' Cyril asked, hearing the Pastoral Symphony in the background.

'I'm fine. Is there any news yet?' Dingle felt in control and he liked the sensation very much.

'Yes, well that's what I was ringing about. The Chief Executive seems to think that you're indispensable; it's causing a spot of bother really but I'm not giving up. I'll think of something else, please don't fret John,' Cyril reassured, flicking his white hair back and feeling quite uncomfortable in this reversed role that he now found himself in. Dingle had no intention of fretting ever again.

'I might be able to help you there, Cyril. I understand that the Mayor and Maisie are very good friends. Do you know what I'm saying? Very good friends indeed,' Dingle informed. Cyril was dumbstruck for the second time that day. His throat felt dry. How could Dingle know so much? Dingle sensed uneasiness in Cyril at the other end of the phone and offered some friendly advice, 'Just mention dildos and Cheatham Royal Infirmary; that should do the trick alright,' Dingle said putting the phone down chuckling.

What Cyril intended to do when Miranda arrived home was a mystery even to himself at that point. Miranda would have the answer to the problem if anyone did. She was a psychiatrist dealing with the demented all day long, she would understand some of Cyril's predicament, specifically those bits that did not include Edith, Cyril thought. The whole Council seemed to be indulging in extra marital relations. Cyril's decided to portray Marcus and Maisie to Miranda as being mentally unwell. He looked at his watch. Where was she? She was normally home by now. Cyril, for the first time in his life found himself clock watching, cursing every single minute that went by. The anxiety he felt building up was so great that he began to feel sick. His blood pressure was going through the roof! It was at this point that a mental picture of Edith appeared.

'Edith doesn't know that Dingle knows. I must contact her straight away,' Cyril trembled

'Edith, bad news, in fact it's very bad news indeed. John Dingle has somehow come by some photographs of us in your greenhouse,' Cyril blurted.

'Conservatory, Cyril. It's a bloody conservatory. How many times do I have to tell you? Greenhouses are what common gardeners have. What photographs?' Edith asked suddenly recalling the rest of Cyril's words.

Cyril now had Edith's full attention and proceeded to fill her in, figuratively.

'Do you remember about ten months ago when we first got together in your conservatory? That kid who was standing outside with the camera was

Biddles. He works for Dingle in the Waste Management Section. I don't know how Dingle has managed to get copies of those photographs but he bloody well has and he's threatening to denounce us both to the world and to Miranda if I don't get him early retirement within the next few weeks. What am I to do? Your political career will be in ruins too,' Cyril was becoming hysterical.

'Cyril, I'm a spinster and if I choose to cavort about my conservatory with no clothes on and not to invite the outside world inside to view me there's nothing the law or the electorate can do about it. I actually think that the local residents would see me in a new and better light. Mainly I'm thought of as a boring, single, sexless creature who couldn't find a man because I'm probably a lesbian. They see me as completely without testosterone I shouldn't wonder. No, Cyril, I think as far as I'm concerned, such an incursion into my privacy would be as good as a makeover and save me spending my life savings on one of those personal image gurus,' Edith said excitedly. Cyril was even more depressed than ever. The only good thing to come out of the phone call was that Edith promised to support his campaign to get Dingle retired as soon as possible.

Miranda arrived home overloaded with plastic carrier bags brim full of groceries. She stood some of the environmentally unfriendly bags on the kitchen floor whilst she finished unloading the car. Cyril would harangue her, she knew, for not taking enough of her own shopping bags to the store. A lecture on depleting the world's oil fields would follow but she had done some research of her own lately and she felt able to defend her decadent use of resources.

'*Plastic bags use only a fraction of the oil recovered. In fact, only four percent of the oil is used for plastic products and the bags can be reused and she would of course, reuse them,*' she rehearsed her little speech. He was bound to ask her how she would reuse all the bags. The kitchen cupboards were full of them. She had thought this one through as well. *Every week I use one for the dust from the vacuum cleaner and I use another five of them each week for my sandwiches. The others would be useful for wrapping things up for storing in the loft.* Miranda locked the car and made her way back into the kitchen. You could have knocked her down with a feather, Cyril was unpacking the shopping.

Miranda could not recall a previous occasion when this had happened. Stranger still, he unpacked the bags in silence until he had placed the last item, a frivolous bottle of salad cream in the cupboard.

'My darling Miranda,' Cyril began. Miranda was gob smacked for a second time and now felt completely unnerved. She could not remember the last time he had called her, *darling*. Cyril's idea of romance was digging for victory in the garden with a basin of mud covered potatoes to show for it at the end and she was not talking about a romantic dig together either. It was normally Miranda who found herself outside on an extremely cold winter's night, torch in hand, harvesting the brussel sprouts.

'Miranda, darling, the most dreadful thing has happened. Dingle wants early retirement and no one wants to give it to him,' Cyril sounded quite jittery and he tried to explain the situation to his wife without spilling the beans of his own rather intimate involvement.

'Cyril, I don't really understand why John Dingle's predicament should move you to tears but since the dilemma of his early retirement is obviously so important to your sanity, I would suggest that you tell me more about the Leader and the Chief Executive's reasons for turning their backs on the issue. You make out the poor man's a saint so why would the Council turn his request down?' Miranda was applying logic as only she might.

'Dingle believes there is an improper relationship going on between Maisie and Marcus,' Cyril blurted out part of the truth and awaited Miranda's response.

Miranda pondered for a second on the words of the little nurse Sadie and taking a deep breath ushered her husband into the lounge.

'Cyril, I think you'd better take a seat,' Miranda advised. Cyril did as he was told. Once Cyril was seated in his raggedy old armchair Miranda revealed Sadie's sad tale. 'Cyril, some months ago I had a patient, a nurse from the Royal Infirmary who'd witnessed a black lady and a man with a chain of office around his neck having sex in a hospital bed. The nurse later recognised the man's picture in the local paper, it was Marcus. Obviously, Cyril, this is confidential. I could be struck off for discussing my patient's affairs, (she chuckled at her apt choice of words). The nurse told me on one occasion that she had a refuse collector boyfriend. I can't quite remember his name, it was something like Gizzard? It might be that Dingle has received his information from this Gizzard person?' Miranda suggested.

'Yes but what do I do about it? Think of the effect on the Council if it gets out. Dingle is adamant that he'll have early retirement and he wants a golden handshake to go with it. I must get Maisie and Marcus to sign on the dotted line because if I don't, this Council's done for,' Cyril lamented thinking that he would be too if Miranda found out about Edith.

Miranda regarded Cyril closely. Poor tired lamb! He really was such a workaholic and was showing such loyalty to his colleagues. Miranda sat on the edge of the armchair and stroking Cyril's hair decided she would do whatever she could to help share Cyril's burden of civic responsibility. She would arrange for him to have some therapy.

'Cyril, I think you should see a colleague of mine, Dr Xia. He's very good and an expert on how to deal with boardroom power struggles and corporate scandals. He'll show you how to stay calm and to see things more clearly. What do you think?' Cyril did not think much at all and he did not trust foreigners at the best of times but he needed to show solidarity with Miranda and agreed to therapy. Miranda took her little red book out from her handbag and telephoned Dr Xia.

At Maisie's flat emotions of a different nature were running high. She had sent for another dvd. Marcus tried to copy some of the interesting positions but at his age the arthritis was a killer.

'Marcus, do you remember I told you about my hot flushes?' Marcus opened his eyes and looked over at her as she continued, 'well, I've really been suffering from them recently. It's so annoying. I've read up on it and it's caused by a drop in my oestrogen levels. I think I'm definitely going through the menopause. What do you think about that, Marcus?' Maisie was expecting sympathy.

'Jolly good is what I say, baby,' Marcus answered jovially.

'Marcus, it's a sad day when a woman can't reproduce anymore. It's like the end of an era. Some women feel that the woman in them has been ripped out and they're no longer attractive to the opposite sex,' Maisie admonished him, 'actually, Marcus, I don't think councils do enough for women going through the menopause. Did you know that some women suffer a sort of temporary memory lapse for people's names and silly little things like that?' Marcus had been suffering major memory lapses for some time and it had nothing to do with going through the menopause. He was not convinced. Maisie went on, 'and not only that Marcus, the menopause can cause mood swings, hair loss, headaches and so many other ailments. It can affect a women's performance you know,' she added. Marcus smiled a knowing smile. There was absolutely nothing wrong with Maisie's performance! Maisie caught the gist of his thoughts, 'I mean work performance, Marcus! I want Cheatham Council to include menopausal women up there with race, religion, age and sexual orientation,' Maisie came to the end of her tirade.

Marcus decided he should explain his position to his lover.

'Maisie, my sweet little chicken, the menopause means that we won't have to worry about you getting pregnant. You'll be able to come off the pill and I won't have to withdraw in such a damn hurry. Our little forays into paradise will be so much more relaxing, my little love bucket,' Marcus cooed, kissing her neck.

'What pill, Marcus? I've never taken the pill. I rely totally on you dear,' Maisie returned as she went into the kitchen to put the kettle on. A silent Marcus pondered Maisie's words until she called him to have some tea and told him about an unexpected meeting with Cyril that afternoon.

'Cyril wants Dingle to have early retirement. I don't understand it. We agreed with David that it wasn't quite the right time, what with the wheeled bins fiasco looming and the need to have some senior officers ready to face the guillotine and suddenly Cyril's in favour of Dingle going as soon as possible. Do you know why the sudden change of heart?' Maisie asked.

'Haven't a clue but I could have a word with him, I suppose,' Marcus replied, 'I must say it's a bit unlike Cyril to go around wearing his heart on his sleeve for anyone other than himself,' he concluded.

The Mayor caught up with Cyril, now on Valium courtesy of Dr. Xia, over coffee the next day. Cyril had some disturbing news for Marcus.

'You will remember when Maisie went into the Royal Infirmary for her bunions? It was the time when some of us went up to Crappendale on a Best Value recycling fact finding exercise.' Marcus nodded getting impatient.

'Yes Cyril. Come on spit it out. Did something happen on that little trip? Something that Miranda shouldn't know about eh? I've been thinking you seem to be getting on like a house on fire with that Edith Dickopf,' Marcus jogged Cyril's elbow.

'No, not me you fool! It's you and Maisie. Do you remember a nurse finding you and Maisie in a compromising position? I think a vibrator might have had something to do with it,' Cyril raised his eyebrows for effect. Marcus felt the colour draining from his cheeks as the enormity of the situation sunk in.

'How would you know about any such alleged incident? Marcus asked cautiously.

'The nurse's boyfriend is an HGV driver on the rubbish carts you blithering idiot! You should have restricted your amorous activities to the privacy of Maisie's home. Your actions could put the whole of the Council in jeopardy,' A Valium tablet was called for and another meeting with Dr Xia would definitely not go amiss. Dingle, he anticipated, would not be a problem for much longer.

Maisie, now aware of the impending doom arranged a hurried meeting in the Leader's office to reconsider Dingle's early retirement.

'I've listened to Cyril and I'm convinced that Dingle's health would suffer if he remains in his post much longer. The Council would not be fulfilling its role as a caring employer if it regards staff such as Dingle as workhorses. Dingle needs care and attention and it is up to us to make quite sure that he gets it,' Maisie spoke with her hands clasped together as in prayer. The Leader could not believe his ears but agreed with Maisie, naturally, since he already knew that Cyril had got himself into quite a predicament. However, he could not quite work out why the Mayor and the Chief Executive were so keen to get Dingle out all of a sudden. Such a concern for the staff was unprecedented in spite of all the posters up around the Civic Offices reminding everyone that they were an asset. No one actually believed all that stuff did they? Maisie, Marcus and Cyril must all be on something and whatever it was, he wanted some for himself.

Sir David wrote a billydo on his pad asking Pamela to fix up an appointment for Dingle with the Council's doctor. He told Cyril to liaise with Finance on any final settlement bearing in mind that whatever was agreed would have to be met from Cyril's own overall departmental budget. Just as they all prepared to leave, Sir David proposed another recycling project for consideration.

'Cyril, have we ever thought about recycling plastic condoms? I read somewhere that they can be recycled through some new chemical cracking process. Takes them back to their original building blocks and recovers the plastic that way. They're already doing it in China – making them into hair bands apparently. Do you think it's worth putting young Moses-Pomfrey on the job?' The Leader asked in his usual enthusiastic and naive way.

'No David, not just at the moment. Condoms are not something I want to concentrate on just now and in any case, they're not plastic, they're rubber,' Cyril replied forlornly as he turned to leave. Maisie and Marcus declined to comment.

Cyril went to see John Dingle to discuss the terms of his early retirement deal. They met in the Express Café in the High Street, John's choice. It was not exactly Cyril's usual haunt. All day breakfasts and silly sixth form girls with their boyfriends from the local comprehensive was hardly the sort of place that a Professor of Palaeoecology liked to frequent. John was smart. He read a lot of spy novels and he would not have put it passed Huckett and Cheatham Council to have planted listening devices in order to catch him on a charge of blackmail. The Express Café, known colloquially as the Greasy Spoon was the perfect and unlikely place for a rendezvous. Cyril knew he needed to meet with Dingle sooner rather than later. He needed to be convinced that the pictures in Dingle's possession would be destroyed forever once the early retirement package was confirmed. John gave Cyril his word that this would happen as soon as his first pension payment had been received by his bank.

The Executive Head of Waste Management no longer trusted anyone on the Council. Gone were the days when a council job was a job for life. The days when you could trust the local authority as an employer to look after you into your old age were long gone. No longer did working for local government make you feel valued, he thought; even the gold watches for forty years service had disappeared. The most you could hope for nowadays was flexi time and umpteen working parties on how to improve staff communication. Dingle's brow furrowed but then he brightened, he had other fish to fry. His talents and experiences were vast and he was even now in contact with a legal friend who was setting up a consultancy for the likes of himself, a disaffected waste manager. The consultancy was to be called, Wasted Opportunities Ltd. and the aim was to catapult senior managers into posts that were temporarily vacant because of reorganisations or because some poor sod had been blamed for a service failing and parachuted into early retirement. Dingle had seen no end of his colleagues suffer this fate. It was a bit like the Mobius Recycling Loop, a full circle of events; a chicken and egg story, where you could not be sure what came first, the egg or the chicken, the reorganisation or the consultant.

Dingle had one other matter he needed to speak to Cyril about. There was something missing and that something was absolutely vital if he was to make a real success of his new enterprise. That something was some sort of title that told everyone that he was an expert in his field. Mr Experienced Top Executive Dingle needed a gong, an honour, a New Year's Honour to be more precise. A knighthood would have gone down a treat but it was unlikely so he would be just as happy to accept a CBE, an MBE or an OBE or whatever was appropriate for a middling civil servant. The latter sounded rather good, John Dingle, OBE. He liked it and it would stand him in good stead for building up his new business. He brought the subject up when he next met Cyril.

'John, an honour is something I cannot in any way influence. You must know that?' Cyril was boiling over inside, 'recommendations are sent to the Queen's Lieutenant, I believe. What I'm trying to say, John, is that I can't just promise you an honour.' Cyril was in turmoil. How could this situation have arisen? It was him, Cyril Huckett, who should be getting a public award, not his senior officer. He had worked his fingers to the bone to get himself an accolade. What would Sir David Hooper have to say? Sir David was looking for a place in the House of Lords. There was a limit to just how many honours the Queen would bestow for Cheatham's waste and recycling work.

Chapter 27

The Cheatham Star, the Recycling Champions, their research student, Matthew and Hannah Hanson from the Green Evangelists met together to thrash out how they would attack the Council's announcement that they were now recycling over fifty five percent of the borough's waste. The Cheatham Star had links to the national Daily Post and the Green Evangelists were keen to work with the Press on a story that could be verified if need be and get the widest circulation. Augustus Aurelia agreed to be an expert witness and was keen to take it as far as a court of law if necessary. Matthew hawked himself around government offices speaking to various people who knew something about waste and how to calculate a recycling rate. He discovered a booklet that the government had produced some years before which clearly explained how it should be done. Matthew scrutinised the list of recycling materials that could be included in the calculation and there did seem to be some glaring discrepancies. Cheatham listed road planings, metal from abandoned cars and an inordinately large tonnage for garden waste which residents were supposedly composting at home. None of these categories were listed in the government guidance. Matthew had all the ammunition he needed to make the LIP a laughing stock.

Adrian Moses-Pomfrey was invited out for a pub lunch by Tim Baldwin under the pretext of writing a feature on recycling for a new green page appearing each week in the Star. Adrian believed it could only be good for his CV, so he agreed. Tim used his charm to lull Adrian into a false sense of security. They chatted generally about recycling and in particular Adrian was keen to mention the creativity of Crappendale City Council's arms length production company.

'You've seen the really super plastic trees that Sir David has put up in Cheatham and Needham High Streets? Well there's more on the way. Sir David has commissioned the very latest from the Crappendale City Council's recycled products catalogue. The Leader has worked so hard to reduce the menace and health risk of dogs and what he plans now is a set of fierce looking plastic bull terriers padlocked to the trees to deter other dogs from peeing up their trunks. That man is so ahead of his time,' Adrian said admiringly, downing his third glass of expensive Cloudy Bay wine from a bottle with a real cork stopper.

Tim made a point of jollying Adrian along, gently bringing the conversation round to the recycling rate, congratulating him for his part in such a high achievement.

'I understand Adrian that builders' rubble, old tarmac and abandoned cars are not part of the calculation? Strange that we can't include these materials especially as we have so much of them to get rid of and of course, it can all be recycled. Cheatham's record is truly admiral,' Tim piled on the praise, 'I must say that Cheatham has shown true grit in excluding the forbidden categories, because most councils do and they get away with it. More wine Adrian?' Tim asked.

'Actually, Tim,' Adrian began hesitantly after taking another good gulp of the excellent wine, 'we do include them. Of course, I wouldn't if it was up to me but Councillor Huckett is very keen and insists that I do,' Adrian paused. He was never known for being able to hold his drink and he was certainly becoming a bit squiffy. He was determined to enjoy his free lunch and would be damned if he was going to declare it. Anything over two pounds fifty had to be written in the little red book but a sandwich costs more than that! Lunch on the Star's expense account suited him well and may there be many more to come, he decided. He raised his glass, focussing as best he could on Tim, 'cheers, Tim! You're not half as bad as Huckett paints you!' Adrian took another sip, grinning broadly.

A determined Tim Baldwin continued with his subtle inquisition of Cheatham's Recycling Officer.

'Tell me Adrian, how much truth is there...' Tim paused, 'in the rumour that the recyclables are ninety percent shit, if you'll pardon my expression. People are saying that the recycling rate is a pack of lies and that all the waste is coming out of the sorting plant and going to landfill.' Tim poured Adrian another glass of wine and ordered a couple of liqueurs, Cointreau, from a passing waiter. Adrian was decidedly slurring his speech but he attempted an answer.

'Well, Tim, what can I say? I have to tell you, my friend, that it's true. Cyril has ordered totters to search through the rubbish or re-s-h-hidue we call it, did you know that Tim? We call it res-s-shidue,' Adrian was sounding ridiculously drunk.

'What's this resshidue?' Tim enquired.

'No, not reshhhidue. It's r-e-s-i-d-u-e,' Adrian corrected, taking pains to get it right himself, 'actually Tim, my friend, they're not happy at the MRF and d'yer know why mate?' Adrian asked. Tim shook his head and edged closer to concentrate on Adrian's drunken revelations, 'the MRF's sorters don't like it because the totters are making a bit of money out of the stuff they find in the rubbish, like copper wire. You see Tim, the Merrrrrrf workers used to sell the stuff themselves. They've had their noses put out of joint. Do yer see Tim?' Adrian asked looking at Tim wide eyed and quite oblivious of the alcoholic daze he was in.

Tim listened as Adrian waffled incoherently until it really was time to get him back to base before his drunken stupor made him totally incapable.

'Don't worry, Ady, I can call you Ady can't I? Tim asked.

'Of course you can. I don't let anyone call me Ady you know but I like you Tim. You're an honest fella,' the inebriated Recycling Officer mumbled.

'Your secrets are safe with me. Let's call you a cab and get you home,' Tim suggested although he did not expect a lucid reply as Adrian's condition was rapidly deteriorating. As soon as his drunken friend was safely on his way home Tim telephoned his office to say that Adrian was feeling unwell and would not be back until the next morning.

Years of heavy smoking had left a legacy of circulation problems for Micky Brown. His declining health was taking its toll on him and Reg encouraged him to take a few days off to undergo some tests and just chill out. The brief change to his routine was as good as a rest and he returned from his mini break refreshed. This wonderful feeling of being invincible soon wore off as Larry Wright filled him in on the troubles that had befallen the depot during his brief absence.

'Larry what did Reg say about it?' Micky asked.

'Well I don't know if he knows actually Mick. It's not something that he'd want to hear,' Larry returned.

'Larry, for Gawd's sake, mate, you've been 'ere long enough to know that smoking cannabis at work is not allowed. Smoking it whilst driving a refuse freighter is certainly not on,' Micky could not believe his ears.

'But Mick, it's OK now. It's legal. I've 'eard it on the telly. In Lambeth I think, it's OK,' Larry defended himself, 'anyways, cannabis is just the same as smoking those strong French ciggys,' he reassured himself.

'No Larry, it's illegal. It's still an offence and the Council's rules on drugs are crystal clear, zero tolerance. Anyway, smoking cannabis is much worse. It goes into the blood stream and affects the way you act. Really Larry, do you honestly think that Cheatham's residents want their dustmen high on drugs? They're driving expensive pieces of kit, mate. Let alone the damage they can do to people. No, I'm sorry, I want a list of names and dates. Reg will have to know. Anyway, who was it?' Micky asked.

'Gazza,' Larry replied.

The next problem arrived via a telephone call from Slump.

'Mick, whose supposed to be on with that agency driver delivering the wheeled bins? Only I've just seen him in the Highways Depot picking up the bins and there's a woman with him. I asked who the lady was and he says it's his wife. Do we know this bloke has his wife going round in the lorry with him?' Slump asked perplexed.

'Thanks Slump. No, he's not bloody well supposed to have his wife in the flipping lorry with him. What does he think we are a bloody holiday camp?' Micky put down the phone and radioed out to Gary Green who he knew was in the area.

'....and Gary, I'd be obliged if you would tell 'im that the lady walks, and now,' Micky put down the phone and getting his sandwiches out of his plastic carrier bag settled down to a belated petit dejeuner.

Micky's break was interrupted by an irate caller put through from Robin in the upstairs office.

'I want the organ grinder not the ruddy organ grinder's monkey,' Mrs Angry of Cheatham said.

'Yes madam, I'm the Senior Refuse Supervisor. How can I help you?' Micky answered in his best customer care voice.

'I want to complain about your uncovered trucks. I was walking along the bypass this morning when one of your trucks full of garden waste rushed out of your Civic Amenity Site and covered me from head to toe with grass and I don't know what else,' Mrs Angry said describing the scene. Micky tried hard to suppress a laugh at the thought of an *Incredible Green Hulk* walking down Cheatham's main artery. Mrs Angry was not finished with Micky yet. 'I want compensation for being made to look such a fool. It's against the law to drive around like that,' she moaned. There was nothing more to be said except to apologise and give Mrs Angry Cheatham's Insurance Section's number to ring. Such enraged callers were the norm now. It was never like this in the old days. What with budget cuts, staff shortages and scatter brained new schemes, Mick was dreaming of the day when he could walk away from Cheatham Council and put his feet up permanently.

The day could only get better. Micky called Kelly and Robin downstairs to look after the office whilst he popped over to the MRF. He needed to speak to Reggie.

'I Knew I'd catch you 'ere, boss. Ever since June started working 'ere you've hardly put in an appearance at the depot. We miss you Reg. I nearly forgot what yer face looked like,' Micky said curtly.

'Cut the clap trap, Micky. Here, have one of my rock cakes,' Reggie offered a tin full of interestingly shaped fruit buns. Micky decided not to partake.

'Thanks Reg, but I've just eaten me dinner and I wouldn't want to waste it by throwing up after one of your cakes, mate. Thanks all the same,' Micky said thinking he would rather have another ciggy. 'Look Reg, what d'yer think we should do about Gazza and the alleged cannabis joint?' Reggie's attention was not fully on Mick but he gave him an answer whilst staring across to the other side of the MRF.

'The Council's policy is quite clear, immediate suspension. It's a disciplinary offence. You need to get him in and interview him. Make sure you have Personnel with you. Gazza of course can choose to invite the Union along. I'm not losing my job because some idiot chooses to flout the rules and drive whilst under the influence of narcotics, Mick, and you shouldn't either.' Reg was focussed on a storeroom across the way with its windows covered by blinds.

'What yer looking at Reg?' Micky asked.

'Nothing interesting. I'm a bit busy now Mick so I'll see you later.' Reggie stated rather matter of factly whilst dodging the mechanical shovel as he made his way to the storeroom.

Mick was dismayed at Reggie's apparent disinterest in the Gazza problem and just looked on as his line manager walked away. The urge for a ciggy overcame him and he went outside but curiosity soon got the better of him and he headed back inside and peered through the one tiny crack he could find between the vertical blinds.

'Bloody hell,' Micky gasped, this was not the Reg he knew and loved. He looked again. Reggie, the normally boring Victoria Sponge baker was clearly in ecstasy. June had at long last awoken emotions deep down inside him. So where else did they do it? Micky wondered; in the lifts, out in his van, where? The slimy bastard! Mick thought. Meanwhile outside in the belly of the MRF, rivers of newspapers mixed with rank food waste were being passed noisily along the conveyors just metres away from this sexually charged couple in the storeroom quite unbeknown to the MRF workers. Mick was perplexed. Voyeurism was never his thing so he left. Mick's own wife would have a nice dinner waiting for him with his slippers by the gas fire he thought and wondered whether this was taking the moral high ground or just him feeling rather old and tired.

The shit did hit the fan a couple of weeks later. The Cheatham Star ran banner headlines, *Recycling Rate Lies*. It was all great fun. The Green Evangelists had called in the Audit Commission to check the borough's recycling figures and they were quick to declare them to be complete codswallop. The professional journals ran the story with double page spreads. The Leader had been asked to explain himself and whilst he tried to give the job over to Russell, the buck was truly stopping with Cheatham Council, a situation which could not continue. Sneaked photographs of the muck entering the MRF illustrated the professional journals. It was difficult to find a convincing excuse to wangle their way out of the deceit. The local and national newspapers continued the tirade for what seemed like a month of Sundays.

Cheatham Council today denied that it has deliberately misled the public with false claims about its recycling rate. The Star has evidence that it has no more reached a recycling rate of sixty percent than it has put a man on Mars. The Star also has evidence that ninety seven percent of the waste going into the MRF is coming out again as rubbish. In fact, the rubbish is stinking, foul, Sh** and a health hazard to its factory workers. What's more, the Star has conclusive evidence that the MRF muck is then sent to landfill but still counted as being recycled and is therefore being doubly counted. Shame on you Cheatham Council! Sir David Hooper, the tax payers of Cheatham call for your resignation...

The Star has faithfully covered the wheeled bin story since its inception and was the first to bring the public news of the general chaos brought by the fiasco. Cheatham residents have a lot to thank the campaigning groups for. The Green Evangelists have been in the High Street for months obtaining signatures in wind and rain and the Cheatham Recycling Champions have run their website and kept people informed. We are truly indebted for without them we might never have known the truth. Let it go on record that per se, we are not against recycling. We are against the stupid idea of having our rubbish putrefying for two weeks before collection. Bring back our weekly collection, or else! Follow the Star next week for the unexpurgated account of a council in crisis and perhaps a response from this irresponsible administration of ours. More photographs to come.

Adrian knew instinctively where some of the information had come and was bitterly disappointed with himself. What bloody good luck that Augustus Aurelia had offered him a job at the Middlesex waste plant! Adrian thought it might be apropos to start as soon as possible. Councillor Merryweather was also devastated by the Star's revelations. He was the Council's Lead Member for Environment and Local Agenda 21; he was also President of the Institution of Environmental Affairs and could not allow his reputation to be sullied. Such sacrilegious betrayal by his colleagues was unbearable. He had put his faith in them and in particular Cyril's scatty idea of a fortnightly rubbish collection. As for Sir David Hooper and his incredulous ideas for plastic trees and plastic dogs, how idiotic it all sounded now. It reminded him of the Emperor's New Clothes, where no one had the nerve to say what they really thought until the end. Sir David could not remain as Leader; that was for sure. The Leader's job was one which he had himself fancied for a while now. Perhaps this current predicament was not all bad. He needed to garner support. He left the LIP Group Room to speak informally to fellow Councillors, whom he knew would be enjoying a nightcap in the Social Club bar. The following week the Council did respond to the allegations. A reply appeared from Maisie in her capacity as Chief Executive.

The Council wishes to state that it has undertaken a preliminary investigation into the serious allegations of fraud made in the Star last week. It has found that there is a substantial amount of contamination in the recycling wheelie bins, which has resulted in a large percentage of the recyclables having to be landfilled. The Council was not made aware of this problem until the Star's report. Following the Council's own initial investigation it has found that officers were aware of the problem but had chosen to hide it from Councillors. The result is rising costs for the recycling service. The Council has appointed an outside

*consultant to investigate more thoroughly the likely outcome of the
contamination and to establish culpability.*

To stave off another coup by the Star, Maisie was instructed by Sir David to
announce that the grey wheelie bins for rubbish would be collected weekly
from October the first. Russell wrote the press release. Judy knew it was
coming and alerted Tim who went to town with the following editorial.

Council Backs Down.
*Cheatham Council has given in. People power wins! Waste will be collected
weekly from October.*
*Waste Managers Dumped! R*an the headline on the next page. *The Executive
Head of Waste Management and the Refuse and Recycling Factory Manager
have been suspended pending an investigation into how the Council managed
to run up a debt of two million pounds caused mainly by wholesale
contamination of the recyclates. Councillors maintain that they had nothing to
hide and that they have been duped by their senior officers. The Council had no
intention of misleading Cheatham's residents by claiming it was recycling more
than it really was.*

The latter bit did not go down well with John Dingle. He was about to hold his
retirement party and this article was a definite defamation of his character. He
picked up the telephone.
    'Cyril, I'm outraged to read in the newspaper that I'm guilty of causing the
Council's overspend. Do something now. I want to see an apology next week
and if I don't you know what to expect, don't you?' Dingle had Cyril by the
short and curlies and this lead councillor lost no time in advising Russell that
an apology was necessary from the Star. The apology was to clearly state that
the Executive Head of Waste Management had not been suspended but was
leaving because he had been granted early retirement, which had nothing to
do with the problems facing the Council. Dingle's ruffled feathers were
smoothed down. The whole Council had gone stark, staring mad as far as the
Leader could see. That weekend he went down to Pets Safari in Cheatham
High Street and consoled himself with a new budgie which he named, Killer. It
was a necessary act of sheer self indulgence and cheered him up no end.

Councillor Merryweather's sly campaigning was going well. He had a little
book in which he ticked off the names of those who professed to be in his
camp. The next group meeting came round and some brave member was
selected to stand up and declare a lack of confidence in Sir David. A
devastated Leader visibly shook. It was suggested that it might be better for
the party if they tried to repair the damage with a new leader at the helm.
What could he do? It was over. There would be no seat in the House of Lords
now. He reluctantly agreed and it was decided that he would announce the
following week that he would be stepping down. The deputy, who just
happened to be Councillor Tom Merryweather himself, would take over the
reins until it was possible to hold a proper election within the Party.
Reluctantly, a piteous Sir David Hooper decided that he would stand down as
a councillor too. A by-election would have to be held in due course.

The Star enjoyed every minute of the charades being played out by the
Council. *Leader's Head Rolls with By-Election Shock,* the headline ran. Micky
and those at the depot were in shock too. If was so unfair of the Council to

blame the contamination on officers like Reggie or even Dingle for that matter. How could they be to blame? It was residents who put the contaminated waste in the bins! Suddenly the world seemed to make no sense at all and there just seemed to be no justice. Reggie was not the brightest star in the sky but he was not all bad either. He had only held the MRF post for a few months after all.

'It's not fair. This Council has tarred everyone with the same brush. They should've taken some of the blame on themselves. They're the stupid bastards who introduced the scheme in the first place. If they'd have asked us we would've told them it wasn't gonna work,' Micky moaned.

'Yeah Mick, you are definitely right there. That waste course I went on learnt us a bit about the 'istory of it. Years ago people used to die of diseases because their waste wasn't collected regular like. It used to get infested with maggots just like Cheatham's bleeding wheeled bins,' Larry impressed his colleague with his knowledge.

'Ah well, I don't suppose there's anything we can do about it except hope they don't finds anyfink to pin on us,' Micky said morosely.

'What about these bloody consultants the Council keeps employing? Did you know they're paying them £1000 a day? You've got more experience than those university blokes,' Larry said making Mick feel even more depressed.

'£1000 a day? I couldn't live on that, mate,' Mick said.

The wheelie bin soap opera and public backlash grew like Topsy. The Mayor was not a particularly religious man but found himself praying that the attention might be deflected from himself and Maisie with whom he kept in regular contact.

'How awful everything is my love. I quite get the jitters every time the phone rings. One just can't be sure that Dingle will keep his word,' Marcus bemoaned, fretfully.

'Quite,' Maisie returned, 'actually Marcus, I need to speak to you and I don't think we should discuss private matters over the phone. Could you call round tonight?' Maisie asked.

'Do you think that would be wise? The Press are all over the place looking for scapegoats and I'd rather not give myself to them on a plate. At times like this it only takes one small mistake for someone to put two and two together,' Marcus explained.

'Marcus, I rather think we've already made your so called, *one small mistake* and I'm sure if you knew the full extent of the problem *you would feel like disappearing into a big black hole!*' Maisie said tersely. It was all that was needed. Marcus, concentrating on the words, big black hole, went weak at the knees. He did like it when his concubine talked dirty. She was such a tease.

Marcus got on his mayoral bike as soon as darkness fell and made his way to Maisie's flat.

'Poppet, come here and let me give you a cuddle,' Marcus said throwing his arms around as much of Maisie as he could manage in one go.

'Marcus, take a seat. I've got something to tell you,' Maisie said sounding serious as Marcus perched his wiry frame on a dining room chair, 'there is no easy way of telling you this. I'm pregnant,' Maisie waited for his reaction.

'Pregnant! How can you be pregnant? You're far too old and we took precautions didn't we? What was all that nonsense the other day about the menopause?' Marcus was confused.

'Obviously we didn't take precautions. I did tell you recently that I wasn't on the pill so somehow you must have misunderstood the situation. At my age my fertility is not supposed to be as good as it was in my younger days so it was ten to one I wouldn't get pregnant. The menopause doesn't mean you don't have to worry at all at least not for several years. The question is what do we do about it?' Maisie, level headed as always set out their predicament in a calm and business like fashion.

'God knows. Are you keeping the baby? I mean at my age Maisie, I'm sixty eight years old for goodness sake. Virginia will take me to the cleaners,' Marcus wailed.

'Marcus, our baby was created in joyous circumstances,' she reminded him bursting into song and singing, one night in heaven, by the pop group, M People.

Marcus, the Mayor of Cheatham suddenly became aware of the larger picture. It was bad enough being tarnished by all this wheeled bin nonsense but to be labelled an adulterer and the father of an illegitimate child whose mother he had absolutely no intention of marrying was the stuff of TV comedy drama. He would have to think fast. Maisie was still singing in the background. Who was it who said it's not over until the fat lady sings!

Cyril needed to confide his innermost thoughts to Edith. This Xia person was not doing him any good at all. He could hardly go to Miranda's friend and pour out the intimate details of his crazy year long affair now could he?

'Edith, let me come round, please. I'm missing you dreadfully and I don't know which way to turn,' Cyril blurted out.

'Oh come on then. I'm just putting dad to bed so give me an hour,' Edith said. She was rather cross about the possibility of being named as the other woman in divorce proceedings and she certainly did not want to end up with Cyril camped out on her doorstep for ever more. After so many years of being foot loose and fancy free she rather wanted to stay that way. She did not need a man to mess it up for her, as past experience had shown they normally did. She believed the philosophy extolled by Nancy Astor that all women marry beneath them.

Cyril arrived ashened faced at Edith's place and she yanked him inside to avoid any prying eyes.

'Cyril, get a grip,' an exasperated Edith shrieked at him, 'think things through carefully and decide where you want to go,' she advised.

'What shall we do?' Cyril asked. In spite of not seeing a future in their union, the sassy Edith decided that the night was too good an opportunity to miss out on. She had dressed appropriately for their ménage a deux in sexy underwear which she had covered up with the usual pleated skirt, one of the many from her inexhaustible seventies wardrobe. Cyril brushed his long white hair back with his hand and with the help of a little music from Frank Sinatra they enjoyed one last fling.

When the time came for Cyril to leave, Edith dropped the bombshell he had been dreading.

'Cyril, I rather think it would be a good idea if we cooled off for a bit and perhaps, just perhaps, you shouldn't contact me again for the time being. When the time is right I'll give you a ring, my love,' Edith spoke softly. She knew really that the time would never be right to ring Cyril again. As she closed the door on Cyril she was remembering all too well the nice mature man with the faded blonde hair called, Alfred whom she had met the day before at B&Q. She fancied him rotten and he would be delivering her new bedroom mirror in the morning. It was nice that do-it-yourself shops employed older people nowadays, she thought. She could see the value in it. They had so much more practical experience and knew how important it was to insert the right sized screws. Her mind wandered on to what she would wear tomorrow; the black fishnet tights perhaps? And there was that new lipstick she'd bought at the chemist when collecting her dad's incontinence pads. It was fun being single and middle aged.

Sir David was not well. He kept suffering bouts of sickness and keeling over in sudden faints. The doctor said it was stress and gave him some pick-me-up tablets. He also advised the Leader to buy himself a pet to replace the budgie. A nice little pooch that he could cuddle would be exactly right for him, the doctor suggested. Sir David had spent the best part of the past two years trying to rid the borough of dirty little mongrels and the thought of encouraging them by becoming an owner made him vomit on the surgery floor.

Pamela Peters was concerned about her mentor and on his return to work kept a careful watch on Sir David. Zombie like he packed up his cardboard boxes in readiness to leave office.

'Excuse me, Sir David but Tom Merryweather is here,' she decided not to tell him that he was clutching his own set of cardboard boxes ready to slip into Sir David's shoes in the most seamless way.

'Oh is he,' the ex-leader replied and then ignoring his secretary's announcement, 'Pamela,' it was the first time he had addressed her by her first name. Familiarity breeds contempt had always been his motto. Pity his colleagues had not minded his words, he judged. The rumours about Marcus and Maisie and Cyril and Edith were all over the place, 'Pamela, do you see that cloud up there in that beautiful blue sky?' Pamela agreed that it was a lovely cloud. She thought that humouring him was probably just as well.

'I think it looks just like a cat, don't you?' Sir David asked.

'Well, I suppose it does if you look at it from some angles,' Pamela agreed hesitantly.

'I've just bought myself a gorgeous Burmese Tom Cat,' Sir David revealed.

'Really, Leader,' she said then checking herself mentally remembering that he was no longer the Council's Leader, 'I do hope the new cat gets on with _Killer_ and doesn't eat him,' she tittered and then seeing his sad face she became serious.

'Pamela, dogs have owners, cats have staff!' Sir David said smiling wanly.

'What have you named your new cat?' Pamela asked.

'Cyril!' Sir David replied, 'I thought it appropriate. I can kick him up the arse every time he gets under my feet,' Sir David said feeling better already.

Sir David was determined to walk out of his office with as much dignity as possible. He stood tall as he passed through his office doorway for the last time.

Cyril Huckett was left holding the baby as the failings of Cheatham's Waste Strategy began to surface in the national press. Dingle had departed in due course for pastures new and his consultancy, Wasted Opportunities Ltd. was doing well. It was registered to Dingle Design Associates, a partnership of Dingle's old industry friends who guaranteed to develop systems that would achieve a modest thirty percent recycling rate without any gimmicks. The new company's chief researcher, Adrian Moses-Pomfrey worked on an ad hoc basis for Dingle Design Associates or DDA as it became known since his time was limited in his new capacity as managing director for a new arm of Aurelia Waste Handling Ltd.

Baby Atichitawomba was growing fast. The scan had shown the most perfect little soul and her mother was already very proud of her. Marcus feigned interest in the photo of his unborn child as he tried to come to terms with his new situation. When the time came, Maisie kept her baby. She employed a nanny and stayed in her job. Marcus' mayoral year should have finished in May but due to delays over bringing in the new Cabinet system, he had agreed to stay on for the summer. He felt worn out. Virginia had changed, often surprising him by ripping his clothes off as she found her sexual urges recharged. She decided that she wanted to retire to a cottage by the sea in a warm climate since working at the Citizens Advice Bureau had suddenly lost its appeal. Marcus decided he would never understand women. They were one of the mysteries of the universe.

Virginia worked under her maiden name, Halpin. She had adopted her maiden name for work purposes in the eighties. It just seemed like the fashionable thing to do at the time. A few weeks earlier she had interviewed a refuse truck driver called Gazza seeking legal advice on account of the Council suspending him without any proof that he had been using cannabis whilst at work. The whole disciplinary process had been a farce from start to finish and Gazza, being well acquainted with his rights being a paid up union man and all that, sought Virginia's assistance in seeking justice. It was whilst Gazza was in his melodramatic state that Virginia encouraged him to spill the beans about anything else in his life that might be affecting his normally good natured and laid back personality. Treat the whole person, was Virginia's mantra. It was at this point that he revealed something else that had been bothering him. The nice lady in front of him at the CAB, whose name plate said she was Mrs V Halpin, was all ears.

'Well, it's my girlfriend, Sadie,' Gazza began, 'she works in an old people's home, The Crest, just off Needham High Street. You might know it?' Gazza asked. Virginia wondered why she should know the old people's home. Did she look old enough to know it? Gazza continued, 'a year ago she worked at Cheatham's Royal Infirmary and the black woman who runs the town council came in to have her bunions done but she didn't come alone, she brought a friend with her. My Sadie found her in the hospital bed with that Mayor bloke, Marcus Bullman. They were 'aving sexual relations and they were using a fake penis,' Gazza explained. Virginia was in shock. Her usually warm complexion drained away. 'My Sadie's been having psychiatric treatment with some doctor at the Royal, a Dr Miranda somebody,' Gazza said. Virginia was dumbstruck.

'That cow was in on it and never said a word to me at the last Party gathering,' she blurted out causing Gazza to sit upright. Virginia contemplated her options. She needed to protect herself at least and then there was Gazza who had come to her for advice. She made an appointment for him to see the Bureau's industrial tribunal expert, which would at least get him out of her hair.

On Virginia's way home, she called at an estate agent with property investments on the Spanish Costa Blanca. A bijou residence in the sun might be just what the doctor ordered. Her decision was made. She allowed Marcus to think that her idea was just for consideration but in fact she had within days put down a substantial deposit and planned an imminent departure. Their children would let the house unless of course Marcus decided to stay on which was doubtful since the money was all hers, inherited from her side of the family. Marcus went to Spain and he went with Maisie's blessing just as Virginia had predicted.

The first job Tom Merryweather did as Council Leader was to assess the financial damage caused by Cyril's wayward recycling scheme. Life was not easy for Cyril either. He was still on the Council but his self esteem had taken a hard knock. Some days he could not face walking through the Civic Offices' front doors. It was only his sense of commitment, one of his most endearing qualities that forced him to carry on. Miranda had noticed Cyril's diffidence. The garden was being neglected and becoming a haven for weeds. He had started purchasing chocolate bars and all the forbidden fruits that his own children had been banned from eating during their youth and was slipping into a deep depression. It was as though he had nothing to anything to live for. Miranda was very concerned.

'Miranda my dear shall we go to church today?' Cyril asked one Sunday morning. Church! Miranda's hair bristled. The last time they had set foot in a church was when they were looking for medieval brasses. Cyril was against *going to church.* He felt that church goers were full of their own egos. The very thought of anything to do with *church* brought Miranda out in goose bumps and she found herself reaching for the stress busting pills.

'Cyril, I think St John's service is at 10am. We're too late,' Miranda advised him.

'Yes I know. I've looked the times up in the local newspaper. I think I'd like to go the Stonebridge Baptist Church. The service starts at 11am and I believe they accept sinners readily,' Cyril was seriously in need of help.

'You're not a sinner, Cyril,' Miranda tried to reason with her penitent husband. If she was going to have to go to church, she would have preferred the Church of England. St. John's on occasion still swung that smelly incense stuff around which made it bit more special. The Baptist Church was all doom and gloom, she thought, remembering the stern Baptist Sunday School of her youth. She agonised, hoping she was wrong. As the weeks passed Cyril read the bible from cover to cover and contemplated the meaning of his life. He went to church regularly and started helping the minister at mid-week services. The Cheatham Baptist Old Peoples' Fellowship needed drivers for their minibus outings and Cyril was the first person to offer his help. He chaired a working party on organising a *Church Event in a Tent* type of bonanza which was due to take place on Cheatham Heath the following July, indeed, he was so unstinting in his duties that he was fast becoming the church's right arm.

The months passed by and Cyril's pious nature convinced the Minister that here was a man who would be an asset to the Church. It came, then, as no surprise when Cyril asked him to support his application to join the church as a student at a Baptist college. Miranda liked the idea. Cyril would be away for three years, only coming home at Easter and Christmas. She had been getting on famously with a divorcee she had met at her psychology classes, a rather distinguished gentleman who shared her interest in the workings of the human mind. His name was Augustus Aurelia. Cyril would never know and would probably not be interested! Anyway, what the eye doesn't see, the heart doesn't grieve over, she consoled herself. Cyril resigned as a ward councillor and at his last LIP group meeting he quoted Francis of Assisi, *Lord, make me an instrument of thine peace. Where there is hate, that I may bring love; where there is offence that I may bring pardon....it is in pardoning that one is pardoned,'* Cyril was showing true signs of remorse.

The hum drum life working at the rubbish coal face continued for Micky Brown. His coughs, colds and circulation problems plagued him more so than ever before and it was clear to his doctor that the stresses of the job were a great deal to blame.

'That's a nice chair you're laying on Mick,' Slump commented one morning.

'Yeah, I got it from the bulky boys yesterday. They picked up a settee and two armchairs. We can't fit the lot in 'ere so I got rid of that old cottage suite and Bob's yer uncle! It ain't arf comfy, Slump,' Mick said as he nestled further into the cushions. Mick sat whenever he could thesedays to stop his legs from hurting.

'You shouldn't be here Mick. Why don't you have a word with Dingle's temporary replacement? Tell 'em straight, you want to be put out to grass, mate. If anyone deserves it, Mick, it's you. I'm sure you could swing early retirement. How many years have you done, thirty five? Just ask them sods in HR. You know what they say, don't ask, don't get, mate. You don't want to be here. I certainly don't want to be here, so I'm bloody well sure you don't want to be here any more,' Slump insisted.

Slumps' words of wisdom set Micky thinking. He went to see the interim Executive Head of Waste, Dingle's temporary replacement following his rapidly arranged retirement. Armed with a letter from his doctor he was not kept in suspense for long. Within the week he had received a letter from Human Resources but it was not quite the letter he was expecting. Instead, it was a letter congratulating him for giving over thirty year's service and inviting him to a celebratory evening with councillors. As if that was not enough, another letter arrived the next day telling him he would be losing the three days extra leave he had acquired for long service. It was being taken away to make his annual leave allowance the same as that of the manual workers in the race to have equality amongst blue and white collar workers alike. It was part of the drive towards what they were calling 'Single Status.' Mick could not believe his eyes. What crazy HR specialist had thought that one up?

The first letter Micky had received was from the new Leader, Merryweather, inviting him to write down a few of the highlights from his extensive years of service. Micky stared at the words in front of him bursting into uncontrollable laughter. The other supervisors just looked on as he waved his piece of paper at them.

'You see lads the worries are all worthwhile in the end. The Council appreciates me so much they're giving me a certificate for long service. What am I gonna do with a certificate? I haven't got a wall to put the bloody thing on!' Mick vented his sarcasm on them. 'Just who do they think they are? A friend of mine who works for Jupiter Demolition got three months salary for being loyal to his firm. He offered me a job years back and how I wish I'd taken it,' Micky sighed.

'Could be worse, Mick. They could've given you a kick in the teeth,' Larry suggested.

'Yeah, I suppose you're right Larry. My lady wife will enjoy the chance to hob nob with the hoy polloi at the celebration. Trouble is though, she's likely to tell the Council just what she thinks of 'em. I'll have to make sure she's on her best behaviour. Mind you, if by then I've had me letter about me retirement, I won't much care will I?' Micky reasoned. A few days later Mick received the awaited letter awarding him early retirement on the grounds of ill health. He would be free, out to pasture by the end of the month.

You may be wondering what happened to Reginald Turner and his sexually indulgent but beautiful wife, June? Reggie was used as a scapegoat by the Council for getting things wrong at the Recycling Factory. No surprises there you might be thinking; councils will be councils but this council had plenty to pin on him. To say that Micky had been surprised when he had found Reg and Juney in a compromising situation at the MRF was one thing but the reaction of the local residents' association being shown around just minutes after Micky's departure, was scary. The scene that greeted them as they entered the paper sorting cabin could have been taken from the Candid Camera TV show. The prime intention of the visiting group was to see what went on at the factory and thus remove the mystique that surrounded this secret place on the Beverly Estate. Amongst the group were two maiden ladies from the local church who left believing that the lustful eye of Satan was embedded in the very fabric of the Recycling Factory, making it an evil place; they would never recycle again!

The Disciplinary Procedure was used to charge Reggie and June with gross misconduct and both were dismissed with immediate effect. Poor Reg! All he had wanted to do was rekindle some of the magic of his youth and satisfy his insatiable wife. Did this fact not count for something? They lost their appeal. They were advised not to talk to the Press or else they would forfeit their generous pension entitlement. With Reggie safely dispensed with, the Council blamed an unnamed senior officer with special responsibility for managing the MRF for all the contamination and overspend problems. A report, written naturally by independent consultants who charged the Council over a thousand pounds a day and who were brought in to show that the LIP administration was faultless, was published on the Council's website with a double page spread in the Cheatham Star. Reggie managed to secure a job at Padwick Council working as a consultant on their new Waste Strategy and at a meagre seven hundred pounds a day, he was far better off than he had ever been before.

Micky Brown tried to forget about his last few years at the depot. One afternoon when he was taking advantage of the sunshine on his garden lounger, one of his retirement presents, he picked up the local paper and thought he would just take a peak at what *that bloody council was up to now*. He read the front page.

Zero Waste. It's no longer a pipe dream. It's the only way to a sustainable lifestyle. Join the Cheatham revolution! The new Council Leader, Tom Merryweather has engaged a consultancy to research the feasibility of various forms of incineration. Emerging technologies such as pyrolosis, gasification and anaerobic digestion would be part of the investigation into the use of incineration as a disposal method for the borough's waste. In addition, Councillor Merryweather is keen to look at the possibility of using chicken waste to fuel a planned new mini incinerator for the Civic Offices. 'Chicken waste is as cheap as chips,' says Tom Merryweather, 'and will provide a very economical form of energy for the Council. Cheatham Council will be the first to utilise this new technology. A chicken shed could be built on the Civic Offices car park.'

Micky could feel the pressure mounting inside his chest. His heart was thumping as deja vu raised its ugly head.

'When will they ever learn? They just go round in bloody circles,' he muttered to himself, putting the paper down and dozing in the warm air.

Cyril, Marcus and Sir David still received newsletters from the Council keeping them up to date with civic developments. In the January of the following year they each opened their copies to see the following headline,

Two of Cheatham's citizen's in New Year's Honours List.
John Dingle, recently retired from his position as Executive Head of Waste Management was awarded an OBE for his sterling environmental work in introducing a comprehensive recycling service to borough residents and Mrs Carter, the Mayor's Mace Bearer was awarded an MBE for unstinting services to local government.

C'est la vie!